WE ARE US

TARA LEIGH

Tara Leigh

www.taraleighbooks.com

Cover Design: Regina Wamba, Mae I Design

Editing: Lexi Smail, BookSmart

Copyediting: Marla Esposito, Proofing Style

Print ISBN: 978-1-7328010-9-7

eBook ISBN: 978-1-7328010-8-0

❀ Created with Vellum

To those who are unable to forget what they cannot actually remember.

The hurt and horror might never go away. But leave the shame for the one who mistook your silence for consent. An inability to say no is never the same as saying yes.

PROLOGUE

*S*ounds break through my insulated cocoon of unconsciousness. Harsh sounds. Ugly sounds. Buzzing. Beeping. Humming.

The fingers of my left hand twitch with the impulse to swat at... something. An alarm clock? The television remote? But although my wedding rings slide around my finger, my arm doesn't move. Almost as if the platinum bands have turned into lead, weighing me down.

Panic whispers at the edge of my mind, though there is no corresponding pulse of adrenaline through my veins, forcing me into action. My limbs are heavy and uncooperative.

Make it stop. Make it stop. Make it stop.

Despite my silent pleas, the unwelcome orchestra continues its assault. *Buzz. Beep. Hum.*

It's been a long time since I've felt this awful, this lethargic. Filled with an all-encompassing exhaustion that has seeped into the marrow of my bones.

Survivor's guilt, apparently. Sleeping the day away is preferable to facing what happened, what I've done. The dawn of a new day isn't a fresh start, a new beginning.

It is a violation. A betrayal.

Make it stop.

Finally, I manage to clutch at my covers, dragging them over my head. Egyptian cotton, a thread count so high it could be spun of silk. Surely it will muffle the noise.

But something is wrong. The fabric is rough beneath my fingertips. It doesn't smell of the lavender and verbena packets tucked into the shelves of the linen closet. And there is a sterilized stench to the air I didn't notice before.

The whisper of panic becomes more of a murmur, then a shout. *This isn't my bed.*

The beeping noises pick up, racing now. My breaths quicken, my lungs throbbing from the sharp bite of bleach with each shallow inhale.

Hospital. I am in a hospital. The buzzing and beeping and humming. Those are machines.

What happened? *Think, think.*

My mind is frustratingly blank even as my skin prickles with memories of another time. Another confused awakening. Another frantic search for memories. Did he… *No.* He wouldn't dare. Not again. Not ever again.

I will my eyes open. Needing to see. Needing other sensory inputs before I get lost inside my brain. Trapped within the shadowy net of my own past.

My corneas sting in protest as I squint against the harsh daylight streaming through the open window, my pupils slowly retracting until the room comes into focus. Various machines stand sentry against pale mint walls, their screens lit by flashes of color—jagged lines and blinking dots. Red and white and neon green.

I turn my head, looking for the door, or a chair where my husband is probably sleeping. A sharp pain explodes in my temple at the small movement, taking me off guard. I gasp, my vision going dark at the edges. Not only does my head hurt, my back is on fire.

"Look who's awake." A woman in scrubs the same color as the walls peers at me. Her hair is pulled back in a ponytail, curly wisps escaping like weeds. A stethoscope swings from her neck as she wraps warm fingers around my wrist. "Are you in pain?"

I consider nodding, then think better of it. My mouth opens on a squeak. "Head. Back." My throat hurts, too. "Legs," I add.

She nods. "That's normal for the injuries you've sustained."

Normal?

"Are you thirsty?"

This time I don't nod, or speak. I just open my mouth. She disappears from my vision briefly and I hear the sound of water being poured into a plastic cup. Then she's back, moving my bed into a more upright position with the press of a button, guiding a straw between my parched lips. I clamp down on it, sucking greedily. Too soon, there is only a gurgling sound as the straw catches the last few droplets at the bottom.

She takes away the cup. "I know, I'm sorry. You can have more later. Not just yet, though."

"Hello, hello." Another woman enters my room. Clutching a clipboard, she is wearing a white lab coat over a navy blue dress.

I swallow, croak a greeting.

"I'm Dr. Carlson. Do you know why you're here?"

Tears prick my eyelids. *No.*

She isn't fazed. "How about your name? Can you tell me your name?"

A wave of relief washes over me. That I know. "Poppy."

"How about the name of the president and the city where you were born?"

I answer both questions and she beams. "Excellent."

"More water?" I ask, hoping I've earned a reward.

"Sure, sure." She looks over at the nurse, who obligingly refills

3

the cup, though not nearly as full as I would have liked. Two pulls of the straw and it is gone.

"My... My husband?" My voice is coming back, although it sounds as if it belongs to a ninety-year-old man with advanced emphysema.

The two women share a glance I don't understand, and the nurse lays her hand on my arm. "No need to worry about anyone else but yourself right now, sweetie."

The affectionate term is as offensive to me as the cheap, scratchy sheets. I stopped being anyone's sweetie, or sweet at all, nine months ago.

I'm distracted by a sharp pain in my foot. "Ow!"

"Sorry," the doctor says, a smile belying her apology as she holds up a pin. "You passed with flying colors."

I pull my feet away. "Why am I here?"

"You had an accident. Do you remember?"

"No." I run a tongue across my dry lips. "Am I— What happened?"

"When you were brought in, we had to give you some pretty heavy doses of antibiotics, painkillers, and, of course, fluids. Additionally, we've kept you sedated for the past forty-eight hours to monitor the swelling in your brain which was, thankfully, relatively minor."

"Forty-eight hours," I repeat. "I've been sleeping for two days?"

"Not exactly sleeping. Medically sedated. But all of these factors—high doses of strong medications, bruising and swelling of your brain, lacerations to your scalp, back, and legs—these things tend to reduce your ability to store memories of the causal event."

Brain bruising and swelling. Lacerations. A causal event.
What event?

Anxiety threads beneath my nerve endings, pushing them up crookedly like roots distorting a flagstone walkway. She continues, as if I'm not already struggling to absorb her explanation. "In some cases, memory loss can go back further, impacting the days or weeks preceding the event. Those memories are most likely stored in your mind, although recalling them can be difficult."

I glance beyond her, looking for a movie camera and a director's slate board. Am I being pranked? Thrust into a bad soap opera?

"Are you—? I don't—" My head isn't just pounding, it is spinning. I can't keep a straight thought.

"Why don't you tell us the last thing you do remember, okay? We can go from there."

The last thing I remember...

I stare unseeingly through the window, images floating up from the darkened recesses of my mind.

A silken smudge of horizon, sea meeting sky, no land in sight.

Ships. At least a dozen of them. Then one in particular, with glossy teak decks. Its hull gleaming bright white, mast arrogantly pointing toward an azure blue sky.

The flashes of memory appear and disappear like a shark's fin cutting through the ocean. Furtive and ominous. I turn my confused gaze back to the doctor. "I—"

"Poppy!" My sister screeches to a halt at my bedside, her concerned hazel eyes taking in the tubes and wires, the doctor and nurse and my bandaged head and body, all at once. "Did you — When did you wake up?"

Dr. Carlson scowls at her. "Just now. I know you've been anxiously waiting, but if you—"

"Sadie," I interrupt. "What's going on?"

She presses her lips together, scrutinizing my face. "Don't say anything else. Not until after we talk." She shoots the doctor and nurse a warning glare. "Privately."

A scream would rip through my throat like a fistful of razor blades, but I can feel it building. If someone doesn't tell me something... I suck in a deep breath, ignoring the ache in my lungs.

One of the machines gives an angry buzz. "Calm down, Mrs. Stockton."

Sadie's arm creeps around the back of my neck, drawing me into a gentle embrace. "Just relax. I'll explain everything."

Bright spots appear at the periphery of my vision, and there is another angry buzz. *Can't they just unplug the damn machines already?* In her ear, I whisper, "What happened? Why am I here?"

Sadie pulls back, a strange expression on her face. "You don't remember?"

"No." My heart pounds against my lungs, trying to escape. "Tell me."

Dr. Carlson clears her throat, scribbling something on the papers affixed to her clipboard. "There is an FBI Agent waiting outside. He's asked to speak with you as soon as you're awake."

"Absolutely not," my sister answers immediately.

"FBI agent?" My whisper is barely audible against the blare of the machines.

"Yes. Given the circumstances, he's quite insistent." She pulls a card out of her pocket and reads from it. "Special Agent Gavin Cross. He said you know him."

Gavin. My cracked lips form the shape of a name I so rarely allow myself to think, let alone say aloud.

Sadie merely scoffs. "And you believed him?"

As the machines continue their frantic alarm, I turn pleading eyes on the nurse. *Gavin. Get Gavin.* But she doesn't look at me as she injects a needle into my IV bag.

A drugged numbness charges through my bloodstream, Sadie's voice becoming distant. "No one is going to accuse my sister of murder until…"

The warm embrace of sleep rolls over me and I surrender to dreams of a stolen past. A beautiful, broken boy. An enchanted forest. And a love that evaporated like mist in the morning sun.

PART I

CHAPTER 1

SACKETT, CONNECTICUT

FALL, EIGHTH GRADE

I slip into the woods unnoticed, pine needles scratching at my cheeks and catching in my hair as I duck between branches. The bright, nearly cloudless afternoon sky recedes as the tree-lined perimeter settles into place behind me, interlocking like an evergreen zipper. I am immediately swallowed up by the forest, enveloped within the hushed quiet of this natural sanctuary.

The ground underfoot is still springy, covered by a thin layer of maple and oak leaves that doesn't yet crunch beneath my feet like it will in a few weeks. As I make my way deeper into the woodlands, erratic streaks of sunshine dart through the shuddering canopy overhead like bolts of lightning, breaking up the dense shadows.

It's been two months since I moved to Sackett, Connecticut with my mother and sister, and the nature preserve behind our house is the only good thing about this entire town. There aren't any other kids in the neighborhood to play with. None that have shown an interest in me, anyway. I'm still the *new girl*.

I've spent hours wandering these woods, studying the trees and plants and especially the birds, when I can get a good look at them. The wide sprawl of maples, their bark dripping with untapped sap, perfumes the air with a sweet musk. White oaks, as broad and tall and straight as soldiers, tower over their shorter, more eccentric looking cousins, the red and chestnut oaks. And beneath the broad, rounded crowns of the yellow birch tree's drooping branches, determined roots climb over rotting stumps and logs, making the trunk appear as if it is standing on legs.

There is life in this forest. A peaceful energy that soaks deeper into my skin every afternoon, as if this is a place where good things happen.

They're not happening anywhere else, that's for sure.

My younger sister, Sadie, doesn't ever come with me. I've asked her a few times, but she's content to pass her afternoons lost in the pages of books. That's her safe place, I guess. And my mother… well, she just seems lost. Once I hear the *clink* of a wine bottle on the edge of her chipped coffee mug, I know she won't notice I've gone.

I'm admiring a particularly stubborn sweet pepperbush, pale pink petals still clinging to its stems, when the harsh crack of a snapping twig has me spinning around, every muscle in my body on alert, poised between fight or flight. I've heard there are bears in these woods. Deer and coyotes and bobcats, too.

But it's not an animal that's come up behind me.

It's a boy. A boy I've never seen before, although he looks about my age. He's dressed like I am, in jeans and a long-sleeved T-shirt. But if mine are secondhand, his are third or fourth. His hair is unruly, a motley mix of blond and bronze and copper that springs from his scalp in all directions. Even so, it doesn't quite cover the bruise on his cheek.

But it's his eyes I find most interesting of all. They are a vivid blue, surrounded by a thick fringe of lashes that look like they've been painted by an artist's hand, each one long and perfectly curved. The expression in them is wary, guarded.

Curiosity unspools inside of me, like a roll of twine I've lost hold of. I lick my lips, hoping they will form words. Any words.

I'm not naturally outgoing, which is unfortunate when you start a new school in eighth grade. My life would be a hell of a lot easier if I could go up to other kids and just start talking.

The court-mandated therapists I've been dragged to over the years have all said different versions of the same thing. *Imagine the girl you want to be, and then* be *her.*

As if life is a performance, and I can choose the role I'll play.

So far, I haven't managed to work up the nerve to audition. Which is probably why I'm in the woods right now, silently staring at a boy who looks every bit as uncertain and suspicious as I am.

I could turn away. Give a half-hearted wave and dart down a trail until I'm alone again, with only the trees and wildlife for company. But for some strange, fluttery, completely inexplicable reason—I don't want to do that. The desire to reach out, to impress him, to *know* him, is as undeniable as the scent of fertile soil, musky sap, and crisp autumn air filling my lungs with each breath.

Finally, I force myself to speak. "There's a raspberry bush a little further down this trail. It's where I'm going, if you want to come with me." Pivoting on my heel, my heart races, and my head fills with self-recrimination. *What makes you think he'll want to be your friend?*

A stream murmurs nearby but it's my own breath and the rapid *whoosh* of my pulse that sounds loudest inside my ears.

A fallen tree, it's decomposing bark spongy and damp, acts as a bridge over a shallow ravine. I'm halfway across it, my arms outstretched for balance, when I feel the vibration of footfalls behind me.

The surge of relief, of excitement, nearly makes me fall into the water. The few times I've gathered up the nerve to ask a classmate or someone on the school bus if they wanted to play, I'd been blown off.

I quicken my steps, jumping onto solid ground, and after a few minutes, we come to a small clearing marked by an outcropping of enormous rocks and a single bush. Yesterday, it was a raspberry bush. Today, the leaves are picked clean, barren of any fruit. "There were berries," I say, feeling stupid for not knowing someone, or some animal, would have gotten to them.

He shrugs, one hand pushing his hair out of his face. "I don't like raspberries, anyway."

Embarrassment gives way to confusion. "Then why did you come with me?"

Another shrug. "Nothing better to do."

His matter-of-fact delivery shouldn't hurt my feelings—I don't even know him—but it does.

At my wince, he shoves his hands in his pockets and kicks at a cluster of fallen acorns on the ground. "Hey, that's not— That's not what I meant."

Ducking my head to hide the redness creeping up my cheeks, I scramble toward the largest rock in the clearing and duck behind it, pulling out the metal shovel I've hidden beneath a layer of dirt and leaves. I can feel the boy's eyes on my shoulder blades as I dig, his scrutiny penetrating the thin fabric of my shirt. "What are you doing?"

I don't answer until metal strikes metal, then I set the shovel aside and wipe off the remaining dirt covering a box I hid here a few weeks ago. I lift the lid and pull out a deck of cards. "Sometimes I play Solitaire…"

But maybe today I won't have to.

I dare a glance at his face as he peers at the cards. I can't tell if he's interested—but he doesn't look *un*interested, either. "Do you know how to play Gin Rummy?"

"No," he answers, a frown tugging at a corner of his lips, an edge to his voice that I immediately want to soothe.

By necessity, I am sensitive to the moods of others. My mother can go from happy and engaged to violent and enraged in the blink of an eye, depending on whether she is drunk or high or both. I learned tricks to pacify, or at least distract her, at an early age. And I developed a sixth sense for whether the people she hung out with—the dealers and addicts she considered her friends—would treat Sadie and I like pets, welcomed with a smile and a pat on the head, or like pests, quick with a slap and a shove.

Before I can talk myself out of it, I shuffle the cards and say, "That's okay, I can teach you."

Once I start to deal, he sits down across from me. "What's your name?"

"Poppy."

"I'm Gavin," he says, watching my movements. "How old are you?"

"Thirteen."

He regards me skeptically. "You don't look thirteen."

I've always been on the shorter side of average, and while other girls my age have started filling out, I barely have even a suggestion of curves. "How old are you?"

"I'm fourteen."

"Well, you don't look your age either," I shoot back. He looks older, actually.

Gavin is tall, and while I don't see any scruff on his jaw, there is a quiet maturity in the thick ridge of his brow line and the calm sweep of his stare.

My gaze lingers too long on Gavin's face, the first stirrings of attraction taking me by surprise. I've never felt this way before, jittery and tingly. A little bit breathless. Because of a *boy*.

My tongue is unwieldy inside my mouth as I force myself to explain the rules of the game, my fingers fumbling over the cards.

Once there are seven in front of each of us, I quickly position the remaining deck down in the middle.

Removing an unwanted card from my own hand, I place it face up beside what remains of the deck, and take a new card from the top. Then I motion for Gavin to do the same. *Talk, Poppy. Say something. Something besides the rules of a stupid card game.* "I've never seen you at school before."

"I started at West Sackett last week."

"Oh. I'm at East. I started last month."

This nature preserve acts as a dividing line between the two school districts within our town. Gavin must live on the other side. I haven't been here long enough to know if there's much of a difference between the two.

For a while, we focus on the game. But as I deal out another hand, I ask, "How are you liking it?"

He studies his cards. "School's all right, I guess."

There's a reluctance to Gavin's tone. A defensiveness, too. As if he's used to telling people things are fine when they're really not.

It's a habit I recognize, because I do it too.

He looks up and our eyes catch, a tenuous line of connection forming between us. Warmth blooms inside my chest. I bite my lip as a grin pulls at the corners of my mouth, not sure I'm ready to share even this tiny flare of happiness with him. It feels too fragile, too new. And in my experience, if something can be broken, you'd better hide it from anyone with the power to break it.

Because they will.

Gavin wins our next game, gathering the cards before I do. His shuffle is awkward at first, but after a few tries, they make a waterfall noise as the bridge collapses within his hands. "How long are you allowed to stay out here?" I notice his shoulders rising up toward his ears with each word, like he's guarding himself against disappointment if I give the wrong answer.

I glance away from him reluctantly, squinting up at the patches of sky visible through the trees. My mom works at a dentist's office, but spends most afternoons on the couch, sipping wine and watching reality TV that's as far from our reality as we are from the moon. As long as I'm back before dark, which is about when Sadie wanders out of her room to poke around the kitchen, they won't even notice I'm gone. "Not for another hour or so. You?"

Gavin's shoulders drop back down, the crease that had gathered between his brows easing. "I have time," he says.

The relief in his tone is as comforting as a warm flame, though it also gives the impression that Gavin has even less supervision than I do. "Where did you move from?" I ask, arranging my cards. I have two pairs.

"Vermont. But before that we lived in Oklahoma and Texas. Maine for a couple of years. Then here last month."

Connecticut is small, and Sackett is right in the middle of it. I glance up at him. "That's a lot of places. Your dad in the army or something?" With each of Gavin's answers it gets easier to ask the next question, like we're playing catch and all I have to do is toss the ball back in his direction.

He scratches at his neck with fingernails bitten to the quick, the tips of his ears turning pink. "No. My parents just liked to move a lot."

There is tension between us that didn't exist a moment ago and I hurry to erase it, offering up details I don't usually share. "I was born in Massachusetts. Me and my sister. But my mom said she wanted a fresh start, so she moved us here two months ago."

He makes a noncommittal grunt. "Yeah, I've heard that before."

My hand stills as I discard a Jack. "What do you mean?"

He picks it up. "My mom used to say that, too. But then we'd move to a new place and the only thing that changed was our address. After a while, it felt pretty pointless." He glares at the cards in his hands before reluctantly meeting my eyes. "None of my parents' fresh starts worked. They finally gave up. I don't live with them anymore."

My stomach twists in empathy. Years ago, a neighbor who was all too aware of just how frequently Sadie and I were left alone had called the police. A social worker showed up and took us away. For too long, before my mom got clean and moved us here, Sadie and I were shuffled back and forth between a group home and relatives we barely knew.

My mom still drinks. And our house now isn't in great shape —the roof leaks, the water never gets above lukewarm, and the front steps look like they're about to collapse into a pile of splintered wood. But anything is better than living with strangers, wondering if we'd ever see our mom again.

"Sometimes they come back," I say. At least... physically. There is a part of my mom that never returned. A part I haven't seen in so many years I'm beginning to think it never actually existed. That I only imagined the joy of her spontaneous laugh, the pulse of genuine love in her embrace.

My voice is soft, gentle. But Gavin's blue eyes cloud over anyway, his mouth pressing into a horizontal line as he shakes his head. "I'm not holding my breath."

CHAPTER 2

SACKETT, CONNECTICUT

SPRING, EIGHTH GRADE

"You're late," Gavin says, glancing up from the cards in his hands. He can shuffle like a blackjack dealer now.

"You're early," I shoot back, grinning. In this forest, time feels irrelevant. Whoever gets here first is early and whoever gets here last is late. It's simple. Easy.

Just like the friendship that has sprung up between us.

I sit down on the ground across from Gavin, crisscrossing my legs as he begins dealing the cards. There are plenty of days when I arrive in what has become our spot, only to spend an hour playing Solitaire before heading home to my mom and sister, not knowing what kept Gavin away.

Sometimes I wonder whether he ever does the same.

I wonder… because I haven't asked. The question has occasionally hovered on the tip of my tongue, heavy and awkward. But I've never allowed it to escape.

Because I like to think of Gavin waiting for me, in *our* place. When I can't get away, I can at least retreat inside my mind and

17

imagine him here. Picture his nimble fingers touching each card, dappled light falling over his shoulders as he listens for the tell-tale crunch of my footsteps on the overgrown dirt trail leading to this clearing.

During much of the winter, walking through the woods was impossible. After we'd spent a dozen autumn afternoons together, a series of snowstorms turned Sackett Preserve into a beautiful, but inaccessible, winter wonderland. By March I was beginning to wonder if Gavin was just a boy I'd made up, if our wooded haven was merely a fantasy that existed inside my mind.

But the snow finally started melting and, except for the deepest drifts, it's mostly gone. We returned to the woods a few weeks ago, although the afternoon temperatures are still pretty brutal. Today it's barely above freezing and Gavin isn't wearing a coat. He's trying not to show it, but every so often, a tremble shakes his spine.

Once there are seven cards in front of me, I arrange them in a fan and organize them by suit. I have a decent hand, but I throw the game to end it quickly. Before Gavin can deal another, I shove the deck into the Ziplock bag and put it inside the metal box.

Gavin frowns at me, his disappointment obvious. "You have to leave already?"

"No. Not yet." I stand up, extending my ungloved hand in his direction. Gavin takes it, sending a little shiver of energy clanging against my nerve endings. "But I'm not in the mood for cards. Let's go exploring."

Truthfully, I've been looking forward to playing cards with Gavin all day. Each class felt like a lifetime, the bus ride home a trip across the country. I couldn't wait to be right where I am now, in our little clearing, stealing glances at Gavin's inky black eyelashes and crazy untamed hair, at the sharp slashes of his cheekbones and the bright glint of his smile.

I don't think Gavin has a clue how attractive he is. But I do.

Gavin's bold, dramatic features remind me of a charcoal drawing, the kind I saw on a field trip to the Metropolitan Museum of Art earlier this year. But someone took a paintbrush to his black and white portrait, giving him honey hued skin, piercing blue eyes, and endless shades of gold that spring from his head like a lion's mane.

And right now, Gavin's lips are turning violet. We need to move.

It's only as he stands up that I notice his wince. "Are you—"

He drops my hand and averts his face, shaking his head until his eyes are hidden beneath that unruly mop of hair. "I'm fine." Ignoring my hesitation, Gavin sets off for the nearest trail. "I saw a couple of deer on my way in. If we're quiet, maybe we can find them."

I follow after him, my gaze sweeping through the dense woods as I keep a few steps behind.

We don't find the deer.

But we do find an enormous rock ledge that looks over half the preserve, maybe more. Not all of the trees have regained their leaves yet, and our vantage point allows us to see more of the forest than we will months or even weeks from now. Naked gray and brown tree trunks stand desolately beside their lush, evergreen brothers, hiking paths twisting between them like an enchanted maze.

Gavin points at a spot just beyond the nearest ridge. "What do you think that is?"

I squint into the shadowed basin. "I don't know. Could it be the graveyard?"

"Graveyard?" He sounds skeptical.

"Yeah. There's a cemetery over in that direction, just beyond the northeast corner of the preserve. I noticed it on a map a while ago but I haven't worked up the nerve to go looking for it yet."

He grins and jumps down, turning back to me with his hands extended. "Let's find out."

Grabbing hold of Gavin's shoulders, I ease forward until he's caught me by my waist, swinging me to the ground. When he lets go, my sides tingle from his touch.

We follow a trail that wanders through the wetland valley and across rolling open woodlands. Around us, peeking out from behind trees and beneath exposed roots, the forest floor is covered in thickets of mountain laurel and skunk cabbage, maple-leafed viburnum and swamp azalea. Nothing has bloomed yet, but in another month or two the preserve will be a riot of green leaves and colorful flowers.

But right now, it's a flash of silver that catches my eye from above. I come to a complete standstill, throwing my head back for a better glimpse. As if the bird knows he has an audience, he lands on a branch over our heads, flapping his wings and showing off a dappled white and pale blue belly, opening his beak to give a warbled cry. "It's a mockingbird," I say, pointing. "Look at him, he's preening."

Gavin follows the trajectory of my finger and quirks a smile. "Does that mean there's a *she* around here somewhere he's trying to impress?"

I scan the trees around us as the mockingbird's mating call echoes off the deciduous hardwoods rising sixty, eighty, one hundred feet above us. "I don't know, but he's sure giving it his best shot."

The exertion of our afternoon hike has worked, and I can feel the warmth of Gavin's body beside me. I have to fight the urge to move closer, to drape his arm around my shoulders and curve into his side like I see the girls at school do with their boyfriends.

Yearning scrapes my skin, as abrasive as a thorny vine. *What would it be like to call Gavin my boyfriend?*

But it's another thought that steals my breath, sending pain twisting through my stomach. *What if he already* has *a girlfriend?*

Gavin and I don't go to the same school. We don't even know

any of the same people. What if I'm just someone he meets in the woods when he has nothing better to do?

I almost don't notice the second bird that lands beside the first in a wild flapping of feathers.

"I guess he's met his match," Gavin says, watching as they dance on the tree limb, flashing their white wing patches, chittering and warbling like long-lost lovers.

"They make a cute couple, don't you think?" My voice is strained as I ask about the birds. Because what I really want to ask is: Don't *we* make a cute couple?

But do I dare risk what we have now—an easy, relaxed friendship that doesn't need a label—for a chance at something else? The couples at school change every other week. Gavin and I have only known each other a few months. And yet, I feel like I *know* him, and he *knows* me in a way that can't be measured by arbitrary standards.

Isn't he— No. Aren't *we* worth the risk?

Before I can find the words or gather my courage, Gavin waves me forward. "Come on, let's keep going."

With a last look at the flirting mockingbirds, feeling both confused and deflated, despite the fact that nothing has actually happened between us, I follow Gavin's footsteps.

There's no one else in the woods with us today. At least no one we see or hear. Sometimes we run into locals taking their dogs for a hike, but this preserve isn't big enough to attract tourists. There's no parking lot or visitor's station. Most of the time, like today, it's all ours.

A few minutes later, we come to a creek cutting straight through the trail. There's no footbridge or downed tree in sight, just a series of uneven, slippery stones jutting out of the water at odd intervals.

Gavin's brows furrow in concentration as he evaluates their placement. Finally, he reaches for my hand, his fingers interlocking with mine, his thumb rhythmically sweeping along the underside of my palm. "Don't let go, okay?"

Sparks shoot up my arm, igniting tiny fires throughout my body. "I won't."

Together, we scramble across the makeshift path, and when my foot does slip a bit, Gavin tightens his grip and pulls me against him. "I've got you."

The heavy thrum of my heartbeat pulses in response. *Yes, you do.*

Back on land, we walk the rest of the way in silence, our hands still clasped.

"It's a cave," Gavin says, when we get closer to what he'd pointed at from the ridge.

"Can you see inside?" I ask in a whisper, squinting my eyes and trying to make out anything in the thick darkness.

"No." He picks up a rock from the ground and tosses it inside, then pulls me back behind a tree.

"What are you—"

He presses a finger to my mouth, silencing me. I freeze, my lips tingling from his touch, my heartbeat stuttering and then taking off at a gallop.

Gavin appears unaffected. His attention is on the mouth of the cave, watching it intently. Only after we hear the rock clatter against the ground does he pull his hand away. "Just checking."

My lips purse with disappointment. "For what?"

"Bears."

A soft laugh slips from my throat. "And what would you have done if a bear came charging out at us?"

"Same as you," Gavin says, the dark sweep of his lashes fanning his cheeks. And then he's cracking up, too. "Run."

The mingled sound of our shared humor bounces off the trees surrounding us, reverberating inside my ears as we cling to each other, our shoulders shaking, sides heaving.

Just as suddenly as the moment came, it's gone. Exhilaration evaporates inside our throats, the energy between us turning turbulent.

Gavin's eyes swirl with confusion and surprise, just as mine must have when he pressed his finger to my lips.

So, not unaffected after all.

After an awkward, expectant moment, we step away from each other and walk back to the cave. It's narrow, forcing us to sit side by side, our arms and legged pressed up against each other, our feet stretched out in front of us.

We've only ever sat across from each other, our card games like a wall we'd build and rearrange and tear down, only to build again.

The two of us look out at the forest, as if an explanation for the sudden change in atmosphere might be hidden in the shape of the leaves, the sway of the branches. My sneakers are muddy and wet, and my feet are so cold I can't feel them anymore. The boots I had last winter don't fit me anymore, and I had to give them to my little sister.

Gavin isn't wearing boots either. His sneakers are just as wet and muddy as mine, and he has a tear on the right one, the tip of his sock peeking out.

"I guess we can try to find the cemetery another day," I say, breaking the strained silence. "I think they have gravestones from the civil war."

He nods, then tilts his head further back to look up at the sky. I'd been avoiding evidence of the day pulling away from us. "We should probably go soon."

"Yeah." My stomach clenches with reluctance as I agree. "I just wish…" I let my voice trail off, feeling dumb. I've made plenty of wishes. On fallen eyelashes, holding a tiny black hair on the tip on my finger and blowing it into the wind. On birthday candles, if anyone remembered to mark the occasion. Even on a four-leaf clover I found once.

"What, Poppy? What do you wish?"

I turn to find Gavin regarding me with intense interest, as if my wishes are the most important thing in the world. And suddenly, I don't need verbal confirmation of the connection between us. I feel it in my bones.

"I wish we could live here. That this was our home."

A faint smile crosses his face, and I notice a yellowish tinge around his left eye. The remnants of a fading bruise. But then Gavin sees me looking and he gives a little shake of his head, his hair sliding forward. "That'd be nice," he says, softly. "Real nice."

CHAPTER 3

SACKETT, CONNECTICUT

SUMMER, FRESHMAN YEAR, HIGH SCHOOL

"*I* can't believe we start high school tomorrow." I practically groan the words.

"Oh, I don't know. I'm looking forward to it," Gavin says, his tone much lighter than mine. "Homework, tests, hanging out with people whose names don't start with *P* and end in Oppy."

I give him a not-so-playful shove. "Hey!"

At my faux outrage, Gavin tips his head back and laughs. A low, rolling, entirely endearing laugh that sends goose bumps scattering across my skin. I take advantage of the opportunity to step a little closer, pulling the scent of him into my lungs. As always, Gavin smells like pinecones and clean laundry, but now layered with sunscreen and bug repellant—a necessity until we hit sweater weather.

I let out a little sigh of pleasure. At his laugh, at his scent, at his proximity. *I've missed you.*

Gavin and I have barely seen each other this entire summer. I've been working as a counselor for the local camp organized by

Sackett's parks and rec department. It runs every week of summer break, from eight in the morning until six at night. And he's spent nearly every day pumping gas and stocking shelves at the gas station and convenience store his foster dad manages.

The thought is still pulsing inside my mind when Gavin nudges me with his elbow, pointing at something outside the cave. "Look."

I look over just in time to see a red fox scurrying through the underbrush. Two baby fox kits, not much bigger than squirrels, trail behind, their tiny legs racing to keep up.

"A family," I whisper softly, watching until they disappear from sight.

In an odd way, I am struck by the similarity to my own. My sister and I, chasing after our mother, sticking as close as we can in the hopes that she won't lose us, leave us behind.

I'm certain that's why Sadie has never followed me into the woods. She's afraid that if she leaves the house too, my mother won't be home when we return. In the beginning, those first few weeks we'd lived in Sackett, I'd been a little put off that Sadie refused to join me in exploring our new neighborhood. But everything changed the day I met Gavin. Now I'm glad she's content to stay at home. And I'm glad I don't have to share my best friend with anyone, even my sister.

"You think the dad's around here somewhere?" I ask. "Or did he lose interest after the fun part of making babies?"

Gavin's shoulders lift in an unconcerned shrug. "I'm not exactly up to speed on the mating habits of foxes. But they look fine to me."

"Better one parent who gives a shit than two who don't, I guess."

The second the words leave my mouth, I feel him tense up beside me. "That's for sure."

Shit. I want to race after my thoughtless remark and stuff it back down my throat.

Before I can apologize, or think of a way to wipe the sad look off Gavin's face, he asks, "You ever see your dad, Poppy?"

I shake my head. "N— No. Not since I was little. I barely remember him."

"Does it bother you that he's not around?"

"Not really." I release a sigh and lean back on my palms. "It's hard to miss something you've never had, I guess."

A lazy breeze barely shakes the green canopy overhead, the leaves reflecting and amplifying the summer sun. Our cave offers a cool haven from the warm, humid air of the forest. Since discovering it last spring, we've turned it into our secret hideaway. I brought a camp light I unearthed at the Salvation Army and Gavin found some old, mismatched cushions that provide a buffer from the cold, damp cave floor.

Despite the direction of our conversation, I feel cozy and comfortable here with Gavin. More cozy and comfortable than I can ever remember being anywhere, or with anyone. And it occurs to me that, for all the time we've spent together—we haven't shared very much about ourselves. Not the important things, anyway.

Strangely, it makes me want to be cozy and *un*-comfortable. To do more than just skirt the truth about why I wound up here, in Sackett. Why I don't know my dad and don't really trust my mom.

She likes to say, "two wrongs don't make a right." But, in this moment, I don't believe her. What feels right is wanting to share all my wrongs with Gavin. And for him to do the same.

I clear my throat, pulling my hair free of its ponytail so it falls over my shoulders in a messy, windswept tumble. "My mom is a drug addict, Gavin. That's why Sadie and I were taken from her."

He turns to me in surprise, his eyes swirling with questions but devoid of judgment. I fill him in on my past, my tone matter-of-fact, eventually linking the initial strand of our conversation by saying, "Things are... okay now. I don't know if my dad was the reason my mom got into drugs, but if seeing him again would make her self-medicate with anything stronger than a bottle of wine—" I pause, my thoughts turning inward as memories scroll through my mind like a slideshow. Memories I wish I knew how to erase.

Gavin pats my hand reassuringly and the urge to intertwine my fingers with his brings me back to the present. "Sorry, I got a little lost in my head for a minute."

"It's okay. I get it." He offers a solemn nod, his gaze remaining warm and steady on mine. "Really."

"How about you?" I ask tentatively, not at all sure Gavin will want to open up to me any more than he already has. "Do you miss your parents?"

Gavin is quiet for several beats, and my stomach gurgles with uneasiness and self-recrimination. What if my feelings are one-sided? What if Gavin isn't interested in being *un*comfortable—at least, not with me?

But then he rubs his palms on his knees, little brackets shaped like crescent moons appearing at the edges of his mouth as he presses his lips together. "Sometimes. But then I remember how things were and I'm glad to be away from them. I probably could have dealt with being my father's punching bag. It was covering for him that was the worst. Lying to the nurse as she was stitching me up. Backing up my mom's stories about falling down stairs or walking into cabinet doors."

"Why did you?"

"Because my mom asked me to. And I thought I was doing the right thing." He exhales a heavy breath. "I should have told the truth—I know that now. My dad's a real piece of shit. But my mom accepted it. She loved him—even though he hurt her, hurt me. Sometimes, I swear she'd pick a fight just for the adrenaline rush of an argument, and the apologies and attention she'd get afterward."

"I'm sorry," I say, wishing I could come up with something better. "Do you think you'll ever see them again?"

"Doubtful." He blinks a few times, the outline of his iris deepening to a rich cobalt while the inside gets lighter, as pale as a robin's egg. "I don't know that I want to."

He breaks our stare, rubbing at the frown crossing his forehead. "I wish I knew how my mom was doing though. If things are better for her without me around. I hope they are, anyway."

When my mom chose drugs over Sadie and me, at least I could tell myself that her addiction was a disease, that she was sick.

But Gavin... what is the voice inside his head telling him?

Whatever it is, I'm sure it's not kind.

"Every once in a while, my mom would talk about running away. Going someplace he'd never find us. But in the end, it was me she ran away from."

My heart breaks for Gavin as he confirms my suspicions—that he feels abandoned. "Maybe she stayed with your dad to keep you safe."

He throws a dubious stare my way. "How do you figure?"

"Well, maybe your mom was worried he would come after her, after you both. Maybe leaving you was the best option to keep you safe."

"I'm not a little kid anymore. If she left him, I'd protect her." A vein pulses at Gavin's neck, tension pulling his shoulders closer to his ears. "Whatever it took."

"Well, that's probably—"

"I get what you're trying to do, Poppy. And thanks. But it's fine. I'm fine," Gavin insists.

"I'm not—"

"If my mom showed up one day, wanting help to get away from my dad—I'd drop everything to go with her, to keep her safe. But it's never going to happen."

"It might. Never say never."

29

He releases a humorless half-laugh. "Your mom fought her demons and won—and that's awesome. But she's the exception, not the rule."

I know when I'm beat. Even if the theory I proposed just to give Gavin an alternate narrative to consider is true—I have no way of knowing, or proving, that it is. "I think, at least in my mom's case... I think every day is another fight. Addiction is a battle you never really win. And maybe that's why my dad didn't stick around."

"She's clean now though, right?"

The sharp cry of a hawk makes me think about the mama fox and her babies, and I hope they're all safe. "She still drinks, but she doesn't do any of that other stuff. And she doesn't have guys over anymore."

Noticing the shudder I can't quite suppress, Gavin frowns. "Did someone—"

I shake my head, hurrying to reassure him. "No. It wasn't like that."

I don't tell Gavin how close it came. Sometimes, I wake up in the middle of the night to find my mother in my bed, slurring apologies about what she put us through. During the day though, she pretends like none of it happened at all.

He sighs. "There are some really shitty people in the world."

"Yeah. But luckily, there are some really good ones, too." I am drawn back into the intense vortex of Gavin's stare and I feel myself leaning into him, inch by inch, until his breath is a welcome caress against my lips. I stop myself from kissing him just in time, swallowing hard.

"So..." I search for something else to say, anything else, and decide to broach a subject I attempted once before, the day a rough branch had ripped Gavin's shirt, exposing a dark blue bruise that stained the skin over his ribcage. He'd rebuffed me then, but I sense an opening now. "Have you considered telling your foster parents about—"

Gavin's brows pull together over the bridge of his nose in a fierce scowl and he moves away from me. "No."

"Why? He's not your mom, you don't have to protect him."

"I'm not protecting him."

"Then why not say something? He's hurting you."

"I only let Doug get a punch in every once in a while so he won't do worse, like convince his parents to send me back. And they love him. Do you really think they'd keep me around if I tell them their kid is a dick?"

"But—"

"No. I can't take the chance." He runs a hand through his hair. "Leaving here would mean leaving *you*, Poppy."

The sweetness of Gavin's admission is almost lost as the truth behind it slaps me in the face. For the first time, it occurs to me how tenuous our relationship is.

We might be hunkered down inside this cave, shielded by thick walls, but our relationship is hardly invulnerable. Like a spider's web, the connection Gavin and I have forged is intricate and beautiful. And so very, very fragile.

"For now, it's enough that you know the truth," he continues. "And when the time is right, he'll get what's coming to him." His voice lowers to a gritted rasp. "They all will."

A breath of chilled air wafts across the back of my neck, skating across taut nerves and sending a tremor down my spine.

Gavin glances at me with concern. "Cold?"

I blink dully, ignoring the question. I'm not sure what I am right now. Knowing what Gavin is dealing with, just to stay here, just to be with me, is a lot to take in. And so is knowing that, all the while, his resentment is brewing. "Remind me never to get on your bad side." I mean it as a lighthearted joke, but it doesn't come out that way.

Gavin pins me in place with a broody stare, stilling the breath in my chest. And then his face breaks into a grin, as bright as the sun sliding out from behind a cloud. What he says is just as blinding, taking me completely by surprise. "I think it's impossible for anyone to have a bad side around you, Poppy. You're kind and funny and smart. And I'm pretty sure it's contagious, because when I'm with you, that's how you make me feel too."

A tangled knot of gratitude laced with fear expands inside my chest. Gratitude at the confirmation that my feelings aren't entirely one-sided. Gavin likes me, too.

Thank God, because I can't even imagine my life without him in it.

And fear, for exactly the same reason. What if Gavin's mom returns for him? Or Doug succeeds in getting his parents to send Gavin away? "Promise me we'll always be friends, okay?"

"Always," he says.

Maybe because I know it's a promise he might not be able to keep, I lift my hand, pinkie extended.

Gavin laughs. "You're going to make me pinkie swear?"

"I am."

And he does, locking fingers with me and giving me a little tug forward. "Poppy?"

"Yes?"

"What if I want to be more than friends?"

My throat is suddenly dry, my voice quivering from an excess of emotions I'm not quite sure I can contain. "Do you?"

"Yeah. I do."

A gust of wind suddenly whips through the trees, sending leaves fluttering to the ground like confetti. "I think... I think I'd like that." Talk about an understatement.

"Okay."

"Okay," I repeat. Gavin's grip on my finger loosens, his hand sliding over my wrist and along my forearm until it curves around the back of my shoulder and I'm floating inside the ocean of his eyes, my heart thudding with the knowledge that this moment—*this very moment*—is exactly what I've been waiting for.

My wish is actually coming true.

I've never been kissed. And I've wanted to be kissed by Gavin for almost as long as I've known him.

It's a yearning I've grown accustomed to, like the tug on my heart every time our eyes connect, or the way his smile warms me to my core. I've dreamed about this moment, fantasized about it so many times. And now that it's finally here, I realize I don't quite know what to do.

Gavin's fingers push through my hair to cradle my head. We are so close, I can see flecks of black and gold around Gavin's pupils, and the way each iris is made up of layered, interlocking rings of blue, from pale morning sky to deepest midnight—like the circular growth rings of a tree. His eyes are the doors to a world that calls to me. A future we'll share, together.

At first, Gavin's mouth merely hovers over mine. I'm not at all sure he'll actually kiss me. Maybe his breath is all I'll get.

But, after a moment, I feel the soft press of Gavin's lips on mine. It's enough, more than enough, for the thrill of possession to weave through me, for the spark of infatuation to burst into a more enduring flame, for me to be forever marked by my first kiss.

Initially, we're both clumsy and stiff, my neck cocked at a strange angle and his fingertips digging into my ribs. But eagerness and enthusiasm win out.

Our mouths open, our tongues tentatively sliding together. His grip relaxes, and I loop my wrists over his shoulders.

And that's when I feel *it*. Something so powerful it doesn't have a name. A certainty.

A certainty that we are meant to be together. Today. Tomorrow. All the tomorrows to come.

That this kiss, our first kiss, and the next one, and the one after that, and the thousands in between until our very last, is inevitable.

CHAPTER 4

SACKETT, CONNECTICUT

SPRING, FRESHMAN YEAR, HIGH SCHOOL

"What's that?" I ask, glancing over Gavin's shoulder as I sit down beside him. We don't play cards as often as we used to. These days, we come into the woods with bulging backpacks. I like studying to the sound of Gavin's pencil scratching on paper, the low hum he makes in the back of his throat when he's concentrating, his satisfied grunt when he gets an answer right.

"Just a list of electives for next year. We have to put in our requests tomorrow."

"We got ours, too." I pull out a sheet of paper that looks nearly identical to Gavin's.

As he reads mine, I say what we're both thinking. "I wish they would just combine our schools already."

Last year, a proposal to merge East Sackett and West Sackett into one school system was voted down. Local politicians had played up the fact that, with the cost savings generated by sharing facilities and overhead, there would be more money to spend on extracurriculars and special programming, not to mention a wider array of elective offerings.

But our town, like much of New England, is set in its ways.

Gavin sighs, and then circles *Business Law*. "Never going to happen. Most of the people who bother to vote grew up in Sackett, went to school in Sackett, and either stayed here or came back because they want the same for their kids. They're not going to fix what they don't think is broken. And they don't think two high schools, two middle schools, and two elementary schools in one town is broken—because that's how it's always been."

"In this case, breaking something would mean putting it together," I grumble.

"The only way we'll be in the same school is to go to the same college."

I smile at the thought. "I can't wait to get out of here, Gavin. This place is stifling." Most days, I still feel like the new girl. Probably because only three other kids have entered my grade in the year and a half since we moved here—all of them boys.

That advice I'd been given before moving to Sackett—*Imagine the girl you want to be, and then* be *her*—is impossible to follow in this town.

At first I thought I was the problem, that I was shy or gave off unfriendly vibes. But I've realized that it isn't all my fault. I'm not failing at friend auditions. In Sackett, the stage just isn't big enough.

I don't have nice clothes or a big house or a mother on the PTA. I don't play sports. I'm not particularly artsy or rebellious.

There are only a few cliques to choose from... and I don't fit into any of them.

Gavin waves his hand at the forest exploding around us. "It is. But I'm sure you want to come right back here after college."

"No way. Never."

"Never say never," he echoes my own words teasingly as I roll my eyes. "Okay, fine. Some other place where you can build a treehouse and live off the land."

A laugh bursts from my throat. "Nope. Urban jungle or bust." Well, that's not entirely true. For Gavin, I would definitely compromise. But this is a conversation about dreams, not written-in-stone destinations.

I crave the freedom of anonymity and the benefits of a big city. I want to live in a skyscraper, dine in gourmet restaurants, and browse through art galleries and museums on a whim. I want to live in a place where secondhand is called vintage. Where being new makes me interesting, not an outcast.

"You?" Skepticism oozes off him in waves. "Poppy, there are thirty-three acres in this preserve, and I think you can name every single species of tree and flower."

I highly doubt that, but I play along. "Don't forget about the shrubs."

"My point exactly. How many shrubs will you find in a city?"

"A lot. New York has Central Park and the Botanical Gardens. Boston has the Public Garden and the Emerald Necklace. Chicago has—"

"It's not the same," he says dryly.

"I know. And I love it out here, I do. But..." I duck my head, feeling a wave of embarrassment come over me. Of all the confidences I've shared with Gavin, I've never told him just how pitiful my social life at school really is. "I'm not exactly a bookworm, but I hide in the library during lunch. Usually, behind the biggest book I've found—an oversized field guide to native New England geography."

My cheeks are already burning but I keep talking. "I only started coming into the forest because it was better than sitting in my room, alone. I pretended the trees and flowers and shrubs were my friends."

Gavin's hand snakes around my waist and pulls me into his

side. He whispers in my ear, "You were smarter than me. I sat alone in the cafeteria my first week, reading *Lord of the Flies*."

"The entire first week?" I ask doubtfully, pushing away my own embarrassment. I can't imagine the girls at West Sackett High aren't vying for Gavin's attention every chance they get.

His lips curl into a rueful grin that makes my chest ache. "Almost."

My lungs swell with the scent of the fertile ground beneath our feet, the fresh forest air, and the clean, bracing scent of Gavin himself. The heady rush makes me sink my teeth into my bottom lip until the sizzle of pleasure is tempered by pain. Because I don't know how to handle the feelings that rise up inside me at the most innocuous things Gavin does. A look, a touch, a smile. "How about you—city mouse or country mouse?"

He leans forward and nibbles on the lobe of my ear, sending a shiver down my spine. "I don't care, as long as this mouse gets his cheese."

"Way too *cheesy*, Romeo." I laugh, poking a finger into his stomach.

A pained, hissing sound erupts from behind Gavin's clenched teeth, his eyes narrowing in a wince.

"What—" I draw back immediately. "What did he do this time?"

"It's nothing."

"Show me."

"Poppy—"

"If it's really nothing, show me."

Reluctance is etched into the sharp lines and hard angles of Gavin's face as he slowly lifts his shirt, revealing a bruise bleeding into his belly button.

"I hate him," I say, as soon as I catch my breath. I've never met Doug, the son of Gavin's foster parents, but I despise him with an intensity that runs bone-deep.

"That makes two of us," Gavin says, his tone smooth and

soothing as he lets the hem of his shirt fall. "He was pissed when he found out his dad had slipped me some money on the side to help out at the gas station this summer."

"You were there practically every day, of course he should pay you."

"Well, not according to Doug. He demanded I give it to him. When I refused, he got in a sucker punch."

"They should know what an awful kid they've raised," I grumble, relaxing into his hold as he pulls me forward.

"One day," Gavin says. "But today, I have money hidden in a place Doug will never find, and I have you. I have nothing to complain about."

Gavin plants tender kisses along the curve of my neck, then makes his way to my mouth. We have yet to do much more than kissing, but his mouth wreaks such havoc with my senses I'm not sure I can handle anything else.

When he pulls away, I let out a disappointed moan. My eyes flutter open, about to tell him not to stop. But Gavin's head is cocked to the side, an air of intense concentration on his face. I know that look. "Thunder?"

He waits a moment, still listening, then says, "I'm not sure. If it was, it's really far away."

Thunder means lightening, and a forest is the last place you want to be in a storm. "Let's wait it out a few minutes. Maybe it was something else."

He gives a shallow nod, the spell of his kiss broken. I grab for his pencil and circle *Personal Finance*, *Public Speaking*, and *Practical Writing* on my sheet.

"That was fast," Gavin says.

I shrug. "I don't want to open my mail and see bills with Past Due stamped in red across the front, I want to get more comfortable talking to people, and I happen to be a very practical person."

He holds out his hand and I give him back the pencil. After a minute of frowning at the list, Gavin circles *Computer Programming* and *Accounting*.

"Law, computers, and accounting? Are you moving straight from sophomore year to grad school?" Although it wouldn't surprise me. Gavin is already taking the most advanced math and science classes his school offers. Next year, he'll enroll in a few college-level courses.

"I wish," he jokes, but his lips are pressed together as if he's holding in a secret.

"What?" I ask. "What aren't you saying?"

"It's dumb. A pipe dream. It's probably never going to happen anyway so—"

"Gavin, there's nothing dumb about dreams. Tell me."

He doesn't answer immediately and I think he's probably hoping for a crack of thunder to save him, but there are only the normal forest sounds: rustling leaves, water cascading over rocky creek beds, the twitter and chirp of birds. Finally, he exhales a breath and mutters something completely inaudible.

I have no intention of letting him off the hook. "What was that?" I prod.

"FBI, all right. I want to be an FBI agent."

I'm puzzled. "What's wrong with that?"

"Wrong?' He blinks several times, as if I'm the one who is confusing him. "Do you know how hard it is to get into the Academy? It's basically impossible. I have next to no chance."

Not that I've ever considered a career in law enforcement, but in my opinion, Gavin has every chance. "Why the FBI?"

"Because... Because they get to solve the toughest cases, put away the worst criminals. And I want to be a part of that."

Gavin is still and serious, as if this is something he's thought about for a very long time. "So, basically, you want to be a real-life hero."

He ducks his head, a self-conscious grin pulling at his mouth.

I loop my wrists over his neck, forcing him to meet my eyes. "Promise me one thing."

"What's that?"

"Never forget that you were my hero first, okay?"

The look he gives me is so filled with heat, it melts the marrow inside my bones. "I can do that."

I feel myself unraveling, coming apart in places I instinctively want to protect. To lighten the moment, I take one hand from behind his neck and bring it between us. "Pinkie swear?"

But Gavin doesn't take the bait. "We can do better than that, don't you think?"

From the minute we met, and probably without even knowing it, Gavin has been breaking down my walls and sanding away my protective veneer. He's the reason I can go to school every day, knowing I'm an unwanted outcast, and still have something to smile about when I go to sleep. He's the best part of my present, and the most important part of my future.

Despite the low rumble of thunder that accompanies the press of Gavin's lips on mine, we linger in each other's arms until we're both breathless and panting.

Gavin finally wrenches away from me when the breath we share is as electric as the storm-charged air. And despite my protests that he should hurry home, he walks me all the way to the edge of the woods behind my house.

Blue light flickers from the living room window and I picture my mom sprawled on the couch, a half-empty wine bottle beside her, watching the Kardashians complain about their hair and their clothes and their multi-million-dollar houses.

Although it hasn't started raining yet, the clouds hovering just above the tree line are dark and bloated, and our feet are nearly obscured by heavy mist. I turn around when another bolt of lightning leaves a jagged scar across the sky. "You had better make it home safe, Gavin. I might need you to rescue me one day."

≈

"Is that you, Poppy?" my mom calls when I shut the door behind me.

I sigh. The impending storm forced me home earlier than usual, before wine made her sleepy and inattentive. "Yep. I'm just going to finish my homework."

"Can you start dinner first?"

"Sure." I open the refrigerator, hoping that maybe she swung by the grocery store on her way home but… no. We have two apples, a container of yogurt, and a dozen half-empty condiment bottles. I open the cabinet over the stove. "Mac and cheese okay?"

"There's nothing else?"

I look back inside the cabinet. A box of cereal and a bottle of olive oil. "Nope."

"Fine. Will you—"

"Yeah. I'll pick up a few things this weekend." I automatically swallow the resentment that coils through me, thinking of the babysitting money I'll have to shell out at the supermarket.

I'm grateful my mom is home with us, and that we have a home at all. I just wish it were easier, I guess.

When I have kids, I never want them to feel like they're parenting me. I'll have a career, not just a job, although my family will always come first. There will be plenty of food in the refrigerator, a basketball hoop at the end of the driveway, and one of those huge calendars in the kitchen—filled with soccer games, dance classes, and date nights.

Fifteen minutes later, I divide the pasta between three bowls and bring one to my mother. She puts her mug down and takes it from me, barely glancing away from the TV.

I want to ask her: When did *this*—dinner out of a box, eaten in front of a screen, passing out on a couch—become enough? Had she never wanted anything better for herself? For us?

41

They are questions I don't bother asking. Even if my mom could give me an answer, I'm not sure I want to know.

Instead, I carry the other two bowls down the hall, tapping on Sadie's door with the toe of my sneaker. "Come on in."

"I can't, my hands are full."

I hear Sadie's feet hit the ground; the door swinging open a moment later. "Well, this is a surprise." She takes the bowl I extend to her.

"That we're having mac and cheese for dinner?"

She rolls eyes that are nearly identical to mine. Almost everything about us is *nearly identical*, but not quite. Both of us can be called strawberry blondes, but mine veers more to the auburn end of the spectrum. We both have hazel eyes, but mine are green edged with amber and Sadie's are amber edged with green. Our skin tone is the same, but she has a scattering of freckles across the bridge of her nose that I love and she hates. She's slightly curvier, I'm an inch taller.

The differences between my sister and I feel glaring to me, but they often go unnoticed. Sadie is a daredevil, I am a rule follower; she is loud, I am reserved; she writes with her left, I with my right.

Since we are so close in age and appearance, most people assume we're twins. But I've been a surrogate parent to her for my entire life, so to me, the eighteen months separating us sometimes feels more like years.

"No. I mean that you're home before dark." She scoops a bite of bright orange shells into her mouth. "Seriously, Pops. What do you do in the woods for hours on end?"

I shoot a pointed look toward the stack of library books beside her bed. I think she devours one a day. "You stay in your room all afternoon, reading about imaginary people."

"Is playing with leprechauns and fairy sprites better?"

I shrug my shoulders. "Better than being cooped up inside."

"Who are you avoiding—me or Mom?"

Her question takes me by surprise, and so does the streak of hurt that flashes across her face, so quickly that if I'd been anyone else, I would never have noticed it. "I'm not avoiding anyone. I just like to go exploring, Sadie. That's all."

Guilt roils inside my stomach. Until Gavin, I'd never kept a secret from my sister.

We shared everything. Food, clothes, toys when we had any at all. Before we moved to this house, we shared a room, sometimes even a bed.

Sadie narrows her eyes at me. "Why are you lying to me? Do you think I'm stupid? Or that I'll tell mom whatever your secret is?"

If I wasn't holding my dinner, I'd throw up my hands in exasperation. "I'm not lying," I insist. "And even if it was, why do I have to tell you everything? One of the best parts about moving here is that I don't have to watch over you every second anymore."

The blood drains from her face, only to reappear in blotchy pink patches on her cheeks. "If that's the way you really feel, then get out," she yells.

Damn it. "I didn't mean it like that, Sadie. I'm sorry." My frustration evaporates instantly. I hate that I've hurt her, even unintentionally.

But... is it so horrible that I'm finally carving out a life of my own? For the first time, I have a secret. Someone who belongs just to me. I'm not ready to share Gavin with anyone. Even Sadie.

Yet. Eventually, I want him to meet my sister. And it would be nice to walk through town, hand in hand. To go to the movies or out for ice cream.

For now though, he's the best kind of secret.

Mine.

CHAPTER 5

SACKETT, CONNECTICUT

FALL, SOPHOMORE YEAR, HIGH SCHOOL

a s I grab for my science notes, the pages I'd ripped from a magazine while I was at the dentist's office last week fall to the ground.

Before I can tuck them back inside my bag, Gavin glances over my shoulder. "Class project?"

"Not exactly." I feel a flush creeping up my cheeks, as if he's caught me with my sister's tattered copy of *Fifty Shades of Grey* instead of a double page spread from an interior design magazine. "I thought they looked a little like us, actually."

It's become a habit of mine, ripping out pages from magazines and squirreling them away in a drawer at home. Photos of people and places and clothes. A woman ice skating in the snow. A pair of black slingback stilettos with red soles. The setting sun melting into a placid lake, turning the water into a violet cauldron. Sometimes, I spread them out on my bed, trying to find some thread of connection, a common similarity. The ones I like best, I pin to a bulletin board on my wall.

Gavin frowns at the couple embracing beneath a chandelier dripping with crystal beads and pendants. "If you say so."

I run my finger over the glossy photographs taken in the couple's newly renovated apartment and sigh. So many glamorous, elegant things in one place—furniture, artwork, high ceilings and thick, carved molding. Especially the couple themselves, who are dressed as if they're going to a ball, he in a fitted black tuxedo and she in a strapless evening gown glimmering from thousands of tiny sequins and seed pearls threaded through the lush fabric.

The only consistency I've found is not in the captured subjects themselves, but the response they evoke in me. Awe. Maybe a little envy. A desire to see what's on the page with my own eyes. Feel it, touch it, experience it.

Obviously sensing I'm more interested than I'm letting on, Gavin sets aside his own homework and reaches for the pages. His lips move silently as he skims the article. When he's finished, his gaze lifts to mine. "What is it you liked so much about this apartment, these people?" Gavin's expression is earnest, and he asks the question as if he really wants to know the answer, as if it's important to him. Because *I'm* important to him.

When I'm with Gavin, there's just the two of us. No one else is vying for his attention. He makes me feel like I'm the only girl in the world. But beyond our wooded sanctuary, in my high school, in Sackett, I'm nobody.

Moving back and forth between these two worlds—somebody to nobody, nobody to somebody—just amplifies the best and worst of them both.

Lately, I've wondered if my mom ever experienced this kind of elation. If she'd ever felt the way Gavin makes me feel.

Because if she had, and then been forced to live without the one person who makes her feel happy and welcomed and interesting... Well, maybe then I'd understand her need to dull the sharp edge of loss with a bottle of wine every night.

Even thinking about living without Gavin makes pressure build up inside my chest, constricting my airway and blood vessels. To distract myself from the sudden rush of fear clawing at my neck, I return my attention on the pages in Gavin's hands.

Unlike Gavin's dream of becoming an FBI agent, I don't know exactly *what* I want to do. But I do know who I want to *be*.

Someone who is invited to glamorous parties.

Someone who fills her home with beautiful things.

Someone who drinks coffee—not wine—out of an unchipped mug.

Someone who builds a life with a man who loves her. A man who will never abandon her.

I hesitate, trying to put my feelings into words. "It's more than just the apartment. Look at the expressions on their faces. Look at how he's holding her, as if he'll never let her go. And the way she has one of her hands on his chest, right over his heart. They just," I pause for a moment, sighing at the photograph. "They look so... perfect. Meant to be, you know. Like nothing bad has ever happened to them. Like nothing bad ever will."

He frowns. "Bad things happen to everyone."

"Not everyone." I shake my head stiffly, the movement conveying my absolute certainty. "Some people were born to live charmed lives. I mean, do you think that couple would ever have their kids taken away from them, or voluntarily give them up?"

Gavin considers what I've said for a minute, then shrugs. "That's the thing about pictures. They capture one moment in time, and only what's within the frame. That couple—in that moment, in that picture—they may look like they lead perfect lives. But it's just an image. It's what they want us to see. We have no idea what really happened before the photographer got there or after he left."

I blink back the unexpected sting of tears. There are times, like now, when the worry I'll never escape the cycle of my past—abandonment and fear and a constant yearning for things I'll never have, a life I'll never lead—weighs on me like a boulder, the pressure slowly crushing me.

I need to believe that not all images are illusions. Some are true snapshots of the kind of life I can have—if I want it badly enough, if I work hard enough. One day.

"Well, you might not believe in them," I say, looking back down at the couple in the photograph, "but I do."

Gavin sets the torn pages aside and gently sweeps a lock of hair behind my ear. "I believe in you, Poppy. And I believe in us, too. We all have… *stuff* we keep hidden from view. If you didn't have yours and I didn't have mine—maybe we wouldn't be here, together. But you do, and I do, and *we are*.

"I want to get the fuck out of this town, too. I want to get my diploma, do whatever it takes to get to Quantico, and go wherever the FBI sends me. I want to solve crimes the bad guys think they've gotten away with. But our past is an engine, not an anchor. It's what will drive us forward, not what holds us back."

Gavin's arm encircles my waist as he positions my palm over his chest, just like the couple in the picture. "You are strong, Poppy. Stronger than you think you are." The steady thrum of his heart is both reassuring and terrifying.

A heart can ache. A heart can break. A heart can harden.

A heart can stop beating, stop loving.

In an instant.

"I don't feel strong," I admit in a choked rasp, doubt crashing over me. What if my mom once had the same dreams as I do right now? What if I'm just a bad breakup away from a life of alcohol and addiction?

Gavin presses a kiss to my forehead. "You are," he assures me. "It's what I love most about you. Well, besides your laugh. And your smile that shines from your entire face, not just your mouth. I love that you don't just walk through the woods, you're always looking around, noticing birds' nests and blooming flowers and trees with the perfect amount of shade."

My breath catches in the back of my throat as I study Gavin's face, wanting so badly to believe what he's saying. "You *love* me?"

His eyes twinkle at my question. "I do. I have for a while now."

Why? My doubts are like dry leaves on a blustery day, swirling around with no apparent order or reason. "But—"

"You don't have to say you love me back. Not if you don't."

I might not understand why Gavin loves me, but I understand what he needs. Hope is threaded through his voice and shining from his eyes. *Love me back.*

And there's an unspoken plea etched into the tiny creases bracketing his lips. *But don't lie to me.*

No lies are necessary. I love Gavin with every breath in my body.

"I do. I love you so much." Tears streak down my cheeks as I say the words, the salt only adding to the sweetness of the moment.

CHAPTER 6

SACKETT, CONNECTICUT

SUMMER BETWEEN SOPHOMORE AND JUNIOR YEAR, HIGH SCHOOL

"*T*hanks, Jim." I smile appreciatively at the bus driver and give a last wave to the kids crowded into each row before stepping back outside into the summer heat. We take a field trip every other Friday and when I realized we'd be driving right past the gas station Gavin's foster dad manages, I asked if I could end my shift a little early and be dropped off on our way back to the community center. I've never visited Gavin at work before, but he said his foster dad had been splitting time between this station and one in another town so he's often alone in the afternoons. I decided to take a chance and surprise him.

Herding my group of eight, eight-year-old girls through lines and rides, sunscreen applications, and bathroom breaks, all while not losing any of them, was exhausting. My skin is sticky and sunburned—because I didn't have a chance to reapply *my* sunscreen—and my hair is a wind-blown mess, but I fully intend to wrap my arms around Gavin's neck and kiss him until my coconut lip balm is gone.

The two pumps outside are empty and I walk past them, toward the small convenience store with a pickup truck parked in front.

I have one hand outstretched toward the door when I see Gavin through the window. He's behind the cash register... but he's not alone.

From the mix of defiance and aggravation coloring Gavin's expression, I'm certain the rough-looking guy with the bushy eyebrows, snub nose, and backward-facing baseball cap is Doug, Gavin's foster dad's son.

I yank at the door handle just as Doug's fist bangs the cash register, open hostility rising between them like a mushroom cloud. Two heads swivel my way and Doug's leer makes me entirely too aware of the sheer cover-up clinging to my still damp bathing suit. "Well now, how can I help—"

"Poppy." Gavin's voice is thick with strain. "What are you doing here?"

Doug's eyes widen for a brief second, then narrow into slits. "Little orphan Gavin, why don't you introduce me to your friend?"

Gavin is neither little, even compared to the stockier Doug, nor an orphan, but nausea roils in my stomach at this small taste of what Gavin deals with in order to continue living with his foster parents.

"Don't talk to her," Gavin growls.

"Or what? Don't forget—one word from me and I'll have you kicked back to wherever you came from."

"Say all the words you want." Gavin points at a security camera positioned in the wall. "They won't mean anything when I have proof you're trying to steal money from the register."

Doug scoffs, unconcerned. "Shows how much you know, that thing hasn't worked in years."

"Really?" Keeping his eye on Doug, Gavin enters a command into the monitor sitting just to the left of the cash register. I can't see the screen, but whatever's on it makes Doug go pale.

"Son of a bitch." His hands clench into fists as he spins around, stopping just short of slamming one of them into Gavin's face.

Gavin doesn't even flinch. "Do it," he spits, moving even closer to Doug. I've never seen him like this, aggressive and angry. "We're on camera. Hit me now, so I can finally hit you back."

Their tense standoff continues for one beat, then two. My feet are glued to the ground, the breath still in my chest. Finally, Doug barrels out from behind the register.

His expression is mutinous as he hurls the door open, yelling, "This isn't over!"

But for now, it is. And I have to resist the urge to applaud as a blast of sultry summer air rushes through the gap, sending the edges of my cover-up dancing over my thighs.

I run over to Gavin, throwing myself into his arms. "Are you okay?" he whispers against my neck, holding me tightly.

"Yeah." The squeal of Doug's tires as he peels out of the parking lot makes me wince, even as proof that he's gone sends a tidal wave of relief through me. "Are *you* okay? How long was he here?"

"Just a few minutes. I'm fine."

"What a lucky break with the camera—when did it start working again?"

"When I replaced the lens and rewired it. I knew it was only a matter of time before Doug showed up when he knew I was here alone. Figured it wouldn't hurt to take precautions."

I pull away, staring into the deep, inky blue of Gavin's gaze that's still the exact same as the day I met him. He's taller now, his muscles lean but strong. And the almost cocky confidence I glimpsed when he stood up to Doug—a little bit brash, a little bit disdainful—wasn't just an act.

My beautiful, broken boy isn't so broken anymore.

He's not really a boy anymore, either. But still beautiful.

And definitely mine.

I interlock my fingers behind Gavin's shoulders, my thumbs stroking his neck. "So, not luck then. You outsmarted him."

"For now." He shrugs. "I know how to fight battles with my fists, I learned from the best. But, as much as I'd like to break every bone in Doug's face, I'm better off doing things this way."

Any lingering thoughts of Doug are chased away by the promise of Gavin's kiss, but his lips have barely grazed mine when a bell from outside lets out a sharp ring. Gavin's groan of disappointment sends a shiver down my spine, his forehead resting against mine for a moment before we turn to look through the window.

A Jeep has pulled up to the pump labeled: FULL SERVICE. Before Gavin lets go of me, the car doors open.

I recognize the five girls who get out. We've gone to school together for the past three years, although they're in the grade ahead of me. They'll be seniors when school starts again in a month.

Clarissa, the queen bee of East Sackett High, struts inside wearing jean cutoffs and a bikini top, her long blond hair perfectly tousled as it falls down her back. "Hi, Gavin," she coos, taking her Ray-Bans off and making a show of suspending them from the tiny string connecting the two triangles barely covering her breasts.

Her syrupy-sweet *Hi, Gavin* is echoed four more times as the other girls file in behind her.

"Hey." Gavin acknowledges them all, though his eyes quickly return to Clarissa. I note with pleasure that they don't drop below her face. "You use up a whole tank already?"

She frowns briefly at me, a flicker of irritation creasing her forehead. "Not quite. But you know me, I feel safer driving around with a full tank."

Really? I roll my eyes, though Clarissa doesn't notice. *I'd have thought she had better game than that.*

When Gavin doesn't comment, she adds, "We just got back from the beach—you should really come with us next time."

"Thanks." His lips tug upward in a grin, his hand squeezing mine. "But I'm more of a hiking kind of guy."

"Hiking, huh?" Clarissa's high-pitched giggle makes me cringe, although I have to admire her persistence when she adds, "You'll have to show me the best spots around here."

"Actually, Poppy's the expert." His face lights up as he turns to me and makes the connection between us. "You must know each other already since you're both at East Sackett."

Five sets of eyes immediately turn my way, and despite the coolness of the air-conditioned store, I flush bright red.

Clarissa isn't the type to admit when she doesn't know something. Instead, she drags her gaze up and down my body, trying to place me. "Of course," she says, just before pivoting away from us, the ends of her hair slapping my upper arm as she heads for the refrigerated section.

After they buy an impressive amount of drinks and junk food, Gavin follows them outside to gas up Clarissa's jeep while I pretend to be engrossed in a tabloid. When he returns, he plants his feet behind me and wraps his arms around my waist, nuzzling the sensitive patch of skin behind my ear. "So, where were we?"

"Would you really rather hike than go to the beach?" I've only been to the ocean a few times, and there's something unsettling about it. Like it's just a vast, yawning mouth waiting to swallow me whole.

He lifts his head, settling his chin on my shoulder. "I don't know. I like both, I guess. So long as it's not with *them.*"

I let out a surprised laugh. "I think most guys would be pretty happy to get in that car."

If I'm being honest, I would too. Not because I like Clarissa or any of the other girls who walked in here—I don't even know them. But I envy their easy banter, their shared history, their cohesive group. I've never had that.

Gavin moves his hands to my hips and gently turns me to face him. "I'm not most guys... And why would I be interested in anyone but you?"

CHAPTER 7

SACKETT, CONNECTICUT

SPRING, JUNIOR YEAR, HIGH SCHOOL

"*Y*ou're late."

Today, instead of saying *you're early*, I just agree. "I know. I couldn't help it. My mom was in a real mood."

Gavin throws his arm around my shoulders as I sit down beside him, still panting after nearly sprinting all the way here. "What's wrong—anything serious? Did she…"

The concern on his face has my chest cracking open just a little bit wider, my heart filling up with even more love than I thought possible. "No, she didn't do anything. Or take anything." *Yet*.

Like always, I silently tack that word onto any response concerning my mom's addiction. I don't think she's used drugs since we've lived in Sackett, but the first thirteen years of my life are impossible to forget. She hasn't left us *yet*. She hasn't relapsed *yet*.

It's like there's a ticking clock inside my head that only I can hear. *It's just a matter of time.*

"She was fired up about a letter that went around to all the parents." Two towns over, a girl was found unconscious behind the bleachers of the football field. One of the players, a high school senior, was arrested and everyone is saying something different, except for the girl herself, who was so drunk she doesn't remember anything. But apparently there are pictures and texts confirming that *something* happened.

Gavin merely nods. "The incident with the football player?"

I pull back to meet his eyes. "You've heard already?"

"We had a school assembly about it today."

"We'll probably have one tomorrow then."

"It's too bad the douchebag isn't eighteen." Gavin's shoulders are tense, his tone dripping with disgust. "If he did do it, he should get more than just a year or two in juvie."

"From the way my mom was talking, it's the girl's fault for getting drunk."

I shake my head, wishing it was possible to dislodge my mom's voice from inside my ears.

I didn't raise my girls to be so stupid. If you lose control, you'd better be prepared for what happens. Never trust anyone but each other.

Gavin scoffs as he grabs a nearby twig and snaps it in two, then throws the pieces back into the woods. "Nothing against your mom, but that's bullshit. The only thing you deserve for drinking too much is a hangover."

I hesitate, analyzing my feelings about something I haven't faced and can barely even imagine. I don't know any of the people involved. I've never had a drink in my life. And I've never had sex.

When my mom gets drunk, I blame her for the things she does, the things she says. I blame her for unscrewing the bottle, for every splash of wine into her damned mug, and for every time she lifts it to her mouth. I blame *her*.

I blame her for the years Sadie and I spent in foster care, the situations she put us in when she was doing drugs. Sometimes I even blame her for my reluctance to talk to strangers, and for Sadie preferring fictional worlds to our real one. As far as I know, no one has ever made my mom swallow a pill or smoke a pipe or take a drink.

"You don't think it's the girl's fault?" I ask, wincing at the tentativeness of my question, at my lack of conviction regarding what's right and what's wrong when a situation is distorted through an alcoholic lens.

"You mean for getting attacked while she was unconscious? No, I don't. Poison ivy from puking in the bushes, grounded by her parents for missing curfew, losing her phone—any of those, yeah. But assaulted, no. Definitely not her fault."

I let his words sink in. If someone took advantage of my mom when she was drunk or high, hurt her while she was vulnerable—even if she was in that state because of her own actions—I wouldn't blame her. I wouldn't say, *she was asking for it.*

But that's what my mom is saying about a high school girl she's never even met. That's what a lot of people are saying about her.

I nudge him softly. "You're a good guy, Gavin Cross."

"Yeah, yeah. That's what all the girls say."

Girls. The word is like a laser beam to a kitten, distracting me from the topic at hand. I think about Clarissa and all the other girls who have probably gone out of their way to have Gavin pump their gas since last summer, inviting him to the beach or their pool or a party. Probably into their pants.

Clarissa even cornered me in the bathroom once last semester, peppering me with questions about Gavin. Implying that if I was willing to bring him along, I'd be welcome to hang out with her and her friends.

I wanted friends… but I wasn't about to fall for her blatant ruse. If anything, it only made me even more protective of what Gavin and I had. What we share together.

"Um… Have you ever…" I clear my throat, not sure I really want to know the answer to the question. "…you know."

"Have I ever…"

I look around furtively, then whisper, "Had *sex*."

Gavin's brows edge upward until they disappear behind the hair falling over his forehead. "No. Not yet."

I blink at him, strangely unsatisfied. "Why not?"

"Why not?" he repeats my question, but doesn't answer it. "Have you?"

"No," I shoot back. "Of course not."

"Then why are you asking me if *I* have? I kind of figured it's something I should do with my girlfriend. You know, when you're ready."

Instantly, my lungs feel like they've been replaced with tanks of helium, my lips curving in what I can only imagine is a stupid grin. "You just called me your girlfriend." A word I'd been hoping to hear from his lips since the cold spring day we'd witnessed a very vocal mockingbird find his mate. After spotting them together several times since, either stoically protecting their nest or warbling and chirping at each other as they danced from tree to tree, we'd nicknamed them Fred and Wilma.

Gavin makes an exasperated sound. "Of course I did. You are, aren't you?"

Hell yes, I am. "But you've never said it before."

"Oh. Well, now I have."

"I guess that makes you my boyfriend, huh?"

"It sure as hell d—"

I cut Gavin off with a kiss, savoring the press of his lips on mine, the warm slide of his tongue. Ribbons of desire unspool inside me as his hands wind through my hair, gathering fistfuls of it as he cradles my head within his grasp.

The last lingering thoughts of a girl I don't know and a football player I don't want to know evaporate from my mind. There is only us, in our cozy cave, in our enchanted forest.

"You know, speaking as your girlfriend, if you wanted to do something… *more* than kissing, I wouldn't mind."

The blaze inside Gavin's eyes sets my face on fire… until his groan douses the flames. "I wish you hadn't told me that."

I let my forehead fall against his neck. "Why?"

"Because I've been doing a damn good job convincing myself *more* isn't on the menu."

"Why?"

"Because I love you. And you're my best friend. And the things I want to do to you…"

Intrigue wraps around me like a net of silken strands and shimmering fairy lights. "What do you want to do to me?"

"Everything." Guilt is written into the sharp slice of his cheekbones, the chiseled set of his jaw.

"I want that, too," I say urgently. "We don't have to make a big deal of it. Everyone says their first time isn't all that special, anyway."

"Maybe not, but you sure as hell are." He cups my chin in his hand, bringing my gaze back to his face. "Don't settle for anything less than what you deserve. Your first time—your *every* time—should be special."

"I love you." My words emerge as a whisper, although I could gleefully shout them at the sky.

Gavin echoes them against my lips, drawing me into another kiss. The sounds of the forest swell around us, mimicking my own restlessness and impatience.

Wind tugs at gnarled branches that arc over our heads, their leaves swishing. Birds twitter and chirp, their wings flapping as they jump from one perch to the next. Not even the shrubs clinging to the forest floor are silent, their verdant depths rustling as chipmunks and squirrels scavenge for fallen acorns.

But I'm not paying attention to any of it.

Because within our wild universe, Gavin is my sun. The biggest, brightest, most beautiful star. I am pulled to him by gravitational forces that exist just between us. Our own atmosphere, our own electrical currents. We are a galaxy unto ourselves.

Throwing a knee over Gavin's legs, I push my hands into the hair at the back of his neck and sit astride his lap. Gavin's fingers slide beneath my shirt, following the ladder of my spine until he reaches my bra. Unclasping it, he cups my breasts in his hands and I let out a wanton, yearning cry as his thumbs sweep over the sensitive peaks of my nipples. Between my legs, there is a pulsing, a second heartbeat that grows more insistent with each kiss, each caress.

Pressed up against me is proof that Gavin feels the same way. I rock my hips against him, his moan sending a tremble through my bones. My hands become greedy, reaching beneath his shirt to explore his muscles. Gavin has filled out in the past three years, he's no longer the lanky boy I first met.

I've changed, too. Last winter, my breasts appeared almost overnight. My hips curving enough that I needed a bigger jean size.

When I reach for my own hem, intending to pull off my shirt, Gavin stops me. "No, Poppy. We can't."

Shaken by a mix of frustration, disappointment, and embarrassment, I blink back the sting of tears. "Why not?"

He takes a few ragged breaths. "I don't want to roll around in a cave with you. You deserve better."

I shake my head in protest, desperate to both allay Gavin's concerns and satisfy the primitive mating instinct surging through my veins. "We found this place together; we've made it our own. And besides, all I need is you."

For a moment, I think Gavin will change his mind. That love and lust will win out. But then his features harden, his voice modulating. "Not yet, Poppy. I want to make it special for you. And I'm not... I'm not prepared."

"Not..." It takes me a minute, but I finally realize what he's saying. "Oh," is the only thing that comes out of my mouth. Condoms. Of course. Why would he carry them around if we aren't having sex? *Yet.*

The determination filling my lungs evaporates in a rush and I slide off his lap, adjusting my clothes. The heavy weight of our awkward silence presses down on my shoulders.

Eventually, Gavin breaks it. "There's something I need to tell you."

I immediately think the worst. "Oh, God—what's he done?" *He* is Doug, of course. After that afternoon last summer, Doug had apparently spent the next few hours drinking before slamming his truck into a tree.

He walked away without a scratch. Well, technically he didn't walk since he was unconscious when police arrived on the scene. They brought him to the hospital to rule out internal injuries, then to the local jail when his bloodwork revealed an alcohol content twice the legal limit. Since it was Doug's second DUI, he spent a few months in jail and has been on probation ever since.

Mostly, he's avoided Gavin. But, like so many other things— it's probably just a matter of time before he returns to his old tricks. Although now, Doug has to know he won't emerge from a fight with Gavin unscathed.

"Yeah?"

"I got a job. A second job, at a warehouse," he amends. "For the days Bill doesn't need me at the gas station. The shifts are right after school, and the pay is pretty good."

A second job means more demands on his time and less of it for me. For us. "Wow. Um, congratulations."

My attempt at feigning excitement isn't very convincing and Gavin easily sees through it, running agitated fingers through his already messy hair. "Yeah. I know, it's not ideal,"

"S-so when am I going to see you," I stutter. As it is, we only have one or two afternoons to spend together now, and when school lets out in a couple of months, we'll have even less.

"We'll find time."

My shoulders slump. I love our afternoons in the woods together.

Sure, sometimes it's frustrating as hell when the weather gets in the way.

But mostly, it feels romantic. Old-fashioned, but in a good way.

This past winter, when the preserve was impassable for months at a time, we'd arranged to meet up at the library every Wednesday. Not coincidentally, this was the day Sadie stayed after school for her creative writing club. Otherwise, I knew she would want to come with me—the library was her favorite place —and even though Gavin and I were venturing out of the forest, I still wasn't ready to share him with my sister yet. And sometimes on the weekends, I pretended to have a babysitting job but met Gavin at the movies instead.

"When do you start?"

He swallows, the bob of his Adam's apple making me wary. "Tomorrow."

CHAPTER 8

SACKETT, CONNECTICUT

FALL, SENIOR YEAR, HIGH SCHOOL

"*H*appy birthday," Gavin says with a beaming smile, meeting me at the clearing where we played our very first game of Gin Rummy. Except that today, instead of a deck of cards, he's holding a small, wrapped box.

I don't take it right away. In my world, birthday presents aren't expected. At least, not the kind bought in a store.

Last year, Gavin surprised me with a bouquet of wildflowers. And this year, what I've been hoping for can't be wrapped with a bow.

"Does this mean you don't want…" *me*, is the word that comes to mind. I manage to hold it back, although the hot sting of disappointed tears pricks my eyes.

I am so in love with Gavin that it almost hurts… and I've been hoping this would be the day we finally…

I have an unsettling sense that time is running out for us. That this idyll we've shared won't last forever. I'm sure it's just me, just the ridiculous clock inside my head that no one else hears. *Tick, tick, tick.*

Usually, I can shake it off. We've spent hours planning our future together, sharing our hopes and dreams.

We leave for college at the end of summer. Thankfully, we both got into Worthington University. We'll still be together, but so much will be different. There will be other people around. Other girls. We'll be living on the same campus, where we can see each other anytime we want. That's a good thing, it's what I want …

But I'm scared of losing what's made us special.

Sometimes, like now, the urgency vibrating through my bones is impossible to ignore. I want to lose my virginity to Gavin *now.*

Before we leave for college.

Before the next phase of our lives begins.

Before what we have right now, here in our very own enchanted forest, slips away.

He shakes his head at me. "I promise, tonight you'll have everything you want." The grin stretched across Gavin's face, coupled with his familiar low laugh, breaks up some of the tightness curving around my ribcage. "And so will I."

But not all of it. I'm still not entirely reassured. "I only want you."

His eyes crinkle at their corners, his voice lowering like he's sharing a secret. "Poppy, trust me. Open your present."

I take the box as if it might explode in my hands, carefully plucking at the tape so the paper comes apart in one piece. But my stare shoots back to him when a jewelry box is revealed. "You shouldn't have spent—"

"I wanted to," he reassures me.

I told Gavin not to buy me anything. He's been working so much these past few months, and I don't want him spending his hard-earned money on me. Not when I know he's trying to save every penny for school. And maybe, hopefully, the future we'll build together.

I'm working every spare second too, just like Gavin. I nanny for two girls who live down the street, getting them off the bus almost every afternoon and taking care of them until their parents get home from work. And I babysit for other families most Friday and Saturday nights.

Gavin and I don't see each other nearly as much as we'd like. But sometimes, like today, we make the time.

I give him a last stern look, but when I lift the lid, all my reservations evaporate as suddenly as morning mist on a sunny day. In the center of the velvet cushion is a milky stone, carved into the shape of a teardrop and suspended from a delicate silver chain. As the light catches it, shades of blue and green give the pendant an ethereal effect. "Gavin, this is beautiful," I say in an awed whisper, running my finger over the smooth surface.

"It's moonstone," Gavin tells me, "one of the birthstones for June."

Gavin's birthday is June twenty-eighth. Tears spring to my eyes. In my seventeen years, I've never received such an extraordinary, extravagant gift. "I'll have a reminder of you with me, always."

His cheeks are tinged pink, and he shifts nervously from foot to foot. "Yeah... but if you don't like it—"

"I love it," I interrupt, overwhelmed by his thoughtfulness and generosity. Gently, I remove the necklace from the box and hand it to Gavin. "Will you help me?"

Lifting my hair up, I spin around and close my eyes. After he fastens the clasp at the back of my neck, he kisses my skin, sending a bolt of electricity racing down my spine. My head lolls forward as I moan, savoring the scrape of his teeth and the swipe of his tongue. Gavin's kisses are a gift, too. There is nowhere I don't want to feel his mouth on my body.

Gavin's touch makes me feel like I'm at the precipice of something magical and dangerous.

But with him, I am safe. I have no doubts about that.

I am the luckiest girl in the world.

Slowly, so slowly, I turn in his arms, my head thrown back, my neck exposed and vulnerable. A supplicant embracing her salvation.

Gavin's lips track up my neck, drawing my earlobe between his teeth and nibbling on it. "You taste so good, Poppy," he murmurs, his warm breath sending goose bumps skating over my skin. "You always taste so damn good."

My body responds to his words, and to the need threaded through each syllable. His sexy rasp sends a flood of heat between my thighs, a craving for friction, an aching to be filled.

Proof of Gavin's lust, the bulge in his jeans pressing against me, compounds my own. A lit match tossed onto an oil slick.

He brushes his lips against mine, releasing a shuddering breath. I swallow his exhale, filling my lungs with his minty warmth.

"Let's go to our cave."

~

"Close your eyes."

I slant a curious look at Gavin, taking in his kiss-swollen lips and flushed skin, his untamable mop of hair and the blaze of excitement lighting up the blue of his corneas.

Gavin squeezes my hand reassuringly as I do what he's asked, then slowly walks me the remaining few steps toward our cave. Without vision, my other senses are heightened. The cry of birds sounds closer, like they are perched just overhead instead of on branches thirty or forty feet above. The bite of the breeze on my skin is sharper, each gust sending a chill racing along already sensitive nerve endings. The smell of ripe earth and rich evergreen and the clean, bracing scent of Gavin himself is downright intoxicating, my head swimming as I pull breaths deep into my lungs.

Most of all, the moonstone pendant laying against my collarbone is making my chest tingle, my heart fluttering against my ribcage.

"Okay, open them."

I do, immediately gasping in surprise at what Gavin's done to our little cave. There are candles burning and scattered rose petals—no, *poppy* petals—and a basket filled with drinks and snacks. A pile of blankets and pillows.

"You did all this for me?" I ask, my voice sounding whispery and weird.

I *feel* whispery and weird.

I've never had a birthday like this. I've never even *imagined* a birthday like this. First the necklace and now, seeing the lengths Gavin has gone for me...

Beneath the surface of my skin, I'm a chaotic mess of emotions. I don't know what to say, how to act. This is uncharted territory for me.

"Of course," he says, as if it's nothing. But it's not nothing. It's *everything*.

Before I dissolve into a teary puddle, Gavin reaches into his pocket and pulls out a deck of cards. "You taught me how to play gin rummy—how about I teach you to play poker?"

A strangled laugh leaves my throat. "I think that's fair."

We sit down and Gavin spends a few minutes going over the basics of the game before dealing out the cards. It's not as easy as gin rummy, but I get the hang of it after a few rounds.

And when Gavin lifts a mischievous brow and asks, "Want to make things interesting?" I know exactly what he's doing. Not just poker. Strip poker.

That's when I realize just how much planning has gone into tonight. Beyond buying me an expensive present. Beyond

67

pimping out our cave. Gavin found a way to make my first time —our first time—a mix of old and new. An experience evoking our past and celebrating our future.

I've imagined the night Gavin and I would finally go *all the way* a million times. But I'd only focused on the physical aspects. Would it hurt? Will there be blood? What if I do it wrong?

It never crossed my mind that he would take such care with… everything.

But, of course, it should have.

Gavin Cross is one of a kind.

And he's mine.

After his pair of aces beats my pair of queens, I stand up to shimmy my jeans down my thighs. Watching me, Gavin's fingers fumble with the cards, his eyes glazing over with appreciation. Before he can deal out another hand, I crawl into his lap and throw my arms around his neck. "I'll tell you again later, but just so you know, this is the best night of my life."

"Don't say that yet. We haven't—" Gavin breaks off, and a nervous expression pulls at his features.

My heart softens. In all this, I've almost forgotten that tonight is Gavin's first time, too.

"Strike that," I say, his hair caressing my fingertips. "It's the best night of *our* lives."

At that, I sense Gavin's nerves easing. "So far."

I echo his sentiment just as his lips claim mine, his mouth devouring all of my hopes and wishes and questions and fears. They are no longer mine, they are ours.

I am his and he is mine and we are us.

I must have spoken my thought aloud, because Gavin cups my face in his hands, the intensity of his gaze searing my soul. "I am hers and she is mine and—"

"—We are us." My voice joins his, our hushed whispers leaving our lips like a prayer. We are wrapped up in each other, our bodies connected, our eyes locked, our hearts beating in tune.

The moment stretches out. One second, then two, then three. Time is irrelevant.

But the time for playing cards is definitely past.

He finally relinquishes eye contact to press a kiss to the top of my head, his breath fanning my hair and sending a rush of goose bumps over my flesh. Then his mouth moves to my temple, along the curve of my cheekbone, and finally to that sensitive patch of skin between my jaw and earlobe.

I moan softly, allowing my head to fall back. Gavin's tongue sweeps across my pulse point and he chuckles, the sound as thick and decadent as the sap seeping out of the maple trees surrounding us. "Your heart is beating so fast."

"I'm excited," I whisper. And nervous, though I don't want to admit it.

"Me too," Gavin says as I slide my hands over his chest. His skin is warm, the stacked muscles of his abdomen tense and tight, the trail of hair leading south tickling my palms in a way that sends primal desire unspooling through my body.

I'm wearing only the pale pink lace bra and panty set I bought for tonight. Gavin takes a minute to admire it, to admire me. His teeth sink into the fullness of that lower lip I love so much, pupils dilating as his fingers trace my curves through the diaphanous fabric. "Fuck, Poppy. You're so …"

I'm expecting Gavin to say something simple, like pretty or beautiful. But instead he says, "perfect."

I immediately roll my eyes and look away. Perfect is definitely not the word that springs to mind when I look in the mirror. My hair, including my eyelashes and eyebrows, is a strange shade of copper. My mouth is too wide, my hips not wide enough. I blush too easily, and find talking to most people too hard. But knowing that Gavin thinks I'm perfect, or at least perfect for him, is satisfying in a way I can't even explain.

He cups my chin in a gentle hold and forces my gaze back to his own. "I'm serious, Poppy. It's like every inch of you, every ounce of you, was made just for me."

If I'd heard that line in a movie, or written in a card, I would cringe. But there is only reverence in the husky rasp of Gavin's voice. Reverence... and love.

His hands run down my ribcage, his light touch on my sensitive skin making me suck in a breath as tingling sensations light up my nerve endings.

"Still so ticklish."

I am. Over the years, there have been plenty of times when Gavin has pinned me to the ground, his fingertips dancing across every inch of exposed skin he could find. I'd laughed until I couldn't breathe.

But I'm not laughing now.

And I'm definitely not laughing when Gavin bends down and rolls his tongue over my nipples, making them harden into desperately needy buds, turning the already sheer fabric completely transparent.

A gentle breeze enters our cave and sends my hair swaying over my back and shoulders, caressing my bare skin. I cling to Gavin's shoulders, interlocking my fingers behind his neck.

I am trembling with anticipation. Shivering from an avalanche of sensations.

He unclasps my bra, a moan ripping from my throat as my breasts spill into the palms of Gavin's hands. His touch feels so good, so right.

I'm smiling when Gavin pulls away from me, his fathomless blue gaze, as mysterious and mesmerizing as the night sky, capturing mine. And for a moment, the way he's looking at me almost makes me want to cover up, to turn away and shield myself because I've never before felt so exposed, so vulnerable. So *seen*.

70

Like I'm giving him my body but what he's really taking is my very soul.

"Are you sure you want to do this?" he asks, so very earnestly. "We don't have to. I can stop right now... Why are you looking at me like that?"

The truth is, Gavin isn't taking my soul, I'm giving it to him.

But that's not true either. It's already his.

Everything I am, my hopes and dreams and fears and needs, I've entrusted into Gavin's hands, into his heart.

He will hold them safe.

And tonight, my body belongs to Gavin too.

"Because I want to do this more than anything else in the world. Because I don't want to stop. And because you are everything I've ever wanted."

He stares at me, jaw just slightly slack, a corona of indigo encircling the black abyss of his blown pupils. And then he nods, as if he finally, finally understands that the river of emotion running through me is just as wide and deep as his own. "We are us," he says, his voice clear and strong, reverberating in the crisp autumn air.

"We are us," I repeat.

Gavin gathers me into his arms so tenderly I feel tears gather in the corner of my eyes, like distilled drops of love and trust that cannot be contained inside my body for another second. Candlelight flickers on his face, illuminating his chiseled features as he deposits me carefully onto the mound of blankets he's assembled.

I'm naked, except for the last bit of lace between my thighs, but the heat of Gavin's stare keeps me warm. And it burns away my worry about what will happen when we leave Sackett.

I know now that I have nothing to fear. Every day since we've met has created a tiny filament of trust. Gossamer thin strings that have woven together, becoming a braid, and then a rope. As days became weeks, weeks became months, and months became years, Gavin and I forged an irrevocable connection.

Changing locations won't change who we are or how we feel or what we want.

"Come here," I whisper, needing to feel more than Gavin's eyes on me. I want his weight, I want his kisses, I want his love.

And I want to *be* his. In every way.

Gavin shucks off his clothes as I watch, then drops back to his knees to crawl over me. His elbows land at the indent of my waist, his head lowering to my belly button, his tongue sneaking out to lap at the shallow groove. "Gavin," I beg, writhing beneath him. It feels ticklish, but not *ha ha* ticklish. His tongue is awakening an illicit, furtive sexuality in me, bands of desire curling and coiling, spreading throughout my body.

And those unfurling threads are making *me* needy and wanton, greedy and desperate. I plunge my hands into Gavin's hair, tugging on his head as he moves across my stomach to tenderly nip at my hip bones, then lower still.

There's no rush to Gavin's pace, he is slow and thorough, ensuring that every inch of me is treated to the wet lap of his tongue, the enticing pressure of his teeth, the roughened abrasion of his chin and jaw.

This is the first time we've been naked together, instead of just exposing pieces of ourselves, one at a time. It feels different somehow. Deeper. But the hours we've spent exploring each other's bodies has taught us what brings pleasure and what doesn't. What leads to rapture and what just makes us laugh. I've climaxed from Gavin's fingers, from his tongue. His sticky wetness has coated my hands, covered my breasts, slid down my throat.

Gavin knows exactly what it takes to make me lose control, abandoning all thought and reason and worry to exist solely in *us*.

And now he pauses, gently resting his chin on the rise of my pelvic bone. "Look at me, Poppy."

I do. I stare intently at Gavin, my eyes roving over his wild hair and fevered eyes and the impossibly sexy smirk tugging at his kiss-swollen lips.

"I see you," I say.

"Yeah." He shifts down another two inches, his tongue licking the already damp lace between my thighs. "You always have."

A whimper falls from my open mouth. Then another as he moves the fabric aside and his tongue meets my skin directly, without any barrier between us.

Electricity shoots through me, jagged and white hot as it burns away the last of my already tenuous hold on reality. My panties disappear and I barely blink as Gavin opens his mouth over me, ravenously devouring me.

I climax with my eyes trained on Gavin, this broken boy who's somehow always been a man, whose wounds and scars align so perfectly with mine that we've healed each other.

He draws out every last delicious pulse of my orgasm, my thighs pressed tightly around his ears, my heels tapping out a staccato drumbeat against his back as waves of pleasure crash over me. And when they finally recede, when he finally pulls a condom out of seemingly nowhere, I watch him roll it over his length with hands that aren't quite steady. "I love you, Poppy. I've loved you since the moment you looked like you were going to cry when there were no raspberries on that damn bush."

Gavin's weight settles over me, pressing me down into the pile of blankets and pillows he must have made countless trips to carry though the forest, along with the candles and snacks and drinks and even the damn poppy petals. I wrap my hands around his neck, pulling his face down to mine as I feel the tip of his sheathed crown knock at an entrance that hasn't yet been entered. "I felt awful. Well, at least until you said you didn't like raspberries."

He chuckles, his thickness stretching me wide, then impossibly wider. There is a pinch of pain, and then a deeper wrenching sting. I cry out and Gavin captures my mouth, hungrily swallowing my hurt. He kisses me with deep, claiming strokes of his tongue and then, when the pain has faded into a murky fog hovering just at the edge of pleasure, nebulous and indistinct, Gavin releases my mouth and gently, reverently, kisses my cheeks and neck, my eyelids and the tip of my nose. He kisses me until I'm rolling my hips, wanting more of him, more of us. Wanting to feel full, so very full.

Later, after Gavin gives one final surge of his hips and bellows a deep, satisfied growl, his head dropping into the curve of my neck, his breath a heated gust over my dewy skin... only then does he whisper, "Poppy, I love raspberries."

CHAPTER 9

SACKETT, CONNECTICUT

SPRING, SENIOR YEAR, HIGH SCHOOL

I left something for you in our place. It explains everything.
I will be out of touch for a while. I'm sorry.
I love you.
I love us.

I feel Gavin's texts come in, one after the other, while I'm taking a test. My phone is in my pocket, and although I feel the buzzing against my thigh, checking it during a test would mean an automatic F.

I read them as I navigate the crowded halls on the way to my next class, barely paying attention to where I'm going or who I'm bumping into.

I left something for you in our place. It explains everything.

Gavin should be in school, like me. It's a Thursday morning. We were together, in the woods, in our cave, *our place*, yesterday afternoon. Why would he skip school today to leave something for me when I just saw him yesterday?

I will be out of touch for a while. I'm sorry.

We have plans to see each other this weekend. Where is Gavin going? How long will he be gone?

I try calling during lunch, over and over, but he doesn't pick up. I send texts.

> Hey, what's going on? Your messages don't make sense.
> I'm at lunch right now. Call me.
> Lunch is over and I'm in class for the next few hours. Call me,
> I'll pick up.
> Come on, Gav. This is not cool.
> Where are you?

Gunmetal gray clouds roll in during Spanish class, enveloping the sun in a thick layer of gauze. Within minutes the brightness that shined through the windows has been extinguished, befitting my mood. The only incoming text I receive is from the mother of the girls I babysit telling me that I don't need to work today.

> This isn't funny.
> Where are you?

By the time my AP History class is over, the clouds hang even lower and their color has deepened to a bleak charcoal. Mist swirls around my feet when I walk to the bus, its headlights barely penetrating the thick drifts of vapor.

> I'm heading home now. Whatever you've left for me better be
> good.

And by good, I meant—it had better explain what the hell is going on.

Sadie drops heavily into the seat beside me, her backpack knocking my phone out of my hands. "Sadie, Jeez! Watch it!"

Her head jerks back. "Wow. Someone's got their panties in a twist. What's with you?"

I glare at her as I bend down to grab my phone from the sticky bus floor. Once it's in my hand, I gesture at all the empty seats. Our bus is only half full in the mornings and even less in the afternoons. "There are plenty of places to sit—you don't always have to be right next to me. We're sisters, not Siamese twins."

Hurt pinches her features as she stands up and flings herself into the seat across from me. "Thanks, sis. Love you, too."

Guilt cuts through me for taking my frustration with Gavin out on Sadie. She doesn't deserve it. A deep sigh rattles from my lungs as I slide next to her. "I'm sorry—"

A flash of light breaks through the layer of dirt and condensation covering the bus's windows, illuminating my sister's face for a brief second before a *boom* vibrates through the seat. I curse, peering anxiously through the fogged windows.

The corners of Sadie's lips turn down as she hugs her bag to her chest. "No running into the woods today for you, huh? Guess you're stuck in the house with me and mom." She clucks her tongue. "It must really suck for you."

Logically, I know she's speaking from a place of hurt. I yelled at her for no reason, and couldn't even finish my apology without being distracted by the incoming storm and what it means for my plans to head straight for the cave to find out what is behind Gavin's cryptic texts.

But I'm not feeling very logical right now. "Forget it," I say, shaking my head in disgust and checking my phone again.

I don't have any new texts, but I do have an email I'd missed. It's from the drug store in town with the one-hour photo booth in the back, a notice that the pictures I'd ordered are ready for pickup.

I dismiss it as a mix-up. I didn't order any pictures.

By the time Eddie, our driver, starts the engine and pulls slowly out of the bus loop in front of school, rain is coming down in heavy sheets, through an inky darkness that feels like night.

It doesn't let up as we wind through the uneven terrain that is northern Connecticut. Our rolling hills and jagged coastline are the result of glaciers cutting through this land thousands of years ago, which is why most of the roads in our town are narrow and windy, with sharp inclines and steep curves.

It takes twice as long to get home as it normally does, though I don't blame Eddie for going well below the speed limit.

There are five cars waiting at our bus stop. My mom's isn't one of them. Sadie and I run down the street with our backpacks over our heads, but it doesn't matter. By the time we walk in the door, we are soaked to the skin.

"Hey, girls," my mom calls from the kitchen.

"Hi, mom," we chorus, taking off our shoes and jackets and slicking back our wet hair.

"I just got home, too. It's really coming down out there," she says, eyeing us after we leave our things by the door and join her in the kitchen. She takes a sip of wine from her coffee mug and opens a drawer, throwing a dish towel at me.

"Thanks," I wipe my face with it.

"Oh, honey. No. Use that to wipe up the puddle by the door, I noticed some water leaking in."

I have to fight the familiar tug of resentment that pulls at me on days like these. Why can't my mother be normal? Or even just slightly more considerate? I'm sure it never even crossed her mind to wait at the bus stop for us instead of coming straight home after work. Even if she noticed the other cars parked there, she probably had no idea that they were parents waiting for their kids.

But I don't let myself get too far. I know I'm lucky to have her at all. If she ever disappeared on us again, walking home in the rain would be the least of my problems.

I mop up the water on the floor and then carry my backpack to my room, changing out of my wet clothes and pulling my hair into a messy bun.

Through the window over my bed, I watch the rain come down, bolts of lightning piercing the sky in jagged white streaks, illuminating the band of trees swaying and shivering against an angry wind. *Please, let the storm end. Send the sun back out.*

When my phone vibrates in my hand, I nearly jump out of my skin.

Gavin. Thank G—

But it's not Gavin. It's a weather alert, warning of flash flooding in our area. *Great.*

I'm home. I can't get to our place until the storm is over.
Call me.
This isn't funny.
I'm not kidding.
Where the hell are you?
Are you ok? I'm scared. Please call me.
I love you.
I love us.

Twenty minutes passes, forty, an hour. I read all of Gavin's texts again. And then all of mine.

Where the hell is he?

I open up my backpack, attempt to concentrate on homework. After reading the same sentence five times, I pick up my phone again and call the number of the photo shop. "Hi, I received an email from you earlier today."

"Sure. How can I help you?"

"Well, I didn't order any photos."

"Oh. Can you give me your order number?"

TARA LEIGH

I rattle off the number referenced in the email and he puts me on hold. The synchronized music drones on for several minutes before cutting off abruptly. "It says here this order was paid for by a Gavin Cross. Do you—"

I don't wait for him to finish his sentence. "I'll be right there."

Running down the hall, I skid into the living room on socked feet to find my mother dozing on the couch, her mouth partially open, empty coffee mug on the table beside her. *Shit.* I know better than to wake her.

I jog back down the hall, to Sadie's room. "Hey—"

"Don't you even knock?" She's lying on her bed, holding a book with a half-naked man on it a few inches from her face.

"Can you cover for me if Mom wakes up? I need to take the car into town—I won't be long."

Sadie sits up and looks pointedly outside her window. "Poppy, you only just got your license and you want to go driving in that?"

Urgency clutches at the tendons of my throat, turning my voice into a croak. "I have to."

"What for?"

"I—" Glancing down at my watch I see that I only have twenty minutes to get into town before the store closes. It takes fifteen on a sunny afternoon. "I'll tell you later. *Please.*"

Her features soften. "Go. I'll handle mom if she wakes up." After shooting her a grateful smile, I'm halfway to the back door when I hear her call softly. "Just be safe."

I make it to the store just as the manager is coming around the register with a set of keys. Her shoulders slump, a heavy sigh hallowing out her chest. "We're closing."

"I'm sorry, I called a few minutes ago?" My voice ends higher like I'm asking a question. "I'm just picking up a photo order. I'll only be a minute."

My heart is practically crashing against my ribcage by the time I'm back in my mom's car, soaked to the skin. I grab the

80

plastic bag and rip open the envelope containing photos Gavin must have taken with the camera of his phone. There are only fifteen, that's all his phone would store, and he said he wished he'd gotten one with more memory a dozen times.

But as I flip through each one, the tears fall harder until my vision is as blurry as the windshield of my mom's car.

Gavin and I, lying in a pile of fallen leaves we'd raked with our hands. Our heads are touching, our hair mingling together. Huge grins stretch across our faces, a halo of red and yellow and copper leaves forming around us. I run a finger over Gavin's lips now. We were so happy that day. So happy whenever we were together.

There's a photo of me, my eyes closed, lying on a bed of blankets in our cave. My shoulders are naked, and I know the rest of me is too, although the picture frame ends just below my collarbone. I don't remember him taking this picture, though I'm almost certain I know he did—the night we made love for the first time. My moonstone pendant is visible in the shot, although my hair is partially covering it. And there's a softness to my features, a sated kind of blissfulness that shows even in this photograph.

There's a selfie of us in front of my favorite tree, a yellow birch with thick, exposed roots that we sometimes sit on like chairs. Another where we're sitting on the high rock ridge we climbed that led us to our cave all those years ago. And another of us standing on either side of the GC + PW Gavin had carved into the smooth, mouse-gray trunk of a beech tree.

The rain is still coming down when I finally drive home, the sky sludgy and even darker than before. Sadie is waiting for me in the kitchen, and she tosses me a box of tampons as I come into the room.

"Thanks, Poppy. You're a lifesaver," she says loudly, jerking her head toward the living room and taking the tampons back. "Mom, Poppy's home."

My mom stumbles into the kitchen, clutching her coffee cup and weaving slightly. "Sadie, that is the last time you'll send your sister out into a storm." Her voice trails off as she gestures with her mug at the window rattling from the wind. "And Poppy, you should have told her to stuff her underwear with paper towels."

Sadie heads back to her room, I'm sure biting her tongue.

"It's okay, Mom. It was no problem."

Pouring the last of her bottle into her mug, she returns to the comfort of her couch, shaking her head and mumbling. "There's no reason to be out in this. That girl, just no consideration."

A few moments later, I tap lightly on Sadie's bedroom door, waiting until I hear, "come in," to open it.

"Thank you. I—" A wave of remorse pierces the thick veil of worry and confusion that has blinded me since reading Gavin's texts. "I'm really sorry, Sadie. For earlier, and for the million other times I've bitten your head off for no good reason."

Sadie accepts my apology more easily than I deserve. "It's fine, sis. We're stuck with each other, for better or worse."

A soggy laugh tumbles from my throat. When we were younger, we joked about marriage vows being pointless because, in our case, they certainly hadn't kept our parents together. I'm not even sure my parents were actually married. We've never seen any pictures of my mom in a white dress, and her answers are always vague. But sisters, we said, would always be together, for better or worse, no matter what.

"I'm lucky to be stuck with you, Sadie. I owe you."

"Not as much as I owe you. But don't worry, I'll get even with you one day."

"I, um…" I look down at the wrapped bag of photographs in my hand. I promised Sadie an explanation. "These are—"

Our stare is broken when her phone chimes. She picks it up and glances at the screen. "Can we—"

"Of course." I flash a quick smile and back out of Sadie's

room, clutching at any excuse to delay a conversation I'm in no condition to have.

I spend the night staring at Gavin's photographs, finally easing out the back door when the first light of dawn streaks through the sky.

The storm wreaked havoc in the preserve. The hiking trails are slippery, muddy rivers. Decades old trees are uprooted, twigs and branches and huge sheared-off limbs scattered over the forest floor like LEGO bricks.

But nothing is going to keep me from the woods today.

I left something for you in our place. It explains everything.

It better, Gavin. Because if it doesn't, I don't know what I'm going to do.

PART II

CHAPTER 10

WORTHINGTON UNIVERSITY

FALL SEMESTER, FRESHMAN YEAR

"*I* think that's the last of it," my mom says, blowing a piece of hair off her damp forehead and surveying the bags and boxes we'd stacked near the narrow closet.

She's taken the day off work to drive me to school, but I can tell all the happy, two-parent families—especially the fathers hauling suitcases and trunks up and down the stairs, their sweaty faces beaming with pride—are making her uncomfortable. Now that her car is unpacked, she's hovering by the open door, half in, half out of my dorm room. Eager to escape.

I don't have it in me to manage my mother's emotions right now. I can barely manage my own.

Frankly, I just want her and my sister to leave so I can walk over to the administration building. I've called several times, but no one will tell me whether Gavin has registered as an incoming freshman yet. If I don't have more success in person, I'm prepared to stake out every dorm until I find him…

If he's here.

Out of habit, I lift my hand to my neck, my fingers closing over the moonstone pendant Gavin gave me for my birthday. This necklace, a few pictures, and hope are all I have left of him. Hope that he'll show up here, to Worthington University. Just like we'd planned.

Last spring, when I finally made it into the preserve after the Nor'easter storm slammed Sackett, I'd found our cave completely flooded. I returned every day for weeks, searching the cave itself and the surrounding area as the water receded. But it was no use. The only thing I found of even the slightest interest was a phone, the kind you buy at a gas station. It was caked in mud a few feet from the entrance to our cave. I tried to turn it on, but the wiring must have short-circuited after being submerged for so long.

Whatever Gavin left for me was either destroyed or lost.

As of today, I'm officially a Worth U student. I've been dreaming about it for as long as I can remember. Dreaming of starting a new life. But without Gavin, everything about this place, this day, this new life... feels all wrong.

"Thanks for your help." I muster up what I hope is at least a shadow of an appreciative grin for my mom and sister. "Why don't I walk you out—"

But Sadie is in no hurry to leave. She crosses the room, running her hand over my roommate's crisp white duvet and navy pillows. "I should have known you would wind up with the best roommate, Poppy." A trace of envy is threaded through her voice.

Surveying the other side of my room, my spirits sink even lower. Of course, I would get paired with a diva.

By the looks of it, an advance team of interior designers had arrived at dawn to renovate exactly fifty percent of our shared room. Both sides have a bed, nightstand, dresser, and desk. But mine are clearly school-issued and hers are... not.

Real artwork, as opposed to sticky-taped posters, hang on the wall behind her upholstered headboard. And the bed itself has been raised off the floor, three bunching chests arranged beneath. Her chair is sleek white leather, her desk made of glass and chrome. And above her dresser, the mirror is extra-wide, with lighting strips adhered to the perimeter, like it belongs in a backstage dressing room.

The overall effect is disconcerting, like standing inside a Before and After photo.

I frown as Sadie sits down on the bed, bouncing a little on the mattress. "We haven't even met her yet."

"Yeah, but look at all her stuff. She must be loaded."

Finally, picking up on the disparity my sister pointed out, my mom's bloodshot eyes bounce from one side of the room to the other. "Maybe you can pick up a few things to brighten things up."

What this room really needs is a wall down the middle of it.

"You know, if she decides not to show, I could probably come up here on weekends and—"

I flash Sadie an exasperated look. "If you really want to be here, you should spend more time reading textbooks than romance novels."

Sadie just rolls her eyes. Studying is not her thing. If she's not obsessing over her current crush, she's curled up with a fictional book boyfriend. I think all those contrived endings have Sadie convinced that her life will play out like a plot written by her favorite author. The cute, quirky girl lands the sexy, brilliant, rich sports star and they live happily ever after.

I used to believe in happy endings, too.

Now I know better.

Fairy tales don't come true for everyone. Some girls kiss their prince and he turns into a frog, then hops away.

"Excuse me." The polite words are delivered like a reprimand by a tall, thin blonde standing in the hall.

My mom steps aside, my sister jumping off the bed, wearing a guilty expression as she crosses back to my side of the room.

The blonde strides into the room, immediately followed by her slightly younger looking replica. They are both wearing dark jeans, narrow belts, and fitted white shirts.

"Which of you girls is Poppy?" says the one who is either an older sister or a mother with a plastic surgeon on speed dial.

Feeling at a disadvantage, I immediately regret ignoring the letter I'd received with my roommate's contact information. It was sent a few weeks ago, to encourage incoming freshmen to get to know each other before move-in day.

Then again, she hadn't reached out to me either.

"That's me," I say.

"Lovely." She gestures at her mini-me. "I'm sure you and Wren will have a fantastic year together."

Wren and I regard each other silently, mutual doubts piling up between us.

"I'm Sadie, Poppy's sister." For once, I appreciate Sadie's unwillingness to be ignored.

"Lovely. I'm Cecelia Knowles, Wren's mother." Her slender neck twists back toward the door. "And you must be …"

"Poppy's mom," she acknowledges, a hand fluttering over her throat.

Mrs. Knowles's polite smile drops a bit when my mom shows no sign of volunteering her first name. I almost want to explain that my mom doesn't mean to be unfriendly, it's just the way she is. Always an extension of something—Sadie's mom, Poppy's mom, Dr. Rankin's receptionist. I don't know that I've ever heard her introduce herself as herself, Emily Whitman.

But, of course, I don't, and the awkward moment ends when Mrs. Knowles turns her attention to her daughter's side of the room, opening drawers and peering into the closet, flicking on the desk lamp.

Wren is only carrying a backpack, which she sets on her chair.

"I have orientation soon," I say, shifting impatiently from foot to foot. There's nothing left for my mom and sister to do, and if Gavin is here, I need to find him.

He has to be here.

Eager to be off, my mom comes toward me with outstretched arms, smelling slightly acidic and oaky, like Chardonnay. "Take care of yourself, okay? Study hard and make good choices."

I walk them back down to the parking lot, smiling and waving as if there isn't a fist of fear twisting and turning inside my stomach. I'm not scared about being on my own or getting good grades. I'm terrified that today is the day I'll have to face a truth I've been denying for months. That Gavin is gone… and he's never coming back.

Once the taillights of my mom's battered Honda disappear into a line of receding cars, I jog across campus toward the main quad. A perennial favorite on lists of "America's Most Beautiful Universities," Worthington was modeled after Cambridge and Oxford Universities in England. But today I barely notice the beautiful gothic architecture that had me sighing over the brochures, dreaming of the moment this place would become my home.

"Hi." I don't wait for the gray-haired, heavyset woman sitting behind the front desk to look up before I begin speaking. "I'm an incoming freshman and I hope you can help—"

She lifts the glasses hanging on a beaded necklace to her face and peers up at me. "Did you just move into your dorm?"

"Yes. Crawford Hall."

"And will you be attending orientation this afternoon?"

"Of course."

"Well then, my dear, you are no longer incoming. You are here." She beams at me. "Welcome to Worthington University."

"Thank you," I say, the depressed fog I've been living in fragmenting the slightest bit in the face of her unexpected warmth. "I'm glad to be here." Regardless of what happens with Gavin, I *am* grateful to be taking this first step away from Sackett.

"How can I help you?"

"I'm looking for a friend. He was supposed to be here, too. I mean, we applied together and we both got in but..." Sadness and fear and confusion come rushing back, the emotions slamming into me like a rogue wave. I sway on my feet, feeling the blood drain from my face.

The administrator comes rushing around her desk and guides me into a chair. "There, there. If your friend is here, we'll find him. You just sit down right next to me." She reaches into her desk drawer and pulls out a handful of Hershey kisses and plastic-wrapped butterscotch candies. "Have a little treat, dear. Sugar makes everything sweeter."

I unwrap a butterscotch with trembling fingers and place it on my tongue, grateful for the explosion of flavor that somehow manages to help me focus. She looks at me with an encouraging smile. "There you go. All better?"

No. But I nod anyway. "Thank you," I glance at the nameplate on her desk, "Mrs. McGill."

"Just call me Roz. Everyone does." Her chair squeaks as she settles back into it and turns her attention to her computer screen. "Now, you just tell me who you're looking for and I'll see what I can do."

"Gavin. Gavin Cross."

As Roz's fingers dance across the keyboard, I allow myself to imagine that she'll turn to me with an ebullient smile, announcing his dorm and room number.

I'll smile and clap my hands. I'll say, *I know exactly where that is. Thank you, I'll go find him right now.*

We'll share a laugh and she'll insist that I take a few more candies with me, maybe remind me to keep a pack of Lifesavers and a water bottle in my backpack.

And then I'll go find Gavin and...

But her keyboard goes quiet, and I know what she's going to say before the words leave her mouth. She says them anyway.

"I'm sorry dear. There's no Gavin Cross in our system. He isn't here."

He isn't here.

I manage to nod and thank her again before stumbling back into the sunshine, a fistful of candy melting inside my hand.

He isn't here.

And I realize that my mom's advice will be hard to follow. Not the studying part. It's the "making good choices" part that I need to work on.

My track record is shit.

I entrusted my heart to a beautiful, broken boy. Gavin's kisses left me loose-limbed and starry-eyed, but his whispered words of love were the cruelest of illusions.

I am his and he is mine and we are us.

I am hers and she is mine and we are us.

We are us.

Lies. All lies.

CHAPTER 11

WORTHINGTON UNIVERSITY

FALL SEMESTER, FRESHMAN YEAR

"*A*re you going to close that?" Wren's voice is a mix of bored and disdainful as she points a manicured fingernail behind me.

I ease my backpack onto my bed, nearly groaning as the heavy weight slides off my shoulders. "Sure thing."

We've been sleeping less than ten feet away from each other for a month and our relationship is just as formal and stilted now as it was the day we moved in. I can't say I'm surprised. I knew from the moment I saw her side of the room that we'd never be friends.

I can't blame it all on Wren, though. I'm no better at making friends here than I was in Sackett.

I miss Gavin.

So damn much.

I still find myself looking for him around every corner. I'll see a flash of blond hair sliding against a square jawline or the shadow of sooty black lashes fanning the rise of a cheekbone, and

94

a sharp blade of longing slides right through my rib cage to pierce my heart.

But it's never him. No one else has the same unruly golden mane as Gavin. No one else has eyes the exact shade of my heartbreak. No one else has sculpted lips that whispered such sweet, sweet lies.

I know I should be moving forward and making friends and acting like a typical college freshman—studying and partying and eating too much late night pizza.

But I've never been a typical anything.

And even though Gavin doesn't deserve my tears, I can't seem to stop shedding them. Missing him is an ache that never subsides.

Before I can close the door I've left ajar, it flies open, hitting the adjacent wall with a slap. Holding a bottle of tequila in one hand and a folded slice of pizza in the other, Tucker Stockton—Wren's closest guy friend who finds a reason to stop by at least once a day—walks in, trailed by one of his lacrosse team buddies. "Thought we'd pre-party here."

Wren's glossy lips curve into a smile as she sets her enormous art history textbook aside. "It's about time."

"Hey, Poppy." Tucker sits at the end of Wren's bed while his friend yanks my chair from under my desk, spins it around, then straddles it.

"Hi." I give an awkward wave from my side of the room.

Tucker holds his pizza a few inches from Wren's mouth and she takes a small bite from the edge. "You brought the shot glasses, right, Sully?"

"'Course." Tucker tosses Sully the bottle and he catches it midair.

I stand up, throwing my backpack over my shoulder before this gets any more awkward. There's no need to wait until I'm the only one without a shot. "See you later. Have f—"

I spin around, almost knocking the glass out Tucker's hand.

The one extended toward me. "Oh." I feel my cheeks turning pink. "That's okay, I don't want to impose."

What I want is to hide in the library until I'm certain they're gone. Tucker and Wren finish each other's sentences and laugh at shared jokes I don't understand. I asked Wren if Tucker was her boyfriend, but she just replied, *There's no label for what we are.* Being around them is like taking a salt bath with open wounds.

"Impose," Tucker repeats softly, looking back at Wren with an amused expression on his face. "I like your roommate, Wren."

"She's a keeper," Wren responds, her tone droll.

I take the glass from Tucker. "Um, thanks." I'll just have the one and go.

Sully lifts the bottle overhead. "Let's get drunk!"

Let's not. After Gavin left, I'd occasionally broken down and retreated to my bedroom with a bottle of my mom's wine. And I regretted it every time. I don't want to be the kind of person who drowns their sorrows with alcohol, and I know I'll never find solace at the bottom of a bottle.

But tonight, I swallow the tequila gratefully. It burns a path down my throat, exploding into flames inside my stomach.

I cough as I wave a hand in front of my mouth, my eyes watering.

"For God's sake, be quiet," Wren hisses. "You'll have Michael running in here any minute."

Michael is the resident advisor assigned to our floor—an upperclassman who gets free room and board in exchange for keeping an eye on about thirty freshmen. He seems nice enough, but if he spots us with alcohol, he'll have to confiscate it and make a report to campus security.

I grab for the water bottle beside my bed. "Sorry. That one just... went down wrong."

Sully refills my glass. "Here, have another before we head to The Hill."

"Oh, no thanks." I gulp at my water. "I'm going back to the library."

"Of course, you are," Wren says, managing to look both pleased and irritated at the same time.

"On a Friday night?" Tucker asks. "You should come with us."

Wren's hand closes over Tucker's shoulder and gives it a squeeze. "I don't think it's really her scene, Tuck." And then she slants a look at me, one eyebrow raised in challenge.

Something inside me bristles at my roommate's dismissive tone, at her scornful glance. But I shrug it off. "I wouldn't know," I admit. "I've never been to The Hill."

"Never?" Sully's dumfounded expression is almost comical.

"It's only been a month. I'm still settling in."

"Then you definitely have to come with us." Tucker turns to Wren. "Tell her."

Wren arches a perfectly plucked brow, her lips flattening into a thin line. "Tell her what?"

"Tell her to come with us. That she'll have fun."

She squirms slightly, then glares at me. "What he said."

Sully saves me from responding when he taps the rim of his shot glass against mine. Without thinking, I pour the tequila down my throat, coughing a little less this time.

"So," Sully moves his chair closer to my bed, "if you haven't been partying at The Hill, where do you go?"

I can already feel the alcohol slowing down my brain. "Go… ?"

"Yeah, to party." Sully looks genuinely interested, his eyes only flicking away from mine long enough to pour refills for everyone else.

Tucker kicks his legs out in front of him. "She's probably hanging out with her boyfriend, dumb-ass."

I bite down on the inside of my cheek, pain slicing through me at the reminder of Gavin. Sometimes, I miss him so much my bones pulse with loneliness. This is one of those times. "Um, no. No boyfriend," I mumble, flushing with embarrassment even as I continue babbling. "Not anymore. I did though. He was supposed to be here with me at Worthington. But he's not. He just... He left."

I finally stop talking, mortified. And sad. So very sad.

For a moment, the room is quiet. And then Sully, Tucker, and Wren all burst into laughter. "Seriously, where did you find her?" Tucker eventually asks Wren.

She lifts her shoulders in a nonchalant shrug. "I didn't. She was just here when I arrived."

My cheeks burn as they laugh—at me—again. I can't believe I opened up to them about Gavin. I haven't told my own sister about him and tonight, with people I barely know—and in Wren's case, don't even like—I open up like I'm at a high school slumber party. The kind I'd never been invited to.

Before I can change my mind, I make a decision. If on-campus parties aren't my *scene*, then why am I here? I need to move on. Try to make actual friends. Worthington isn't a big school, but it's certainly bigger that East Sackett. There has to be someone I can connect with. Someone who will distract me from missing Gavin.

The serene smile I force onto my face contradicts the defiance in my gaze as I meet Wren's stare. "Actually, I think I've studied enough for today. A party sounds fun."

Tucker tips the edge of his glass at me. "Good call," he says, before tossing it down his throat.

I mirror his actions. And this time, I manage to hold back the cough.

CHAPTER 12

WORTHINGTON UNIVERSITY

FALL SEMESTER, FRESHMAN YEAR

*B*uoyed by the tequila buzz warming my blood and the cold autumn breeze at my back, I'm feeling excited about this unexpected turn of events. My first party.

A fraternity party, to boot.

Tonight will be a good night. Maybe even a fresh start.

This is what I've been missing. Not Gavin.

College life. Parties. Hanging out with friends.

Well… Wren, Tucker, and Sully aren't my friends. But maybe tonight I'll meet someone who will be.

It's about a fifteen-minute walk from our freshman dorm to the row of fraternity houses on The Hill, and we head straight to the one with lights and music blaring. Two kegs are set up behind it and within minutes I'm holding a beer. I like beer about as much as I like tequila. But it's comforting to hold on to something—even if that something is a red Solo cup.

Sully lingers by the kegs and I follow Wren and Tucker inside, where the press of too many bodies crammed into a narrow, low-ceilinged space makes the house hot and humid. Jackets and sweatshirts are piled on a couch pushed up against a wall, and a guy wearing medical scrubs works the room, doling out "shots" of Jägermeister.

"Want one?" Tucker asks.

I grimace. "Isn't that the stuff that tastes like black licorice?"

"It's fucking awesome," Scrubs yells, holding the bottle over my head until I tilt it back. I almost fall, but Tucker steadies me with an arm around my waist. I hate black licorice and the mouthful makes me want to gag. I manage to swallow it, wiping my mouth with the back of my hand in the hopes of erasing the horrible taste. It doesn't work.

Scrubs moves on to his next "patient" and I frown at Tucker. "Where's your shot?"

He lets go of me and grins. "I hate black licorice."

I should be mad at him. Or at least annoyed.

But I am so tired of *feeling*.

Mad. Sad. Annoyed. Abandoned. Betrayed.

Feeling sucks.

It's painful, and pointless.

I find myself instinctively reaching for the pendant that sits just inside the hollow of my collarbone, sweeping my thumb over the smooth moonstone like a talisman.

Tucker notices. "What is that?" he asks, peering closer to get a better look, his fingertips brushing mine as he takes the necklace from my grasp.

"It—it was a gift." I stumble over my words, taken aback by his interest. And his closeness.

Tucker's face is just inches from mine, his dark gaze scrutinizing first my pendant, then me. "From that guy? Your boyfriend?"

I can't move away. If I do, the delicate chain will snap. I manage a shallow nod. "Yes."

He finally lets go, straightening to his full height. "You said he left you. Why are you still wearing it?"

I blink in surprise. *Why am I still wearing it?* How could I possibly take off Gavin's necklace? The moonstone represents June, the month he was born. It's like having a piece of him with me at all times. I hate not having it around my neck when I shower, but to just stop wearing it altogether… No. Just, no.

A memory flashes in my mind. The day Gavin and I hiked to the cemetery just beyond the northeast corner of the preserve, to check out the gravestones dating back to the Civil War. It had been a bright, sunny spring afternoon and the burial ground wasn't creepy. It was peaceful, actually. Surrounded by towering oaks almost overgrown with blooming mountain laurel. We read the epitaphs that hadn't been eroded by time and weather, making up stories about people they commemorated. We left later than we should have, at dusk, and I'd tripped over a small headstone. An infant, likely stillborn. The birth date and death date the same.

The pain that shuddered through me had nothing to do with my scraped knee, and Gavin had dropped to my side, his face a mask of concern. He took one look at my wet eyes and trembling chin and pulled me into his arms, kissing away my tears. And later, when he noticed me limping, he got down on bended knees, pulled me onto his back, and with my hands wrapped around his neck and my ankles crossed at his waist, he whistled the sweetest, saddest melody as he carried me home.

"I love him. And one day, he'll come back." I'm not sure if it's the alcohol talking, but in this moment I'm certain my answer is the truth. One day, Gavin will come back to me.

Tucker's expression is indecipherable. "He's a lucky guy."

"No," I blink away the memory even as the haunting echo of it swirls inside my ears, "I'm a lucky girl."

A shadow falls over Tucker's face. It's Sully, being dragged by an irritated-looking Wren. "Poppy, entertain Sully," she orders, then reaches for Tucker's arm. "Come on, Tuck. I want to dance."

"Time for a refill," Sully says, tilting his empty cup toward me as if I need verification. "Want to come with me?"

I glance back toward Tucker but my eyes find Wren instead. She is at the fringes of the dance floor, a small disco light flashing pink and blue from the ceiling above her head. When she meets my gaze, not even the spastic lighting can disguise her triumphant expression.

"Sure." I join Sully outside, the transition from sweaty hothouse to frostbitten tundra making my head swim. He catches me as I stumble on the steps. "You okay there?"

I brush him off. "Someone spilled beer, just a little slippery is all."

"You sure? Wren told me to take care of you—I can't have you falling and cracking your head."

More like, she told you to get me out of her way.

He refills his cup from the keg and then I follow Sully back into the house, where he heads to the basement. A speaker near the stairs pumps in the same music as on the main floor but it isn't nearly as crowded. Another set of inebriated undergrads are playing beer pong and flip cup, and in the corner, a few girls are stirring the contents of a lobster pot with a metal spatula, the kind used to flip burgers on a grill.

I eye the empty Crystal Light canisters and fine yellow powder dusting the countertop behind them with relief. Lemonade is exactly what I need. Anything that doesn't have alcohol.

"Can I have some of that?" I pour out my beer into a garbage can.

"We've got ourselves a guinea pig!" one of them chirps, grabbing my cup and dunking it into the mixture. She hands it back to me, still dripping. "Tell us, is it too strong?"

I prepare myself for the overwhelming taste of sweetener, but it's not nearly as noticeable as I would have thought. "It's good. Thanks." I take another sip. "What else is in this?"

"Just Everclear and ice," she says, lifting her own Solo cup.

Everclear? Is that a new energy drink I haven't heard of yet? I take another sip. It doesn't taste like alcohol, but it doesn't taste like a soft drink either. *Whatever it is, it has to be better than straight shots.*

I walk back toward Sully, who has migrated from the ping-pong table to a dartboard. By the time I've finished half the cup, I'm leaning against the nearest wall.

One of Sully's darts flies smoothly through the air, jutting out dead center. Scott hikes a fist in the air. "Yeah-ah! Bull's-eye!"

I squint at the dartboard, the colored circles moving in front of my eyes.

Jesus, Poppy. Pull yourself together.

The girl who gave me my lemonade saunters over, running her hand possessively along Sully's back. "I call winner," she says, pointedly glancing my way.

I'm not interested in Sully, but it still chafes to be shoved aside. Again. "He's all yours," I say, deciding that it's time to call it a night.

I make my way upstairs and head for the front door. By the time I get outside, I can't focus on any of the faces around me. I'm just grateful that the ground rises up to meet my feet as I put one in front of the other.

I haven't made it very far when I hear my name from behind me. I stop, turning carefully.

"Hey, there." Tucker jogs over. "I was wondering where you went."

I take another sip of lemonade, then peer behind him. "Where's Wren?"

"She got sidelined by some chicks from the sorority she's planning to pledge next semester," he says. "You're heading back already?"

"Yeah." I turn away, toward the dorms.

"If your boyfriend was here, I bet he wouldn't let you walk home alone."

I flinch at the unnecessary reminder. "Well, he's not here, is he?"

"His loss."

Exactly. His loss. I take another sip of lemonade, feeling almost belligerent.

I turn away from Tucker, toward the dorms. I'm not worried about walking back alone. Worthington is one of the safest schools in the country, a fact they extoll in every campus tour and marketing packet.

In two strides Tucker catches up. "Mind if I come with you? I feel bad. I convinced you to come to the party and you obviously didn't have a very good time."

"Not your fault. Wren was right. It really wasn't my scene, after all," I say. "And you don't have to babysit me."

"I'm not babysitting. I'm just looking out for you."

"Don't tell Wren that. She wants you all to herself."

Tucker reaches for my free hand, entwining his fingers through mine. "Don't mind her. She's a little possessive, I know. But she's not who I want." He glances at my drink. "What's that?"

"This?" I extend the red cup in his direction. "Lemonade and… something else. Eversomething."

He sniffs it, then takes a healthy swallow. "Jesus, you don't mess around."

I frown. "What do you mean?"

"Nothing. You've just got a hell of a tolerance, is all." He gives the cup back to me, grinning. "Pretty impressive, for a girl."

Alcohol and elation buzz through my veins. *Impressive.* I like the sound of that. It's the same word that comes to mind when I look at people like Tucker and Wren. They have a confidence about them, an assuredness that surrounds them like a protective bubble.

Next to them, I'm just so… insignificant.

I down the rest of the lemonade mix, toss my cup to the side. *Drunk Poppy is a litterer.*

Is that even a word? Before I can ask Tucker for his opinion, he wraps his arms around my waist, pulling me into his side.

I forget all about my misdemeanor. One moment there is a cloud of vapor between our lips, the next he's swallowing my sigh. Tucker tastes like beer with just a hint of sweetness from the lemonade.

Not like Gavin at all.

Damn it. Stop thinking about Gavin. No matter how many good memories I have, nothing can change the fact that he left me. It's been months, and he hasn't come back. *Maybe I won't get over him —but I have to at least try.*

Tucker's tongue is warm and insistent, and I cling to his shoulders as a tremble shakes my frame.

He breaks away. "Cold?"

I know it's cold outside, but I can't feel it. Maybe because I'm feeling so many other things. Dizzy. Aroused. Nervous. Guilty. Slightly sick. And very, very drunk. "Maybe a little."

But I don't feel mad or sad or annoyed or betrayed or abandoned.

It's an improvement.

"Come on, let's get you home."

Holding hands, we walk the rest of the way, thoughts of Gavin and Wren as distant as the stars suspended within the obsidian dome of the night sky.

Our dorm is practically empty when we return. "Want to come back to my room? We could watch a movie or something?" I ask. Tucker is Wren's friend, but that doesn't mean he can't be mine too.

Oh, please. You never had friends. You had Gavin.

But Gavin's gone. He doesn't love you anymore. Maybe he never did.

Liar! He loved me, I know he did.

Then why isn't he here?

I squeeze my eyes closed, shake my head. *Stop it, Poppy.*

"Poppy?"

Shit. I blink them open to find Tucker staring down at me. And I like how he's looking at me. Concerned. Interested. "Yeah?"

"Let's go back to mine. My roommate's almost never there." He lifts his dark brows and kisses me again. I sway in Tucker's arms, grabbing hold of his biceps to steady myself.

Gavin's probably kissed someone else by now. He's probably forgotten all about me.

Tucker's room is on the opposite end of Caldwell from mine, although we are on the same floor. And it's immediately obvious we both have odd roommate situations, too. One side of the room is perfectly neat. Bed made, books on the desk aligned with their spines facing out, dresser drawers all pushed in, the top free of debris. The other side looks like a tornado has ripped through it, scattering clothes and books and bedding everywhere. A pile of laundry—dirty or clean, I can't tell—is heaped on the unmade bed. "Which side is yours?"

"You think I could live like that?" His full lips twist in disgust as he walks to a small refrigerator tucked beside the spotless desk. "No freakin' way."

I take the can of beer, even though I know I should ask for a soda instead. Or better yet, water. I sit down on the bed. It's soft. Too soft. My stomach lurches, and I edge forward, lowering myself to the floor, needing to feel something solid beneath me.

Tucker looks at me quizzically. "You okay?"

His face breaks apart into two, then fuses back together. "Yeah, yeah. S'fine." He sits down beside me, one hand cupping my jaw, his thumb sweeping over my cheekbone.

"We shouldn't do this. Wren wrants—" I catch the slur and pause. "Wren wants you. I'm breaking girl code. S'big time."

"You and Wren are friends?"

My tongue feels heavy and awkward in my mouth. "No. I don't have any…"

"You don't have any… what?"

"Friends. I don't—I don't have any friends."

Tucker's features blur again. "Poor Poppy. No friends. No boyfriend. You're all alone, aren't you?"

Sadness coils like a spring inside me and I feel a tear slide down my cheek. "No."

He brushes it away with the calloused pad of his thumb. "I can be your friend."

Tucker moves forward, or maybe I do. And then we're kissing, his arms wrapping around my waist, my almost untouched beer forgotten. Once I close my eyes, I feel like I'm on the Tilt-a-Whirl at a cheap, fly-by-night carnival. I pull away, needing space.

But Tucker is so close. Too close. "You're so fucking perfect," he whispers. "And I have you all to myself, don't I?"

"Need to lie down." My words are barely a mumble. I'm holding onto consciousness by my fingernails.

Tucker follows, his lips on mine, his body heavy on top of me. I whimper, trying to draw a deep breath. But I can't.

I press my palms flat against his chest. But I have no strength to push, my fingers wrapping around the collar of his shirt, his skin hot against my knuckles.

I want to speak, to say the words pulsing in my brain like street lights. *Stop. No. Get off.*

But the sounds I make aren't words. They aren't anything at all.

And soon, I am silent.

CHAPTER 13

WORTHINGTON UNIVERSITY

FALL SEMESTER, FRESHMAN YEAR

*T*he smell wakes me. Vomit and chemicals. Urine and sweat.

My brain is on fire, my tongue thick and fuzzy inside my mouth.

Forcing my eyes open, I'm immediately assaulted by bright lights that stab at my corneas.

"Ah, finally. You're awake." A woman dressed in scrubs appears at my side.

Scrubs.

Jägermeister.

Last night.

Last night... What happened last night?

My mind instinctively pivots away from the locked door of my memory and goes into triage mode, focusing on what I do know. I am in a hospital. Everything hurts, but I'm alive. And, beneath a thin sheet... I am naked.

"Hi. Um—" My throat closes as my eyes fill with tears.

She passes me a tissue before thinking better of it and handing over the whole box. "You don't remember much, do you?"

I shake my head, the slight movement sending a bullet ricocheting through my skull. "No," I whisper, taking the tissues with shaking hands. *Lemonade. Dartboard. Piled laundry. Soft bed. Tucker. Kissing Tucker.*

"You were brought in a few hours ago because you had a seizure in your dorm. Not really surprising, if you want to know the truth. Your blood could have been bottled as a wine cooler." She clucks her tongue at me. "Unfortunately, I see girls like you all the time, young kids away from home for the first time, drinking whatever anyone hands you."

"I— I'm really sorry."

"Don't have to apologize to me. This is my job." Disappointment is etched into the lines around her mouth. "But it's your life. Pull a stunt like that again, and next time it might just kill you."

Her ring, a simple gold wedding band, taps against the handrail as she reaches for the clipboard hanging from its side. "Oh, and something else. We found evidence of sexual activity. A condom… inside your clothes." Her pen hovers over the attached paper as her eyes probe mine. "Does that sound about right to you?"

Right? No, no, it doesn't. It sounds wrong. Very, very wrong.

I look away. "I-I guess so."

There is the scratch of pen on paper. "Well, I guess that's that." She puts the clipboard back. "I have a bag with your clothes. And there is a boy waiting to bring you back to school."

Air leaves my lungs in a dizzying whoosh. "Tucker?" The thought of seeing him right now makes me… confused. I can't wrap my head around what the nurse just told me. *Did he… ? Did we… ?*

She scrunches up her face. "No, something with an M, I think. He's an advisor from your dorm—"

Relief and disappointment fight a turf war inside my chest. Not Tucker. "My RA, Michael."

"Yes, that's it. He asked your roommate for a change of clothes so you won't have to go home in scrubs."

Scrubs. My mouth fills with the taste of black licorice and I make a gagging noise, clamping a hand over my face.

The nurse grabs for a plastic bucket and thrusts it below my chin. "There shouldn't be anything left in your stomach but if you need to be sick, go right ahead."

She is right, I have nothing left to throw up. Dry heaves shake my shoulders for several minutes until I finally flop back against the mattress, clutching the bucket to my chest like a life vest. "Thank you."

She gives my arm a final pat. "A doctor will be by in a minute to speak with you. Assuming he signs off, you'll be back home within the hour."

Home. I let the word sink in. Caldwell Hall isn't my home. The little house in Sackett never felt like home either. Home isn't here or there.

Home is a cave inside an enchanted forest. Home is Gavin, his arms wrapped securely around me.

But Gavin's gone. I don't have a home anymore. This isn't a movie and I'm not Dorothy, wearing red slippers and skipping along a yellow brick road. The tornado that's brought me here is all of my own making, my mind a funnel cloud of questions and regrets.

What happened between me and Tucker last night?

Does Wren know?

What about everyone else on the floor? In my dorm? At WU?

Yesterday I'd been just another freshman. But after last night, being rushed to the hospital in an ambulance—

The doctor appears, looking busy and frazzled. I answer his questions, look into the light he shines at my eyes, and recite my name, birthday, and today's date. He walks away and I take a quick, fortifying breath. Once he talks to the nurse, I can leave.

But he doesn't go far. Just a few steps to grab a stool on wheels, pushing it beside my bed. He sits. "You know, I have a daughter almost your age. I'm hoping she'll go to Worthington, too." He pauses, crossing his leg over his knee. I stare at his sock. It's argyle.

I want to look away, cover my ears, make the world stop turning. A few minutes ago my heart was racing but now it's just a slow, dull thud inside my chest. Whatever he's about to say, I don't want to hear it.

But there's nowhere to go. I can't escape. I'm trapped.

"I'm going to tell you what I would tell her. You were in no condition to have sex last night. I'd like you to consent to a rape kit. It won't take very long, just an exam and some paperwork. And, of course, the police—"

A shiver vibrates through me, and I recoil. "No." I stop to swallow a golf ball-sized lump of panic. "I don't want a," I can't even say the word, skipping over it entirely, "a kit. Or another exam. There's no need to call the police. Really." My voice is high, my sentences short and choppy. Tears overflow my lashes.

I want this to be over. The sooner I leave, the sooner I can pretend last night never happened.

The doctor's shoulders drop, and he exhales a defeated sigh. "That's your right. But you should consider counseling. Sometimes it takes a while to process trauma like this, and you don't have to do it alone." He lifts a transparent bag containing a yellowish... My breath sticks in the back of my throat as I realize what it is. The condom. "Stay away from whoever this belongs to, okay?"

I manage a jerky nod, speech beyond my capacity.

At the door, he sends a final glance my way, one last chance to change my mind. But I don't.

And then he drops the bag into a trash can and walks away.

I am staring at it, trying to catch my breath, when the nurse comes back in carrying my backpack and a plastic grocery bag, knotted at the top. She sets the bag at the end of the bed. "Your clothes from last night are in here. I recommend washing them as soon as possible." Gently placing my backpack on my lap, she offers a kind smile. "Best of luck to you, Poppy. Don't take this the wrong way, but I hope I never see you again."

A feeble croak shudders from my lungs. "Me, too."

CHAPTER 14

WORTHINGTON UNIVERSITY

FALL SEMESTER, FRESHMAN YEAR

*A*s soon as she leaves, I gingerly get out of the hospital bed and change into my jeans and sweatshirt. My entire body aches, and I feel like an octogenarian instead of an eighteen-year-old college student.

I reach for the bag containing my clothes from last night but, even knotted tightly, the smell emanating from it is nauseating. After one whiff, I throw it in the garbage.

It seems fitting that all the physical evidence of… whatever transpired, is in the same trash bin together. I'm glad to leave it behind.

Emerging into the main waiting room, I cross my arms in front of me, trying to make myself as small as possible. Right now, I wish I could disappear.

Michael is waiting in a chair, and he jumps up when he sees me. "Poppy, hey. So glad you're okay."

I hold up a hand to keep him from coming too close. "Believe me, you want to stay as far away as you can." The sour smell of vomit clings to my skin, like Linus's dirt cloud in a Peanuts cartoon.

He freezes, his soft brown eyes shining with concern behind rectangular framed glasses. "Don't worry about that. Come on, let's get you back to the dorm."

I follow Michael out the exit and into the parking lot. "Thanks for coming to get me."

It's a dreary November day, and I swallow another wave of nausea as a cold wind gusts, blowing my disgusting hair into my face.

Will I ever not feel like I'm on the verge of throwing up?

"Of course, of course." He fishes his keys out of his pocket, pointing them at a red Honda. There is a click as the doors unlock and I slide in, immediately lowering the window. "I'm so sorry. I can't imagine this was a part of the job description when you signed up."

Michael lowers his window, too, and pulls slowly out of his parking spot. "Poppy, really. It's not a problem."

Tears prick my eyes. Everyone is being so nice—the nurse, the doctor, Michael—but I'm pretty sure things will change once I get back on campus. Teenagers are vicious. "Can I ask you." I take a quick breath, not knowing where to start. "About last night? What you saw. What others saw."

"Um, yeah. Sure." Michael pulls onto a main road, busies himself adjusting his mirrors. "Not much. Tucker came running into my room, said you were sick. As soon as I saw you, I called the campus emergency line. You were on the floor, shaking."

Shame wraps around my chest, compressing my lungs. "Was anyone else around?"

"In the room with you? No, just Tucker. By the time the ambulance arrived, there were a few people on the floor. But only a few."

A few could mean three or thirteen, but I don't press for a more exact number. "Did they see?"

"In the room—no. But they did see you get taken out." He glances over at me. "Listen, you're not the first person to wind up in the hospital after a night of binge drinking your freshman year and, unfortunately, I'm sure you won't be the last. It happened, but you're fine and now life can go on."

I don't feel fine. I feel like an idiot. And fragile. And like I've lost something, something I can't even define but that is important. Self-respect. Confidence. Feeling safe in my own skin. "You're right," I lie. "Thanks."

We arrive on campus a few minutes later, and it is exactly the same and yet completely different. Not nearly as innocuous as it looked the first day I arrived, with my mom and sister, feeling like all I needed to do was focus on my schoolwork and try to forget about Gavin.

Gavin.

The trees have begun to turn colors, vibrant reds and golds bursting from within the lush green landscape. Memories of another autumn day press heavily on my heart. Leaves fluttering to the ground like confetti. Broken shards of sunlight piercing through a shadowy, mysterious forest. And a boy who had treated my body as if it was sacred and special. A precious gift.

My hand flies to my throat, needing proof that those memories are real. Tactile confirmation of the best, most sacred moments of my life. Maybe it was just an illusion, but right now, I need to believe that I was once loved.

But instead of grasping moonstone, my fingers close around empty air, my nails scratching skin.

Horror hits me like a mallet striking bone, shattering my remaining strength.

My pendant is gone.

Just like Gavin.

Could it have been ripped away by the paramedics? Was it in the bag of filthy clothes I'd thrown away?

I'll call the hospital as soon as I get back to my room.

A brutal cold penetrates my clothes and I swathe my terror in silence. Is this karma? Maybe I've lost the right to wear Gavin's necklace. It represents something I no longer deserve.

Trudging upstairs, I am weighed down by guilt and regret and disgust. I keep my eyes on my shoes, not wanting to see anyone until I've showered. Or maybe ever. But it's Saturday, and the dorm is filled with students. I walk silently, my head bowed, hurrying to my closed door. My closed, locked door.

Shit.

But Michael holds up the universal key all RA's are given. "No worries." Lock-outs aren't uncommon.

I mumble another thanks and slip inside, quickly grabbing my robe, towel, and shower caddy full of toiletries.

Although the floor is co-ed, the bathrooms are not. Inside the girl's bathroom, one of the showers is in use, but other than that, it is empty. Turning the water to its hottest setting, I quickly undress and slip beneath the spray. It stings my skin, but I welcome the pain. If I could make it hotter, I would.

The heat doesn't penetrate where I need it most though. Places deep inside my body that are crusted with ice. Permanently stained by something I can't even remember.

But the pain on my skin somewhat balances out the pain in my heart. Scrubbing my body dulls, if only slightly, the ragged edges of my shame.

I shampoo and condition my hair once, twice, three times, letting the sudsy water drip down my face and sting my eyes. I scratch at my scalp with my fingernails until I'm sure the skin is flayed and raw. Until I've created a thousand shallow cuts that no one but me will know are there.

I don't want to leave this small enclosure. Here, my tears run straight into the drain, and I can stuff my fist in my mouth to stifle my sobs. Here, I am alone, the sound of the water a buffer between me and whatever is waiting beyond these three walls and the thin white shower curtain.

Eventually, the water cools. Only a few degrees, but it feels like a betrayal. Another one.

When I return to my room, skin pink, eyes bloodshot and red-rimmed, Wren and Tucker—*Tucker*—are both there. My stomach lurches as I clutch my bathrobe to my chest, squeezing the terrycloth inside my fist.

They sit on her bed, their penetrating stares ripping into me.

God, I want to disappear. Either invisible or dead, I don't care.

"You're back," Wren says, stating the obvious.

I nod.

Tucker glances at Wren and then jerks his chin toward the door. Her lips snap together in a straight line and she stands, striding past me without saying another word, her expression glacial.

My roommate is the last person I would ask for support or comfort, but I want to scream, *Don't go!*

Because once she leaves, I will be alone. With Tucker.

Yesterday, I would have been flattered by his interest.

Today, I'm... not.

Wearing only a pair of squishy flip-flips on my feet and a towel wrapped like a turban around my head, I'm naked beneath my pale pink robe.

My pulse races as I set my shower caddy down on the floor and begin towel-drying my hair, the pain from my raw, scratched scalp the only thing keeping me from passing out.

"Poppy," he begins, "I want you to know that I feel badly for what happened last night. I should have known you were drinking too much. I should have realized you were acting..." He pauses, shrugs. "Out of character."

I think of the doctor with his argyle socks and the condom he'd dropped into the trash bin. I hear his last piece of parting advice in my ears. *Stay away from whoever this belongs to, okay?* I'd nodded, agreed.

I didn't seek out Tucker. But he's here, offering an explanation for what happened last night. Only the two of us were there, but my memory is locked inside my mind. I can practically hear it rattling around inside my brain, like a puzzle piece that's fallen through a grate. If I could, I would bang my head against the wall, remove my skull from my shoulders and shake it until the truth falls out.

But I can't.

"And I want you to know that I'm not mad at you, or anything. I meant what I said last night—I can be your friend. I want to be your friend."

Mad? At me?

My breath hitches in the back of my throat. I'm almost positive he said the same thing to me last night.

But friends don't take advantage of each other. Friends don't... *do* what he did.

There is only one thing I want from Tucker right now. "My necklace... Have you seen it?"

"Your necklace?" He pauses long enough that I feel an obligation to look his way. But I don't. I can't. "Oh, the one you were wearing last night?"

"Yes. The moonstone pendant. It's gone."

"That's a shame. I saw how attached to it you were."

"Could it have come off in your room? Or while the EMTs were working on..." A wave of vertigo slams into me, but I resist its pull. If there's any chance Tucker has Gavin's necklace—I want it back. I may have lost Gavin, I can't lose his necklace too. "Can you check?"

"You saw the way I keep my things. If it's there, I'd know it." Tucker stands up and starts walking toward me. With each step he takes, my heartbeat kicks up a notch, the roaring in my ears growing louder, drowning out any further questions about Gavin's necklace. "Listen, I hope we can get past this. It was a mistake, one I won't ever make again."

Tucker's hands lift, his fingers threading through my still wet hair and pulling me into the well of his chest. Every muscle in my body locks down, oxygen evaporating from my lungs. I can't scream. I can't run.

But my brain is working on overdrive, replaying Tucker's words over and over. One in particular.

Mistake.

I don't dismiss it. I don't ignore it or bat it away.

Mistake.

I find myself reaching for it like a warm blanket on a winter day. Drawing it around my shoulders like a shield. Last night doesn't have to be a four-letter word. R-a-p-e.

No. Last night was a *mistake.*

An error made from defective judgment, deficient knowledge, or carelessness.

A misunderstanding.

Tucker rubs his hand over the terrycloth covering my back as a lone tear, possibly the only one I have left, slides down my cheek and into the corner of my mouth.

I am standing between two doors, marked by two different labels, leading to two very different places. Do I choose r-a-p-e, or *mistake?*

But... Am I really choosing? Haven't I already made my choice, back in the hospital?

I didn't consent to the rape kit, therefore I am not a rape victim. Even if I wanted to walk through that door right now, to wrap my hand around the knob, cross over that threshold—the door wouldn't budge. It's been sealed shut by what I didn't say, what I chose not to do.

And, really, does anyone *want* to walk through that door? No. No one does.

So, I back away from it, this door marked by the four-letter-word I can't say. I embrace the power of this new word, this new place.

Mistakes don't come with trauma. They don't require counselors and kits.

I can move on from a *mistake.*

I am not ruined.

I am not broken.

I. Am. Not. A. Victim.

CHAPTER 15

WORTHINGTON UNIVERSITY

FALL SEMESTER, FRESHMAN YEAR

"*D*on't you ever sleep?" Wren grumbles as she rolls over in the middle of the night, her question more of a complaint.

I can't exactly blame her. It's been a week since Tucker's *mistake*.

"Sorry." I utter the apology as the nightlight clipped to my headboard remains lit, as the tears silently streaming down my face remain unchecked, as my body remains rigid, sleep far beyond my grasp.

I no longer take comfort in unconsciousness. Not here, anyway. Not when I know Tucker is just down the hall.

My mouth is dry but I don't allow myself a sip of water. If I could bring back the days of chamber pots beneath beds, I would.

Getting up to pee in the middle of the night means leaving this locked room. I'm not drunk, but my breasts are braless beneath an oversized T-shirt, my pink pajama pants are stamped with Hello Kitty's smiling face, and my feet are bare. What if Tucker, or anyone else, thinks it's an invitation?

The truth is, no matter what I wear, I feel exposed. Like my skin is an undressed, open wound.

I wipe my face on my comforter, laying with the tip of my nose tilted to the ceiling, resisting the Kleenex so that I don't further piss off my roommate.

Wren tosses again, sighs. "Are you... okay?"

I almost want to laugh. *Okay? Will I ever be okay again?* But I say, "I'm fine."

"You know, if you want to talk..." She doesn't finish her sentence, and I'm not sure if she would have said *I'm here to listen* or *there's a student counseling service you could call.*

"Thanks." Since she's obviously awake, I decide to blow my nose.

After a few minutes pass, she says, "It must have been scary, waking up in the hospital like that."

My already tense muscles clench even tighter. "Like what?"

"Like, I don't know. Just waking up after passing out, but in a new, strange place."

"Has that... has that ever happened to you?"

"Waking up in a hospital, no. But passing out and not remembering where I am or how I got there, yeah."

Is Wren saying... ? My breath is a heavy, choking mist inside my throat. "With Tucker?"

She releases a low laugh, unaware that my lungs are barely moving up and down in the dark, so still is my chest. "Sure. Whenever I try to keep up with him, I get in trouble. I should really know better by now."

"Trouble? What do you mean?"

"Just the stupid shit we've pulled over the years. Last winter, we took the kayak at his parents' lake house out in the middle of the night. I woke up in the bottom of the boat, completely hungover, with no memory of what we did with the oars and no way to get back to the house that didn't involve swimming in fucking freezing water."

"Oh." No, Wren isn't implying what I thought she was. Not even close.

"Yeah. I finally shoved Tucker overboard and made him swim back to the dock for an extra set of oars." She sighs. "Tucker is a troublemaker. I honestly don't know why I love him, but I do."

"You love him?" Shame gnaws at me as I recall enjoying Tucker's attention. Flirting with him. Kissing him.

If I'd been a better person, his *mistake* never would have happened.

His mistake is *my* fault.

"Of course. We've grown up together. He was the first guy I ever kissed. I can't imagine my life without him."

Wren could be me, talking about Gavin.

"I-I didn't realize—"

"Wait, did something happen between you and Tucker? Before the hospital?"

"I—"

"Whatever, it's fine if it did," she says, although her voice has a layer of strain to it that wasn't there before. "We haven't hooked up since we both decided to come to Worth U. He wants to see other people and so do I."

She makes a high-pitched sound that's not a laugh. "I mean, we'll pick back up eventually though. Our families have been planning our wedding for years. Don't get too attached, Poppy. If you guys are having some kind of *thing*... just know he's only on loan."

I cough. "You don't have to worry about that."

"So," Wren sounds wide awake now, "what did happen between you two?"

"Um, what did Tucker say?"

"Nothing. Just that he thinks you're cool. And he felt bad that you got sick."

I don't even know how to respond.

"So, did you?"

"What?"

She huffs in annoyance. "You tell me."

"I don't know." My voice is quiet.

"What… what does that mean?"

"I don't remember."

"You don't remember? Nothing?"

I close my eyes, the face of the doctor and nurse projecting onto the blank walls of my eyelids.

We found evidence of sexual activity. A condom… inside your clothes. Does that sound right to you?

I'd like you to consent to a rape kit. It won't take very long, it—

I blink my eyes open. "I don't remember," I say again, a little louder.

"Well, you can rule out sex then. If you had sex with Tucker, you'd remember it."

"How do you know?" This time my voice is sharp, slicing through the still, stale air of our small room. I need to know what Wren knows, if there's a possibility that nothing happened. Not even a *mistake.*

"Just that Tucker's damn good at it. He's not like other guys. He makes sure I come, every time. The few times I haven't, he goes down on me until—"

I feel sick. "Okay, I get it."

Wren laughs. "No need to be a prude about it. Sex isn't anything to be ashamed of."

"I'm not ashamed." Not about sex itself. With Gavin, it was beautiful and tender and poignant. Sex was special. He made it special.

Pain claws at my heart, ripping my soul into shreds. What happened last week was the opposite of special. I don't remember it, but I can't forget it.

Why can't I forget something I don't even remember?

This is just one of the many questions that have been keeping me up at night. *Why didn't I go back to the library like I wanted to? Why did I act on the petty impulse to prove Wren wrong? Why didn't I realize that Everclear is a grain alcohol twice as strong as vodka?*

Why didn't I go back to my room, alone?

How could I have been so stupid?

Questions that pulse inside my brain on an endless loop. So many, every night. I've started fantasizing about drilling a hole through my skull and pouring a gallon of bleach into my brain. *Will I sleep then?*

"Do you like him?" The question comes after at least twenty minutes, startling me. I thought Wren had fallen back asleep.

"No."

"You liked him enough to go back to his room."

"It was a mistake," I say quickly, firmly.

Suddenly, her night light turns on and she bolts upright in her bed. "Wait. Do you think Tucker... Do you think he hurt you?"

I roll over so she won't see my swollen eyes, my tear-stained cheeks. "I think it's late. Go back to bed."

She does the opposite, her feet hitting the floor and padding over to the light switch on the wall. "Ow." I cover my face with my comforter at the sudden brightness. Small night lights clipped to headboards are one thing, but unforgiving fluorescent bulbs suspended from the ceiling are completely different.

Wren sits on my bed.

Wren never sits on my bed.

"This is serious." She yanks at my blanket. "You've been different, ever since you came home from the hospital. Did you accuse Tucker of something when you were there?"

I don't know what comes over me. Maybe it's because it's late and Wren, who isn't my friend, is in my face. Maybe it's because I've barely slept, barely eaten, and have no idea what to do with my body and my brain and the fear and the shame.

"I didn't have to. I didn't have to because the nurse, the doctor

—they already knew. *They* told *me!*" Words I've been pushing down and pushing down and pushing down come up in a violent heave.

Wren recoils from me as if I've slapped her. "That's bullshit. You're disgusting. Tucker *saved* you."

Some volcanos explode in a massive torrent of steam and fire and lava. Others release intermittent eruptions of exhaust, just enough to alleviate whatever pressure is no longer tolerable. Some never explode at all, keeping their churning, virulent chaos completely hidden.

I must be the middle. Because my three heated sentences are enough. I shrink back against the wall, clutching my sheet and comforter to my chest. Wishing I'd said nothing at all.

"Just forget it," I say, my body already shutting down.

"Tucker can have anyone he wants. He doesn't need to force himself on an unconscious girl, practically a warm corpse."

"I said, forget it."

"Not until you promise to forget about this crazy idea of yours. Think about it, Poppy. If you're pissed at Tucker because he hasn't come back for seconds—"

I gasp but Wren ignores me.

"—and you turn this into something it isn't, Tucker will be embarrassed, his parents furious. But do you think the school will kick him out, or do anything really? I mean, come on. He's a Stockton, for God's sake."

I let her words pummel me, reminding me of everything I already know.

"And you… who the hell are you? You'll be just another slut looking for a payout from a rich jock."

The tremble starts in my bones, shaking me like a twig in a windstorm. "Thanks for the perspective. I get the picture."

I'm quivering so hard even my teeth are chattering.

Wren slides off my bed, sighs, then turns back to face me. "Listen, I know I come off like a bitch. I am a bitch, I guess. But I know Tucker, better than anyone. You're wrong about him. He would never..."

Her voice chokes up, and I can see the glisten of unshed tears in her eyes. The idea of Wren Knowles crying is just as shocking to me as our having this talk at all. "If you really think he did... *something*, you should talk to him about it."

I shake my head. "No. I don't want to talk to him, or to anyone. I just want to forget about it, all right."

Her features harden into a resolute expression that practically screams, *If you won't, then I will.*

"Don't," I warn. "I'm serious, if you breathe a word about this conversation to him, or to anyone else, then so will I. I'll tell everyone, and even if nothing comes of it officially, it will be a black mark against Tucker."

Wren is still glaring at me, nothing about her posture indicating that she'll back down. I pull another threat out of thin air. "You know an accusation like that would follow him forever. So if you really mean it about wanting to marry him one day, you'll keep your mouth shut."

It works. Her eyes blaze with indignation but after a minute she straightens her spine and walks back to me, hand extended. "I won't say anything. But you better keep your word, Whitman."

It feels strange to mark this mutual code of silence with a handshake, of all things. But it makes our promise feel more official than it would have otherwise, more than just a pre-dawn secret between two college freshman.

She slaps at the wall switch, crawls back into bed, and turns off her own night light.

But not me. I leave mine on until the whisper of a new day is written in the streaks of milky light coming through our closed shades.

CHAPTER 16

WORTHINGTON UNIVERSITY

FALL SEMESTER, FRESHMAN YEAR

*M*ichael pokes his head through my door. "Hey, do you have a minute?"

I'm sitting cross-legged on my bed, re-reading an essay I finished at three in the morning last night. "Of course." After I email it to my professor, I'll pack a bag and catch the shuttle to the train station.

I've been counting down the days until I can get off campus for Thanksgiving break, and yet I'm terrified of going back to Sackett, too.

Will my mom and sister sense the change in me? I look exactly the same, physically. Mentally, though, it's like I'm an entirely different person. And frankly, I don't like this new Poppy. She's a stranger living inside my skin.

She's so afraid of saying the wrong thing, she doesn't say much at all. She doesn't like studying at the library or going for long walks on campus. Even fully clothed, she feels exposed and vulnerable. Rushing from Caldwell to class and then straight back again, she takes no comfort beneath the shade of a gnarled elm tree on the quad.

It's driving Wren nuts, I know. Every time my roommate walks in the door she gives me a look like, *You're still here?*

I am.

But not for much longer. Soon I will be back in the town I couldn't wait to escape. Back in my old room, my bulletin board filled with pictures of things I'd torn from the pages of magazines. Things I wanted. Things I thought would make me happy.

They mean nothing now. They belong to the person I used to be. The person I will never be again.

I set the essay aside as Michael steps into my room. He's holding a folder, and the expression on his face tells me I won't like what is in it. "Mind if I close the door?"

Panic claws at my composure. I don't want to be alone with Michael, or with any guy. But explaining why is impossible. "Yeah, sure." At least no one from my dorm will overhear this conversation.

He pulls out the chair from my desk and sits down, nodding his head toward the other half of my room. "Wren left already?"

"She did. Last night."

Michael exhales, then passes me the folder. It's blue, with the WU emblem stamped in gold on the front.

I take it reluctantly. "Am I being expelled?"

Michael shakes his head. "No, no. Of course not." With nothing left to hold, he wraps his hands over his knees, palms rubbing at his worn jeans. "They wanted me to give this to you personally, walk you through everything and then, you know, if you have any questions, direct you to the relevant person."

I want to ask who *they* is, but the question shrivels on my tongue as I open the folder and pull out the papers inside with stiff fingers. The first is an invoice. My eyes are immediately drawn to the line item at the bottom of the page. Ambulatory medical services. The amount listed makes my breath catch in the back of my throat. Nearly a thousand dollars. Money I don't have. "Michael, I, um, I don't—" I take another breath, try again. "How am I going to…"

"I know. I'm really sorry. Apparently, insurance covered your hospital costs, but not the ambulance ride from campus." He stands up, reaches in his pocket and opens a folded sheet of loose-leaf paper. "I wrote down the case officer assigned to you if you have any questions."

This time, I make no effort to reach for it, so Michael places the creased paper on my bed and sits back down. My lungs feel like they've shrunk in the past two minutes, I can't get a deep breath. "It's not fair. How can they expect me to pay for…"

But I don't finish the sentence. Won't say the four-letter word that starts with *r* and ends in *ape*. That night is a *mistake*.

I don't need Wren to tell me that I can't point my finger at Tucker, levy an accusation that will affect me as much as him. Maybe more. He's a Stockton and I'm a scholarship student. If I speak up, regardless of who is right and who is wrong, his family can easily buy another building or pay a team of lawyers to slant the facts to his advantage. No. Much better to keep my mouth shut and my head down.

If that makes me a coward, so be it.

Pushing out a breath heavy with desperation, I set the invoice aside. Next is an appointment confirmation with a WU Judicial Administrator. I look up at Michael. "What's this?"

"Well, any time a student is found to have violated school alcohol policies, you have to go before the WUJA Board."

I feel the blood draining from my face. "So, I *am* in trouble for what happened."

"No. Of course not."

"Then why do they want to see me?"

"I think it's just policy, really."

"Policy." I let the word sink in. "Have you ever gone before the…"

"The WUJA Board," he fills in. "No. But it's not all that uncommon."

"Has anyone from our floor had to?"

"Well, no."

"The dorm?"

"Poppy, I really can't say."

"Can you at least tell me what I should expect? Will I have to tell them everything that happened?" *I'm not telling anyone what happened. I just want to get my lies straight.*

He gives a slow nod, the paper in his hands rustling. "Um, yeah. I think so. Tucker will talk to them, too, because there was alcohol in his room that night."

I swallow. "Will we have to go together?"

"No, no. You each have your own appointment."

Beyond my closed door, I hear the shouts of students as they celebrate coming back from an exam, or turning in a final paper. Suitcases are knocked into walls, there is yelling up and down the hall, music is playing, various songs clashing so that I can barely differentiate between them. Noise. But mostly what I hear is a buzzing in my ears, and the hurried *thump-thump-thumping* of my heartbeat.

I turn my attention back to the remaining piece of paper in the folder. Worthington University Counseling Services is printed at the top, with a date and time written in by hand below. "Another appointment?"

"Yeah. It's a session with a counselor, so you can talk about what happened."

I look into Michael's face, imagining what he would say to me if he knew what *actually* happened. "Isn't that what I have to do in front of the WUJ whatever people?"

His face reddens. "Yeah. Kind of. But they're different. It's mandatory for anyone caught with alcohol to see a counselor. I think they evaluate you to decide on the best course of action for moving forward."

"The best course..." my voice trails off.

"Like, whether you need to take an alcohol abuse class. Or—"

I interrupt. "It's fine. Forget it." A tear drips onto the page in my hands and I let go of it, then press the heels of my palms against my eyes.

How can I pretend *that night* never happened if everyone else won't let me?

After all, it was just a mistake.

"Was any of this sent to my mother?"

"No. You're over eighteen so it's up to you what, or how much..." Michael's voice trails away and I sense him stand up. A moment later, he places a box of tissues in my lap. "I'm sorry, really."

Something deep inside me breaks, cleaves completely away. I manage to grab a handful of tissues and hold them to my face. I need to be alone. "Please, just go."

"Are you sure? We can talk about this. I can stay."

He means well, I know that. But I'm falling apart and I don't want any witnesses. My hands drop and I glare at him through a veil of tears. "Go," I repeat in a strange kind of gurgling growl.

Michael blinks twice, nods once, then backs away until his heel hits the door. Opening it just until there is enough room for him to squeeze through, he disappears into the hall.

I wish I could escape, too.

There is a speaker on the shelf above my bed and I start the Spotify playlist I've recently created. KoRn, Rage Against the Machine, Nine Inch Nails, Betty X, Rollins Band. The manic rhythms and angry lyrics tunnel deep inside me, assuaging the broken bits I hide from everyone else. I turn up the volume, and then I let go.

I'm crying, choking. Drawing deep, ragged breaths that do a terrible job of getting oxygen into my lungs, into my brain. My chest hurts and my brain is sludge. A scummy, noxious puddle. At the back of my throat, bile rises up, burning the delicate tissue.

Kleenex is no match for my tears. It's like defending a nuclear attack with a pocket knife. Useless. I flip over on my bed, pressing my face into the pillow. And scream.

Over and over and over.

Until my throat is a ragged tube, destroyed. My lungs ache, sharp pains lancing through my heart with each rasped breath.

I can't handle this.

I can't, I can't, I can't.

That night was a *mistake*. A foolish freshman fuckup. I don't even remember it.

Maybe it di—

But no. I picture the clear plastic bag, the yellowish condom.

The nurse's question. The doctor's urging. Tucker's explanation.

It happened.

Even as tears transform my pillow into a damp sponge, the logical part of my brain can't understand why this hurts so badly. Why *I* hurt so badly. If I don't remember Tucker unzipping my jeans, pushing them down my thighs, taking off my underwear— why can't I pretend it never happened?

If I didn't hear the sound of plastic tearing, see him sheathe himself in latex, feel him enter me—why does knowing he did hurt so fucking much?

But it does.

I asked Tucker about it last week, when he stopped by my room looking for Wren. I hadn't seen him since the morning I came home from the hospital.

The question popped out of my mouth before I realized what I was saying. I'd wanted to race after my words, grab them in my hands and shove them back down my throat. Send them back where they came from, never to emerge again. Instead, I bit the inside of my cheek so hard I tasted blood, waiting for Tucker to answer me.

Well, of course I used one. But then you started to shake, so I stopped. When you got sick, I rolled you to the side so you didn't choke. I pulled the condom off and made sure you were dressed, then went to get help.

It wasn't an apology.

It wasn't even an acknowledgment that he'd been wrong.

Then he'd shaken his head. *The first time we have sex and neither one of us gets off. Kind of sad, don't you think?*

Recalling Tucker's words, my lungs constrict. He genuinely believed I wanted to have sex with him. He must have, to be so cavalier about it all.

And why wouldn't he?

I flirted with him, didn't I? I did shots with him and smiled at him and held his hand. I wanted Tucker to kiss me. And when he did, I kissed him back.

The shame running though my veins calcifies. *How could I have betrayed Gavin so quickly?* Wherever he is, he's better off without me in his life.

The embers of hope I'd been stubbornly guarding give a final flicker before dying completely. Even if Gavin were to come back, with a perfectly reasonable explanation for leaving, a reason for every day he's spent somewhere else, it doesn't matter anymore.

Because *I* have betrayed *him.*

I have betrayed *us.*

We aren't us.

We are nothing.

Legs shaking, I stand up and go to my mirror. I'm pink-faced and blotchy. My hair is a riot of tangles, wet around my temples and forehead. Snot is smeared above my puffy lips. My eyes are red and swollen, as is the tip of my nose, like a clown.

And my neck is naked. No silver necklace, no iridescent sliver of moonstone perched on the subtle rise of my collarbone.

This is what I will remember about *that night*. Not the act itself. But my ruined, almost unrecognizable face. My blotchy, unadorned neck.

I am nothing.

CHAPTER 17

SACKETT, CONNECTICUT

THANKSGIVING BREAK, FRESHMAN YEAR

*T*hanksgiving in the Whitman household is a simple affair. Normally, I envy those who celebrate the holiday with chaotic gatherings of extended family. But this year, I am grateful it's just the three of us at our small kitchen table.

My mom mostly sips her wine quietly, for once poured into an actual wineglass, while Sadie quizzes me on every last detail about my life at Worthington. Somehow, I manage to plaster the mask of a happy, carefree college co-ed on my face, sprinkling lies in with the truth. *School is great. Wren is an acquired taste but she's fine. Sure, I've made tons of friends. My professors are tough, but fair. Yes, there is a lot of work but it's manageable. No, I don't have a boyfriend. No, I haven't been to any fraternity parties.*

She's applying to colleges now, and has already submitted her application to Worthington, early decision. Sadie is convinced she'll get in because, according to her, she's a legacy now. I decide not to remind her that getting in isn't the hard part. Without the same kind of financial aid package they gave to me, there's no way she can afford to go.

Finally, dinner is over. Sadie and I insist on cleaning up, and our mother tops up her glass and heads into the living room.

"Please tell me you're too full for cake," Sadie urges quietly, as we gather up the dishes and bring them into the kitchen. "I don't want us to get there late."

"Get where late?"

"There's a party—"

"No. I'm not going anywhere."

"Are you serious?" The plates in Sadie's hands clatter to the countertop as she spins around to face me. "*Everyone's* going out tonight!"

"Well, *everyone* won't include me." My full stomach churns with an unsettling mix of guilt and exasperation. Over the past year, Sadie's interests have expanded to include real boyfriends as well as fictional ones. Her current boyfriend is on the football team, which has her embracing an entirely new social circle.

I'm glad she's happy and having fun. But her plans don't have to include me.

"I thought things would change once you went off to college, that maybe you would miss me." My sister's face is pinched, her lips set in an angry pout. "But I guess you're still too good to hang out with me."

"What?" I don't know what to make of her accusation. "Where is this coming from?"

"I'm just telling it like it is. You haven't wanted to spend time with me in years."

"That's not true! I—"

"Oh, please. Stop lying. You're always hiding things from me, keeping secrets. We're a year and a half apart, Poppy. Stop treating me like I'm a baby."

"I don't." But I know I do. After so many years caring for

Sadie, watching out for her, protecting her, it's a hard habit to break.

"It is true," she insists, the gold in her hazel eyes flashing brightly, the venom in her voice cutting deep.

"Girls!" our mom admonishes from the other room. "Do I need to come in there?"

"No," we say, in unison, turning away from each other. Grateful for something to do with my hands, I begin washing the pots from the stovetop.

For a few minutes, there is only the sound of running water, stacking plates, and the muted hum of the television coming from the living room. Sadie disappears for a minute to wipe off the table. When she returns, she slaps me with the dish towel in her hand. "I just miss you, you know."

I jerk back, nearly dropping the slippery pot cover I was washing. I set it down in the sink and turn off the water. "I miss you too, Sadie."

I hate fighting with my sister. Especially within earshot of our mother. And I know Sadie does too. The fear that she'll leave us again has never truly dissipated. When DCSF came for us, my mother had been gone for three days. A neighbor finally called the police, hearing Sadie crying for food and my unsuccessful attempts to soothe her through the thin walls of our government-subsidized apartment.

We were taken away, but only after she left us behind.

My sister and I have had plenty of arguments before, but I'm not the person I was just a few months ago. Though I'm standing upright, it's taking every ounce of self-control I have not to drop to the ground and curl up in a ball.

"I'm sorry," I say, looking directly at Sadie. And I am. I resented my sister when she was young. I was a kid myself, tasked with caring for Sadie as if I were her parent. And it's clear that she resents me now, mistaking my indifference for apathy.

But as much as I love her, I can't be the sister she needs right now.

Sadie nods her head. "I'm sorry, too."

She gives me a hard hug and I feel awful for not being a better sister. I want to say that I'll go out with her tonight. That I'll drink with her and her friends, make conversation with whatever guy she's currently crushing on, tell everyone how great college is and how I can't wait for Sadie to join me at Worth U next year.

But I can't do that. I wish I could. But I *can't*.

I can't explain why either. I've always shielded Sadie from ugly truths. I turned my mother's extended absences into elaborate games, made long nights pass quickly with Scheherazade-like stories, and protected her from bullies at the group home.

I've backed myself into a corner, and now I'm caught in a trap of my own making. How can I confide in Sadie about Tucker with telling her about Gavin, too? I'll have to admit that I've been lying to her for years.

Losing Gavin nearly broke me. And what happened with Tucker is a hot stone I can barely carry. If Sadie turns away from me now, I—

I don't even want to think about it.

"Want to go to a movie tomorrow?" I ask. It's a peace offering. A flimsy one.

Sadie takes the lid from me, though she rebuffs my olive branch. "I'd much rather grab a cup of coffee and actually talk about what's going on with you."

I avoid her tenacious gaze by looking around for something else to wash, but the sink and counters are clear. "Nothing's going on with me."

"You were moping around here before you went away, and you're still moping now that you're back." She lowers her voice to a stage-whisper. "It's a guy, right?"

Elbowing Sadie aside, I reach into the cabinet below the sink for the spray cleaner. "Jesus, Sadie." Why won't she just drop it?

She leans back against the counter, interpreting my non-answer as a *yes*. "Who is he?" I hear her suck in a breath just before she hits me with the dish towel again. "You finally hooked up with your roommate's guy, didn't you? That hottie lacrosse player? Come on, tell me everything."

She may as well have tossed a bucket of ice water over my head. "Sadie, stop looking for dirt. Especially since there's none to find." A chill penetrates my spine and I shiver, regretting letting Sadie come visit when Wren decided she needed some "retail therapy" and spent a weekend shopping in New York City. Sadie had practically drooled over Tucker when she saw him.

To avoid looking my sister in the face, I spray every inch of the countertop with cleaning solution, the plastic bottle belching with each squeeze. Ripping off a wad of paper towels, I attack the fake granite, rubbing so hard the finish starts flaking off.

Sadie watches me, looking entirely unconvinced.

I'm saved by a bell. Well, technically, it's a horn.

Exchanging the dish towel for her purse, Sadie is halfway through the door before she turns back, pointing at me. "We're not finished, by the way."

"Be home by midnight," Mom yells, although whether Sadie heard, or intends to abide by her curfew, is anyone's guess.

Mom comes back into the kitchen, empty wineglass in hand. "Thanks, hon. It's nice having you back home."

I fold the towel Sadie haphazardly tossed onto the counter. "Even when I fight with Sadie?"

A crooked smile wobbles on her lips as she leans back against the cabinets, swaying slightly. "Even then," she says, refilling her glass. "So, now that she's gone… Tell me about the boy."

My mom is usually more interested in reality TV than actual reality. But every once in a while, she is cheerful and animated. An almost perfect replica of a sitcom mom, actively interested in her children.

I frown, not trusting this version of her. "What boy?" I never told her about Gavin, and I'm definitely not telling her about Tucker.

"I overheard you and Sadie." Her voice is light, almost teasing.

"She's wrong, Mom. There's no boy."

My mother huffs. "Well, hopefully you'll find someone soon. It would be nice for you to leave there with more than just a degree."

I think she means a ring on my finger. Or, at the very least, a serious boyfriend.

What I'll take from Worthington isn't a pretty bauble or a handsome guy. It's not something to be envied or admired. It's an experience I never expected to have, an invisible wound I don't know how to heal.

Sometimes it takes a while to process trauma like this, and you don't have to do it alone.

My resolve to keep everything bottled up inside me weakens. What if my mother is strong enough to lift me up, for once? "Well, there is something I wanted to ask you about…"

If I tell my mom what happened to me, if I explain the mess I've made of my life—what would happen?

"Yes?"

"Actually, never mind. It's nothing."

"Poppy, just say it."

I'm squeezing the damp dish towel like a stress ball. "I guess… when you were… I mean, years ago, before we came to Sackett—"

She looks up sharply. "You know I don't like to talk about the past, Poppy."

"I know, Mom." The food in my stomach has become a roiling vat of acid. "But, maybe when you were drinking or… Did anything ever happen that you regret?"

My mother stiffens, wineglass halfway to her now pursed lips. "What do you mean by regret?"

"I don't know exactly," I lie. Because I do know. Exactly. I just don't know how to say it.

Setting her glass down on the table, she reaches for my hand. "Well, then—"

I suck in a breath and force the jammed words through my throat and out of my mouth. "I can't remember, Mom. That's the problem. I drank too much and I think something happened. Actually, I know something happened. But I just—I can't remember it. Except that I can't forget it either."

"What are you trying to tell me? That you— That he..."

I swallow the heavy lump of shame rising up my throat. "Yes."

"And something happened. Something you now regret."

"Yes."

She levels her gaze at me, lips puckering in distaste. "Blaming someone else for your problems is a dangerous thing. What did you expect, Poppy?"

I shouldn't have brought this up. My mother has the same opinion now as she did two years ago, when our entire state was in an uproar about a football player and the girl behind the bleachers. A judge found him guilty of rape, but he only served a few months.

Gavin had been disgusted, I remember. But my mother, like most people in town, was upset that the boy's bright future had been tarnished by a "ridiculous" accusation. She blamed the girl for "making a fuss."

Was it really so ridiculous? Just because she drank too much, did that give anyone the right to lead her into the shadows, to touch her? Didn't she have every right to "make a fuss"?

I want to argue with my mother now. To defend a girl I don't know. To defend myself.

But my brain flashes a warning. *Abort, abort, abort.* "Y-yeah. I'm sure you're right."

Relief sweeps over her features, smoothing out the surface of her skin. In the Whitman household, a certain amount of sibling bickering might be tolerated, but difficult truths are to be avoided at all costs. Her shoulders lower a notch and she begins backing out of the kitchen. "Good, I'm glad that's settled."

"Yeah, me too." Another lie. Nothing is settled.

CHAPTER 18

WORTHINGTON UNIVERSITY

SPRING SEMESTER, FRESHMAN YEAR

*M*y mother's words are still fresh in my mind when I return to Worthington. *What did you expect, Poppy?*

If I had any doubts about who to blame for *that night,* my mother cleared them up.

Me. I'm to blame. My own mother thinks so.

And so I take it. I carry the blame. In front of the Worthington University Judicial Administration board, I admit that I drank too much. I say I'm sorry, and that I'm grateful Tucker was with me to get help. That he saved my life. He's a hero, really.

These are the half-lies and distorted truths that have become my made-up memory.

I drank too much. I'm sorry. I'm grateful Tucker was there to get help. He saved my life.

I wonder how long it will be until I forget they're not actual memories. That I'm just selling the story everyone wants to hear.

Even me.

The WUJA review process was a streamlined, official affair. They didn't ask whether a condom was found on my body. Or about the doctor who sat down at my bedside, a pained expression on his face as he spoke to me like I was his daughter, putting a name to what had happened. Asking—no, suggesting—that I consent to a rape kit.

But I wasn't his daughter. I'm my mother's daughter.

Whitmans don't face difficult truths head-on. And we don't make a fuss.

We make allowances and excuses. We go along to get along.

Even when, inside, we're falling apart.

Even when every lie, every allowance, and every excuse that leaves our tongues sends another drop of poison sliding down our throats.

A few days later, at my required student counseling session, I am escorted into a small office with barely enough room for a desk and two chairs. "My name is Johanna Gregory. I'm a graduate student here at Worthington."

I take a seat, concerned that in this tiny space, I won't have the luxury of hiding behind my made-up answers. That this will be a more intimate exploration of my actions. That Johanna Gregory won't buy the story I'm selling.

After she gives me the broad strokes of her biography and responsibilities at WU's student counseling service, she flashes an overly bright smile that I'm guessing she thinks is reassuring. It's not. "So, now that you know a little about me, let's talk about you, Poppy."

"There's not much to tell. I'm a freshman, I made bad choices and wound up in the hospital." I don't want this intimacy. I resent this forced vulnerability, this unwanted intrusion. And I want her to know it. So I add, "I'm here today because I have to be."

Her only reaction is to make a note on the yellow legal pad balanced over her crossed legs. "Have you ever been in therapy?"

"Not therapy, exactly. But I have met with counselors and psychologists before."

"Oh? Tell me about that."

I outline my family history as if I'm reading from a résumé. Dates and places with one or two bullet points. She fills up the first page and flips to another. Then another. "And would you say your life stabilized with the move to Sackett at thirteen?"

"Yes. I guess so."

"Does your mother still engage in any of the activities that made her incapable of caring for you and your sister prior to your move?"

"She drinks wine occasionally, but that's all."

"Occasionally," she repeats. "Can you be more specific?"

"Well, after work. Or weekends. Afternoons."

"Every afternoon?"

"No. Not every afternoon." I can't remember a day without the *tap* of her bottle on the edge of her coffee mug, but I'm sure there must have been a few.

"Once or twice a week... Every other afternoon... More, less?"

The vent behind me is blowing dry, heated air that smells vaguely of burned toast. I shift in my chair, trying and failing to find a comfortable position. "Maybe every other."

"And are we talking about a glass, two glasses, the bottle, more than that?"

I bite off a ragged cuticle, suck out the blood that wells up in the gauge beside my nail bed. "I really don't keep track of my mother's drinking."

"Okay. Well, on those afternoons, what did you do?"

"What did I *do*?"

"Yes. Did you sit with her, talk to her, take some wine for yourself, hide in your room... ?"

"What does it matter?"

She tilts her head to the side. "Humor me."

146

I sigh. "I went to my room, I guess. Did my homework. If the weather was nice, I'd go outside."

"To play with friends in the neighborhood?"

"Ah, yeah."

"Did you hang out at their houses?"

"N—Why?"

"I'm curious if you had other parental role models."

"Oh."

"Well, did you?"

"I mostly hung out in the woods. A nature preserve behind our house."

"Ah." She tries for a conspiratorial grin this time, though it drops when I don't return it. "A parent-free zone."

"I guess." *Please don't ask who I was with.* If I have to talk about Gavin, I might lose it.

"Did you drink too?"

"No," I say immediately, before correcting myself. "Well, only a few times."

"A few times a week?"

"No, a few times in total. Not until the end of my senior year."

"And what precipitated that?"

"What pre... ? Nothing. I just started, I guess."

"So, you were around your mother's drinking for years and you just started one day, out of the blue."

I shrink lower in my chair. "Yeah."

"What about with your friends?"

"What do you mean?"

"Before coming to Worthington, did you drink with your friends? Or with your sister?"

"No." I shake my head. "I only drank a few times before coming here. I poured myself a glass and went to my room." Drinking and crying and looking through the photos Gavin left for me.

She pauses to underline something on her page and then flips to a fresh one. "Okay. That gives me a feel for your life before you came here. Let's talk about what your life has been like at Worthington. It's a big adjustment, going from living with your family to a freshmen dorm. How is your roommate?"

"She's fine."

Johanna waits for me to expand on my answer. When I don't, she reaches for a folder on her desk and opens it. "And your classes? I see you have a three point one GPA for your first semester."

My scholarship requires that I maintain a 3.0 average. I barely squeaked by and I know it. "They're fine. Harder than high school but I'll get used to it."

She nods in understanding, then pulls a pamphlet out of a drawer and hands it to me. "There is a student tutoring service you might want to look into."

I accept the glossy folded paper with two smiling students beaming from the front, my stomach clenching as we work closer to *that night.* "Thank you."

"Let's get a little more specific, regarding your alcohol use here on campus. Prior to the incident, had you been drinking on other occasions?"

"No."

"No? Are you sure? Because you won't get in trouble for telling the truth. My role in this process isn't punitive, Poppy. The reason we're talking is to evaluate the extent that alcohol has affected your life at Worth U, and ensure you have the best chances for a safe and successful future here."

Safe and successful. I wonder what she would say if I told her I've already failed on both counts.

"That was the only time I had anything to drink on campus."

One eyebrow tics upward, and I sense her skepticism. "So you're saying that this was a one-time event, that it won't happen again?"

The thought of going through this again sends a wave of nausea crashing into me. "Yes."

Her eyes flick to the clock on her desk. "We have a few more minutes. I'd like to ask about the student you were with, Tucker Stockton."

The way she says his name makes me think that she's been told to tread lightly here. That further revelations concerning him will not be appreciated.

I don't say anything, waiting for an actual question.

"Is there anything that happened in Tucker's room, prior to him seeking out your resident advisor for help, that you were uncomfortable with?"

"Uncomfortable..." My throat feels like it's been reduced to the width of a straw, and I have to force the syllables out. "No. We were just hanging out."

"And have you spent time together since then?"

"Not—not really," I stammer. "He's mostly my roommate's friend."

Johanna pauses, rolling her pen over her knuckles. "When someone, especially someone who isn't family or a close friend, does something selfless, such as risking disciplinary action to get help for a friend with whom he'd been drinking, it often leads to feelings of indebtedness or discomfort around that person. Would you say that's been the case for you?"

I shake my head. "N-no."

Uncrossing her legs, Johanna leans forward in her chair as if she's going to get up but then hesitates. Her eyes hold mine, more gently than before. "Can you describe your feelings then?"

"My feelings for Tucker?" The air in my lungs evaporates, the synapses in my brain screeching to a halt. I hadn't anticipated this question. And I have no idea how to answer it—because I can't begin to put my feelings for Tucker into words. They are an assembly of emotions that attack me like overzealous wasps, stinging over and over with relentless, unerring accuracy.

Fear. Anger. Regret. Grief. Confusion. Shame.

"I, um." I notice her looking at my hands, which are curled into fists, my nails digging into my palms. Awareness flickers on her face, sympathy warming her gaze. But there is something else, too. Reluctance. If I tell her what really happened, if I confirm her suspicions, then she'll have to do something about it. She'll have to take my story to people only interested in accolades about a Stockton. Make a case against Tucker on behalf of a drunken scholarship student who refused a rape kit and hasn't told anyone the truth of what happened. Has actively lied about it to everyone who's asked.

Johanna Gregory is just a grad student. She has her whole career to consider. Why would she throw it away for me? I'm nobody.

I quickly unclench my fists and slide my fingers beneath my thighs, saving her the trouble. "I'm just grateful Tucker went for help. He saved my life."

What I see next on Johanna's face is relief.

I don't blame her. If I won't fight for myself, why should anyone else?

CHAPTER 19

WORTHINGTON UNIVERSITY

SPRING SEMESTER, FRESHMAN YEAR

"*H*i, I have a—"

The upperclassman sitting at the reception desk of the Student Services office taps the clipboard facing me on her desk. "Sign in right there and someone will be with you in a minute."

"Great." I pick up the pencil attached to the metal clasp by a rubber band and write my name. "Thanks."

I'm early. My appointment with the Dean of Student Affairs isn't for another ten minutes, so I find a seat and pull a textbook out of my bag.

I received an email with the findings of Johanna Gregory and the WUJA just before heading home for Christmas break. In addition to my schoolwork and work study hours this semester, I will have to fit in thirty hours of community service and ten alcohol education classes.

I don't know where I'm going to find a spare thirty hours this semester, but I want to get it over with. Once freshman year is behind me, I don't want to think about *that night*, or Tucker Stockton, ever again.

"Poppy Whitman?" A gray-haired, African-American man in khakis and a tweed sport coat rests his elbow on the front desk and scans the students slumped around the room in various poses.

"That's me," I say, picking up my backpack and slinging it over my shoulder.

"Come on back." He holds open the door to a hallway. I walk through it, but he doesn't let it close behind me. "We're just waiting on one more."

The hair at the back of my neck rises, my heartbeat suddenly accelerating. *No.*

I don't need to hear the dean say it, I already know who will be joining us.

"Tucker." He elongates the word so that it sounds like there are three *r*'s on the end, not just one, then follows it up with a combination shoulder clap and squeeze, just in case I was in any doubt about the relationship between them. "Good to see you again, son."

Tucker Stockton, the dark-haired golden boy of Worth U. *Barf.*

According to Wren, because beer was present in Tucker's room, he's been assigned ten hours of community service and one alcohol education class.

"Hey, Dean Johnson." The hallway is narrow, and I have to make a distinct effort not to shrink away from Tucker. This is the first time I've seen him since last semester.

The dean's office is bigger than Johanna Gregory's, but not by much. He takes a seat in the room's only chair, motioning us toward a couch pushed up against the far wall. I sit down at the very edge and instead of putting my backpack on the floor, I set it on the seam between the two cushions to create a barrier between Tucker and me.

"I don't always see students together, but after reading your intake forms I thought it would make the most sense."

My tongue is the consistency of cardboard. "Intake forms?"

"The questionnaire I emailed you. About your—"

"Oh, right. Sure. Sorry." I'd forgotten about the survey I received, asking about my interests and skills. My palms are sweating and my breath is too fast, too shallow. I dare a glance at Tucker. He is perfectly at ease, wearing jeans and a Henley, one foot crossed over his knee.

"Now, Poppy, you were a camp counselor, is that correct?"

I nod. "And Tucker, you coached a boys lacrosse team, right?"

"Just a clinic. It was part of an—"

Dean Johnson beams. "Clinic, right. The point is, you've both worked with kids. And, it just so happens I've found a perfect opportunity to fulfill your community service hours. Since you'll be working together, it made sense to go over the details together, too."

Working. Together.

This can't be happening.

But it is.

"As I'm sure you know, Worthington University prides itself on our community outreach. TeenCharter is a nonprofit that runs several group homes in our area. Their facilities support teenagers who, for whatever reason, cannot live with their own families and haven't been placed with a foster family. I recently met with their program director to set up a tutoring service for them and she shared some of her other concerns with me as well. We've decided that the youths could benefit from more direct contact with Worth U students, unrelated to academic objectives."

"Are these kids—"

"What kind of—"

Tucker and I both talk at once. He grins at me as if we're sharing an inside joke.

153

I flinch, spinning back to face the dean.

We found evidence of sexual activity. A condom... inside your clothes. Does that sound about right to you?

We shared one night, one mistake. That's all.

Focus on the kids, Poppy. "TeenCharter... they work with the Department of Children and Families?"

"Yes. Each of their homes can support eight to twelve teenagers, but they're not large facilities, and the director thinks it would be helpful to bring them to the Worth U campus one afternoon every weekend. The kids..."

I listen to him explain the necessity for places like these, housing children who don't have anywhere else to go. I don't admit that I know exactly what kind of homes they are, and the children who live there. I was once one of them.

"How can we help?" Tucker asks.

I listen carefully for any note of scorn in his voice, any indication that he intends to do only the bare minimum to fulfill his obligations. But I don't find any. Tucker sounds intrigued, even enthusiastic.

"The specifics are up to you and Poppy. But the main problem, as I understand it, is—"

"Boredom," I interject. "These kids attend school, but there's no organized sports, playdates with friends, or even errands with their parents. They're scared, and they feel abandoned." TeenCharter didn't manage the home Sadie and I were placed in, but the issues children face are universal.

Two pairs of eyes swing my way. Dean Johnson speaks first. "That's exactly right. What I'd like you both to work on is setting up an ongoing outreach program, where interested Worthington students will spend time with the TeenCharter children one afternoon every weekend. You can organize games or crafts, anything to put smiles on their faces. Sound good?"

"Yes," Tucker and I both agree.

Aside from actually working with Tucker, it sounds great.

CHAPTER 20

WORTHINGTON UNIVERSITY

FALL SEMESTER, SOPHOMORE YEAR

"*H*ave you ever shot one of those before?" Jenny regards me dubiously, her eyes traveling from my helmet and thick safety goggles to my camouflage coveralls and the gun I'm clutching to my chest with gloved hands.

She is wearing an identical getup, and I grin at her. I've grown close to many of the teenagers from TeenCharter, especially Jenny. She reminds me a little of me, actually. Absentee father, addict mother, few relatives or foster families willing to take on a teenage girl who'd basically raised herself and didn't believe normal rules—curfews, bedtimes, chores—applied to her.

When I first met Jenny, she was angry at the world—and I was no exception. But over time, we've come to an understanding. I don't try to act like a parent or even an older sister—no judgment, no advice. When she wants, she participates in the activities Tucker and I plan, and when she thinks they're dumb, she sulks in a corner and seeks me out afterward.

Jenny is skittish, especially around Tucker and the lacrosse buddies he's enlisted to work with the TeenCharter kids once a week. But she's also smart and strong, and when she smiles, her entire face radiates joy. Jenny's laugh is my favorite part of the week.

Working with Tucker is my least favorite.

Jenny had picked up on my discomfort almost immediately. "Why don't you like him?" she'd asked me in a whisper the second afternoon we spent together.

"Who?" I played dumb, though I knew exactly who she meant.

Jenny knew I was lying. "Fine, don't tell me," she'd huffed, then stalked off.

But she brought it up again the following week. "If you don't want to be around Tucker, why do you come here with him?"

"Well, if I didn't, then I wouldn't get to see you, would I?" Jenny's eyes had filled with reproach at my half-answer and I'd sighed, looking away. "Things with Tucker are... complicated."

Jenny didn't push further, though I could tell she wanted to. If anyone understands complicated, it's a teenager in a group home.

To get this program off the ground, I'd had to put my feelings about Tucker aside. They were still there, of course, otherwise Jenny wouldn't have noticed anything.

It's hard to look at Tucker without feeling ashamed of my own behavior that night. And angry at him for, knowingly or unknowingly, taking advantage of my intoxication.

But it's been months, and while it's definitely not *easy* to see him every weekend, to text and email and coordinate about TeenCharter events, it has gotten *easier*.

In my Intro to Psychology course, we learned about Exposure Therapy. It's a treatment developed to help people confront their fears, by repeatedly exposing them to the object of their fear. It's extremely effective.

And I think that's what our TeenCharter program has done for me. At first, it was just a means to fulfill my community service hours. But it's become so much more. My commitment to the kids we help has far outweighed my aversion to dealing with Tucker.

The truth is, I couldn't have asked for a better partner. Tucker is great with them, and generous with his time. He fulfilled his community service hours within the first few weeks, but hasn't once mentioned pulling away from the program.

At this point, more than just "complicated," my feelings for Tucker can best be summed up in one word: discomfort. I don't want to like him. But it's hard to hate someone who dressed up in a bunny suit for Easter last semester and spent two hours hopping around the main quad, pretending to "lay" plastic eggs we'd spent hours filling with candy, stickers, and temporary tattoos.

When Tucker first proposed the idea, I tried to shut it down. *They're teenagers. They don't believe in the Easter Bunny*, I'd said. But Tucker rented the bunny suit anyway, and he was right. Most of these kids didn't grow up with novelties like the Easter Bunny or Santa Claus. They had a blast.

Just like they did at the Monster Mash he suggested for Halloween.

And coming to Paintball-Palooza today was Tucker's idea, too. He'd convinced the owner to comp our fees and Dean Johnson arranged for transport using one of our campus shuttle buses.

Now I wink at Jenny through the thick lenses. "Believe me, I know exactly what I'm doing."

At Paintball-Palooza, games are played on four and a half acres of thick woodlands, with natural cover coming from trees and boulders, piles of logs and tires, as well as manmade wooden shelters.

As a camp counselor for five summers in a row, it would be impossible not to be at least somewhat proficient at paintball. Although, after finding out we were coming here today, I made a solo trip to acclimate myself to the terrain and equipment.

I'm glad I did. The second I pulled the scent of pinecones and damp earth unto my lungs, a wave of nostalgia sent me reeling. I closed my eyes, trying to focus on the good rather than the bad. Because almost all of my memories of Gavin are good. Incredibly great, actually. Our hikes, our talks, our card games. Kissing and touching and exploring each other's bodies. Stolen moments. Shared jokes. Laughing and loving.

The Sackett Preserve had been a little slice of paradise. *Our* little slice of paradise.

And I want to remember that. The smiles Gavin put on my face. The joy he brought into my life.

It took a while, but I thought I'd pulled myself together. I really did.

So, I let go of the maple tree I'd used to steady myself, and my palm came away sticky from untapped sap.

And suddenly... I wasn't okay. My hand felt like it was on fire. Pain ripped through me, sharp-edged and fierce, as if I'd been gutted by a hot poker.

Gavin.

I spent the entire session hiding beneath that tree, my paintball gun forgotten on my lap. Finally accepting that his absence is a gaping wound I might never recover from.

Even knowing I don't deserve him anymore. That, in the truest sense of the word, I'd been unfaithful. Regardless of what came after, I flirted with Tucker. I kissed Tucker. I invited him back to my room before agreeing to go to his.

I don't know whether Gavin has been with anyone else. Or why he left. But I would take him back in a heartbeat... if he'd have me.

If he'd only come back. Or call. Send a message via carrier pigeon. Anything.

I left without answers or closure. The only saving grace was that got my breakdown out of the way. So far, I've managed to maintain a relatively calm, composed facade in front of the Teen-Charter kids. And Tucker.

We split up into teams, then paired off to find cover. I led Jenny behind a stack of several enormous Goodyear tires, our guns blending in with the black rubber, cautioning her, "Most people run around like lunatics, shooting at random. If we stay focused, we'll take out the other team like fish in a barrel."

The fog horn blares, and as I suspected, everyone starts running like children let loose on a playground. Which, let's face it, is entirely accurate in this situation. I take aim, fire, watch the bloom of neon pain strike a shoulder. I find another target and repeat.

Jenny fires off half a dozen shots, cursing when she only hits trees.

I put my gun down. "Here, let me show you." I go over the rudiments of aligning her sight and firing in the space between her breaths.

"Should I be scared that you're a little too good at shooting people?"

I pick my weapon back up. "Only if you decide to switch teams."

This time, when Jenny squeezes the trigger, she makes contact. "Got one!" she squeals… a little too loudly.

Shit. From the corner of my eye, I see Tucker drop out of a tree. I swivel, pointing my gun in his direction and firing. Tucker rocks backward, his chest splattered with yellow, just as a green paintball from his gun slams into my upper arm.

We're playing the game with seven lives, which means we can get hit seven times before we're out. But after each hit, we have to walk back to *home base*, and wait three minutes before returning to the field.

"I'll be back," I say to Jenny.

"You're leaving?"

I shift so that she can see the paint covering my arm. "I won't be long, but in the meantime," I point at a shed behind us, "head over there. And don't announce every hit, okay?"

She nods and I wait for her to reposition herself before standing up. "Dead man walking!" I yell, shouldering my gun and heading back to home base.

Home base is a bench positioned beneath a metal overhang, near the entrance to the course. Shawn and Terrell, two of the TeenCharter boys, glance at me briefly before returning their attention to the clock.

"Good shot," Tucker says when I show up just as he's sitting down, rubbing his chest.

My arm is already aching where he hit me, but I don't admit it. "Yeah, you too."

"I'm free!" Shawn yells a few seconds later, rushing out onto the field without a backward glance. Terrell follows behind not long after.

"You know, I tried to convince Wren to come with us today but she was pretty adamant that paintball isn't her sport."

"Wren?" I try and fail to picture my former roommate wearing dirty coveralls and safety goggles, hiding behind trees and crawling through mud. "This is hardly her scene."

Tucker's lip twitches. "Even if you tried baiting her with that line, I don't think she would have come."

I shrug. "Guess she's smarter than I am."

"That's not true, Poppy. Wren is just... well, she already knows who she is. She doesn't have to prove herself to anyone."

"Are you implying that I don't know who I am?"

"No. Well, not exactly."

"You don't even know me!" When it comes to Tucker, my emotions are on a hair trigger.

"Because I fucked things up the first night we hung out. I hate what happened as much as you do."

My eyebrows lift so high I feel them disappear into my hairline. "I doubt that," I say, every syllable dripping with disdain.

"Fuck." Tucker lets his head fall back and sighs. "There's something about you. I've never met anyone else who makes me get everything wrong, every single time."

I release a hoarse chuckle. "It's a gift."

He brings his head level again and turns to me. "What I'm trying to say is that you're open to different people, different experiences. You're still trying to figure out your path while people like me and Wren, well, ours was laid out before we were even born."

"And you think that's a bad thing? Please. You have no idea how lucky you are, Tucker."

He shakes his head. "Lucky? It's like wearing a goddamned straitjacket."

My head twists back to him like it's on a swivel. "Are you seriously expecting sympathy for the silver spoon jammed in your mouth when you were born? Or your perfect pedigree?"

"No," Tucker practically growls. "I'm not looking for sympathy from you or anyone else. But I didn't realize I had to filter my experiences and opinions through your lens, Poppy. If you're only interested in hanging out with people who are just like you, then I have news for you—you're just as judgmental as Wren."

Tucker's words land heavily and sit like stones inside my chest, the truth of them an unexpected weight.

Is that why I've always had a hard time making friends— because I'm only comfortable with people who are just like me?

I'd found one when I was thirteen, practically in my backyard. Gavin and I were so alike. My mother an addict, his father an alcoholic. Years in the foster system. Abandonment issues. Trust issues. Growing up with barely two nickels to rub together.

I scratch at the paint drying on my face. "You're right."

Tucker remains expressionless for a moment and then, to my surprise, he grins at me. "It killed you to say that, didn't it?"

"It kind of did," I admit, fighting a smile of my own.

Tucker taps his temple. "In here, we're our own worst enemies."

The timer goes off, putting an end to our conversation. I sprint out onto the field without another glance at Tucker. Out here, battle lines are clear, the rules of the game defined. Tucker Stockton is my enemy and I spend the rest of the hour shooting at him.

CHAPTER 21

SACKETT, CONNECTICUT & NEW YORK CITY

HOLIDAY BREAK, SOPHOMORE YEAR

*M*y phone rings on the morning of New Year's Eve. I put it to my ear before I'm fully awake, my *hello* more of a yawn.

"Good morning." Tucker's deep voice jolts me awake, a surge of adrenaline rushing through me.

"What's wrong? Did something happen?" My thoughts immediately turn to the TeenCharter program. Besides Christmas Day itself, I've been working practically nonstop since coming home for break, and I had to miss the holiday party we'd planned for them.

I feel terrible about it. This time of year is rough for anyone going through family drama, and especially for kids who feel like the entire world has abandoned them.

"No. Everything's fine."

"The party? And the Secret Santa gifts?"

"Went off without a hitch."

I breathe a sigh of relief, letting myself fall back against my

163

pillow. "How is Jenny?" Not long after our day at Paintball-Palooza, her father showed up and she'd left with him. But it didn't last. A few weeks ago, she showed up outside my door with a tear-streaked face and a black eye. She's back at TeenCharter now.

"She's doing okay. And I think she really liked her present."

I smile. "Yeah?" I had bought Jenny's gift myself—a rose gold journal and a pack of metallic, flare-tip pens. She isn't good at talking about her feelings, so I thought writing them down my might be helpful for her.

"Definitely."

As I wait for Tucker to tell me why he's calling, my mind starts flipping through my schedule. Maybe I can stop by to see Jenny before our next planned weekend afternoon…

"I was just calling to say hi."

"Oh." I have no idea what to say back. For the most part, I've barricaded *that night* into a dark part of my past, pretending it's a mistake I've moved beyond, a strange anomaly that doesn't define who I am today. Most days, I even believe it. I have to. Anger and fear are heavy burdens that only weigh me down. "Hi."

And I've forgiven Tucker. We don't live in the same dorm anymore and our interactions are purposeful, focused solely on TeenCharter. We don't hang out. We don't share confidences. He's not my friend.

"What are you doing tonight?"

"Tonight?"

"It's New Year's Eve."

Right. I'd forgotten. But I don't need to think about my answer because I haven't made any plans. "Nothing much. I'm staying in."

"Can I pick you up, bring you into New York City? I was going to hit up a few parties."

I must still be dreaming. Because the last time I went to a party with Tucker, I woke up in a nightmare.

"Um, I don't think that would really be—"

"Please, Poppy. Just hear me out."

I take a breath and push it out through my teeth. "Okay."

"What happened last year, that's not… that's not who I am."

"I know, Tucker. It's fine. We're fine."

"No, we're not. Every time you look at me, I see myself through your eyes. And I hate who I see."

I bristle. "That's really not my problem."

"I'm not— That's not what I'm saying." He sighs, and it occurs to me that, while I have forgiven Tucker, I haven't truly moved on.

It's been over a year, fourteen months, since I went to that fraternity party with Tucker, and yet in some ways, I'm still there. Still lying in a hospital bed, naked and confused. Still reeking of vomit and drowning in shame.

"Give me a chance to set things right, Poppy. It's a new year, let's start it off together, with a clean slate."

A clean slate. Is that even possible?

If it is… if there's even a chance, isn't it what I want?

To finally disconnect the guy who undressed me from the guy who dressed up in a bunny suit.

"Does it have to involve a party? Can't we just—"

"Just what?"

"I don't know. Go for a walk or ice skating or something?"

"You skate?"

"No." A nervous laugh slips from my mouth.

"How about this—I come pick you up, we'll drive into the city, and we'll figure out what to do together?"

A red flag goes up, my nerve endings twanging in alarm. "And then what? I'm not—I won't stay—"

"What? No. God, of course not. I'll get you a hotel room and bring you back home in the morning."

A few long beats of silence pass. "My own room?" I ask, my

voice sounding tinny and strained. *Am I crazy for even considering this?*

"Yes. I promise."

"I-I don't know, Tucker. We go back to school in a few days. How about we just get together for coffee then?"

"That's not the same." He exhales heavily. "And I don't want to wait until we're back at school. Come on, say yes. New year, new beginnings, a chance to reset the clock. Please."

I cave. "Okay."

"Okay? Yes?"

I cave because I want that fresh start, too. I want to rewrite what happened last year, replace it with something different. Something better.

I want to be more than just a drunk girl who flirted with Tucker, kissed him, and then woke up in a hospital bed, told she'd been sexually assaulted.

And it's clear Tucker doesn't want to be the guy who brought that drunk girl back to his bedroom, gave her a beer she definitely didn't need, and thought her inability to say *no* was the same as saying *yes*.

"Yes." I say it now, immediately feeling lighter somehow. Like I've shed some of the weight I've been dragging around for the past fourteen months. Not all. Not even a lot. But some.

LATER THAT AFTERNOON, Tucker pulls up to our modest house in a sleek black Porsche. Sliding out of his sports car, he saunters up our icy walkway wearing a thick black overcoat, a cashmere scarf draped around his neck, and expensive looking leather gloves. "You didn't tell me *Tucker* was picking you up," Sadie hisses, turning away from the window to gape at me.

I'd forgotten that she met him last year, and I don't have time to respond before my sister races to the front door and throws it open. "Hey," she says, popping her hip and running a hand through her hair.

"Hey. Sadie, right?"

Her eyes gleam with pleasure. "Right."

My mother wanders in from the living room, stopping short when she sees Tucker stepping through the narrow opening.

"So nice to meet you, Mrs. Whitman. I'm Tucker." He comes across like a young Manhattan mogul, all traces of the lacrosse-playing frat boy he is at Worthington erased.

"H-Hello," my mother stutters out a greeting, then turns to Sadie. "Sadie, for God's sake, close that door. No need to heat the front yard."

My sister's cheeks flush at the rebuke, but Tucker distracts her. "A house full of gorgeous women, why haven't I been here before?"

Sadie swats me. "Because my sister kept you from us."

Already dreading the firing squad of questions I'll get when I come home, especially from Sadie, I grab my coat. My sister didn't get into Worthington, and the financial aid packages she received from other schools were almost laughable. She decided to enroll at a community college for now and reapply next year. But I know it bothers her that I'm at Worthington and she's not.

Growing up, if I got a cookie, I'd give her half. If I had a shirt she liked, it was hers before I'd even outgrown it. But I can't give Sadie an acceptance letter and it's an unspoken point of contention between us.

Tucker takes my coat from my hands, holding it by the collar for me to slip my arms into the sleeves. My hair gets caught beneath the heavy wool and he pulls it out, smoothing it down my back. "Ready to go?"

My mouth suddenly dry, I can only nod.

Sadie doesn't have that problem. "Where are you going?" she asks.

Tucker offers a mischievous smile. "I'm sure she'll tell you everything tomorrow."

My sister only scoffs as we walk through the door. "I doubt that."

Halfway to his car I slip on the walkway, my heel coming out from under me. Tucker catches me by my elbow. "Gotcha," he says.

It's not just the ice that has me feeling off balance and tentative. It feels like Tucker and I are entering strange, uncharted territory. We moved from mutual avoidance to stilted cordiality when Dean Johnson brought us together to work with Teen-Charter. And now, it seems like Tucker wants to move beyond that, too.

But I don't know what *beyond* will look like. What kind of relationship am I willing, or even capable, of having with him?

After sliding into Tucker's low car, the steady thrum of the engine buzzed through my veins as he merges onto the highway. Two hours later we are on the Henry Hudson Parkway, then in Manhattan.

Tucker navigates the crowded city streets with the ease of a veteran cab driver. Meanwhile, I act like a typical tourist, pressing my forehead to the window and admiring the skyscrapers pointing their steely tips at the sky.

He is comfortable in his role, and I am almost, or at least pretending to be, comfortable in mine. But the truth is—I'm scared to death I'm making an even bigger mistake today than I did *that night.*

"Here we are," Tucker finally says, pulling up outside the most iconic hotel in New York.

I blink at him. "The Plaza?"

He flashes a playful grin. "Don't all girls grow up wishing they could be Eloise, at least for a night?"

My wishes had been so much more complicated than having the run of this enormous Manhattan landmark, but I nod in spite of the knot of anxiety twisting my stomach. "Of course." *Am I stupid to trust Tucker? Did he reserve separate rooms?*

My thoughts are coiling their way around my throat, cutting off my air supply, when a uniformed bellman opens my door. "Good afternoon, miss."

"Good afternoon," I manage to whisper, feeling lightheaded.

My boots tread silently on the red carpet covering the entrance stairs, a doorman ushering us inside.

Immediately, the noise and grittiness of New York City fall away. It's as if I've walked into a French chateau, or at least what I imagine a French chateau would look like. Endless marble, crystal chandeliers, velvet sofas, gilded everything.

I barely notice when Tucker says, "Wait here," and leaves me standing in the center of the enormous lobby. My neck cranes up at the ceiling as I turn in a small circle.

He comes back a few moments later, a discreet envelope in his hand. "Ready?"

And just like that, I'm back to reality.

Are there two key cards in there? "Um, Tucker." My feet are rooted to the floor. Even though we've just spent two hours in the car together, I cannot make myself walk into a hotel room with him. "I don't think…"

There's a flash of hurt on Tucker's face, but it fades almost immediately. "Of course. I understand." He hands the envelope to me. "The room number is on the front. My parents' place is just a couple of blocks away. I was going to walk up with you before heading back home to change, but if you would rather—"

Suddenly, I feel ridiculous. Tucker invited me here for a fresh start, and I want that too. "No. It's fine. I'm sorry. I didn't realize — I thought—"

I stop talking as Tucker's arm lands on my shoulders and he steers me toward the elevator bank. His touch sends my senses into overdrive—a disconcerting mix of pure panic and unexpected pleasure. "I'll only stay a few minutes."

We take the elevator to the fourteenth floor and walk halfway down a corridor painted the color of butter and adorned with gilt-edged paintings. Chandeliers, smaller than the ones in the lobby, hang from the ceiling at even intervals.

Tucker opens the door to my room and I step inside, standing awkwardly by the dresser. He brushes by me and sinks into one of the chairs by the window, pulling out his phone. "We have options for tonight."

"Options?" I'm staring at the wide bed that dominates this room, but I'm remembering a different room, a smaller bed.

It's soft. Too soft. My stomach lurches, and I edge forward, lowering myself to the floor, needing to feel something solid beneath me.

Tucker looks at me quizzically. "You okay?"

His face breaks apart into two, then fuses back together. "Yeah."

"Yeah." Tucker's real voice takes the place of the echo inside my head. "New Year's Eve parties."

My mouth is dry, the hairs on the back of my neck are standing on end. "Oh, right. Okay."

"Or, if none of them sound appealing, we can go for a walk, like you said. See the tree, even go ice skating."

Tucker glances up from his phone. "You don't want to see the ball drop in Times Square, do you?" At my pause, he adds, "I mean, we could. If—"

"No." Times Square is packed with drunk tourists on New Year's Eve. It's the last place I'd want to be. "Anywhere but there."

We share a smile and I take my duffel bag from where Tucker left it by the door, setting it down on the bed. Unzipping the top, I begin pulling out the clothes I brought. Once the mattress is obscured, I feel a little better. "Does Wren know I'm here?"

Tucker shrugs. "Dunno. Can't remember if I told her or not. Anyway. There's also…"

I pretend to pay attention as he itemizes the various invitations. But when he asks, "Do any of those sound good?"

"Ah, yeah."

"Which ones?"

"Um." I make up an answer. "The first and last sound great. Really fun."

He sets his phone aside and stands. "What's wrong?"

Me. Him.

Not every story has a happy ending. And not everyone deserves a new beginning. What if we're *beyond* a fresh start?

What if, no matter how badly Tucker wants to be the hero of our story, he'll only ever be a villain?

CHAPTER 22

NEW YORK CITY

HOLIDAY BREAK, SOPHOMORE YEAR

*A*fter Tucker heads back to his parents' place to change, it takes forever before my heartbeat returns to normal. I'm walking the edge of something that's either dangerous, or stupid, or both.

But it's better than the way I've been living. Dismissing memories that aren't real and yet won't be suppressed. Ignoring emotions that don't make sense and yet can't be denied.

Maybe I've been approaching this all wrong. Maybe what I need to do is accept what happened, take control of it, and shift the narrative.

Can I bury the Tucker of the past—the Tucker who hurt me, who took something from me? Separate that guy from the Tucker who invited me into New York City to celebrate New Year's with him.

If I allow Tucker to move on from who he was, maybe I can become a different person, too.

Stronger. Less naïve. Maybe even... brave.

Last year, I didn't go out on New Year's. I certainly wasn't in the mood to celebrate.

It was a far cry from the year before. After Sadie left for a sleepover with a friend and my mom passed out on the couch, I snuck Gavin into my bedroom. We had done plenty of celebrating then.

Gavin. I rub at the familiar hollow ache in my chest that plagues me whenever I think about the beautiful, broken boy I once loved, sending up a quick prayer that he's safe. That he's happy. My anger at being abandoned has faded, but the hurt is still there. I will always love Gavin, probably always long for him. But I am done mourning him. I have to be, because I cannot go on living a half-life, feeling like half of me—the best part—is missing.

No matter where Gavin is now, why he left, or who he's with —I deserve to welcome this new year to come. I deserve a new beginning. He would want that for me, I know he would.

An old memory pops into my mind. The magazine article I'd shown Gavin all those years ago. Photographs of a beautiful couple I'd found so intriguing, their sheen of glamour and sophistication shining from the pages.

They look so perfect.

Meant to be.

Like nothing bad has ever happened to them. Like nothing bad ever will.

The woman in that photograph wouldn't be rushed to a hospital, her blood the alcohol content of a wine cooler. She wouldn't learn that a condom had been found beneath her clothes. She wouldn't cry herself to sleep, night after night, for weeks and months on end.

"Imagine the person you want to be, and then be her," I whisper feverishly, just like the child psychologists advised when I was younger. Their version of *fake it till you make it*, I guess.

A few hours later, when my phone lights up with a text from

Tucker, I take a last look at myself in the oversized, cheval mirror tucked into a corner of the room, running my hands along my sides. I had to cut the tags off my dress because I'd never worn it before. It had been shoved to the back of my closet, something I bought on impulse because it was so deeply discounted. But I've never had a reason to wear it. Until tonight.

The black material hugs my curves, but not too closely. The sweetheart neckline isn't too low, just barely skimming the rise of my breasts. The hem is a little shorter than I'd like, a few inches above my knees, but I'd borrowed a pair of stockings from Sadie that were almost opaque, but not quite, so the effect isn't as racy as it could have been. And my heels do nice things to the shape of my legs, even though they pinch my toes.

Simple studs adorn my ears, but my throat is bare. My arm lifts, my fingers automatically tracing the hollow of my collarbone where Gavin's necklace should have sat. That familiar sting of loss makes me meet my own eyes in the glass. They look very green tonight, the gold flecks glinting brightly. I see sadness and fear. But also… hope.

Sadness for the man I've lost and the girl I used to be.

Fear that I'll never recover. Never move on.

And hope that I will. That tonight really will be a fresh start. A new beginning.

I take a deep breath, pushing a smile onto my face. It trembles a bit, but it stays.

"I want to be happy," I say to my reflection. "And I want to be whole."

And then I grab my wrap and meet Tucker in the lobby. He's wearing a perfectly cut black suit that accentuates his broad shoulders and slim hips. His snowy white shirt is open at the neck, unencumbered by a tie. He looks entitled and arrogant, and too handsome for his own good.

"You look fantastic," he says, wearing a pleased expression as he takes my hand.

"Really? Are you sure?" I glance down at my dress, smoothing out the fabric as fresh needles of doubt and insecurity prick my spine. "I know it's not all that fancy—"

"It's perfect," Tucker answers easily, his gaze skimming my figure before returning to my face. "When you came out of the elevator just now, you looked for me. And from the moment our eyes met, you never once looked away."

A half-laugh makes it up my throat. "Well, I don't—I don't know anyone here."

"True. But you're different than other girls who seem to travel in packs. Always surrounded by other girls. It's the first thing I noticed about you. Your… comfort at being alone."

I don't bother explaining that it's not comfort so much as acceptance. Because being alone gets really lonely.

But Tucker takes my silence as agreement.

He shakes his head, his lips curving into a soft smile. "You're very focused, Poppy. And I like when you focus on me."

THE FIRST PARTY Tucker takes me to can only be considered "small" by State Dinner standards. At least a hundred people meander through expansive rooms, although security guards with earbuds and closed-circuit mics are posted every few feet and at the openings to certain hallways. The crowd is a mix of young and old. I try oysters for the first time, a cold and slimy mouthful I don't intend to repeat, and caviar, which tastes like a briny, delicious bite of the sea. We are offered champagne several times, though we both stick with club soda.

After an hour of pretending like I don't feel horribly out of place, Tucker nudges me with his elbow and bends down to my ear. "Please tell me you're as bored as I am."

I hide my laugh with my hand, goose bumps from his breath

skating over the back of my neck. "Does that mean you want to leave?"

"Ready when you are," he says with a nod, pulling his phone out of his pocket and ushering me into the elevator. "Wren's been texting me. I'll tell her we're on our way."

Wren. My stomach immediately sours. I don't miss my old roommate, though I'd expected to see her tonight. Anticipating it with a slow creeping dread. "Sure."

As the doors open onto the lobby, Tucker glances up at me and scrutinizes my expression. "That *sure* sounded an awful lot like *I'd rather shotgun a dozen oysters.*"

I exhale an awkward sigh. "I'm sorry. I know she's one of your closest friends. We should go."

Tucker's expression is inscrutable as he thumbs off a quick text. After he puts his phone back in his pocket, he reaches for my hand. "Come on."

The midtown loft he brings me to isn't far, and when we get inside, Tucker points to the windows on the far wall. "Times Square is just a few blocks away."

I look over in that direction, though I'm just searching the crowd for Wren's face. But the party is dark, lit mainly by strobe lights and the city skyline rising up around us. I tug on Tucker's arm. "It feels like we're in a club," I shout. The music is so loud we could hear it from the hallway.

"The DJ was flown in from London, just for tonight."

"I guess Wren went all out."

"This isn't Wren's place."

"But I thought—"

"New beginnings, remember?"

Surprise twists through me. Surprise and a pleasant feeling of relief. "New beginnings," I repeat.

For the next couple of hours, Tucker holds my hand as he introduces me to people he knows. Which is almost everyone. When I'm not smiling and pretending like I can hear over the music, we're dancing to a blend of hip-hop and pop, most of the songs remixed with a techno beat. Every once in a while, Tucker's hands graze my body, but he never pulls me too close or grinds up against me.

And even though there is a liquor bar staffed by a bartender in a corner, Tucker bypasses it in favor of the ice bucket beside it, grabbing bottles of water instead.

Finally, the music cuts out. "It's almost midnight, everyone!" someone yells. Tucker grabs my hand and brings me out onto the terrace, positioning himself behind me, his arms wrapping around my waist.

"Ten, nine, eight…" everyone is shouting, counting down the last seconds to midnight. Everyone but me. I can't, I'm frozen in place, the breath still inside my chest.

"Seven, six, five…"

Talons of fear claw at my neck. *What will I do if Tucker kisses me?*

"Four, three, two, one…"

How did I not consider this scenario earlier? Of course, he'll expect a New Year's kiss.

"Happy New Year!" The crowd of partygoers erupts, here on the terrace and below in Times Square.

I imagine Tucker's hands sliding to my hips, turning me around to face him, his mouth crashing down on mine.

"I have you all to myself, don't I?"

"Need to lie down." My words are barely a mumble. I'm holding onto consciousness by my fingernails.

Tucker follows, his lips on mine, his body heavy on top of me. I whimper, trying to draw a deep breath. But I can't.

"Happy New Year," Tucker whispers softly. His breath is an unsettling caress over my temple, but he makes no move to spin me around and the kiss I dreaded is just a gentle press against my cheek. "Thank you for coming tonight, Poppy. It really means the world to me."

177

I manage a nod, and we stay like that. The madness of Times Square below, an indigo sky ablaze with fireworks overhead. Champagne corks popping, ebullient couples kissing.

Tonight has been... nice. Really nice. Tucker has been attentive and charming. And his smile has been doing wicked things to me—like making me all too aware just how good-looking Tucker really is and how much fun I'm having with him. And, when I let myself relax, it feels damn good to be held in his arms.

Which makes me think— If this really is a fresh start, why can't I follow these new feelings wherever they lead? I don't have to stay trapped in the past.

I don't *want* to stay trapped in the past.

Tucker and I are an island in a sea of chaos, standing still even as my turbulent heart thumps wildly against my ribcage. Eventually, I give myself permission to enjoy the feel of his hands around my waist, the gentle press of his chin on the crown of my head.

And after a long while, or maybe only a few minutes, it is me who turns within his embrace. Heat gathers in my belly when our eyes meet, then spreads outward when his gaze drops to my lips. My tongue darts out of one corner, sweeping along the crease. Tucker's eyes follow, chocolate brown melting into amber. "I think I should bring you back."

CHAPTER 23

NEW YORK CITY

HOLIDAY BREAK, SOPHOMORE YEAR

"Can I take you up?" Tucker asks, when we're standing in the lobby of the Plaza.

I nod, and our hands remain clasped together until we're inside my room. "Poppy…" Tucker turns me gently to face him as he leans back against the closed door.

Butterflies dance inside my stomach as I step into Tucker's embrace, sliding my hands up his arms until I'm gripping his biceps. "Will you— Will you kiss me?"

His surprised stare burns into me, his voice a husky rasp that strips away the last of my reservations. "I think that can be arranged."

Our mouths are a breath apart when those reservations slide right back into place. "Just a kiss, that's all." I might be pushing the envelope, but I'm not ready to tear it up entirely.

"Whatever you want, Poppy. Nothing more."

Tilting my head back, I close my eyes and welcome the tender press of Tucker's lips on mine. I don't expect to get swept up in his kiss, to truly relax into his embrace. But I do.

I do more than that. I lock my fingers behind Tucker's neck and moan into his mouth. I meet each stroke of his tongue with one of my own. I arch my spine and press my body against his.

I've forgotten how good it feels to be held like this, kissed like this. It's been so long. Too long.

It's only when Tucker lifts me into his arms and sets me down on the mattress, the springs compressing as his weight is added to mine, that I freeze, panic a vice around my ribs. Tucker immediately pulls away, his face confused. I shake my head, pushing at his shoulders. "I— I can't."

Tucker releases me instantly, his breath loud in the quiet room as he strides to the window and runs a hand through his dark hair. The Manhattan skyline highlights Tucker's strong jaw, clenched fiercely as he stares at something I can't see.

For several minutes, there is only the roar of my pulse in my ears and Tucker's harsh breaths.

Finally, he turns back and crosses the room, falling to his knees beside the bed. "I was drunk, too, Poppy. That night. Not as bad as you, of course. But I never meant... I never meant to hurt you."

There is a grace in Tucker's movements, an urgency to his words. And I am startled at the sight of Tucker Stockton, his head bowed, kneeling before me. This is not the Tucker his lacrosse teammates know. Maybe not even Wren.

I place a hand on his shoulder, my thumb stroking the muscled column of his neck. I look down at him for a long time, weighing my thoughts. Weighing memories of *that night* against this man here with me now. "I believe you."

I feel his shoulders drop slightly, as if my admission sloughed off a burden he's been carrying for a very long time.

"Do you..." He clears his throat and lifts his face until his gaze is holding mine. "Do you want me to take you home?"

Do I? I think for a moment. I don't know exactly what I want, but going back home to my mom and my sister definitely isn't it. "Give me a minute," I say, ducking into the bathroom to change out of my dress and into the yoga pants and oversized hoodie sweatshirt I brought with me.

When I return, Tucker is standing by the window again. "I'd like to stay," I whisper.

"Then you'll stay," he says, nodding. "I'll pick you up in a few hours to drive you home."

"Wait." I hold up a hand. "Don't go yet."

He blinks at me, studying my expression as if trying to figure out what's going on in my confused mind. One corner of his mouth twitches upward as he shrugs out of his jacket and drapes it over an ornately carved chair. He sits down, stretching his legs out and crossing them at the ankles. "Okay. You hungry?"

I shake my head.

"Thirsty?"

Another shake.

"Tired?"

This time my lips purse in a half-smile. "Not really."

Tucker's rich, sable brows pull together and a vertical crease forms just above his nose. "Then what?"

I sit down at the edge of the mattress. "I want to know about this Tucker."

"*This* Tucker?"

"Yeah. The guy who begs for a fresh start and opens doors and treats me like I'm made of glass. The guy who doesn't take anything I'm not ready to give."

Sparks flicker within Tucker's rich brown eyes, glimmers of warmth shaded by the thick sweep of his eyelashes. "I am that guy, Poppy. I know it didn't always seem that way... but I am."

His heat penetrates my skin, burrowing inside the dark, secretive places where I've stored every hurt, every ache. "I'm glad."

For a moment we just stare at each other in silence. "You know what? Let's go for a walk."

"Now?" I laugh.

"Now."

"Okay." I throw on my boots and coat and we practically skip down the Plaza's red carpeted stairs, turning south on Fifth Avenue. Holding hands, we linger in front of elaborately staged holiday window scenes and run across crosswalks, laughing as angry cab drivers honk and swear. Just as we turn around to come back, it starts to snow. Big, thick flakes, so perfectly formed I can see the individual crystals. I tilt my head back and stick out my tongue, pinpricks of cold melting in my mouth.

New Year's Eve in New York City.

With Tucker Stockton.

A little nerve-wracking. A little awkward.

And completely, unexpectedly, magical.

By the time we get back to my room, our cheeks are cold, our noses pink. Just like an hour ago, Tucker leans back against the closed door, looking at me with hungry eyes. But this time, before I tell myself all the reasons to keep him at arm's length, I take his hand and pull him toward the bed. "It's practically morning," I say, "you can *sleep* here."

He gives me one of his knowing smirks, and in this moment it looks adorable rather than arrogant.

Tucker lies on one side, and I lie on the other, leaving a no-man's-land in between that could accommodate another person.

I'm on edge, but not as much as I would have thought I'd be. After a few minutes, I ask, "Do you have any siblings?"

He doesn't answer, and I realize Tucker's breaths have evened out, becoming deep and regular. Rising up on my elbow, I study his aristocratic face. In sleep, his features have softened, and he looks like an oversized boy, innocent and vulnerable. Loveable, even.

There are too many sides to Tucker Stockton, I decide.

Curved slopes that beckon me, hard edges that scare me. The overall package undeniably intriguing.

Eventually I doze off, my cheek on my arm, turned toward the enigma sharing my bed.

I wake up facing the other direction, the room softened by early morning light. Tucker is curled behind me, the heat of his breath fanning the back of my neck, the weight of his arm draped across my hip. My shirt has ridden up, and our thighs are pressed together.

I wait for panic to claw at my throat, a rush of adrenaline to flood my senses.

But neither comes. What does is the low hum of desire, unfurling in my belly like a flower awakening to catch the morning dew.

I run my palm over Tucker's forearm, sliding my fingertips between his much larger ones. He comes awake with a sharp breath. He says my name, his voice husky with sleep and surprise. "Jesus, I—"

When he tries to release me, I press his arm to my ribs. "No. This is... nice."

He exhales a kind of pleased groan. "Very nice."

I smile and shift my leg up, waiting to see if his will follow.

Almost immediately, it does, followed a second later by Tucker's hand along my thigh, his fingers trailing sparks beneath my skin. "Still nice?"

I tilt my head back, into the warm nook between Tucker's neck and shoulder. "Mm-hmm."

His palm cups my hipbone, the tips of his fingers slipping just inside the top band of my panties before stopping there. "Let me make you feel good, Poppy. I owe you at least that."

My heart and my mind are on opposite sides of a chasm so deep I don't even want to peer over the edge. But my body is speaking a language all its own, pressing back against him, my leg inching open. Traitor.

"Good girl," he says, his voice like churned gravel.

I don't feel good. Well, I do. But I don't.

Tucker's hand moves lower as he kisses my neck, his touch gentle and slow. "If you want me to stop, I will."

In response, my hips roll forward, seeking the heat of his hand, the warmth of his touch. "Don't stop," I somehow manage to whisper, before biting my lip as his fingers slide between my slick folds, using my own wetness to make me tremble and twitch.

"Tucker," I cry out, taken aback by the intensity of the orgasm that rocks through me. He continues rubbing me gently to draw out firecrackers of pleasure, like the aftershocks of an earthquake.

When I can't take it anymore, I twist inside his embrace. Throwing my arms around Tucker's neck, I open my mouth to him, letting my kiss convey the fragments of thoughts I haven't yet make sense of.

Thank you and *Christ, you're good at that*, and *Why couldn't this have been our first time together*.

Evidence of Tucker's desire is prodding my belly, and I want him to fill the ache inside me, this need for *more*. I push at the band of his boxers, and they run off in the same direction as my panties. Against my lips, Tucker growls, "Tell me you want this, Poppy."

"I do." I really, really do. And I want to welcome Tucker's weight on me, to engage in intimacy on my own terms.

I hear the crinkle of plastic, and then Tucker pulls away, hiking my legs around his waist and pushing into me. My body tenses as the barbed edge of a memory snags on the periphery of my consciousness. *Wait, wait.*

But I don't say the words. This is our fresh start, a way to rewrite the past and shift our narrative. I won't ruin it by giving into my fears.

Tucker's mouth claims mine as he fills me. Emotions swirl—

fear and lust and shame, the tangled knot laced with glittering shards of pleasure. Pressure builds and recedes, crashing into me with increasing force. Until my inner turmoil is pounded into submission by one enormous tidal wave.

Tucker jerks inside me, then collapses.

We are cheek to cheek, his lips grazing the shell of my ear. His voice is hoarse, a rasp. "This is how it will be, Poppy. How it always should have been."

And I believe him.

CHAPTER 24

WORTHINGTON UNIVERSITY

SPRING SEMESTER, SOPHOMORE YEAR

*I*t's not long after I return to campus for the second semester of my sophomore year that I find out it might be my last.

I'm holding the official-looking letter in my hands, trying to read it in its entirety, but I'm standing in the middle of the mailroom. And no matter where I stand, I'm in someone's way. "Sorry," I say. "Excuse me, sorry. Sorry." My hands are shaking, the words blurring. Some phrases jump out at me. *We regret to inform you* and *your GPA has dropped below what is required to maintain* and *this decision is final and may not be appealed.*

Last year was rough. After *that night,* I had a hard time concentrating on my classes. I barely slept and hardly studied. And once I got involved with TeenCharter, those first few months of working with Tucker, every interaction had left me weak-kneed and nauseous. My grades took a huge hit.

But I pulled myself together last semester. I did well. Better than well. But not, apparently, well enough to compensate for my freshman year.

Catching sight of a familiar blond head out of the corner of my eye, I crumple the letter inside my fist and begin walking toward the exit. But my vision is bleary and I stumble, bumping into the very person I was trying to avoid.

"Hey—" Wren gripes, the vehemence of her glare only intensifying when she realizes it's me.

"Sorry," I say, for the tenth time in the past few minutes.

"Poppy." She looks me over and takes a step back. I can imagine what she sees—glassy eyes, blotchy skin, pink-tipped nose. But maybe she doesn't notice because all she asks is, "I've been meaning to catch up with you. How did you manage it?"

Either my head is more clouded than I thought, or she's not making any sense. "Manage what?"

"Convincing Tucker to stand me up on New Year's."

Winter break was a couple of weeks ago and I'm caught completely off guard by her question. *Had I?* No. Tucker could tell I wasn't excited at the prospect of meeting up with Wren, but the decision had been his. "What makes you think it was up to me?"

Her eyes narrow. "Because I've known girls like you before. Girls who only want what they don't deserve. Who think they can take what isn't theirs."

"Well, I hate to break it to you, but it was Tucker's call." I sniff, wishing I had a pack of tissues on me.

Wren frowns. "Are you sick or something?"

My problem can't be solved with a trip to the infirmary and a bottle of penicillin. But it's easier to agree. "Yeah. You should stay away from me, I'm probably contagious." Hopefully, Wren will spend the next month worrying I gave her the flu every time she sneezes.

It's only later, at a brainstorming session for future Teen-

Charter events, that I regret making the excuse. "What are you doing here?" Tucker asks.

I blink at him in confusion. "Where else would I be?"

"In bed," he says, shoving his hands in his pockets and rocking back on his heels. "I was going to bring you some soup after the meeting."

Wren. Of course. Tucker may have ditched her on New Year's, but they are clearly still close.

"I was wrong. It's not flu." I slide into a chair and pull my notebook out of my bag. "The nurse said it was just allergies."

"Allergies? In February?"

I don't have the energy to make up any more lies. "Can you please just drop it," I hiss quietly.

Tucker's expression changes, his features tightening with hurt.

I was going to bring you some soup.

Guilt hits me like an incoming tide. Ever since we spent New Year's Eve together, Tucker has been nothing but kind and thoughtful. I wouldn't go so far as to say he's my boyfriend... I don't want to put a name to what we are, actually. I spent so much of last year forcing labels on things, on feelings, on people. Hiding behind doors and shoving my emotions into boxes I'd seal shut.

Sometimes Tucker and I study together. Sometimes we eat together. Sometimes we kiss and make out and have sex.

We don't drink together. We don't party together.

We don't argue or tease or stay up all night telling secrets and sharing dreams.

What I have with Tucker is nothing like what I had with Gavin.

But that's okay.

Because what I had with Gavin taught me that passion leads to pain. Promises turn out to be lies. And love... love hurts.

With Tucker, I know what I'm getting. We are careful and cautious with each other. On our best behavior.

After the meeting ends, and I have a page full of notes on possible future events for the TeenCharter kids, I smooth the wrinkles creasing the letter terminating my scholarship and hand it to Tucker. "I saw Wren just after I opened this. I'm sure I looked like crap, and when she asked if I was sick, I just went with it rather than explain why I was upset."

I don't mention the grudge Wren is holding against me. It has more to do with her and Tucker anyway, and I'm not dumb enough to get in the middle of them. As it is, Wren looked ready to scratch my eyes out in the mailroom. There's no reason to put myself on her bad side any more than I have already. I have enough problems of my own.

He quickly scans the page. "But, why did you lie to me?"

I fight the sting of tears. "It's embarrassing, Tucker. I can't afford to stay here without a scholarship. And all I needed to do was maintain a B average. But..." I lose the battle and they overflow my lashes, not in a steady stream but slowly, one tiny droplet at a time. "I couldn't. Last year, I just couldn't."

He holds my gaze, lifting his hands to cup his palms over my cheeks. His calloused thumbs are gentle as they wipe at my skin. "You're not going anywhere, Poppy."

I try to shake my head but Tucker's hands prevent the movement. "I'm not a charity case."

Technically, that's not true. I'm a scholarship student. I *am* a charity case.

"The Stockton Family Foundation gives grants and scholarships all the time. All you have to do is apply."

"But ..."

"No buts," he says. "Welcome to the real world, Poppy. Haven't you ever heard the expression, 'It's not *what* you know, it's *who* you know?'"

"Sure."

"Well, now you know me. And I owe you."

I pull away from him, my stomach churning. "No, you don't."

Tucker drops his hands, his thumbs wet from my tears. "Yeah. I do."

CHAPTER 25

WORTHINGTON UNIVERSITY

FALL SEMESTER, JUNIOR YEAR

"*L*et me guess, you need a little sugar fix today."

I grin at Roz, the woman from the registrar's office I met on my very first day at Worthington. There's something about the warmth of her embrace and her drawer filled with butterscotch candies that I find comforting. "The hug doesn't hurt either," I tease.

There is a plaque on her desk that reads, I GIVE GOOD HUGS, so I have a feeling that I'm not the only student who swings by Roz's desk for reasons that have nothing to do with school and everything to do with her.

Today though, I stopped by because I was meeting with my advisor and his office is right next to the main administration building. I feel... *good*. My grades are back up, I was approved for a scholarship through the Stockton Family Foundation, and our outreach program with TeenCharter is a success.

Tucker and I have continued hanging out, too.

I almost feel like a normal college girl these days. Of course,

I'll never be the same Poppy that came to campus, but I'm finally okay with that.

Roz squeezes my shoulders as she pulls away. "Look at you, Poppy. Is that a genuine smile I see?"

I laugh. "I think it is."

She opens her top drawer but doesn't pull out a candy. "I don't know, I usually reserve these for kids that come in here with their heads hanging low."

I force my lips into a frown and hunch my shoulders. "Will this do?"

Roz clucks her tongue and tosses me the cellophane-wrapped treat. "Don't you dare. Happiness should never be hidden."

After a quick chat and another hug I head back outside, jumping out of the way of a guy holding a Worthington campus map to his face. The door hasn't quite closed yet when I hear, "I'm looking for a student."

I know that voice. It rolls through me like thunder, shaking me to the core.

I would gasp, but the wind's been knocked out of me. Surely, I'm mistaken. Because the man behind the map can't be Gavin. Not now, after all this time. Not now that every thought of him, of *us*, isn't a dull blade shredding my soul to bits.

Not after *that night*. Not after TeenCharter and New Year's Eve and accepting Tucker's help with my new scholarship.

Gavin abandoned me. Tucker took advantage of me.

But I've forgiven them both. And I've forgiven myself.

I might not be healed, though I'm definitely healing. I've stopped looking back, mourning what I've lost. I'm focused on the future now. My future.

The door opens behind me, and I hear Roz yell, "If you hurry, you might catch her."

I am caught.

"Poppy." Gavin says my name and it explodes inside my brain like a bomb. Anger, hot and thick, pollutes my veins as I spin around. I want to shove him away. I want to scream. I want to bombard him with questions. I want to hold him close and never let go. *What the hell are you doing here?* and *Where have you been?* and *Why now?*

But the words shrivel into black, bitter soot that coats my throat. *Gavin.*

It's him. It's really him.

Gavin is here, standing right in front of me. My eyes frantically rove over every inch of him. His gorgeous tawny hair is gone—not shaved, but certainly shorn—which only makes the blue of his eyes stand out more dramatically. Blues, actually. How had I forgotten how many shades existed inside the deep vortex of Gavin's eyes? The pale aquamarine of sea glass, the seductive blue of the autumn sky an hour past sunset, the rich brightness of larkspur springing up from the forest floor like festive blue spires.

I devour Gavin's broad, high forehead, his strong, straight nose, the sharp jut of his cheekbones. There is a scar on his face that wasn't there before, a silvery groove etched into the skin between his chin and lower lip.

I press my own lips together, swallowing the urge to ask about it, to kiss it, and quickly drop my gaze to the broad expanse of his shoulders, the biceps bulging from his shirt. Gavin is taller and wider and stronger than he was the last time I saw him. Muscles bulging in places that were previously flat.

"It's you," I finally whisper, something inside me unlocking. I take a step toward him. He does the same and we meet in the middle, crashing into each other.

Gavin.

Holy shit. Nothing against Roz, but hugging Gavin… it has to be the best feeling in the world. And the worst. It's everything. Every emotion. In his arms, I am lifted by my highest hopes, crushed by my deepest disappointments. Swallowed by our shared dreams and his broken promises.

It's too much.

It's not nearly enough.

I must have pushed at Gavin's chest, or maybe he felt it too. The tiny crack that splintered us apart.

Invisible.

Excruciating.

"You're still perfect," Gavin says, and I can practically hear the unspoken, *for me* that accompanies his words.

I bite down on the tender skin inside my cheek until the coppery taste of my own blood coats my tongue. *I'm not perfect for you, Gavin. Not anymore.*

Our arms drop and we each take a step back. A small one, but it feels like a chasm has opened up between us. "And you." I gesture at him, realizing with a shock that he's wearing military fatigues. My eyes again travel the length of Gavin's body—God, his body—before returning to his face. He is still so damn beautiful. "You're a GI Joe action hero come to life."

An echo of memory cuts into me, hard and fast and deep.

Promise me one thing.

What's that?

Never forget that you were my hero first, okay?

He reaches up to run a hand through his hair. What's left of it, anyway. The last time we were together, he would have tugged at his unruly mane, curls flying every which way. "Well, you know I had to leave to—"

"Know?" I want to sound strong and self-assured but my voice is barely a squeak. "How would I know?"

He frowns. "The letter I left for you in our cave. I told you I had to disappear, that my mom finally decided to leave my father and needed my help. My foster dad understood the situation, and he told me to leave my phone behind, giving me a few burner phones from the gas station. I left one for you, with my new number programmed in it. But you never called. I thought—"

I don't realize I'm crying until I taste salt on my lips. "There was a storm. A nor'easter. Our cave was flooded. I never got your letter, or the…" I pause, remembering. "I did find a phone in the mud, about a week later. But I never even considered that it might be from you."

Gavin's eyes burn into me, and I can see this is a possibly he never considered. "When I didn't hear from you, I figured I had programmed in my number wrong. I cursed myself for not having simply called your phone from mine, then saved the number so there would be no chance of an error."

"Why didn't you call me? I still had *my* phone."

Gavin looks away and shakes his head. "Fuck, Poppy." A student approaches us, obviously heading into the administration building. I step aside, motioning for Gavin to follow me to a gnarled elm tree, the one I'd sat beneath for the first month or so of school, feeling comforted by the reminder of home.

I haven't found comfort in this tree for a very long time.

Gavin continues talking as we sit beneath the unfurled green canopy, the grayish-brown bark rough at my back. "I didn't call because I couldn't take the chance that my father would somehow find you. He showed up at my foster family's house, looking for me and my mom. When they wouldn't tell him, he broke Bill's nose and knocked Mary into a wall."

At my gasp, Gavin sighs. "Doug was there too. My father beat him to a pulp, apparently."

I make a small noise of acknowledgment, although my sympathy lies solely with his foster parents. They were nice people. "I went to the gas station a few times. I tried asking about you but he didn't…"

"Bill didn't say anything to anyone. Especially once he saw the lengths my father was willing to go to track down my mother." Gavin squeezes my hand. "Things were crazy with my mom. Moving from place to place. One minute she'd be crying, thanking me for getting her away from him. The next she'd be yelling, hating me for keeping her away. I didn't want to bring

195

you into my mess and since my note explained everything, I thought you would understand. Then I got shot and—"

Pain shoots through me. "You what?"

He sighs. "Turns out my mom called my dad, told him where we were. He decided to follow through on his threat—that if she ever left him, he'd kill her. Except that I got in the way."

"Oh my God." I narrow in on the scar between his lip and chin. "Did he do that to you?"

He nods, then pulls the collar of his shirt away from his neck. A raised stripe mars the otherwise smooth skin. "We fought. The gun went off, hit me, I survived. It went off again, he died."

"Gavin." I say his name because I don't know what else to say.

"I hated him, Poppy. So much. But after I killed him... I was pretty fucked up. I was in no shape to be with anyone, even you, for a really long time." His voice is a hoarse rasp that scrapes at my nerve endings.

"What about your mom?"

Gavin's features tighten, pain etched into the grooves crossing his forehead, bracketing his mouth. "When she saw what I'd done, she tried to take the gun away from me. She wanted to kill me."

I suck in a deep breath, the air stinging my lungs. "No."

"Yeah. She still hasn't forgiven me."

"But you nearly died protecting *her*." Just like Gavin said he would, years ago.

If she left him, I'd protect her. Whatever it took.

And it nearly took his life.

"She doesn't see it that way."

I shake my head. "I don't understand."

"I thought about finding you then. I missed you so—"

A frisbee whizzes by and I look up, startled by the intrusion of real life. People are going about their day. Walking to class, hanging out with friends, playing fucking frisbee.

"So, what did you do? After..."

"A lot of it's a blur. But, and I know this sounds really weird, the only thing that made sense to me was math. Numbers. We were in Michigan at the time, and the only way I could afford to go back to school was through a program with the military."

"But now you're here, at Worthington. Are you transferring?"

Before my hopes can rise, he dashes them. "No. One of my professors is ex-Coast Guard. He still consults for them and invited me onto one of his projects. Their research facility isn't far from here, so I flew out to get up to speed. I knew I had to come see you. To explain what happened in person, and to see if there was any chance of us—" At my wince, Gavin breaks off.

Us. I'm too confused and overwhelmed with all that I've learned to think about *us* yet. Staring at Gavin's fatigues, I put off grappling with my emotions by trying to follow his timeline. Clinging to facts rather than feelings. "So... you're joining the Coast Guard?"

"Not exactly. But any opportunity to work on cutting-edge applications could be a stepping stone to get where I really want to be."

I take a minute to digest what he just said before asking, "And where's that?"

He looks at me strangely, as if I should know. "The FBI."

Of course. "Always a hero, huh?"

"Not always, Poppy." His eyes drop to my lips, and the yearning inside their depths slays me. "I didn't save us, did I?"

CHAPTER 26

WORTHINGTON UNIVERSITY

FALL SEMESTER, JUNIOR YEAR

*G*avin and I spend the rest of the afternoon under the elm tree, talking and reminiscing. It's like being inside that old John Mellencamp song, "Hurts So Good." I can feel my bones shattering inside my body. Tiny splintered cracks that run the length of my limbs, aching with every laugh, every sigh.

They say that when broken bones heal properly, they are even stronger than before. And by the time Gavin stands up, extending his hand to me, I actually do feel stronger. Healed by seeing him, finally knowing the truth of why he left and what had kept us apart.

I don't tell him about *that night*. I don't even hint at it. While I was kissing and flirting with Tucker, he'd been protecting his mom. Tequila shots had put me in the hospital. Gavin had been shot.

The sun hovers low on the horizon by the time Gavin walks me to my dorm. I tip my head back, marveling at the cumulous clouds set ablaze in shades of pink and lavender like swirls of cotton candy. "Gorgeous, isn't it?"

He's not looking at the sky when he answers. "Stunning."

My breath stills in my lungs. "Gavin, I—"

I lose track of whatever I was about to say when his hand lands on the exposed triangle of skin at the base of my throat. "I don't blame you for not wearing it anymore," he says softly.

"That's not..." Losing the moonstone pendant Gavin gave me for my seventeenth birthday was agonizing. But explaining the circumstances would be worse. A teardrop bursting with shame drops onto the tip of my shoe. "I'm so sorry."

"You must have hated me for leaving you."

"No. I never hated you." The admission is a pained rasp. Every syllable stings.

What Gavin says next just twists the knife deeper. "I never stopped loving you."

My heart clenches, regret and remorse flooding through me. "How do we—" I stop myself. "How *can* we move forward?"

"That's what we'll have to figure out." Gavin smooths a wayward lock of hair behind my ear. "Look, I know we can't go back to the way things were. For now, you're here and I'm in Michigan. But I can't lose you again, Poppy."

Possibilities flutter in the air between us like gossamer-winged butterflies. "When do you go back?"

"Not until tomorrow."

"What are you doing later tonight, or tomorrow before you leave?" I'm not ready to say goodbye yet.

Gavin has a dinner tonight and a briefing tomorrow afternoon, so we arrange to meet under the tree at the quad first thing in the morning. This time, he calls my phone from his so I have his new number *just in case*. I barely glance at the missed calls and texts from Sadie filling my screen. She can wait.

Nothing will keep me from seeing Gavin again. I don't know

what the future holds for us. Maybe just a long-distance friend-ship, with the possibility of something more down the line.

Or maybe nothing.

My chest squeezes at the thought. No. After all this time, surely we deserve *something*. Gavin was my best friend. My *only* friend. And so much more.

I can't lose him again. I won't.

Before heading upstairs to my dorm room, I throw myself into Gavin's arms one last time. And it's even better than it was before. It's *electrifying*.

Everywhere Gavin is touching me, or I am pressed up against him, feels awakened somehow. Like the forest coming alive after a long winter, embracing the warmth of the sun and the kiss of the rain.

As we start to pull apart, there is a moment when Gavin and I are still so close that our mouths are barely an inch apart. His breath ghosts across my lips, that same minty warmth I remember so well, and the urge to kiss him, to be kissed *by* him, is nearly overwhelming.

At the last second, I fight his gravitational pull and avert my face, stepping back. Not because of Tucker—we've never discussed being exclusive. For all I know, he's hanging out with other girls when he's not with me.

I step away from Gavin because our first kiss after too-fuck-ing-long should be *special*. It should mean something. And because if anyone would want that too, it would be Gavin.

He smiles crookedly, as if he understands. "I'll see you tomorrow?"

"See you tomorrow," I agree. Happiness trickles through me like rain as I jog up the stairs, becoming a full-blown storm by the time I get to my door. A storm just as powerful as the nor'easter that ripped through Sackett the night Gavin left. Elation expands in my chest like mist, excitement pulsing though my nerve endings like white-hot bolts of lightning. My heart is racing, my breath coming in fast, shallow gasps.

Gavin came back to me. *Finally.*

It's only when my phone buzzes inside my hand as I'm unlocking my door that I remember the missed calls from Sadie.

I answer, fighting off the tug of irritation at her insistence. Of course, Sadie would demand my attention now, when all I want to do is celebrate Gavin's return and think about our future. Together.

How had I ever thought that what we had—what we *have*—could be washed away in a flood, forgotten by time?

We are us.

Then and now.

Always.

"Hey, S—" I dispense with the greeting when I hear her crying. Not the kind of sappy, mournful, I-just-finished-a-Nicholas-Sparks-novel weeping that I've heard from her a million times. This is full on choking, guttural, something is very, very, wrong sobbing.

My fingers tighten around my phone in a death grip. "Sadie, please," I beg. "I can't understand you right now. Take a breath and tell me what's wrong."

Several seconds pass as she gasps for air. Seconds where I imagine her lying in a hospital bed, all alone, naked beneath a thin sheet. *Sadie, tell me what's happened. I'll make it better, I promise. I'll take care of you, just like always.*

Finally, she is able to enunciate actual words, and they slam into me like bullets. "It's mom. She was arrested. And now the lawyer says, because she was arrested once before, like—forever ago, she's going to jail. Jail! For a long time. Years."

I slump onto my bed. "What... I don't understand. Start at the beginning. Mom was arrested?"

"Yeah. She didn't come home last week, and—"

"No. Go back further. The arrest from forever ago."

"It was from ten years ago, I think. While we were in DCF custody. She got busted in some stash house. I don't know the details."

"Jesus," I groan. "Okay, tell me about this one."

"Well, I had no idea what happened until she didn't come home—"

"What do you mean she didn't come home? Where was she?"

"Mom's entitled to have a life, Poppy. And she does that sometimes, stays away for a night or two. But she always comes back. I thought she'd finally met someone, you know."

"Yeah, like a dealer. For God's sake, Sadie—how could you let this happen?"

"You're gone and I can't watch her every second!"

I know I'm being unreasonable. And blaming Sadie isn't going to get us anywhere. "You're right. Sorry. She disappeared, then what?"

"Then she calls—from jail. Saying she's been arrested." Sadie takes a breath and I steel myself against what's coming next. "For possession, with intent to distribute."

My heartbeat stutters, jumping around erratically inside my chest. "That's… that's…"

"A big fucking deal," she finishes.

I was going to say a felony, but her description is just as accurate. "So, what do we do? How can we fight this?"

"It's done. Her public defender said her best bet was to plead guilty in return for less time. The arraignment is tomorrow."

"That's it? You're telling me all this now, and there's nothing we can do?"

"I only found out yesterday," Sadie says. "And she didn't want me to tell you until everything was settled."

"Settled?" I slap my hand over my eyes and fall back against the mattress. "There has to be some way we can help her, Sadie."

"I'm all ears, sis."

The knock on my door startles me. I tell Sadie to hang on,

wiping my wet cheeks as I cross the room. Seeing Tucker, I only vaguely note the darkly furious expression on his face before I collapse into the same puddle of tears and anguish Sadie was drowning in when she called.

Extracting my phone from my hand, he leads me back to my bed as he talks to Sadie. Asking for details like the name of my mom's arresting officer and her lawyer. The date of her arrest and exactly where she's being held. He sits down at my desk, taking notes on a sheet of loose leaf paper.

"She hasn't entered her plea yet, right?" Tucker asks. Then, "Okay, let me make a call. My uncle was the DA for a few years, but now he's a partner at a big law firm. Maybe he can help."

Gratitude rushes through me. Of course, Tucker has powerful relatives. That's the way his world works. If Tucker's mother got in trouble, she wouldn't throw herself on the mercy of the court. She would make a few calls. Or her husband would. Or her brother or sister or any of her friends in high places.

Tucker gets his uncle on the phone. "My girlfriend's mom is in trouble. I need your help."

I'm a little taken aback by the girlfriend comment, but I chalk it up to standard shorthand. What else would he say—*the mom of a girl I'm kinda-sorta seeing?*

He relays the details he got from Sadie and hangs up. "He said he knows the prosecutor on your mom's case. He'll call me back as soon as they talk."

I exhale a huge sigh. "Thank you, Tucker. I really... I don't know what I would have done without you."

He joins me on my bed. "I haven't done anything yet."

But he will. Just like when I lost my scholarship. People like Tucker have a way of making things work out.

"So, while we wait to hear back, why don't you tell me about the guy I saw you with today."

I give him a blank look, my mind still focused on my mom.

"The guy you were hugging as if your life depended on it."

The furious expression on Tucker's face when I first opened the door—it was because he saw me with Gavin. "He's—He's just an old friend." The edge to Tucker's voice makes me downplay my feelings.

"That's all? Because it looked like more."

I decide against outright lying. I've done nothing wrong. "His name is Gavin. He is—" I correct myself, "*was* my boyfriend before coming here."

"He's the one who gave you that necklace."

I nod, keeping my expression neutral.

But Tucker is scowling. "You said he would come back one day. Is that what you're telling me—that he's back?"

I ignore the instinctive lurch of hope, of happiness, that pulses through me at the thought. "What? No. I mean… Gavin lives in Michigan now. He—"

Tucker tosses his phone up with one hand and catches it with the other, drawing my attention to it. Reminding me of the call he's just made and the one we're waiting for. "I'm doing this because you're important to me, Poppy. But I guess I should probably ask… am I important to you?"

That's when I see it, the inherent quid pro quo in this conversation, in this relationship—whatever its label—between Tucker and me. "Of course, you are," I say. Which is true. Tucker is important to me.

Important for now.

Until this moment, I've never considered the possibility of a future with Tucker. We come from completely separate worlds. Even if I move to Manhattan after school, Tucker and I still won't travel in the same circles. He is oysters and caviar and penthouse parties with DJs flown in from London. I am…

Frankly, I don't have a clue what my life will be like in Manhattan. Just that it won't be anything like Tucker's.

I'm saved from answering when Tucker's uncle calls back. He

says that my mom's deal will be amended. She can either go to prison… or rehab.

For a second, I allow myself to celebrate, until I realize that rehab isn't free. And if my mom couldn't make bail, there's no way she can pay for rehab. "We can't afford—"

Tucker silences me with a gentle kiss. "Don't worry, Poppy. I'll handle it."

"But—"

He runs his fingers through my hair in long, soothing strokes. "Sh. I'm not letting you visit anyone in jail, even your mother. Let me take care of you."

The feminist in me wants to protest his *not letting me* comment. But the part of me that was denied a childhood because no one ever looked out for me is just too damn tired. If Tucker wants to take care of me, of my mom—what's the harm in letting him?

CHAPTER 27

FALL SEMESTER, SENIOR YEAR

"*Happy* Birthday."

A smile tugs at my lips as I look at Tucker, silhouetted in my doorway. A smile I struggle to keep on my face when I notice the shopping bag dangling from his hand.

For my last birthday, Tucker bought me a necklace. A gold *P* that dangles from a thin chain. It's elegant and beautiful. Every time I feel it against my neck I'm reminded of the moonstone pendant I lost.

And the man I turned my back on.

I haven't seen Gavin since the afternoon we spent together under the elm tree. Although we were supposed to meet the following morning, I canceled on him in the middle of the night, explaining the situation with my mother and that I couldn't see him. He said he understood, and that he would come back again as soon as he could.

But as dawn eased gently through the windowpane, illuminating Tucker's sleep-softened face, I knew I could never meet up with Gavin. Not when my feelings for Gavin were so strong, and my debt to Tucker so big.

That morning, Tucker drove me to my mother's arraignment. Afterward, we'd brought her to a rehab facility where she spent the next six months. She's back at home now, with Sadie.

But Gavin hasn't given up on me. Yet.

Like the video he'd sent at precisely 12:01 this morning, singing happy birthday. I've already played it a dozen times.

Sometimes he'll call with updates about his classes and projects and even his running times. I've saved all of his videos and voice mails and texts. And I've lost count of how many hours I've spent, just listening to Gavin's voice, reading through his messages.

But I don't answer his calls. I never respond to his messages. I can't.

It would be so easy to hurl myself off the cliff, straight into Gavin's arms. So easy to let myself fall. Except... I don't know that he could catch me. Not with all my damn baggage anyway. We'd all get hurt.

I can't let myself get too close to the edge. I have to keep my distance.

And so now I step aside, motioning for Tucker to come in my room. "You've already done so much for me, Tucker. You shouldn't have bought me a gift, too."

"If it makes you feel any better, it's an entirely practical present. You have interviews coming up and I wanted to get you something suitable."

A nervous flutter rises up in my stomach. Interviews, right. Unlike a lot of other seniors, I haven't sought out internship opportunities that might lead to a post-graduation job offer because it would have meant cutting back on my TeenCharter responsibilities. But if I want to live in Manhattan, I need to land a well-paying job to afford rent. I'll be a fixture at the campus career counseling center in another month or so.

Tucker closes the door behind him and follows me to the bed I've pushed beneath the room's only window, arranging the pillows so it looks like a couch. I still live on campus, but I have a single room in a dorm reserved for upperclassmen.

I sit down, curling my legs beneath me. He pulls a box out of the bag and sets it on my lap. "Thank you, Tucker. This is so thoughtful."

"Don't thank me until you see what's inside." Tucker aims his chocolate eyes my way and I feel a familiar rush of gratitude toward him. He is always looking out for me, thinking ahead.

We've come a long way since *that night*. There is our work with the TeenCharter kids, of course. And since that first New Year's Eve we spent together, there have been dinners and football games, all-night study sessions and long nights in his bed or mine.

In a strange way, Tucker is the only one who understands me. While it's no secret I was taken from his room on a stretcher and rushed to the hospital in an ambulance our freshman year, Tucker is the only person who knows the extent of what happened that night. I am a different girl than I once was, certainly different than the other girls at Worthington. Even the way they walk around campus—with a carefree kind of recklessness to their step—is foreign to me.

Tucker knows what it's like to stand in front of the WUJA board, feeling embarrassed and ashamed. His penalties weren't as harsh as mine, but he had to do community service and attend an alcohol education class aimed at scaring you into a life of sobriety. We both had to deal with strange looks and judgmental whispers behind our backs.

That we became a couple felt almost like rebellion.

It's an illusion though. A lie I tell myself to feel strong and in control.

If I was really brave, I would have walked away from Tucker. I would have figured out another way to help my mom, another way to stay at school.

I wouldn't have turned my back on Gavin.

But I did. I chose Tucker over Gavin. And I have to live with my decision.

What would *bravery* have gotten me, anyway? Embroiled in a scandal at school. My name dragged through mud just like the girl who was raped behind the bleachers of her high school and then verbally assaulted, over and over again, in the court of public opinion. Moving back home to Sackett, attending community college with Sadie.

There is strength in forgiveness, too. Strength in standing my ground. Staying at Worthington hasn't been easy. Giving Tucker another chance hasn't been easy. Running away from him, running away from what happened here at school, would have been much easier.

It's for the best. Gavin's best, as much as mine. The starry-eyed girl he knew was idealistic and naïve. She believed in fairy tales and soul mates. When he left, Gavin took a piece of me with him.

And *that night* with Tucker, our *mistake*—shattered what was left.

Sometimes my coursework even twisted the knife. I had to white-knuckle my way through an English professor's infatuation with British romantic poetry. According to Albert Lord Tennyson, *'Tis better to have loved and lost than never to have loved at all.*

But, is it really? Who had Tennyson lost? As far as I can tell, when he wrote that line in 1850, he was talking about the death of his best friend, his college buddy. Tennyson hadn't yet lost two of his three children. Had his college friend been more than just a friend?

Either way, I think it's probably bullshit. Poetic mansplaining.

Or maybe I'm wrong. Maybe losing someone to death is different than losing them to a twist of fate.

Because knowing Gavin is a thousand miles away, eating and sleeping and maybe even loving someone else, someone who is not me, is like living with razor blades stuck between my ribs. Every breath delivers oxygen to my brain, but never relief to my heart.

And yet, as hard as losing Gavin—*again*—is, I know loving him would be worse. We're not like the couple in the magazine, unscathed by pain and misfortune.

I am strong, but I'm not a fighter. And if I'm not willing to fight for Gavin, to rebel against the way the world works, I don't deserve him. And he wouldn't like the person I've become. She's brittle and suspicious. She understands that the Stocktons and Knowles of the world play by a different set of rules than the rest of us, and the odds are stacked in their favor.

That's why I accepted a Stockton Family Foundation scholarship. That's why, when Tucker insisted on *taking care of me*, I didn't refuse. I said "thank you."

I understand why Gavin left me back in high school. Why he couldn't contact me. Of course, he had to protect his mother. And he had no way of knowing I wouldn't receive his letter and phone because the cave flooded.

I understand why the implosion of his family made him feel isolated, and why he needed time to process what happened before reaching out to me. And even why he chose to enroll at Michigan and enlist in the military.

I love Gavin. I will always love Gavin. But he purposely left me out of every important decision and moment in his life for almost three years. And he wasn't there for me when I needed him the most.

How can I be sure Gavin won't disappear on me again in the future?

Tucker hurt me, true. But he's also been my biggest supporter.

He helped me with my scholarship, although I have earned it by pulling my grade point average up to nearly a 4.0. And he's been a godsend to my mother who is doing well after going to the fancy rehab Tucker arranged and is now back at home with Sadie.

I do care about Tucker. And I am genuinely attracted to him. Maybe it's his confidence that keeps me so enthralled. Tucker is so damn sure of himself, secure in where he's come from and where he's going. Being with Tucker means I'm relieved of the pressure to pretend I have all the answers. It's freeing, in a way.

Tucker has the safety net of his family's wealth and influence, but he's still ambitious and competitive. On the field, he will stop at nothing to win. And when it comes to school, he shows up, does the work, and is always at the top of his class.

But it's Tucker's work with TeenCharter that impresses me the most. He doesn't have to do it, but he seems to genuinely enjoy his time with the kids—often acting like a big kid himself. He's spent time and his own money, creating programming that's both entertaining and inspiring.

The more sides of Tucker I see, the less I remember the one from *that night*.

Sometimes he's the charmer from our first New Year's Eve together. Sometimes, like after he wins a big game, he's cocky and flirtatious.

He can also be quite a tyrant. Not cruel. Just... bossy. Tucker likes to be in control, always. Surprisingly... I don't mind ceding it.

When we're together, I don't have to think about where to go to dinner or what movie to see. Tucker always has an opinion, and I've realized that I don't miss dealing with the daily minutia that once cluttered my mind.

He's insightful, too. I've learned to listen when he points out which of my study partners is just using me for my notes, or what sweater is best left in my closet. The same goes for which guy is taking my casual smile as an invitation of something more.

We made the decision to become exclusive last semester. Well, Tucker decided to become exclusive. I wasn't seeing anyone else and had no plans to. I am the center of Tucker's attention, his priority. And I like it.

When we walk through campus, hand in hand, I feel the jealous stares of other girls. No more dismissive, disparaging glances that cut me to the quick. I'm not an unwelcome misfit anymore… except to Wren. But I don't care about her. After graduation, Tucker and I will probably go our separate ways and Wren can have him back.

For now, Tucker and I spend almost every night together. I enjoy sex with him, deriving just as much pleasure watching him come apart in my arms as I do when he sends me off that same ledge. Afterward, our limbs tangled beneath the sheets of a twin-sized bed and my head resting on his chest, his heartbeat pounding beneath my cheek, I know I'm exactly where I'm meant to be.

So yeah, I surrendered.

Is this a different kind of love than I knew with Gavin? A less risky kind of love? Maybe. Yes.

Nothing like freshman year has ever happened again. And not just because I rarely drink, and never more than a few sips here and there. Tucker's careful, too. He pays attention to everything I do when we're together. What I eat, how much I drink, who I talk to, what I'm wearing.

A silvery white ribbon is wrapped around the black box, and I pull at it now, my fingers stiff and clumsy beneath the weight of Tucker's stare. There is a frisson of impatience wafting off him, like steam rising from wet asphalt beneath the morning sun, and I concentrate on untying the knot beneath the bow.

Finally, the ribbon comes loose, sliding off the square edges into a silken pile on my lap and fully revealing the name stamped across the top. Giorgio Armani. Folded inside the layers of white tissue is a diaphanous blouse the color of freshly poured cream, practically weightless as I hold it up. "This is beautiful, Tucker."

That impatience disappears and a happy smile splits Tucker's handsome face. I love it when he looks like this. Like he wouldn't know an ulterior motive if he stepped on it. "There's more," he prods.

Setting the blouse aside, I pull out a stunning navy jacket and matching skirt. My mouth opens on an appreciative sigh, both pieces so well-tailored I know it will spoil me for anything I can afford on my own. "Tucker, this is just—"

"Perfect for you," he finishes.

I was going to say "too much," but decide to swallow the words instead. Price tags don't matter to Tucker, and he'll interpret it as criticism. "Thank you, really. I love it."

"Why don't you try it on?" he suggests. I glance at the size, my heart sinking when I see the small number printed on the tag. Not surprisingly, Tucker notices the quick flash of disappointment streak across my face. "What's wrong?"

"Nothing," I say quickly. "Nothing at all."

I get up, crossing the room to my dresser and unobtrusively slipping a Spanx slip from the top drawer. Opening the door of my closet, I position myself behind it. Tucker has seen me naked dozens of times, at least. He likes my curves, or at least that's what he's told me. But I'm worried about the number printed on the tag at my neck. Size four. The one I'd been when I started at Worthington. I've gained at least ten pounds since then. Weight even Spanx might not be able to erase.

I bite back a groan as I tug the modified scuba suit up my hips, and manage to squeeze into the clothes, although the zipper and buttons aren't happy about it. "It's a little tight, I think." Emerging from behind the closet door, I stand awkwardly on the other side of the room.

Tucker rises, walking toward me. I expect him to pull out a gift receipt and encourage me to exchange the clothes for the next size up. He doesn't. "That's okay. You said you wanted to get back into shape, so I bought it a little small."

A disconcerted flush races up my chest to heat my face. I know if I look in the mirror there will be unsightly pink patches on my cheeks. "Oh." I'm at a loss for words. *Thanks?*

"I've got to run to practice." He drops a quick kiss on my lips. "I'll swing by later."

And then he's gone. In the span of Tucker's visit, he's made me feel happy, appreciated, grateful, insecure, and mortified—all within ten minutes.

I don't want to see him later.

I hope he comes back soon.

Scared of popping a button, I suck in my breath and carefully undress. Hanging Tucker's gift in my closet, I practically rip the skin-toned shapewear from my body.

You said you wanted to get back into shape, so I bought it a little small.

Had I said that? I must have.

Rather than slipping back into comfy sweats and opening up my laptop, I dig through my drawer for the workout clothes I haven't worn in ages. Too long, obviously.

At the track, I run until sweat beads my brow and my muscles ache from fatigue.

I run until the chaos clouding my mind is quiet, solely focused on my next step, my next breath.

I run until the pain in my chest is from exertion rather than shame.

CHAPTER 28

WORTHINGTON UNIVERSITY

SPRING SEMESTER, SENIOR YEAR

*T*he cafeteria on campus is practically empty at five o'clock. I know this through careful observation, timing my visits in fifteen-minute intervals to determine the most optimal time to pick up my dinner. If I fill my cardboard take-out container quickly, most days no one will even see what I put inside.

I always tell myself I'll only have a salad. Just some lettuce and chickpeas, a tiny drizzle of vinaigrette. And usually, I listen to that inner voice.

Sometimes, I ignore it completely.

Today is one of those days.

Instead of heading immediately to the salad bar and turning a blind eye to anything else, I do exactly the opposite. The glistening displays of pizza, buckets of French fries, pasta, and stir-fry stations are all I can see. I've eaten nothing but a banana for breakfast and a protein bar for lunch. Because this is what I eat.

Every day, since deciding that squeezing into a size four Armani suit was my most important goal in life.

Having to stand in front of Tucker, literally busting at the seams, was an experience I will do anything not to repeat. That afternoon, while I was sucking wind on Worthington's track for the first time ever, I came up with a plan. No need to research the latest diet fads, or sign up for Weight Watchers. All I needed was willpower. I would eat three meals a day. Banana for breakfast. Protein bar for lunch. Salad for dinner. Plus a half-hour run.

My plan worked. Within a couple of weeks, I didn't need Spanx to close the zipper. And by the time I walked into my interviews, I felt pretty and successful. Being offered a job with a Manhattan-based marketing company was the icing on my cake. Slowly but surely, I'm working toward the goals I set for myself when I applied to Worthington. Goals I set with Gavin, showing him pictures from stolen magazines.

Missing him hurts a little less these days. Mostly because, for my own sanity, I pretend he's *the guy who got away* instead of the guy I turned my back on. Everyone has one of those.

Dieting down to a size four was almost too easy. I felt good, especially after Tucker said that my newly slim figure made me look like I'd been born on the Upper East Side.

Like Wren.

Except, Wren is a size two.

So now I pick the smallest banana in the bunch instead of the biggest. Choose a protein bar with less sugar. Even less salad dressing.

These days, my new suit is a little too big.

Tucker noticed, of course. Just last night he'd swirled his tongue over my protruding hipbones, calling me delicate. He'd been so gentle, pushing into me as though I might shatter in his arms. I liked it.

But I have a secret. I've discovered a trick. One or two nights a week, I hit the cafeteria early, filling my cardboard box full of everything that tempts me. Pizza and pasta. French fries. Egg rolls and fried rice. Bread and cupcakes and chocolate mousse. Everything I can fit into the takeout box, in five minutes or less. And then I race back to my room, lock the door, close the lights, turn off my phone. And I eat.

My bites are determined, mechanically pulverizing each mouthful. I eat until my jaw hurts, until my stomach feels like a five-pound bag stuffed with ten pounds of rocks. By the time I get three-quarters of the way through my super-sized meal, I'm crying. And that feels good, too, like the tears make way for more food.

This is what I'm doing right now. Eating and crying.

I don't stop until I've finished every bite.

The second I'm done, the greasy cardboard stares at me in accusation. I can't get rid of it fast enough. The bathroom would be the easiest way, but it is communal, shared with the other residents of my floor.

I have a system though. With shaking fingers, I line my garbage pail with two grocery bags. Quickly, because every second that passes means more calories are digested.

As soon as the bags are wrapped tight around the edge, I turn up the volume on my speaker and shove the fingers of my right hand down my throat, holding the pail to my chest with my left. My first attempt is unsuccessful. So is my second. There's too much in my stomach, and it's too thick.

Panic spirals through my veins. I have to get this food out of me. Now. I let go of the pail, chug half a bottle of water, jump up and down a few times.

Then I suck in a deep breath and try again. My stomach lurches once, twice, its contents finally rising up and spewing from my mouth before I can get my hand out of the way. Vomit and saliva drip from my fingers, but I don't care. The need to purge myself of every single gluttonous thing I just shoved down my throat is overwhelming, undeniable, irresistible. I want to feel good again. Empty and light.

I shove my fingers back inside my mouth, again and again. Until all that's left are dry heaves and I'm sure there's not a single French fry or bite of cake left inside of me.

It's not just food I'm expelling. It's sadness and shame and self-loathing. Feelings of not being good enough.

The person who ate enough for a family of five—she is disgusting. Undisciplined. Lazy. Coarse.

I am not her.

After tying the bags closed, I put them inside another trash bag, and throw everything down the garbage disposal chute. Half an hour later, I'm at my desk, freshly showered and Listerine'd, with a hot cup of tea at my side while I study. Feeling like a different person. A better person. A person who deserves nice things, and a smart, handsome boyfriend.

A person who's not falling apart on the inside because I'm so determined to keep up with my confident, pulled-together facade on the outside.

I get about an hour's worth of work done before Sadie calls, and I have to stifle my irritation at the interruption. "Hey, sis. How's Mom doing?"

"She's fine. And would it kill you to ask about me occasionally?"

"Whoa. What's gotten into you?"

"Maybe if you'd call me every once in a while instead of the other way around—"

"I call!" If I'd known what kind of mood Sadie was in, I would have sent her straight to voice mail. But ever since our mom's arrest, I pick up right away.

"Only to talk to Mom or ask about Mom. Never me."

I swallow an aggravated sigh, but I know she's right. "Fine. I'm sorry. How are you?"

A few seconds pass. "Well, if you really want to know, why don't I come up this weekend. We could spend some time together and—"

"*This* weekend?" I love my sister but she rips through my life like a hurricane whenever she comes to visit. She wants to hang out with Tucker and explore the campus and go to parties. I miss the days when she was happy to hang out in her own bedroom, her nose buried in a book.

"Yeah, *this* weekend. I haven't seen you in ages."

"On Sunday I have a TeenCharter—"

"Of course you do. You'd rather hang out with those kids than with your own sister."

"Sadie, I made a commitment—"

"Yeah, well, maybe you can recommit to your own family. You've all but abandoned us."

I choke on a mouthful of now lukewarm tea. Doesn't Sadie realize what I've sacrificed for my family? "If that were true, mom would be in jail right now."

Sadie's scoffs. "She's not in jail because the guy you're fucking waved his magic wand. Is his dick just as magical, Poppy? Because maybe I should find someone—"

"Stop it," I cut her off. There is more than a grain of truth to what Sadie is saying, but I won't have my little sister shoving it in my face. "If you only called to say ugly things to me, I'm hanging up."

The sudden silence on the other end of the line means Sadie is biting her lip, hard, to keep quiet.

"How about next weekend?" I offer begrudgingly.

"That depends. Are you going to cancel on me like you did last time, and the time before that?"

"I—" I stop myself from denying it. She's right. "I promise. Now, do you want to come or not?"

She exhales a pent-up sigh. "Fine. I need to get out of Sackett for a while."

I hated Sackett when I lived there, so I can imagine how Sadie feels having never left. Yet the tone of Sadie's voice makes me wonder if there isn't something more to her call than just wanting a brief respite from small-town life.

"What's going on?"

"Nothing. It's stupid."

"Okay," I say, knowing the way to get my sister to talk is to pretend not to be interested.

"It's all a misunderstanding. I mean, I'm not a stalker for God's sake."

I close my laptop. Sadie treats boys like she used to treat her novels—completely enraptured until she's finished, then casting them aside to move onto the next one. I've never known her to pursue a guy before, unless you count checking out his social media history. "Who's accusing you of stalking?"

She groans. "Just some girl."

"A girl?" I have to fight an amused grin. "Is this some kind of love-triangle gone wrong?"

"Oh, please. I only wish it were that scandalous. Life in Sackett might be interesting for once. No, it's just some idiot who's too dumb to realize no one can steal a guy. If he's not happy, he's going to leave. That's not stealing."

My empty stomach clenches. "Sadie, please tell me you're not dating a married man."

"I'm not. They're not even engaged."

"Good."

"But even if I were, what's the problem? He would be the one cheating. Not me."

My jaw sags. "I guess technically, but—"

"But what? It's the truth."

"It may be the truth, but that doesn't make it right."

I can tell she's rolling her eyes at me. "Whatever. See you next weekend, sis."

With a sigh, I check the time. Twenty-three minutes of my life I won't get back.

On the other hand, I am twenty-three minutes closer to my banana breakfast.

CHAPTER 29

WORTHINGTON UNIVERSITY

GRADUATION DAY

"...Earning a diploma from Worthington University is a tremendous accomplishment. Looking out at all of you, I am confident this is only the first of many worthy endeavors, of milestones and crossed finished lines, earned through hard work and tenacity..."

I look around at the sea of navy caps and gowns surrounding me in the main quad. The graduating class is arranged alphabetically, which has landed me in the second to last row. In front of us is a stage with the chancellor and provost and commencement speaker, and a whole bunch of other people I don't recognize.

I hadn't wanted to be here today. The commencement ceremony is really just a formality. If I skipped the event, my diploma would simply be mailed to me. When I floated this concept to

Tucker, he'd been horrified. *If you don't celebrate the big things, you're going to live a very small life, Poppy.*

It is a hot day, especially by New England's usually mild spring standards, and the polyester fabric of my gown isn't helping things. The risers arranged around us are packed with friends and families holding battery-operated fans in one hand and taking photos with their other.

Ahead of me, I can see the back of Tucker's neck, and the glint of Wren's shiny blond hair. I wonder about the other people who might be in these rows. Sully, Tucker's lacrosse buddy who poured me my first tequila shots. The girls from the basement of the fraternity house who'd so generously filled my cup with Everclear lemonade. Everyone that had gathered outside Tucker's room in Crawford Hall, who watched as two EMTs treated my unconscious body.

And I consider who might be up on stage or in the crowd surrounding me. The men and women of the Judicial Administration board, who were so righteous in their judgment. Johanna Gregory, the graduate student from the counseling service who pretended not to see the lies inside my eyes. Dean Johnson, who pushed Tucker and I into working with TeenCharter, and is the reason we're together now. Maybe even Michael, the RA who drove me home from the hospital, graciously pretending not to notice the stench of vomit rising from me like a mushroom cloud.

I'm eager to be moving on from Worthington University. I will definitely miss the TeenCharter kids though, especially Jenny who isn't such a kid anymore. In a few months, she'll be eighteen, which means officially aging out of the foster care system. But I've made her promise to keep in touch.

I listen with half an ear to our commencement speaker. She talks about the world being both a bigger and smaller place than it had been when she graduated from WU twenty-five years ago. Safer and scarier. More interconnected while less intimate.

The world is full of dichotomies.

My years at Worthington have been both more and less than I'd expected. I'm hopeful about my future, and terrified of screwing it up. Excited to head into the real world, and yet uneasy about my place in it. Weighing on me the most heavily, though, is my relationship with Tucker. I am indebted to him, but sometimes slightly resentful of how much he's done for me. Grateful, and yet a little ashamed of the person I've allowed myself to become.

It's a strange way to feel about the guy I will be living with in less than a week.

We're moving into the gorgeous Tribeca loft that was his graduation gift from his parents. Tucker noticed me looking though Craigslist for crappy apartment shares I somehow hoped to afford on my relatively meager entry-level corporate marketing salary, and he'd looked at me as if I'd grown a horn in the middle of my forehead. *Don't waste your time*, he said. *We're moving in together.*

And that was that.

This morning I told my mother that I would be living with Tucker, expecting her to say it was a bad idea and spout a theory involving milk and cows. Instead, she'd simply smiled and congratulated me, handing me a Hallmark card and a Dr. Seuss book, *Oh, the Places You'll Go.*

I'm still not sure if the congratulations was for graduating… or landing a guy like Tucker. I've never explicitly told her that he was responsible for her prison reprieve and months-long stay in rehab… but she's never asked, either.

Sometimes I wonder what Tucker sees in me. He has the world at his feet. I have thousands of dollars in school loans and credit card debt, accumulated despite my financial aid and scholarships. Although, that doesn't include the ambulance bill from freshman year. When I mailed my first installment check of the payment plan I worked out with them, it had been returned, along with a copy of a check made out for the full amount, signed by Tucker. Of all the gifts Tucker has given me over the years, this is the only one I haven't said thank you for.

The speech wraps up and, row by row, we walk to the stage to shake hands with the Chancellor and receive our diploma. And once we are all back in our seats, we throw our caps into the air.

A thousand navy squares, looking almost like a flock of birds, silhouetted against a clear blue, cloudless sky.

Back in Sackett, there was always a day in late fall when it seemed as if every bird in the forest heeded some signal known only to them, fleeing their wooded sanctuary to migrate south together. A few minutes when the sky was a chaotic canvas of outstretched wings. This moment reminded me of that.

Until one of the squares crashes into my face, sending my sunglasses flying and jabbing me in the eye.

I yelp, but with thousands of people yelling and cheering, no one notices. Somehow I manage to find my mom and sister, one hand cupped over my stinging eye, the other one leaking with tears of sympathy for its injured twin.

"What the hell happened to you?" Sadie asks, noticing me lurching their way.

"I didn't look away fast enough, I guess."

My sister shakes her head. "Seriously, Poppy, only you could get injured at your own graduation."

"Here, let me take a look." I let my mom pry my hand away from my face, hear her quick intake of breath.

"Is it bad?"

"No, no. But why don't we swing by the campus medical office, okay?"

My mother hates doctors, so I know it can't look good.

Less than an hour later, a wad of gauze smeared with anti-bacterial medicine is taped over my eye socket. Catching my image in the mirror, I look like a sickly pirate. My good eye wells up again, and I reach for my phone.

"Who are you calling?" Sadie asks.

"There's no way I can show up looking like this tonight. I have to cancel." Tucker and Wren's families have planned a celebratory, post-graduation dinner, and we've been invited to join them.

Sadie snatches the phone out of my hand. "No way. I want to see how the other half lives for a night."

I fix my one-eyed gaze on her. "I thought you came to see me graduate."

"Half a day under the hot sun, just to see you handed a piece of paper? Yeah, that's exactly why I came."

"Sadie, come on. You expect me to hang out with Tucker, Wren, and their parents looking like this?"

Her voice turns into a whine. "Please, take pity on me. The last restaurant I went to was Red Robin."

"How about I take you out in Manhattan—any place you want?"

Sadie crosses her arms over her chest and pulls her trump card. "Mom's been looking forward to this, too. Do you really want to disappoint her?"

Damn it. Sadie knows I would never purposely do anything to upset our mom. Since her return from rehab, she's been working hard to stay sober and build relationships with us, while we try to avoid anything that might set her off. If we lose her a third time, we might never get her back.

My brows knit together over the bridge of my nose, pulling at the tape holding the gauze to my eye. "Sometimes I really wish I'd been an only child," I grumble, not meaning a word of it.

"But most of the time you feel blessed to have such an incredibly fabulous sister, right?"

I shake my head even as a begrudging grin twitches at my lips.

Because inside, I'm nodding. The relationship Sadie and I have is another dichotomy. Nearly identical on the outside yet complete opposites in almost every other way. She drives me nuts, but I love her. We are sisters, for better or worse.

CHAPTER 30

WORTHINGTON UNIVERSITY

GRADUATION DAY

*S*adie forces me to lie down with a cold compress pressed to my good eye for twenty minutes, then she outlines it with liquid liner and mascara, blending half a dozen shades of shadow so that it appears twice as big and green as it usually does.

"You look great," she insists.

Great is definitely not the word I would use. I try to smile but my lips, encased in a thick layer of lipstick and gloss, refuse to cooperate. "Thanks, sis. This is… wow."

She beams. "Finish getting dressed, I'm going to check on mom."

Once Sadie is out of sight, I attack my face with half a box of tissues before changing into my dress, a gift from Tucker. It is a soft pink, fitted at the waist and falling in a straight line to just above my knee. The high neckline is adorned with pearls, making it look as if I'm wearing a beautiful necklace. I tuck the gold *P* he gave me beneath it, out of sight.

I wish I could push thoughts of Gavin out of my head as easily. He sent me a congratulatory message this morning and I feel guilty that he's still keeping in touch with me after all this time. Guilty for not responding to it. Guilty that I want to, even though I'm about to move in with Tucker. And guilty that I haven't told Tucker about any of Gavin's messages.

In the back of my mind, I think I'd convinced myself that if Gavin kept in touch with me until after I'd left Worthington, even with no encouragement from me, it would be proof of a commitment that was lacking when he disappeared from Sackett and I didn't hear from him for nearly two years. Commitment I needed to even consider trusting him again. If there was a chance that we could be an *us* again.

Of course, I'd also assumed that Tucker and I would have broken up by now. But we're still going strong. I'm happy, damn it. Tucker makes me happy. Which is why I shouldn't be thinking about Gavin at all.

Sadie's eyebrows lift when she sees me come out of my room. She says nothing about my muted makeup, but I notice her tugging at the hem of her own dress that is shorter and tighter than mine, more appropriate for a bar-crawl than an elegant dinner.

My mother is wearing a nervous smile and a classic black sheath dress that emphasizes the fragility of her frame. "My girls," she says softly, drawing us into a hug. "It feels like just yesterday that you were two little cuties in pigtails and tutus."

Sadie and I look at each other over her head. *Tutus?* We never had tutus because we couldn't afford dance class. And my mother wasn't the type to sign us up for activities. But we don't disagree. I understand only too well the temptation, the *need*, to rewrite your own history. And if doing so keeps my mother in recovery, I'm all for it.

Dinner is at one of the oldest restaurants in New England. Originally a tavern, it was routinely patronized by Paul Revere,

George Washington, and several other founding fathers, including two that have a place on Tucker's family tree.

Wren's family sports three.

Currently led by a three-star Michelin rated chef, it is harder to get a table here than at the finest restaurants in Manhattan. Unless, of course, your last name is Stockton or Knowles.

Pulling up behind a Mercedes Maybach, my mother leaves her ten-year-old Hyundai hatchback with a teenaged valet who looks just as reluctant to slide behind the wheel as she is to give him the keys. "I hate handing my car over to a stranger," she stage-whispers as we walk in the door. "How do I know he won't drive off in it?"

Sadie laughs. "The competition's pretty stiff here, Mom. I don't think you have to worry about it."

Tucker appears before the hostess can address us. "Wow. You three are almost too beautiful to handle," he says, then winks. "But I love a challenge."

His perfect smile and honeyed, over-the-top words have my mother eating out of his palm, as always. She blushes, batting her lashes and giggling like Scarlett O'Hara in the opening scene of Gone with the Wind.

"Sadie, it's a good thing you chose not to come to Worth U, you'd probably start a war on Fraternity Row."

I cringe inwardly, both at the mention of Fraternity Row, and at the reminder that Sadie didn't get into WU. It is still a sore point for my sister, although she doesn't take offense tonight. "It wouldn't have been fair," she agrees.

Finally, Tucker turns to me, frowning at my bandaged eye. "My broken doll," he murmurs, lifting my chin and giving me a chaste kiss. "You okay?"

"I am now," I say as he wraps his arms around my waist, glad Sadie hadn't let me cancel.

"Well, once we get to New York, I'll have our family doctor look at it."

"No, it's fine, really."

Tucker stiffens, the hands that had been casually draped around my waist becoming a set of pincers. He hates being contradicted, especially in public. *Stupid*, I chide myself. "Actually, you're right. I'd really appreciate that, Tucker. Thank you."

He relaxes, dropping another kiss on my forehead. "No one will ever take care of you like I will, Poppy."

My mother sighs in pleasure. "Don't ever let this one go, honey. He's a keeper."

I push my lips into a smile, but before I can answer, Tucker says, "You don't have to worry about that. I wouldn't let her even if she tried."

Tucker slips my mother's arm through his elbow, then manages to gather both Sadie and me against his other side. He leads us to a large round table seated in front of a bay window with beautiful water views, making introductions all around.

Wren stands up to greet me, pulling me into an unexpected and completely uncharacteristic hug. But I understand why when her harsh whisper hits my ears. "Enjoy your meal, Poppy. It's only a matter of time before Tucker realizes he's just been slumming with you. Remember what I said—he's only yours on loan."

Her eyes are glittering when she releases me and I find my chair somewhat shakily, sitting between my mother and Tucker, with my sister on Tucker's other side. Tucker casually rests his hand over my chair, his thumb sweeping across the back of my neck.

It's not his touch that makes my hair stand on end. It's the fear that Wren is right. Tucker has become such a huge part of my life, I don't even know what I would do without him anymore. Am I just a temporary placeholder until he commits to a life with Wren? I can't deny that she looks a hell of a lot more like pictures I ripped from magazines. Sleek hair, waifishly thin, always so poised, even when she's pulling the rug out from beneath me. And the truce we came to years ago, our handshake agreement, it doesn't matter anymore. I wouldn't say anything to smear Tucker's name, and even if I did—who would believe me?

"What happened to your eye, dear?" Wren's mother asks, interrupting my frantic thoughts. I remember her from freshman move-in day, and she still looks only a few years older than her daughter.

Her father barely glances up from his phone as I recount the cap-throwing incident. Everyone murmurs sympathetically except Wren. "You almost got your eye poked out by your graduation cap... seriously?"

My sister laughs. "I know, right?" I don't enjoy being the butt of their joke, but it does break the ice.

Tucker's father asks to speak with the sommelier and they spend a few minutes discussing various regions and wineries in France, selecting a red and a white older than anyone at our table. I've met Tucker's parents before. Like now, they are polite but aloof.

The waiter hands out menus and I can feel the shock waves rolling off my mother as she peruses it. Even excluding alcohol, our bill will easily come to more than she earns in a week. Tucker has already told me that his and Wren's father will probably argue over who gets to pay the check, and neither expect my mother to pay any portion of it.

I lean toward her discreetly, knowing she will order a garden salad and a cup of soup if I don't say anything. "Mom, don't worry about it, it's taken care of," I whisper.

She looks at me, confused. "What?"

I jerk my chin at the menu. "Order what you want, Tucker said it's their treat tonight."

She stiffens. "We're not a charity case, Poppy."

I almost want to point out that *charity* is exactly why I'm here tonight, celebrating my graduation. It's also why she's not in jail. Heat rushes up my chest to deposit pink patches on my cheeks. "Let's not make this a—"

Wren notices our exchange, nudging her mother. Mrs. Knowles speaks up. "Is everything all right?" she asks.

My throat swells with mortification as the waiter fills my mother's wineglass. She doesn't stop him. *Shit.* Technically, my mom went to rehab for drugs, but I'd foolishly hoped she would give up drinking, too.

My mother looks at me and then back at the menu before taking a fortifying sip of wine. Then another, this one bigger. "I didn't bring my girls here tonight for a free dinner. I'd like to pay our share."

Tucker's dad responds first. "Our kids are going to be living together, we're practically family."

Unaccustomed to standing up for herself, she blinks wetly, like a chipmunk facing down a fox. I expect her to concede, but to my surprise, she clears her throat and then says in a small voice, "Well, until we actually are, I'd like to—"

"Actually, I think that's a great idea." Tucker pushes back his chair. My stomach clenches as I watch him drop down to one knee.

No. I'm not ready for this. Not even close.

Apparently, neither is anyone else at our table. I hear gasps from my mom and sister, choking sounds from Wren, her mother, and Mrs. Stockton, and a sharply delivered, "Tucker, now is not the time," from his father.

"This is the perfect time," Tucker says, in that arrogant, unflappable way of his. Then he looks at Wren. "You will always be in my life, but—"

Wren swallows, her skin so translucent it's like fine china. Fine china that's cracking before my eyes. "But not as your wife."

"Tucker, honey," his mom pleads, her manicured nails curving over his shoulder. "You're so young. There's no rush."

"Aren't you and Dad the ones who told me I should settle down after college, grow up and focus on the business?"

As Mrs. Stockton looks from her son to me to Wren, it's clear that she's torn. Pleased to hear that Tucker is following their advice, but alarmed at the woman he's chosen to settle down with. "Yes, but—"

"I can count on one hand the number of times you've listened to a damn word we've said, son," Mr. Stockton grumbles. "If you're trying to make a point here, it's completely unnecessary. Unless…" My flush deepens when he looks pointedly at my stomach.

Tucker regards his father seriously, then says stiffly, "That's not what this is. I love Poppy, and if you want to be a part of our lives, then you'll respect our choices."

Their protests silenced, Tucker turns his back on his parents and faces me again, an enormous diamond ring appearing in his hand. "Poppy Whitman, it's about time we start building a life together. Will you do me the very great honor of becoming my wife?"

The restaurant is quiet. Not just our table, but the entire room. Horror is gusting my way from the other side of the table, but I'm still processing the contentious exchange that just happened between Tucker and his parents. More importantly, the fact that Tucker stood up for me. He was calm but firm, and he didn't back down an inch. Now Tucker's smile is wide and encouraging, though it falters a bit as I hesitate.

I feel like an overblown balloon, my skin stretched so tightly that I'm in danger of splitting apart. I've only imagined this moment with Gavin. Had pictured him doing something like hiding a ring inside a deck of cards, or proposing during a hike through the nature preserve back in Sackett. It would be just the two of us, and he would tell me all the reasons he loved me, all the reasons we were meant to be.

"Tucker, I—" The diamond shoots a prism of light at my unbandaged eye, blinding me. For a moment, I'm back in that hospital room, waking up naked beneath a sheet. Overwhelmed by terror and pain and confusion. But then the light shifts and I see Tucker's face again. He's spent every moment since that awful morning making up for his mistake. I forgave him the night we walked along Fifth Avenue, snowflakes dusting our eyelashes as we took in the magic and wonder of the holiday window displays. We made our own magic just hours later.

Tucker is as comfortable and confident in a bunny suit as he is in his lacrosse uniform or custom-tailored tux. And now he's offering me exactly what I've craved since I saw it captured so perfectly in the pages of a magazine.

They look so... perfect. Meant to be. Like nothing bad has ever happened to them. Like nothing bad ever will.

I thought Gavin and I were a perfect couple. But he's not here. He left me.

Tucker is here now. He is my future.

With Tucker, I'll have an elegant life, a beautiful home, and the security of knowing I belong.

And with his ring, Tucker is promising something else. Forever.

A lifetime with a man I can count on, a true partner who won't ever leave me. A man who just showed me that he'll always be in my corner, even against his own parents.

That night, his *mistake*, isn't a reason to refuse Tucker's proposal. If anything, it's a reason to accept. I've seen Tucker at his worst. I am part of his deepest regret.

In a very strange, and maybe even bizarre way—it's almost like insurance. Because one day, I am bound to hurt him, to disappoint him. To prove I am not perfect and maybe even unworthy. But Tucker will have to forgive me. He'll have to give me a second chance.

Just like I did for him.

My answer is suddenly at the tip of my tongue, as if it has been there all along. "I will."

CHAPTER 31

NEW YORK CITY

THREE MONTHS LATER

"*Y*ou're meeting with the wedding planner today, right?" Tucker asks, his eyes automatically scanning my outfit.

And your mother. "Yes. What do you think, do I look okay?" I shift anxiously in my Jimmy Choo shoes, as beautiful as they are uncomfortable, watching his face for any sign of disapproval.

I haven't forgotten his parent's unequivocal objection to our engagement. And although I understand their perspective—their only son proposing to a girl they barely know, in front of the girl who's already like a daughter to them—but it still chafes. I am determined to win Mrs. Stockton over.

My dress is probably the least of my concerns though. After all, Tucker bought everything I'm wearing and most of the clothes now hanging in my closet. Not long after we moved in together, he'd insisted on reenacting that scene in Pretty Woman —the one with Julia Roberts trying on clothes and Richard Gere either approving or rejecting each outfit.

It's not as much fun as they made it look. I felt like a mannequin Tucker was dressing up in clothes that fit my body, but didn't fit *me*. Maybe that was the point though. Because Poppy Whitman doesn't live in a Tribeca loft and she certainly can't afford to shop at Saks.

But Tucker's fiancée, Poppy soon-to-be-Stockton, does and can. And that's who I am now. Because of Tucker, I'm becoming the woman I've always wanted to be.

I wear pretty dresses to glamorous parties.

I live in a home filled with beautiful things.

I drink coffee, not wine, from a mug without a single chip.

I am building a life with a man who loves me. A man who will never abandon me.

And… when the director of TeenCharter called with the news that they were expanding into New York City and looking for a programming coordinator, I was able to give notice at the marketing company where I was in the management training program and take a significant pay cut to do something that actually makes a difference in people's lives.

Now, Tucker's lips curve into a smile and he brushes a stray lock of hair behind my ear, his fingers lingering on my neck. "You look beautiful," he says. I kiss him as a wave of relief washes through me. Not quite enough to drown my nerves, but enough to propel me out of the closet and into a cab.

I want our wedding to be above reproach. So perfect that no one will have any excuse to criticize Tucker's choice of bride. Which is why I asked his mother to help plan our wedding. The best way to silence someone's objection is to make them a part of the process. Cecelia immediately hired Xenia, Manhattan's premier wedding planner. She arrives at the Stockton's townhouse in a cloud of perfume and poise, wearing a floor-length fox coat despite the warm weather.

We sit in the formal dining room, though the trays of finger sandwiches and assorted crudités arranged on the sideboard go ignored.

"Let's discuss locations, shall we?" Xenia's voice is vaguely European, although I can't pinpoint the country.

I've been poring over bridal magazines and stalking wedding websites. I have a notebook full of notes with me and a Pinterest board ready to show them. "I was thinking maybe Central Park. Or the Rainbow Room at Rockefeller—"

Cecelia interrupts. "My son will be married at the Metropolitan Club, of course."

My face flushes with embarrassment. How could I be so *stupid*? I hadn't even considered the private, old money social club on the corner of Fifth Avenue and Sixtieth Street, originally founded in the late 1800s by J.P. Morgan and a few other prominent industrialists, whose names are well known to this day. Vanderbilt, Whitney, Roosevelt.

According to Tucker, the men of his family have been members of the Metropolitan Club for over one hundred years. When he brings me there, it's easy to imagine a time when elegant horses would have trotted along a cobblestoned Fifth Avenue and turned onto Sixtieth Street, coming to a halt outside the Sanford White designed building. With its tall Corinthian columns and intricate wrought iron gates, it's a throwback to a different era, the kind of place I never would have known existed if not for Tucker.

Not just anyone can have a wedding at the Metropolitan Club. Exclusive and elegant, it's the perfect place.

Thank God Cecelia is here. Who knows how many mistakes I would have made on my own?

Xenia makes a note in her Hermes portfolio. "Of course. Any thoughts on the menu?"

"Oh. Um, yes, I—"

"I've already arranged to have a private tasting with the chef, but we're thinking lobster, Kobe beef, and duck as the proteins."

"Lovely. How about the date?"

"Tucker and I—"

At this, my future mother-in-law turns to me, her hand hovering over my forearm. "I'm sure you both believe a long engagement is best, right?"

I nod shakily. At this point, I don't trust myself to say my own name. And if Tucker takes issue with it, I'll tell him the delay is due to scheduling rather than his mother's insistence.

She flips through her calendar, murmuring things like "that's the month we'll be in Gstaad, we'd hate to miss the Grand Prix in Monaco, we'll be on the yacht for much of the summer." Finally, she taps a manicured fingernail on a page at the very end of her agenda, eighteen months away.

"What do you think, dear?"

I swallow the heavy knot of uncertainly in my throat. "That's perfect."

Later, when I share the wedding details with Tucker, he only frowns for a moment at the far off date before looking at me with open admiration shining from his eyes. "Come here," he says, pulling me into his arms.

I exhale a relieved sigh, nestling into his embrace.

Tucker lowers his mouth to my ear, his breath sending a shiver down my spine. "I can't wait to make you mine, forever."

CHAPTER 32

NEW YORK CITY

ONE AND A HALF YEARS LATER

*I*t's been ten years since I first met Gavin. A decade since I went for a walk in the woods and was startled by a beautiful boy with wild tawny hair and wide bee-stung lips and a fading bruise beneath his left eye.

A lot has happened in that time. Laughter and love, tears and heartbreak. I went from a child to an adult, from a girl to a woman. Next week, I will be a bride, then a wife.

But whatever maturity I've gained, the experiences that have informed my composure…

All of it is ripped away from me in an instant, as if it had never been there at all.

Stolen by the one man who will always hold a slice of my heart in his hands, a piece of my soul in his stare.

Gavin.

At the sight of him, leaning oh so casually against a marble pillar in the lobby of my apartment building, the blood drains from my face, a ripple of awareness cartwheeling down my spine. *Holy shit, Gavin.* The struggle to process my shock is compounded a thousand times over by an instinctive, unfiltered, undiluted joy.

When my footsteps slow, Gavin closes the distance between us until we are so close that I can see the stubble dusting his jaw like the fine-grained sand. So close that his cerulean gaze cuts right through me. So close that the magnetic pull between us draws me even closer.

Silence stretches out as I force myself to stand my ground. I cannot waver, cannot be swayed by the yearning that flickers in the contours of his face, by the suggestion of a smile chased away, too soon, by his wounded scowl, by hands that almost, *almost*, reach out for me.

I'm so sorry, Gavin. So sorry that I've done this to us.

"Is it true?" he finally blurts, his voice leaden as he pins me with a broken stare.

"Is *what* true?" I finally manage to say, although what I want to do is throw myself at Gavin's feet and beg his forgiveness. To leap into his arms hold on tight.

To find out if Gavin still smells like clean laundry and pinecones. If our hearts will still sync to the same rhythm.

I want to go back in time, to the way we were, to the place we fell in love, to the people we used to be.

I want…

"You're getting married." Gavin's eyes drop to my left hand, not a question but a statement.

"I—" Words fail me and I look over Gavin's shoulder, as if I can make sense of everything that's happened to keep us apart. I don't find an explanation, but I do catch the interested stare of one of the building's security guards. "Let's not do this here. Will you come up?"

I immediately regret it. Not because I don't want to talk with Gavin privately, but because I know Tucker will be furious if he finds out. I should have suggested that we go to the Starbucks around the corner, or for a walk.

But Gavin gives a terse nod, and I lead him to the bank of elevators at the back of the building, the guard's disapproving stare penetrating the thin fabric of my blouse. We stand facing front, the subtle chime as we pass each floor emphasizing our awkward silence.

"Can I get you something?" I ask as soon as we get inside. "Soda, water? Something stronger?" Isla, the housekeeper Tucker hired, was here this morning. Every pillow has been fluffed and puffed, the edges perfectly straight. There is not a speck of dust to be found on any surface. And the airs smells of lemons and bleach.

"I'm fine," he replies.

I drop my purse on the console table and walk to the couch. Gavin follows, taking a seat in the adjacent chair. "I'm sorry. I—" My voice falters and I look down at my hands, fighting the urge to twist my engagement ring around my finger until the sparkling diamond is hidden. Not that it matters, Gavin has already seen it.

"When's the big day?"

I clear my throat. "Next week."

Gavin leans forward, his elbows on his knees. "Poppy, are you sure about this?" His eyes make a quick sweep of the room before landing back on me. "Is *this* really what you want?"

The disapproval in Gavin's tone reminds me uncomfortably of Tucker's parents, and I bristle at the implication that my marriage is merely a ploy to get a nice apartment. Which isn't true. And even if it was, what difference would it make? I've made my decision. Too much has happened, I can't go back now. Gavin deserves to move on, too.

"Yes. I'm happy." I reach for Gavin's arm, stopping myself just in time. I can't bear to know if I'll feel the impact down to my bones.

Because Gavin wouldn't say Tucker's name, I emphasize it now. "*Tucker* makes me happy." The apartment, the clothes, the ease that comes from financial security—all of that is window dressing. Tucker makes me feels safe. Truly. We're building a life together. Gavin needs to know this.

"No." Gavin shakes his head. "Poppy, I don't know what lies you've been feeding yourself but there's no way—" He breaks off, his eyes dragging over my body. But his gaze isn't adoring, it's anguished. As if looking at me physically hurts. "For God's sake, have you been eating? What has he done to you?"

I don't have to look in a mirror to know I look different than I used to. These days I wear designer clothes that have been tailored to fit my body perfectly. I don't buy secondhand clothes or throw my badly cut, tangled hair into a messy pony-tail. My makeup is artfully applied, my hair blown out and pin straight. I'm thin, but not nearly as thin as I could be, as thin as Wren.

Anger wells up inside me, and I embrace the searing warmth that floods my body. It is infinitely preferable to the doubt and uncertainty that are my usual companions. I don't need to explain myself to Gavin. How dare he come back into my life, acting as if I've betrayed him by moving on and forging a life of my own—after he *left* me?

"Get out," I say flatly, pointing at the door. "Get out and don't come back."

Gavin doesn't move. "You can't answer me, can you? You don't even realize what he's done. This… plastic person he's turned you into."

"*He* is going to be my husb—"

Gavin cuts me off. "*I* was supposed to be your husband!"

I stare at him now, slack-jawed and dizzy. Gavin's words have knocked the wind out of me. I fumble for something to say, something to do. And maybe because I'm light-headed and off-balance, my thoughts become disordered and nonsensical, my imagination taking me to a place that doesn't, cannot, exist. A future—with Gavin—that is impossible to achieve.

But, for a moment... No, longer than that. A lifetime, condensed into the span of seconds, I see what we could be, feel the life we *could* have as if I'm holding it in my hands. My heart swells with happiness, and I'm warmed by the glow of the white light that accompanies a near-death moment. But instead of actual memories, I'm flooded with sparkling, mystical glimpses of a path not yet taken. Memories that have yet to be made.

"Poppy?" Gavin's voice cuts into my consciousness, bringing me back to reality.

I open my eyes, blinking away the fantasy even as it slips through my fingers, evaporating in front of me. It's not real, and I'm not in some faraway future. I'm here, in New York City. In Tribeca. In the apartment I share with Tucker.

If it wasn't for Tucker, my mom would still be in jail, or maybe even dead. If it wasn't for Tucker—I couldn't spend my days helping kids thrust into the foster system, as lost and aching as I once was.

I turn my gaze back to Gavin. This sight of him hurts. Oh God, how it hurts. His soldier's body is tense and taut beneath his simple clothes, his face the embodiment of nobility and steadfastness. Life with Gavin would be simpler, maybe even easier. But making the choice to diverge from the path I've taken is not at all simple, not at all easy.

I accepted Tucker's proposal; I have promised him my future. I won't abandon him. Not even for Gavin.

The waxed, parquet floor has turned to mud beneath me, sucking at my heels and squishing between my toes, but I know what I have to do. The past ten years have taught me that not all risks are rewarded and reckless decisions always come with consequences. Harsh, corrosive consequences.

I've learned my lesson. I am taking the safe road, clinging to the highest ground.

Gavin abandoned me once before, and I will not give him the chance to do it again.

Which is why I have to cut the cord between Gavin and I once and for all. I have to, for *us*. If there's any hope of keeping our memories intact, of not ruining our beautiful past with the bitterness of our current reality.

My body is a vault of sadness, filled with nothing but heart-breaking, soul-crushing loss, invisible atoms of wrenching pain tearing me apart. I would give anything to avoid it, to spare Gavin from it, but this is our path. And it ends here. It has to.

"No, Gavin. We were just kids, daydreaming. You don't even know me anymore."

"I do. I know you and I want you and I love you. Come with me, Poppy." He reaches for my hand. "Come with me, we'll—"

"No!" I wrench away from him, gathering all of my resolve to say what needs to be said. "I don't love you anymore, Gavin. I'm sorry." *Shit. Shit. No, don't believe me. Please, don't believe me.*

"You're lying. Why are you lying?"

He knows. Of course, he knows. "I'm not. And you have to leave." *Before I give in and cause us even more pain, even more heartache.*

Gavin's shoulders slump, his military bearing failing him as sadness pulls at his features. "Do you remember that day in the woods? The spring of our freshman year, and we were choosing our electives for fall. I told you I wanted to become an FBI agent…"

I cross my arms warding off the memories. *No. Don't do this. Don't take me back into the woods. Don't make me remember* us.

But Gavin continues anyway. "A thunder storm rolled in and I walked you home. Do you remember what you said to me?"

Yes. A shudder goes through me as I exhale. "No."

"You said, 'I might need you to rescue me one day.'" Unshed tears sting my eyes and I bite down on the inside of my cheek until the taste of copper fill my mouth. *Do not cry. Do not break down.* "That day is today. Let me take you away from all this. Let me rescue you."

The question is like a trip wire, flipping a switch deep inside me. Gavin has no idea how many times I prayed for him to do just that—to appear, like some kind of mythical knight on a white horse, and spirit me away from the clutches of a nightmare.

When he finally did, it was just for a short visit. A few hours. Long enough to catch up. But not long enough to be *my* hero.

And now, he's too late.

A sudden, bitter laugh rips from my throat. "You want to be my hero... now?" I spin away from him, striding toward the floor-to-ceiling windows framing the impressive architectural sprawl of Manhattan. But I'm not really looking at the view. My eye is still turned inward, remembering a time when I did need rescuing, desperately.

"Yes. If you let me, yes. But you can't— *You can't marry him, Poppy.*"

I swallow a scream of regret and turn back around, facing Gavin once again. Maybe for the last time. "I can and I will." There is more distance between us now, though the room is crowded with hurt and recriminations. "When I needed you, you weren't there. So you don't get to wear a cape now, show up at the last second and save the day. You're no hero, Gavin. Not mine, anyway."

CHAPTER 33

THREE HOURS LATER

*A*fter Gavin left, I changed into workout gear and went to the gym, my body a lightning rod of adrenaline and anger. I was too furious to cry, too worked up to sit still.

When I finally return to the apartment, my body is depleted and weak. I need a hot shower, a gallon of water, and a good night's sleep. The security guard on duty is still the same one who saw me with Gavin, and I tell myself his judgmental glare is just my guilty conscience nagging at me.

I know Tucker is in our apartment the second I open the door. I sense his anger as I cross the threshold, like a drop in barometric pressure just before a storm.

I hesitate to close the door, reluctant to trap myself inside with Tucker, but he rises from the couch and closes it for me. "Where have you been?" Tucker is still in his suit, but he's unbuttoned his shirt and loosened his tie. In his hand is a tumbler filled to the brim with amber liquid. Scotch, or maybe bourbon.

Despite being "the boss's son," no one could ever accuse my

fiancé of relying on genetics to get ahead. He leaves for the offices of his family's private investment firm before I wake up and rarely comes home until I'm itching to change into pajamas and binge-watch Netflix. I don't though. Because I discovered that Tucker doesn't appreciate coming home to find me sprawled on the couch with a bag of popcorn and a can of soda. And why shouldn't he deserve my full attention after a long day? Why wouldn't I greet him with a happy kiss when he walks through the door?

Noticing the clench of Tucker's jaw, the tight grip of his fingers on the crystal, my fingers fumble with my coat. "The gym," I answer, talons of anxiety clawing at my neck. Does Tucker know Gavin was here?

"Bullshit," he spits out, crossing the room before I've managed to get my arms out of the sleeves.

I recoil as Tucker reaches behind me to grip both of my wrists, pinning me to the wall. "Hey— Stop!"

"Where were you?" he repeats.

"I was at the gym." My sneakers squeak on the hardwood floor as I squirm against him.

"How do I know you weren't with *him?*" His eyes flash with anger. Just inches from mine, they're bright and the slightest bit glazed.

"Who... ?" My voice trails off. Tucker is drunk. The small hairs on my forearms and at the back of my neck rise up in alarm. Drunk Tucker cannot be trusted.

"Don't make me say his name, Poppy. There are security cameras all over this building, including one aimed straight at our front door."

Could he recognize Gavin from that one time he saw us together, all those years ago? Is that even possible?

But it's Tucker questions that are most disconcerting right now. I don't like his tone. And I definitely don't like the feeling of being cornered, caught. "Then you know he didn't stay long."

"He stayed too damn long. And he never should have been here at all." Tucker pulls at my wrists so that my back arches away from him and my hips jut forward, pressing against his. "Why the fuck was he here, Poppy? Tell me that."

"He heard we were engaged. H-he wanted to congratulate me," I stutter over my words. "To wish us well."

The angry creases at the corner of Tucker's eyes cut even deeper, and he rubs against me, hard enough to feel evidence of a desire I don't yet reciprocate. "Really? And just what did you say?"

I search for a response that would soothe the hard edges of Tucker's temper. "I—"

"Did you thank him?"

"Yes."

"Invite him to our wedding?"

"No. Of course not."

"Did you fuck him? One last taste of his dick before our wedding?"

"Tucker!" I fight against his grip, twisting away from him, but he's too big, too strong. Too drunk. "Stop it. Let go of me, right now."

"After everything I've done for you, for your family. Look where you live, look how far you've come. Because of me, goddamn it. Everything you are, everything you have, is because of me."

I ignore the barbs he's throwing my way, purposely trying to provoke me into a heated exchange. But I refuse to give it to him. Instead, I try another tactic, pushing the tension from my body and forcing myself to relax into his hold. Tucker can be temperamental, but he's never physically hurt me before. At least, not since *that night*. "Tucker, please. This isn't who you are. I love *you*. I'm marrying *you*." I feel tears gathering and I let them fall, staring right at my fiancé as they slide down my cheeks. "You're scaring me."

249

He drops my wrists, his expression one of surprise and shame as he backs away. "Shit. Poppy, I—"

"It's okay," I reassure him, just wanting this moment to be over. There's no point talking about it when he's been drinking.

And, truth be told, I would be pretty rattled myself if Tucker's first love, the woman he thought he'd spend the rest of his life with, showed up the week before our wedding. But there's never been anyone in Tucker's life who compares to what I had with Gavin.

Not even Wren, though she would definitely disagree.

"Come on, let's go to bed." I finally step away from the wall and put my arm around Tucker, leading him into our bedroom.

"I had a shit day, Poppy." He drops onto the mattress with a groan. "Nothing like spotting an opportunity and watching it go down in flames. Too risky, they said. Too speculative, they said. Well, want to know what I say? A bunch of fucking pussies, all of them. My father included."

"They'll come around," I say, keeping my tone light and soothing as I bend down to help Tucker with his shoes.

I showered at the gym, so it only takes me a few minutes to change into pajamas and brush my teeth. When I return, Tucker is sprawled across the mattress, his face relaxed and at peace. I take a moment to stare at him, at his broad forehead and aquiline nose and the cleft in his chin. His dark hair is messy against our pristine white sheets and my hand itches to smooth it away from his face.

Of course, Tucker wanted me home after he'd had a bad day. And I shouldn't blame him for losing his temper. Not only did he arrive home to an empty apartment, he discovered Gavin had been here.

If anything, I'm angry at the stupid security guard. I can't imagine Tucker checks the video footage every day. He must have been tipped off.

Tucker loves me so much, and he counts on me. We're a team.

But when I close my eyes, it's Gavin's face I see. Gavin's touch I crave. And Gavin's hurt that coils through me, pulling so tight I can barely breathe.

I need him to believe what I said. Every word, especially the vicious ones.

Almost as much as I want him to read between my wounded accusations, root out every single lie.

Tick tock, tick tock. One week until my wedding.

WEDDING DAY

"See you soon, *Mrs. Stockton.*" Sadie's bridesmaid dress swishes around her legs as she slips through the door, taking the last shred of my composure with her.

Mrs. Stockton. In a few minutes, that will be me.

I wish I could take a deep breath, but my Monique Lhuillier gown is not constructed to accommodate more oxygen than absolutely necessary. *Tucker will be so embarrassed if I faint in front of everyone.*

Wren regards me with a sour smile plastered to her face. "Last chance to cut and run," she trills, her voice high-pitched with strain. It's probably taking everything she has not to rip off my dress and walk down the aisle herself. Wren is my maid of honor at Tucker and his mother's insistence. We're not friends, not even close. Although, even I can't help but feel a twinge of sympathy for her today. *Our families have been planning our wedding for years. Don't get too attached, he's only on loan.*

I'm about to be as attached as it's possible to be.

"I don't think I'd get very far in this dress." I run my hands over my sides, keeping my voice even and non-confrontational.

There's both anger and pain shining from Wren's icy expression, but when Xenia taps lightly on the door, she lifts her chin at a haughty angle, pushes her shoulders back, and walks through it like she's on a Paris catwalk.

The chords of the premier harpist from the New York Philharmonic Orchestra filter into the small chamber where I'm waiting with Tucker's father. He offers me his arm. "I guess it's now or never."

"I guess so." My stomach flutters nervously as I slip my hand through the crook in Mr. Stockton's elbow. He's told me to call him Hewitt, but I haven't quite gotten used to it yet.

This is it. My wedding day. I keep reminding myself to take it all in. To enjoy every moment.

But it's going by so fast.

Mr. S—*Hewitt* is walking me down the aisle. My mother asked if I wanted her to attempt to contact my father, but I said no. He left when I could barely walk myself, so asking him to give me away felt more than a little disingenuous.

But no more so, I realize now, than asking Tucker's father. Thankfully, both he and his wife have warmed up to me since the day Tucker surprised us all with his proposal. Once they realized I was here to stay, and that I wasn't some flashy gold-digger out to mine their family vault, the Stocktons seemed to accept that I would one day be their daughter-in-law.

For the first time in over a year and a half, there is no ring on my left hand. It's been temporarily displaced to my right, to make way for the wedding band Tucker will soon slip onto my finger. More diamonds, of course.

I'd suggested a simple ring to the salesperson at Harry Winston. She'd looked at me as if I was a traitor to our gender, and placed an eternity band of flawless, emerald-cut stones on a velvet-lined tray. *For women who prefer an understated look*, she'd said to Tucker.

Xenia's minions make a few last-minute adjustments to my appearance, smoothing out the train of my dress and straightening my veil. Someone thrusts a bouquet at me, with the reminder to keep it at hip-height. Any higher and it will conceal the intricate beadwork sewn into the bodice.

These are my last moments as Poppy Whitman.

For the rest of my life I will be Poppy Stockton.

One of the most venerable names in the country, the Stocktons represent safety and security. A life of privilege and invincibility.

Soon the Stockton name, with everything it entails, will be mine.

Xenia waves us forward. "Remember, better slow than fast. And," she tugs at the ribbon-wrapped stems in my right hand, "don't forget to smile. This is the happiest day of your life."

The doors open and all six hundred of our guests, most of whom I've never met, rise in unison.

We step out onto the balcony and I hold tightly to Tucker's father as we make our way down the grand staircase and into the Great Hall with its walls of white marble.

Tucker is waiting for me at the end of a long aisle, along with my sister, Wren, and several Stockton cousins. Tucker's side is filled with a matching number of fraternity brothers.

For a moment, it feels like my feet, in their Louboutin stilettos, have grown roots. Tucker's father looks down on me seriously, his cocoa-colored eyes exact replicas of Tucker's. "Welcome to the family, Poppy."

The tremulous smile I've plastered to my face falters as grateful tears threaten to overflow my lashes. "It's an honor… Hewitt."

He glances over at his son and then back at me. "Shall we?"

Yards of white duchesse satin whisper as I take one tentative step, then another, along an ivory runner liberally sprinkled with soft pink rose petals.

But for one blinding moment, it all disappears, replaced with an image of poppy petals scattered outside the entrance to an abandoned cave. Flickering candles and a pile of mismatched pillows. And *Gavin*.

I stumble slightly, the tip of my heel catching on a wrinkle in the satin runner. Tucker's father tightens his arm, and I doubt anyone even notices. But I do. The slight misstep brings me back to reality.

Gavin isn't here. I have to leave him where he belongs. In the past.

It's an arcane habit, a bride donning a veil to hide her face on the day of her wedding, but I am grateful for it now. It allows me a few extra seconds to compose my features into a serene mask that reveals nothing of my inner turmoil.

Unnecessary turmoil.

I am the luckiest girl in the world to be marrying Tucker Stockton and I know it. I do, really.

By the time Tucker lifts my veil, I've found my equilibrium again. I am the perfect bride he deserves.

CHAPTER 35

BORA BORA, TAHITI

HONEYMOON

*I*t is a long flight to Tahiti, thirteen hours, but from the minute we land, I know it was worth it. French Polynesia is like nothing I've ever experienced. Translucent water, the most perfect shade of aquamarine, sprawls like a glistening blanket below an endless azure sky. The air is sultry and tropical, fragrant with the scent of gardenias, hibiscus, and the faintest hint of vanilla. Coconut palm trees stand like soldiers, their leaves gently swaying in the breeze, a quiet whisper on the wind.

Our home for the next ten days is a luxurious, glass-bottomed villa. It perches on stilts driven into the ocean, and a staircase connects our terrace to a breathtaking lagoon. Everywhere I look is sun and sky and sand and sea.

It is, truly, paradise.

"Do we really have to go home in a week? Can't we stay here forever?" I exhale a contented sigh, staring out at the most breathtaking sunset I've ever seen. Vibrant pinks and purples are smeared across the horizon with the restraint of a toddler's finger painting, shards of color reflected onto the serene surface of the ocean.

Sitting beside me on the deck of our villa, Tucker glances at me with an indulgent smile and takes a sip of his post-swim, pre-dinner cocktail.

It's a moment. Not a moment in time. But a *moment.*

The slow blink of Tucker's inky black lashes, the relaxed slope of his shoulders, the way he holds his glass with barely enough pressure to keep it aloft. Everything about Tucker in this *moment* conveys happiness and comfort. That I make him happy and comfortable.

That I am loved.

And in this moment, *our moment...* everything that happened between us feels preordained. As if we've been pushed together by the hand of fate herself.

The chirp of Tucker's phone interrupts my musings.

"Who was that?" I ask after he ends the call. It's an unnecessary question. Tucker and Wren still finish each other's sentences, still laugh at the same inside jokes. I know it was her on the phone.

"Work." His voice is nonchalant.

"Since when do you and Wren work together?"

The vein that runs along his temple pulses, his jaw clenching as he reaches for the sunglasses he'd idly tossed on the table earlier. "Since always. Wren's an art consultant, I'm an investment advisor. We both hunt the same whales."

"We're on our honeymoon," I remind him.

"Business is business, Poppy. And there are people I'd like to meet while we're out here. People Wren has known for years."

"Here, in Bora Bora?" I hate how needy I sound.

"No. But we've already been here a week. You'll love Indonesia, too."

My head twists so fast I hear a crack, followed immediately by a jolt of pain. "Indonesia?" I repeat, rubbing the ache just below my ear.

"Yes. I'll probably only be busy for a day or two. I'm sure there's plenty of sightseeing tours for you to enjoy. I'll have the concierge look into it." Tucker's lips arrange themselves into a satisfied grin beneath his mirrored sunglasses.

"You're going to send me sightseeing—all by myself?" My eyelids flutter as I blink back tears.

"Of course not. I'll get you a tour guide."

I don't want a tour guide. I want to wallow in paradise with my new husband. An hour ago, we were snorkeling in the water swirling in the lagoon below our villa. Pushing my back against one of the columns, Tucker had untied my bikini bottom and hiked my legs around his hips. We made love to the rhythm of the tide. "You're handing me off to a stranger. Great, thanks."

He shifts in his chair, expelling a disgruntled huff. "Do you have any friends there? Maybe someone from school?"

Tucker's question isn't an unreasonable one. Worthington University attracts students from all over the globe. "No one I've kept in touch with." Besides Tucker and, not by choice, Wren, I've purposely put my years at WU behind me. Except for my work with TeenCharter, of course.

In the distance, kayakers row across the sea, their oars streaking in a graceful arc before disappearing back into the water again. Behind them, Mount Otemanu rises majestically from the mainland, green and lush against the setting sun.

"Do you want another drink?"

I've barely touched the one I have. "No," I answer, the word sharp and quick.

Tucker takes another sip of his. "This is my chance, Poppy. My chance to meet people without…"

I wait for him to continue, finally prompting, "Without…"

"Without anyone from the office looking over my shoulder."

Why is Tucker meeting people he doesn't want anyone else to know about? I wonder, although that's not what I ask. "Who looks over your shoulder?"

A sound rumbles from his throat, like a strangled grunt. "Who doesn't? My father. Everyone else who wants to take his place, but knows they'll have to get rid of me first. It's like walking a goddamn tightrope every day."

I feel myself softening. It can't be easy for Tucker, always having to be perfect. It's why he wants me to be perfect, too. Image means everything to his parents and their friends. Maybe most of all to their rivals in the moneyed world of the Manhattan elite. The least I can do is be supportive. If he wants to go to Indonesia, I'll go too. With a smile.

I try one out now, turning to my new husband once it is steady on my face. "I guess I can manage a day or two without you."

But Tucker isn't looking at me. His phone is back in his hand. "I have a great idea." He taps the screen a few times and brings it to his ear. "Your sister is in-between jobs again, right?"

"Yeah, I think so." Sadie is always in-between something. Jobs, boyfriends, apartments.

"Sadie, hey. Did I wake you?" He pauses, chuckles. "This won't take long. What would you think about joining Poppy in Indonesia for a couple of days?"

I hear an answering screech, which I assume is a yes, and wait for her to ask the obvious question—why is she being invited to join her sister and her new brother-in-law on their honeymoon? But Sadie doesn't ask. "Great. My assistant will call you with the details."

He sets down the phone, a satisfied grin stretching across his lips. "Problem solved. She can fly down with Wren—"

"Wren needs to make her introductions personally?"

"I want her to. And Wren's closest friend from boarding

259

school is the daughter of one of the wealthiest men in Indonesia. It looks good for her to be here with me."

My eyes slide back to his phone, wishing I had the nerve to toss it into the Pacific Ocean. "Fine."

Something else occurs to me. "I didn't realize you had Sadie's contact info."

"You're my wife," Tucker says with a nonchalant shrug. "I have all of your contacts."

The hairs on the back of my neck stand on end. "You do?"

He rattles his glass, slivers of ice clinking against the sides. I stare at him, wondering if he's doing it so that I'll get up and refresh his drink. I remain motionless, waiting for an answer.

The sun dips lower, the shadow of the mountain falling over the kayakers. I know they are there, but I can barely see them anymore.

"Of course. I downloaded all of your information after we got engaged. I didn't tell you?" Tucker's handsome face shows not the slightest trace of remorse.

Is this normal? Do all husbands disregard their wife's privacy?

I have no idea. I've only been a wife for a few days. I don't even have any married friends to ask. My closest friend is my sister. Beyond that, I only have a few casual acquaintances through work. And it's not like I can reach out to Gavin. "No, you didn't," I say.

As if he knows where my thoughts have headed, a frown settles below Tucker's sunglasses. "Is there something you're trying to hide from me, Poppy?"

A thought scurries along the edges of my brain, making my palms damp. Did that *information* include the messages from Gavin I could never bring myself to erase?

I grip the edges of my chair, forcing myself to stand up. "No, Tucker. Nothing."

It's the truth. If he's accessed them, so be it. I cut ties with

Gavin before our wedding even though it nearly killed me to hurt him. Tucker has no right to expect more from me than that.

Though I'm sure Tucker would disagree. Since the day we met, he's taken over so much of my world that practically everything else has been edged out.

Even me.

CHAPTER 36

BALI, INDONESIA

HONEYMOON

*B*ali, Indonesia, is just as beautiful as Bora Bora. For
two days, while Tucker and Wren *work*, Sadie and I
swim and snorkel and scuba, then retreat to the spa to be
pampered like concubines. My skin is tan and glowing, and as
smooth as a newborn.

Tonight, though, we are together for a business dinner. There
are twelve of us around the table. Wren, Tucker, Sadie, and me, of
course. There are also four Indonesian men and their wives, or
maybe their mistresses. The men wear dark suits with flashy gold
Rolexes peeking out from immaculately tailored sleeves. The
women are in elaborate outfits of brightly colored, but mono-
chromatic, silks and sequins. Pink, purple, yellow, red. They sit
quietly, their faces frozen somewhere between surprise and
adoration, picking at their food without actually eating any of it.

A translator hovers nearby, although the men speak nearly
perfect English. The women don't say anything at all. They are
here purely as decorative ornaments, just as I am. We are merely

pawns, used to blunt the hard edges of a high-stakes business negotiation.

No alcohol is offered or served. And so far all talk at the table has been about burdensome government regulations, currency rates, and international trade. It's boring as hell.

I've attended dinners like this with Tucker before and have learned to keep my mind occupied while listening with half an ear in case anyone directs a question or comment my way. Sadie, though, isn't used to being ignored. I glance her way, and nearly laugh at the daggers she is shooting at Wren.

Sadie is at a disadvantage tonight. She left community college after a few semesters and has spent the years since jumping from one dead-end job to another. Meanwhile, Wren is sophisticated and cultured, comfortable discussing issues Sadie has never heard of. She is a party to this negotiation and when Wren speaks, Tucker and the other men at the table listen. Sadie is paying attention too, looking for an opening. Every so often, her lips part as if she's about to take the leap. But the moment passes, and she is left gulping down papaya juice as if it's wine.

Knowing she's attempting to fight a losing battle, I feel sorry for my sister. She is accustomed to men, including my husband, fawning all over her, all the time.

Tonight, however, Tucker is all business. Sadie and I, and the four beautiful, silent women seated across from us, are just window dressing. The only one who doesn't realize this, is Sadie.

She scoots her chair closer to me now, leaning into my ear. "How much longer, Pops? If I have to listen to Wren another minute, I'm going to scratch her eyes out."

I clamp my mouth shut before a giggle can escape. As if he heard it anyway, Tucker glares a warning at me. *Get your sister under control. Now.*

"Be good, Sadie," I whisper, reaching out to squeeze her hand below the table. "This is important to Tucker."

Wren looks our way, raising her voice like a teacher

addressing a misbehaving student without actually addressing him at all. "Before our evening comes to a close, I'm sure Tucker's wife and her sister would love the opportunity to view your recent acquisitions."

One of the men inclines his head, says something to the woman in yellow.

She nods her head in understanding and stands. "You will come with us," she says, addressing Sadie and me in perfect, unaccented English before taking diminutive steps away from the table. The rest of the rainbow jumps to their feet and scurries after her.

I look at Tucker for confirmation that we're expected to do the same, but he is looking at Wren, mouthing the words, *thank you*. I flush, hating that Wren is handling me for my own husband. And that he appreciates it. Appreciates her.

And then I hate myself. Because I merely grab Sadie's hand and follow.

Some battles aren't worth fighting.

CHAPTER 37

NEW YORK CITY

THREE YEARS LATER

"Where should we go for our anniversary next week?" Tucker asks as he comes back from the gym.

I rub the sleep from my eyes and sit up against our upholstered headboard. "Is that a trick question?"

For our first anniversary, Tucker surprised me with a trip to Iceland, to see the northern lights. It had been magical, standing beneath the otherworldly aurora borealis blazing across the sky like the most exquisite laser light show.

For our second, Tucker booked us a suite at an exclusive resort in Belize. We did nothing but lay by the ocean, visit the spa, and eat room service from our private terrace. It was heavenly.

And now, with our third anniversary coming up, I'd assumed Tucker would take the reins again.

He sits down at the edge of the mattress, his hair still damp from a shower, and grins at me. "Gotcha."

265

I laugh. "Can you at least tell me if I'm packing for warm weather or cold?"

My favorite version of Tucker is the one I'm treated to on most weekend mornings. Not that he sleeps in, ever, but he at least moves a little slower. After a 6:00 a.m. session with his personal trainer, Tucker swings by Starbucks to pick up my drink of choice, a Skinny Mocha—iced in the summer, hot in the winter.

He places it on my nightstand now, and I give an appreciative sniff. It's basically sugar-free hot chocolate with a few shots of espresso.

"No. One bag for cold, one for hot. You'll find out when we get there."

Arguing is pointless. Besides, I love that Tucker still enjoys planning special trips for me. And unlike our honeymoon, neither Wren nor Sadie have joined us on an anniversary trip. *Yet.*

"Okay, boss," I say teasingly, reaching for my paper cup. Once it's in my hand, I notice the scrawl of black sharpie on the side. *Decaf.* I groan. "Is the barista punishing me for something?"

"It's better if you give it up now, before the baby."

My breath catches in the back of my throat as I realize that Tucker specifically requested my drink without caffeine, and his reasoning for it. I scoot over so he can sit beside me. "Baby?"

I've never been the type to ooh and aah over infants, and the sight of one within the confined dimensions of a plane has me on pins and needles.

But lately, something has changed. Everywhere I look, women in cute maternity clothes are advertising their round bellies. Strollers surround me, bearing cherubic looking babies with apple cheeks and dimpled thighs. Just hearing a toddler's nasally *I wuv you* to their harried-looking mother sends a pang through my ovaries.

I've been hinting at starting a family to Tucker. Suggesting that our guest bedroom would make a perfect nursery, and mentioning every time someone in our building comes home from the hospital with a baby. But until now, I didn't think he'd noticed.

"That's what you want, isn't it?" Tucker places a hand on the flat plane of my stomach and gives me a gentle smile.

"More than anything."

In the past, I'd rolled my eyes at the term biological clock.

Until mine started ticking. All of a sudden, there was this noise, as even and regular as if it had been there forever. A sound from somewhere deep inside my body, or maybe buried within my brain. Like a heartbeat, but sharper. I hear it in my ears, feel it in the pit of my stomach.

We are young, but not *too* young, I think. And I want to bridge the gap between us that seems to defy definition. We are a couple, but not yet a family. A baby would make us a family.

My coffee forgotten, I throw my arms around Tucker's neck and pepper his face with kisses.

A baby! A little girl with my eyes and Tucker's smile. A little boy with my love of daydreaming and Tucker's athletic prowess. One, or maybe both. *Do I remember something about twins running in Tucker's family?*

One baby or two, I'm ready to become a mother. And Tucker will be a great father. A baby is just the thing to soften his hard edges.

My initial exuberance melts into languorous, loving tenderness. Tucker's palms find purchase in the curve of my hips and slide upward. A moan leaves my lips as his touch trails along the side of my breast, my nipples crying out for attention. But no, his hands are still moving, calloused fingertips dragging over my shoulders and along my neck until they side into my hair, his thumbs gently sweeping over my cheekbones.

Holding my face as if it's a precious thing, the *most* precious thing, Tucker pulls away from me. Just a couple of inches, far enough that I am staring into eyes that look like chocolate and cognac were swirled together in front of a fire. Delicious and intoxicating. A combination you're not quite sure you'll enjoy but quickly become addicted to.

"Are you ready to make the next generation of Stocktons?" Tucker is an acquired taste, and there are those who would say that he's acquired me. Maybe they're right.

But right now, I don't care about anything else but the liquid heat unraveling deep in my belly. I am warm and wanton, putty in my husband's hands.

"Yes, Tucker." My pelvis instinctively rocks forward.

He dips his head, his teeth nipping at the sensitive skin beneath my jaw, below my ear, then soothing the sting with gentle kisses. "Promise me one thing, Poppy."

"Anything."

"Promise I'll never lose you. Not to anyone, even our kids." He stops kissing me long enough to look deep into my eyes. "I couldn't bear it."

I remember that long ago New Year's Eve, our exchange in the lobby of the Plaza.

"When you came out of the elevator just now, you looked for me. And from the moment our eyes met, you never once looked away."

A half-laugh makes it up my throat. "Well, I don't— I don't know anyone here."

"True. But you're different than other girls who seem to travel in packs. Always surrounded by other girls. It's the first thing I noticed about you. Your... comfort at being alone."

Taking my silence as agreement, Tucker shakes his head, his lips curving into a soft smile. "You're very focused, Poppy. And I like when you focus on me."

Tucker needs to be reassured that he's still my priority. "You and me, Tucker. You and me against the world, okay?"

"I come first." It is both a demand and a question.

"You come first," I agree. My tone is firm, leaving no room for doubt.

His hands fall to my thighs, one wrapping around my waist, the other sliding toward the damp triangle of silk between my legs. The material is so thin; I shiver from his touch. "Fall apart for me," Tucker coaxes, increasing the pressure of his caress. Ribbons of pleasure unspool as I throw my head back, my eyes fluttering shut.

"Don't. Open your eyes. Look at me. Let me in, baby."

"Tucker," I groan, focusing on the adoration shining from his heavy-lidded gaze, letting it burrow deep inside my skin.

The sensual storm Tucker has created finally breaks, my body shaking and trembling as my release rolls through me. For Tucker, I fall apart. And then he gathers me gently in his arms, lays me out on our bed like a broken doll, and puts me back together again.

One kiss, one touch, one thrust at a time.

Later, after he's gone into the office, I take my birth control pills from the medicine cabinet in the bathroom. I have seven pills left for the month. One by one, I push them through the thin silver foil and let them drop into the toilet, each one so tiny, it doesn't even make a sound.

Returning to my bedroom, I open my laptop and order a year's supply of the best-selling pre-natal vitamins, shipping them overnight. And then I order a dozen baby books. *What to Expect When You're Expecting, The Pregnancy Journal, Belly Laughs, What to Eat When You're Expecting*, books on breastfeeding, on sleep-training (whatever that is), and several baby name books. And, at the last minute, just before checking out with my electronic shopping cart, I go back to get a few books on fertility. Just so I won't jinx myself by being overconfident.

But I'm sure I won't need them.

I've spent years trying *not* to get pregnant.

How hard can it be?

CHAPTER 38

NEW YORK CITY

ELEVEN MONTHS LATER

I step out of the shower and wipe the foggy mirror with my towel. Lifting my hands to my breasts, I eye their reflection critically. Are my nipples darker, even just slightly? Do they look bigger?

I think so... *yes?*

Shuttering my stare, I weigh them within my palms like fruit at a farmers market. Do they feel heavy? Sore? "Please," I whisper into the steamy, but otherwise empty, room. "Please let this be real."

I feel pregnant. Definitely.

It's been nearly a year since I flushed my birth control pills down the toilet. But every month, before the devastating pink tinge of the toilet paper takes away my hope, my excitement, I *always* feel pregnant.

When my period came that first month, and then the second and third, I'd been disappointed, but chalked it off to the lingering contraceptive chemicals still residing in my body, like unwanted houseguests. I bought a Vitamix and began blending smoothies bursting with kale and antioxidant-rich berries every morning. I switched from coffee to green tea. Caffeine free, of course. I joined a yoga studio.

I put an end to binging and purging, too. It hasn't been easy. There are times when I gnaw on ice chips just to satisfy the urge. But health has become my priority, not solely chasing after a number on a scale.

I didn't become pregnant the fourth or fifth months either. But again, I didn't think too much of it because of what happened with Tucker's parents. After apparently suffering a massive stroke while driving down the highway, Hewitt crashed into a construction zone. Tucker's mother was in the passenger seat. Cecelia died instantly, and his father died in the hospital two days later.

As their sole child and heir, Tucker instantly became the public face of Stockton Capital. He had to project confidence and calm, conveying to employees and clients that it was business as usual at the firm. I stepped in to plan the funeral service and memorial, familiarizing myself with the Stockton Family Foundation and their many charitable obligations.

But more months have slipped by, and I'm still not pregnant.

There are a few tests beneath the sink. I go so far as to open up the cabinet doors and check. Yes. There they are, a neat little stack of boxes. All three are digital, the rectangular indicator box taking away the guesswork of straight lines or plus signs. Either Pregnant, or Not Pregnant.

Should I? Maybe this time…

But instead of a positive test result, I envision only a bold-faced **Not Pregnant**. Again.

I turn away, deciding that, at least this morning, the frustration of not knowing is infinitely better than the crushing disappointment of seeing my failure spelled out in black and white. I can wait. Besides, I'm trying out a meditation class this morning that I overheard a woman in the elevator raving about—a woman with a swollen stomach.

I don't have a job to rush to anymore. I took a leave of absence when Tucker's parents died and had only been back a few weeks when Tucker got angry with me, pointing out that work stress could prevent me from getting pregnant. At first, I ignored him, thinking he was picking a fight with me as some kind of displaced grief over his parents. When that didn't succeed, I tried explaining. My job was important to me. I loved knowing I was making a difference in the lives of kids who had grown up just as I had—not knowing who to trust, feeling unloved and abandoned. Like they didn't matter.

"What about our kids?" he'd shot back angrily. "When are you going to make them a priority?"

"Let's at least put a pin in it until I get pregnant."

"A pin? A fucking pin? How long do you want to wait— No. How long are *you* going to make *me* wait for a family?" The unspoken was obvious. Losing both his parents in one fell swoop had rocked Tucker's world. He was untethered, and desperate for me to replace the family he'd lost.

I knew I was fighting a losing battle, but I wasn't ready to capitulate so quickly. I gave it another try. "Tucker, you know the kind of work I'm doing with TeenCharter. Don't you remember the kids we helped? Please, don't ask me to—"

"What I remember about TeenCharter is *you*. You were the reason I got involved, you were the reason I stuck with it. Those kids aren't my concern. I want kids of my own."

Tucker's caring, playful attitude with the at-risk teens was the reason I gave Tucker a second chance, and I chose to believe it was grief making him sound so heartless. "I do, too."

"Then prove it. Put your pin in TeenCharter and focus on *me*. On us, and the family we both want."

I didn't want to back down. But… was it really such a big ask to take a step back, temporarily? As much as I loved my work, I hated the strain it was putting on my marriage. It was obvious that Tucker needed me now, more than ever. After all he'd done for me, why wouldn't I do this for him? Shouldn't he and our future children be my sole focus?

But now, month after month of not becoming pregnant is a different kind of strain.

Every time I look into Tucker's eyes, knowing I've failed him, that my body has failed us both, is torture. Each pregnant belly I see is an accusation pointed my way. Cherubic infants and tiny toddlers are indictments of my worth.

There are days when it's hard to leave the apartment at all.

My phone rings with an unfamiliar number as I'm choking down a kale and avocado smoothie. I almost let it go straight to voice mail, pulled by the sudden impulse to take a test after all. Maybe I've miscalculated, maybe this is *the* month.

But I force my thumb over the screen. "Hello?"

The voice on the other end of the line is crisp, efficient. "Mrs. Stockton?"

"Yes?" I tuck the phone between my shoulder and ear as I rinse out the blender.

"This is Manhattan Fertility Solutions. You have an appointment with us next month?"

Next month will mark a full year of trying, and failing, to conceive. I made the appointment weeks ago, hoping I would already be pregnant by then. "Yes."

"The doctor will be attending a conference overseas regarding a recent breakthrough. I'm rescheduling all of her appointments that week. We have an opening this afternoon, are you available?"

This afternoon. Today.

No, it's too soon. It hasn't been a full year. I haven't even told Tucker that I've sought professional help. Haven't decided whether to tell him about it unless absolutely necessary, actually. But—how can I say no? "Sure. Yes, of course."

"All right, we'll see you at two o'clock."

I hang up and rush to my meditation class, although I probably shouldn't have bothered. My mind is a chaotic mess. *Should I interrupt Tucker at work to tell him about my appointment?* He hates when I call him during office hours, says he can't flip back and forth between hard-edged rainmaker to loving spouse at the drop of a hat.

But... shouldn't he know the effort I'm putting into creating our little family?

Ultimately, I decide against it. This is probably just an exploratory meeting. There's no reason to get Tucker involved. Yet, anyway.

I arrive at Manhattan Fertility Solutions early to fill out paperwork, plowing through the stack of forms secured to a clipboard as if I am being timed.

Once I hand everything back to the receptionist who, disappointingly, makes no comment on my remarkable form-filling prowess, I take a minute to look around. The designer could have been hired by Tucker's mother. Mid-century modern meets sanitarium. Neutral walls. White leather. Chrome and glass tables with sharp edges. Not child friendly in the slightest. And, oddly enough, there are no pictures of babies anywhere. Instead, the art is abstract and oversized, like enormous Rorschach inkblots on a white canvas. Nothing to indicate that this is a place that caters that in medical miracles. It could have been the waiting room of a psychiatrist, or the lobby of a venture capital firm. I feel cheated, craving visual proof of their successes.

"Mrs. Stockton?"

Vaulting off an Eames chair, I follow a woman dressed all in white, wondering if I should ask whether colors are reserved only for the fertile. Pastels for pregnant women and infants, bright primary colors for toddlers, neon for grade-school aged kids.

Five minutes later, I've peed into a cup, been weighed and measured, and am sitting, shivering, in a flimsy gown. A woman breezes into the room, small and thin with gorgeous black hair cascading to her shoulder blades in a smooth line. "I'm Vivian Lu. Thanks for coming in today, I'd like to examine you first, and then we can talk once you're dressed, all right?" she asks, the breathless rush of her words softened by an open, easy smile.

I like her right away. "Sure." I lie back, putting my feet in the stirrups and chanting nursery rhymes in my head as I'm poked and prodded.

"Okay, all set. You can get dressed and meet me in my office. It's the room right across the hall."

She is gone before I sit up. Anxiety cinches like a too-tight belt around my ribcage. She was very fast. Too fast. She must have found something. Some reason I will never get pregnant.

What will I tell Tucker? Failure, failure, failure.

There are several boxes of tissues in the exam room, and I go through the better part of one as I pull my clothes on and find Dr. Lu in her office, collapsing into a chair facing her desk.

"So, it's not often I say this to new clients at our first meeting…"

My face crumples. "Oh my God, I knew it. I'm never going to have a b—" I can't even get the word out of my clogged throat.

"No, no. Mrs. Stockton, please. That wasn't what I was going to say at all. Your urine sample registered high, but I wanted to confirm it with a physical exam." As I rub at my eyes with a fresh tissue, she announces what I've been waiting eleven months and a lifetime to hear. "You're pregnant."

CHAPTER 39

NEW YORK CITY

SIX MONTHS LATER

*S*tanding in the nursery of our new apartment, I rub my already bursting-at-the-seams belly. Today marks the start of my twenty-third week. Twins. A boy and a girl. I can't even believe it, and yet I can, because my babies will also be Tucker's babies, and that's just how he rolls. An overachiever, born into a charmed life.

My obstetrician uses a 4D sonogram machine on me at each appointment. Over the past few months, seeing their perfect faces, their tiny hands waving at me from an enormous flat screen monitor, I've connected with them in a way I never knew possible.

I became a mother from the minute I learned I was pregnant, but actually seeing my babies growing and thriving inside me… I'm already so in love with them it's overwhelming. I can barely wait for them to be born, to hold them in my arms and breathe in their delicious baby smell.

We moved out of our Tribeca loft last week. Not into his

family's stuffy brownstone, which he'd sold after receiving multiple offers the day their obituary was printed. We chose a four-bedroom high-rise overlooking Central Park. There is still plenty of white furniture, but there are no more sharp corners. It is a home for a family. The family Tucker and I are building, together.

I designed the nursery myself. It's not the biggest room, but it's closest to our master suite, and that is what matters most. Right now, my babies are such a part of me, I can't imagine being separated from them. In the beginning, their movements were the faintest caress of butterfly wings deep inside my belly, but now I can watch their limbs streak across my skin. Sometimes I swear they're having a one-on-one soccer match in there.

The rug beneath my bare feet is a thick pile, an Ikat pattern of white and khaki with just the palest hint of gray. I had the walls painted the exact color of the winter sky, just before it snows, and the wood trim is a glossy white. Two elegant cribs dominate the center of the room, beneath a chandelier that shoots prisms of light around the room like dazzling jewels. Window treatments—long gauzy panels and, of course, blackout shades behind them—are being installed this afternoon.

I haven't been back to Dr. Lu and her cold, quiet office. Once I stopped crying, she referred me to an obstetrician and since then, all of my appointments have gone smoothly.

Tucker is thrilled, although he's been so busy with work he's hardly around. And even when he's not in the office or on a business trip, work is always on his mind.

Tucker is determined to prove, to himself and everyone who doubted him, that he is up for the job. But the long shadow cast by Hewitt Stockton sometimes haunts my husband. Tucker barely sleeps, and when he does, he's so restless. I believe our babies will give him something to come home to, the same sense of stability I found in him. We will be a family.

"Isla, I'm meeting my sister to go shopping, you'll let—"

"Yes, yes. Of course, the drapery installers. I'll take care of it." Tucker hired Isla full time once I became pregnant. She coordinated our move and so much else. I only have to focus on growing two healthy babies and waiting for my belly button to pop, like the timer in a Thanksgiving turkey.

"Thank you." I shoot our housekeeper a grateful smile and grab my purse, deciding to walk the few blocks to the chic Madison Avenue shop that sells the most gorgeous baby clothes and crib bedding I've ever seen. Spending money on my babies doesn't bother me in the slightest, even though I still cannot walk into stores like Louis Vuitton and Gucci without a serious case of sticker shock. Nothing but the best for my Stockton twins.

I'm finally starting to feel good again, now that the morning sickness has subsided. Or, in my case, all day sickness.

Turning the corner onto Madison, I feel a twinge in my back. Maybe it wasn't such a smart idea to walk. But I've remained fairly active, despite the morning sickness and, well, twins. My yoga studio offers pre-natal classes and I'm a regular. Surely a fifteen-minute walk isn't too much?

But then, *Ouch*, there it is again. A little lower this time.

Spotting the familiar dove gray awning emblazoned with white lambs, I push through the door and head straight for the kidney-shaped sofa in the middle of the store. Amanda, the sales clerk with whom I have an appointment, comes right over. "Mrs. Stockton, so nice to see you. I have a few things set aside already, if you would like to come with me?"

"I think I just need a minute," I wheeze, rummaging in my bag for a bottle of water. "Shoot, I forgot—"

"Something to drink? Of course. Water? Or tea? We have green, iced, sweet, or non?"

Her words blur together. "Just water, please. Cold." I close my eyes, resting my head against the back of the couch.

"Here you go." Amanda returns moments later, holding a glass.

My hand shakes as I bring it to my mouth. Water has never tasted so good.

"Mrs. Stockton, I don't think you look very well. Can I call someone for you?"

"No need! I'm right here, sorry I'm late." Sadie breezes in, looking effortlessly pretty in a crisp black top and frayed skinny jeans, a messenger bag slung across her body and oversized sunglasses perched atop her head.

With my mom doing well, she moved to the city from Sackett a few months ago, around the time I found out I was pregnant. I'm glad to have Sadie close. With Tucker so busy at work, my sister has been an absolute godsend. She's been staying in our guest bedroom for the time being, working odd jobs and looking for an apartment. Tucker and I have both offered to help her get on her feet, but selfishly I love knowing she's just down the hall, especially when Tucker's away. And her erratic hours make it easy for her to join me at doctor's appointments and shopping for the babies.

I finish the last of my water and hold out the glass to Amanda. I feel better now. "Hey, sis. I must be turning into a whale. I'm winded just walking here."

She reaches out her hand. "Come on, you've barely crossed the half-way point, it's too soon to be playing the prego card."

I force a laugh and let her help me up. Sadie is right. Twenty-three weeks is too early to become a couch potato, even with twins. Back on my feet, I take a deep breath. "Okay, let's start with bedding. The cribs are all set up and I'd like—" Suddenly, there is a strange, twisting pain deep inside my stomach and warmth rushes down my pants.

Oh my God, have I wet myself? I'll never be able to show my face in this store again.

Then I see their faces, looking first at Sadie and then to Amanda. Identical expressions of horror. I peer down. There is a puddle leeching into the white rug at my feet, and my pants are wet. Glancing back at the gorgeous gray silk couch, I breathe a relieved sigh, thankful that at least that has been spared. And that's when it hits me. Something is wrong. Very wrong. My eyes are drawn back to the rug—the very white rug with a distinctively pinkish puddle. Oh, dear God. No. No, no, no.

Sadie is the first to speak, turning to Amanda. "Get us a cab. Now." Amanda sprints outside as Sadie takes my arm, guiding me though the store and out the front door. A yellow taxi screeches to a halt at the curb and we get in. Sadie barks the name of the nearest hospital to the driver, and I take one last look at the white lambs happily prancing across the store's elegant gray awning before we pull away.

"Just breathe, Poppy. Everything's going to be okay. I promise." Sadie is jabbing at the screen of her phone, and I know she's trying to reach Tucker. I wrap my hands around my belly, telling myself that Sadie is right. Everything is going to be just fine. It has to be. These babies are Tucker's, too.

Of course, they will be fine. Better than just fine, actually. They will be perfect.

CHAPTER 40

NEW YORK CITY

THREE HOURS LATER

he words of a doctor I've never met until today wash over me, leaving a filthy grime.

My son is dead.

According to him, my baby boy was dead when I walked from my apartment to the Madison Avenue store, had probably been dead for several days. Dead, and I didn't know it.

If what he's saying is true, it means that I stood in the nursery this morning, supervising the delivery of the cribs and changing table and dresser. That I'd sat in the rocking chair with my hands over my belly, humming nursery rhymes and envisioning the day I would bring my babies home and put them to my breasts, knowing everything was just as it should be.

But it wasn't. It isn't.

Today, nothing is as it should be. *Nothing.*

My son is dead.

My daughter, though, is very much alive. Through a flat screen hung on the wall of my hospital room, I watch her squirming inside me as tears streak down my face. Does she know, somehow, that her brother is dead? I try to read her expression, looking for signs of distress that her playmate isn't playing with her anymore. My vision is so blurred, I can barely see.

There are tests, tests, and more tests. Hushed whispering by doctors, strained expressions from sonogram technicians, pitying glances from nurses. *Save my daughter, please.*

"I'm afraid there's an infection in your uterus, Mrs. Stockton."

"An infection," I repeat, a tiny pinprick of hope piercing the layers of anguish pressing against me. An infection can be treated. An infection can be cured

"How did she get an infection?" Tucker asks, standing by my side. "My wife hasn't missed a single doctor's appointment. She is getting the best care money can buy."

"Unfortunately, there's no way of knowing. There are some mysteries medicine can't solve."

"What do you know?"

"Well, I believe the infection is what led to fetus A's death. His placenta ruptured this morning, which is what preceded your wife's trip to the hospital today. It was her body's way of attempting to expel the fetus."

I wince at the clinical terms he's using to describe my perfect little boy, now frozen and unmoving inside of me. He looks like he's sleeping. "What does this mean for my daughter?" *Cut me open, do anything you need to, but please, save my daughter.*

"Your daughter is only nine ounces. She has less than a ten percent chance of survival outside of the womb, and a zero percent chance of living without major health problems. If we don't treat this infection immediately, your uterus will be compromised, which will mean a hysterectomy. And if the infection spreads, the toxins will invade your bloodstream. You will die, Mrs. Stockton."

"How long?" I ask, gripping Tucker's hand.

"How long... ?" There are too many variables, the doctor doesn't know what question I'm asking. How could he? He's not a mother.

Through gritted teeth I complete my thought. "How long must my baby girl stay inside of me to have a fighting chance?"

His face twists with impatience. He's tired of my questions and is eager to treat the problem. "By the time she has a chance, you will be dead."

No. No, no, no.

I would trade my life for my daughter's in a heartbeat. But that isn't an option. She can't live outside my body, and if I delay treatment, neither of us will live.

So, no chance. No options. And no time.

After that, I don't have any more questions. Just grief.

Grief for my son, floating inside my belly like a fossil suspended in amber. Grief for my daughter who is still so alive—beautifully, gloriously *alive*, but for whom death is imminent and inevitable.

She is swinging her hands, kicking her feet, bumping into her brother. Sometimes it appears that he is moving, too. But the sepia flutter of his heart is still. So fucking still.

I want to turn away, to close my eyes and hide my head. But I don't. I force myself to watch every last second I have left with my babies. I barely allow myself to blink, needing to sear the memory of them into my brain.

I am numb, and yet electrified with heartache. It's a roar in my skull as I listen to the doctor speaking to Tucker. Nothing to be done, he says, except to suction and scrape every last bit of my babies from me so that I can start over.

Suction. Scrape. Start over.

Foreign, awful, chilling words. I want to put my hands over my ears and scream *fa, la, la, la, la* until the doctors and nurses stop talking. More than that, I want to will myself back in time, to the last minute I felt both babies move inside me. When was that, exactly?

Panic rises up inside me, hot as lava. When was the last time I could feel both of them? Their final soccer match. When? *Think, think.* If I can just remember, I can will myself back to that moment. *Think hard, damn it.* Immerse myself in that last, perfect moment and everything else will fade away, like a terrible nightmare. Because this can't be real, it just can't.

Think, damn it. Think!

And then I remember. Two nights ago, in bed. Tucker was home and he'd rolled over in his sleep, jostling me. His arm had closed around my hip, and I'd pulled it over my belly, pressing his palm against my skin. Our children had danced then, in our darkened bedroom, high above the racing cabs and dirty streets of Manhattan. My little prince and princess.

Their movements thrummed beneath my belly, and Tucker had been roused from sleep when dancing became kicking. He'd moaned, kissing my shoulder and rubbing my belly drowsily. "Go to sleep, babies," he had whispered. They listened, growing quiet soon after.

And I had lain awake for hours, imagining future dance recitals and soccer games. Park playdates. Ice cream cones on sweltering summer days, hot chocolate on bitterly cold ones. Potty training and training wheels. Boo-boo bunnies and Tonka trucks. *Love.*

So much to look forward to.

I want to go back in time. Two days. I wouldn't have let Tucker tell them to go to sleep. No. I would have drank orange juice and lain on my left side. I would have let them play soccer forever.

Two days. Is that really too much to ask? Just two days. I'll stay in bed. I won't move. I'll spend the next few months eating the healthiest foods.

I will be the best mother-to-be ever. A perfect incubator.

Two goddamn days. Please!

"Poppy, look at me." Tucker's breath is hot on my face. I turn away, rolling over and curling my knees up to protect my belly. He's ruining everything. I need to focus. Need to concentrate on that magical hour. I can get back there, I know it.

But his hand is on my shoulder, he is shaking me. "Poppy, enough. Let the doctor take care of you."

"Forget about me. He should be taking care of *them*. The next generation of Stocktons, remember?" I am begging, desperate. Emotions charge at me, thudding in my chest. Fury and fear held together by the thinnest thread of hope. "Tucker, make him understand. We have to save them—don't you understand? They're why we're together. They make *us* make sense."

But I can see that Tucker doesn't understand. He buried both his parents and was back at work the next day. We don't process grief the same way. Is he hurting at all?

Tucker takes a long, ragged breath and for a moment, it's as if I'm looking at a rainy puddle that reflects the sky above, and there is an instant of confusion. Up is down and down is up. What am I looking at—the puddle or the sky? What's real?

"They're gone, Poppy. There's nothing anyone can do. Not you, not me, not any of these doctors." He roughs a hand through his hair, leaving it messy. "Let's just get this over with."

I wince at my husband's artless, and unnecessarily cruel, candor. "Get this over...?"

I have one choice left. One final act that cannot be taken from me. I shift my stare to the doctor. "I want to deliver them."

He draws back. "Mrs. Stockton, that is highly unusual. We can put you under anesthesia right now. When you wake up it will all be over."

I shake my head, my voice a screech. "No. You're not cutting my babies apart and sucking them out of me like garbage."

Every part of me aches for my little boy and girl. There are no pink tutus or soccer balls in their future. *They have no future.*

I will never rub my cheek against their downy, baby-soft skin, give them a bath, or see their smiles on Christmas morning.

I will never hear the sound of their laughter.

The doctor backs away, his face a mask of disapproval that is mirrored by my husband. He starts to protest further, but the pure fury coursing through my veins daunts even him. "Don't you take this from me," I howl. "Don't you dare."

A needle is filled with potassium chloride—the same concoction given to prisoners on death row—and inserted through my stomach. I hurt so much that the physical pain is a welcome reprieve. They are using a sonogram to aim the needle, and I watch it move through the amniotic fluid towards my daughter's translucent skin. In my head, I'm screaming at her, begging her to move, to run, to escape.

But she can't, she's trapped inside of me. Held captive *by* me. As the tip of the needle punctures her placenta, delivering its lethal dose, she extends her arms wide embracing her brother.

It's as if she knows. As if she is seeking comfort from him. Comfort I cannot give her. Because I am killing her.

I might not be holding the needle, but I'm not stopping it.

Her teeny-tiny heart is still visible through her translucent skin. Its flutter slows, becoming weaker and more imperceptible until finally, my baby girl's heart stops altogether.

I watch my daughter die.

In no time at all, she is as still and lifeless as my son.

Two frozen dolls inside my infected womb.

I'm taken to another room, hooked up to a Pitocin drip. An anesthesiologist offers an epidural, which I refuse even as the contractions take my breath away. Each sharp slice of pain brings me closer to holding my babies. I need to see them, touch them, feel their weight in my arms.

It is hours before I am fully dilated. Hours of coiling, crushing, unrelenting agony I don't actually want to end. Once the pain ends, I won't be pregnant anymore.

Not pregnant. But not a mother. At least, not defined as a verb. I will never *mother* my children. I will never nag them or praise them. I will never build sandcastles on the beach with them.

I will never pin their artwork on the refrigerator.

I will do exactly one thing for my babies. I will bury them.

Is there a word for what I am, what I'm experiencing?

Tucker's determined gaze clashes with my turbulent one. He wants this over. I have failed him and he wants to put the proof of it behind him as soon as possible. "You're doing great," Tucker says, holding my hand as I pant and push, trying to will my body into compliance.

I want to slap him. *Great?* Not even close.

I'm in labor but I'm not giving birth. *What the hell am I doing?*

Our children finally slide out of me. Tiny and still and silent. Dead.

A nurse cleans them and wraps them in blankets, placing them gently in my arms before leaving the room.

My boy is bigger than his sister and looks like just Tucker. My little girl looks like me. Their hair is wispy, their eyelids as thin as rose petals, their lips puckered as if there are about to suckle at my breast. They are sleeping angels. Perfect in every way, but one.

They are not breathing, and they never will.

Angels, here on earth.

Tucker doesn't want to hold them, although eventually he reaches out a finger to brush a cheek, touch a delicate ear. He makes a sound, low in his throat, swallowing down a sob. I glance up at him, and for the briefest moment, his grief and fury are exposed for me to see.

It's the first time since the doctor explained what happened with our son, and what we had to do to our daughter, that I've felt in step with Tucker. The first time I see that he is in mourning, too.

Outside the window, the sun meets the horizon, flooding the room in a dreamy, gauzy gold that blurs the edges of Tucker's profile and drenches my babies in light. I blink once, twice, and the room is dim again.

But I feel a wrenching pain, a pulling away. As if the souls of my children have left on that sweeping sunbeam.

Too soon, the nurse returns. She takes my son and my daughter from my arms.

And then I scream. I scream and I scream and I scream. A tortured wail that doesn't sound like it belongs to a human. I am on fire from the inside out, my nerve endings flayed open and exposed. Toxic lava flowing from my broken heart to incinerate my organs and blood vessels, my bones and skin.

But this sound, this anguished scream, it belongs to me. I can't stop screaming. Maybe I never will.

CHAPTER 41

NEW YORK CITY

TWO MONTHS LATER

I've never been so empty in all my life. My body is a vacant, vacuous cavity I can hardly stand to inhabit. My heart is an aching void that beats for no reason, every dull thud a betrayal of the two hearts that don't.

Our glamorous penthouse apartment is nothing but a shell. Because, really, what is it holding? Grief.

Tucker is gone all the time now. Working, traveling, schmoozing. Maybe he's even fucking Wren, too, because he's sure as hell not fucking me. I cannot bear to be touched. Not by him, not by anyone.

I want to laugh, nearly as much as I want to cry. Now that I'm empty inside, have I truly lost Tucker to Wren? We've known each other for nearly a decade now, but I've never considered Wren my friend. Frenemy, maybe. Nemesis is probably a more accurate description.

She would be only too happy to comfort him with open arms.

And her pale, slender thighs with their gap in between when she stands up straight. Every bite of food I haven't eaten, every bite I've thrown up over the years has been because of that gap.

Is that what I've spent so many years chasing? The empty space between Wren's perfectly long, lean legs?

The joke is on me, I guess. I have no interest in food anymore. Not even to binge and purge. It's been a long time since I put a finger down my throat, forcing myself to give up all the things I'd swallowed. Not since I began trying to conceive. This cycle has followed me, I guess. Full, then empty. I am empty now. So empty I don't care if Tucker is having an affair with Wren. She can have him.

All the years I've spent, trying so hard to be the perfect girl-friend, the perfect fiancée, the perfect wife. Now look at me. My empty stomach is no longer as flat and firm as it once was. Stretch marks mar my hips. My hair is greasy and my roots are showing. And my clothes are the same ones I put on after getting home from the hospital and have barely taken off in the weeks since.

I'm an exile from Stepford.

All I want is to be a mother. Even an imperfect one.

Sadie has stopped looking for an apartment of her own, and she's here more often than Tucker. Isla, too, although at least she knows to leave me alone. Sadie, not so much. She is constantly pestering me to take a shower, go for a walk, get some fresh air. Even Wren has taken advantage of the opportunity to come over, to see me at my worst. Oh, she says all the appropriate things, even schools her face into an expression of sympathy. But I know what she's really doing. On the inside, she's gloating. She's saying to herself, *I was right all along. Tucker should have never chosen you over me.*

And maybe she's right.

Wren aside, I don't mind when Sadie and Isla coddle Tucker. These days, I'm certainly not. Sadie is now the one he shares the

Sunday *New York Times* with, handing her the style section while he pores over everything else. And Isla hovers nearby whenever Tucker eats the meals she prepares for him, jumping up to grate fresh pepper over his food or refresh his drink before he can even ask.

I don't want to look at Tucker, let alone cater to him. I don't want to do much at all, actually. I am exhausted just brushing my teeth in the morning, and brushing my hair seems pointless. Why? I'm not going anywhere. The world outside these walls is chaotic, dangerous.

I might never go anywhere, ever again.

Mostly, I sit in my babies' room, in their rocking chair. The drapery panels and blackout shades were installed, probably at the very moment I learned my son was dead and my daughter would be soon.

Offensive sunlight streams through the windows because I'm afraid to pull the shades. I'm afraid to touch anything, actually. Because if I do, I might just keep pulling and pulling. And then I might knock over the never-used furniture, tear apart the cribs, smash the chandelier, rip up the rug.

There is so much rage inside my body I don't know how it hasn't boiled over and consumed me. I am a lobster in a pot, cooking and cooking and cooking. When the water finally evaporates, all that will be left of me is a shell.

I hate Tucker. I hate him.

He brought me here, into his perfect life. And I fell for his trap. He is Tucker Stockton, how could he not have super sperm? I married into his family, knowing our children would be winners of the ultimate DNA lottery.

But I was duped, that dream was a hoax. A mirage.

My body is empty, my husband feels like an enemy, and I am sitting in a room I decorated for two babies who aren't alive to see it.

I think back to all the moments when I should have seen

Tucker for who he really is—a mean, manipulative, controlling son of a bitch who has *ruined* my life.

There is his *mistake*, of course. Our original sin.

And then Tucker stepped in when I lost my scholarship. Later, once I was financially indebted to him—he compounded the fact by putting my mom in the most expensive rehab facility in New England. I know, because the bills came to me... so that every month I had to go to Tucker with my hand out.

Tucker bought me clothes that were too small, so I had to agonize over every calorie.

He hacked into my phone. And by then, I didn't even put up a fight. I just accepted it, as if I didn't deserve a shred of privacy.

Just like I accepted Wren joining us on our honeymoon and practically being a third person in our marriage.

Tucker convinced me to quit a job I loved.

Because of him, I gave up any hope of reconnecting with Gavin. And the worst part about that is that I can't even blame Tucker entirely. I allowed myself to believe in the fantasy world he invited me into. I wanted to, so damn badly. And that's my fault. I was so naïve. So stupid.

But my eyes are wide open now, the veil swept aside. I've been thinking about *that night* again. Going over and over every detail in my head. And all those feelings, all those emotions I pushed down have risen to the surface. They are choking me.

I wouldn't admit it back then, not even to myself, but I know it now. This is what it feels like to be raped.

God, I wish I was dead.

Almost as much as I wish Tucker was.

The only thing keeping me alive is the hatred running through my veins.

So I sit in the beautifully upholstered chair inside my quiet nursery with two empty cribs and walls the color of the winter sky, lit by sunshine and a dazzling crystal chandelier.

I rock and I rock and I rock.
And, one day, I will have my revenge.

PART III

CHAPTER 42

FLORIDA

FIVE MONTHS LATER, PRESENT DAY

I wake to the sound of silence. Well, almost. Hospitals are never quiet, but the low hum of activity beyond my door is infinitely preferable to the riot of beeping and buzzing from earlier. Cautiously, I open my eyes. The room is less bright than before, just a hazy glimmer of late afternoon sunlight filtering through the window. Sadie is curled up in a chair tucked into the corner. For a brief moment, the sight of my sister cheers me. But it also makes me realize who isn't here. *Tucker.*

Where is my husband?

I open my mouth to call out to Sadie but stop short. I don't want to wake her.

Tucker is probably working. Like always.

The blood in my veins is thick with irritation. Things haven't been good between us since the last time I was admitted to a hospital—the day we lost the lives we'd created together. And every breath of ammonia-scented air, every crackling page of the

297

intercom, every check of my vitals and *beep* of a health monitor makes me ache for the perfectly formed babies I'd held for mere moments. Babies that didn't cry or fuss. Babies that didn't breathe.

Tucker and I are still married though. Not in any real sense, but legally. The least he could do is make an appearance at my bedside.

Releasing a quiet sigh, I attempt to crawl back into an unconscious cocoon for another few hours. But it's no use. My head is pounding, half the skin on my body feels as if it's been flayed open, and closing my eyes only makes it worse. And there's something else gnawing at me. Something Sadie said, just before the drugs injected into my IV took effect.

Something about…

The thought disappears before it's fully formed, like fog evaporating inside my fist. I swallow a howl of frustration, resenting both my injuries and the treatment necessary to heal them. If I can't rely on my own mind, what else is there?

I reach for the television remote control on top of the chest beside my bed. If I was in an accident, maybe there will be a report of it on the local news.

I hold my breath as the screen comes to life, quickly muting the volume before scrolling through channels. Weather. CNN. Infomercial. Infomercial. Cartoon. Infomercial. Tucker. Sports Center. Infomercial.

Wait—what?

I jab at the down arrow of the remote.

Suddenly my husband's face fills the screen. Coolly appraising stare, strong nose, perpetually boyish grin. Not a hair out of place.

Really? Tucker's pandering to the media while I'm in a hospital bed?

But… that doesn't make sense. Although he's given the occasional interview to a financial news network, Tucker has never exploited his personal life to get on TV. Since his parent's death especially, he's preferred to keep a low profile and focus solely on work.

And then I notice the word beneath his face, covering the knot of his tie. Bright red letters, all caps.

MISSING

My chest squeezes as I immediately turn on the volume, needing to know more. Roused from sleep, Sadie pops her head up. "You okay?" she asks, clutching the arm of her chair for support and pulling herself upright.

I point a finger at the screen but I'm too late. Tucker's face has been replaced with a commercial for constipation laxatives. A sense of foreboding leaches into my bloodstream as I turn toward my sister. "What happened to Tucker?"

"I'll bet you're thirsty," she says, bouncing over to the table holding stacked plastic cups and a pitcher of water. "Let me pour you a drink first."

I gratefully suck it down before wrapping my fingers around Sadie's bird-like wrist. "For God's sake, stop protecting me. I need to know. What is going on?"

"You really don't remember?"

My head hurts too much to try. "No, I don't."

"Really?" Her lips purse. "Nothing?"

I thrust the remote control at Sadie. "Turn it off, please." The volume is on and the flickering screen over her shoulder is making me nauseous.

She does and I take a moment to appreciate the sudden, blissful quiet before refocusing my attention on my sister. "Nothing that explains why I'm in a hospital, or how I got hurt. If I did, I would tell you."

There is a hint of doubt in her familiar eyes, shadows that make me wonder whether the secrets I've kept from her over the years are really so secret after all.

Eventually, she blinks. "He's gone."

"Gone," I repeat, choking on a gasp. "What do you mean,

gone? Where did he go? Was there an accident? Is he—" I swallow
the word on the tip of my tongue just as the one Sadie used just
after I first woke up pushes its way back to the forefront of my
mind. *Murder.*

Oh my God. Is Tucker *dead?*

But, like a balloon popping, I recall not just the word she used,
but the context in which she'd used it. *No one is going to accuse my
sister of murder until...*

I turn a horrified gaze on Sadie. My sister has been my rock
for months, rarely leaving my side since the last time I'd been
admitted to a hospital. She knows, more than anyone, how bad
things have gotten between Tucker and me. How angry I've been.
"Were you— Did I— I couldn't..."

I don't even bother finishing my third attempt at a sentence,
because the truth is, *I could.*

Since the day I gave birth—or death, as I often think of it—
I've fantasized about killing Tucker a million times, in a million
ways.

But now, facing it as an actual possibility, I feel only horror
and sadness. Horror that I may have taken a life when I know
exactly how precious each breath is. And sadness that Tucker
might really be gone. For all his faults, and there are many, I
loved him once. Deeply.

"Don't, Poppy." Sadie is pale, her voice high-pitched with
strain. "The doctor says you hit your head, badly. And that you
may never recover your memory of the actual incident. If you
push yourself, you'll only get another headache."

I grab at the hand resting on her hip. "I need to remember
what happened." She tries pulling away but I hold firm. "Please,
help me."

My sister flicks a tongue over her lips, and I catch a slight
tremble in her chin. Even after all these years, we still could pass
for twins. Her hair is slightly lighter than mine, and her eyes

more hazel than green. Beyond our looks though, we are a study in opposites.

And we're at opposite sides of this argument now. "Poppy, I don't think you should try to remember. Can't you just leave it?"

"Leave it—are you kidding me? How can I?"

I loosen my grip and Sadie takes advantage, stepping back. She gnaws at her lower lip, deciding how to handle my questions.

I hate waiting, hate being dependent on my younger sister for information, but I keep myself in check. If I push, Sadie will clam up and I'll get nothing at all.

In the end though, that's exactly what she gives me. "Can't you see? If you don't remember anything, then the burden of proof is on the police. The less you remember, the better."

CHAPTER 43

FLORIDA

I'm pulled from sleep by a prickling sensation at the back of my neck. There is a crispness in the room that reminds me of fall. An odd, unsettling awareness of old things ending and new things beginning that, for the moment, are jumbled together.

Almost… an intuitive sense of wrongness.

Outside it is dark, the lights overhead dimmed. It must be the middle of the night. My attention slides to the chair in the corner, expecting to see Sadie curled into a ball, dozing, even though I'd told her to go back to the hotel and get a decent night's sleep in a real bed.

But it's not my sister in the room with me. And the man in a dark suit with blazing blue eyes certainly isn't sleeping.

"Gavin?" Confusion rattles inside my head like an iron chain. *There is an FBI Agent waiting outside. Special Agent Gavin Cross. He said you know him.* "What are you doing here?"

"Hey." Gavin stands up quickly, his hand closing around mine, the sweep of his thumb over my wrist like the stroke of a magic wand, taking me back in time. Back to our enchanted forest, back into the arms of a boy I loved with my whole heart.

So much has happened since then. I'm not prepared for the onslaught of memories and emotions, all of them trampling over raw, exposed nerves that are flayed open by too much hurt, too much heartache.

"Gavin." I say his name again as tears overflow my lashes, running in sheets down my face. He doesn't hesitate, gently gathering me into his arms and holding me to his chest. My sobs are soundless, the kind that break from my body in a torrent of release. My tears drench my skin and his shirt and the skin beneath his shirt. And still they keep flowing, like a tidal wave of grief and fear and shame and even love that keeps crashing over my head, ripping through my body.

I don't know how long I cry, how long Gavin holds me, whispering nonsensical words into my hair, gently rocking me in his embrace. It feels like days have passed before my tears slow and finally cease altogether, before I draw a breath that's not just a hiccup of air. "Oh God, I'm so sorry," I finally say, my throat hollow and raw.

But Gavin just looks down at me, his expression tender. "Does that mean I have to let go of you?"

I give a little shake of my head. "Please don't."

He presses a kiss to my very damp temple. "Then I won't."

We fidget with the buttons of the hospital bed until it's almost like an extra-wide La-Z-Boy recliner and he can squeeze in beside me. The atmosphere of the room is oppressive, weighed down by our past and my present, heavy with hidden memories, unspoken truths, and overlooked lies.

I don't even know where to start, so after a few moments of strained silence, I reach for the lowest hanging fruit. "So, you're an FBI agent now?"

"I am," he says, flashing that crooked grin I remember so well. "Financial Crimes Unit."

A thought crouches in the back of my mind for a split second before leaping off my tongue. "You're investigating Tucker."

It's not a question, and it doesn't even make any sense. Why would my husband be the subject of an FBI investigation? But Gavin nods. "Some of the business practices he implemented at Stockton Capital raised a red flag. We opened a case file on him and I asked to be assigned to it."

The last time I saw Gavin was the week before my wedding, five years ago. Is he here because of me, or Tucker? Because of Tucker's crimes, or his disappearance? "And that's… That's why you're here now?"

He pushes out a deep sigh. "It's *how* I knew to be here, but not *why* I'm here."

I nod, although I'm not entirely sure what he means. "Am I in trouble?" I whisper, keeping my question deliberately vague.

"Not unless you were involved in your husband's money laundering operation."

Serves me right for not getting to the point.

What I really want to know, and I'm too afraid to ask, is whether Gavin suspects, or has any proof, that I've done something a hell of a lot worse than conspiring with my husband to commit white-collar crimes. I pluck at the tape securing my IV to the back of my wrist, deciding I'm in no rush to confirm my worst suspicions. Maybe, if I beat around the bush long enough, I'll have an answer. Or maybe, like Sadie said, I'm better off not knowing. "Tucker was really laundering money?"

"Yes."

"I've been watching the news reports. There's been no mention of that."

"We haven't released anything publicly yet."

"So, you know more than what they're saying on TV."

"About your husband and his business, yes. The incident that put you in here is still under investigation."

Fear digs sharp knuckles into my ribs. "*What incident?* I don't remember anything. I tried to get Sadie to help me, but she said it's best if I *don't* remember."

Gavin's tone is gentle, his stare compassionate. "First, answer me this. If I'm here in an official capacity as an FBI agent, is there anything that you wouldn't, or couldn't, tell me?"

"What do you mean?"

"The charges against your husband are serious. And now, with the suspicions surrounding his disappearance—"

"What suspicions?"

"That it was staged. That he's not dead but in hiding, somewhere without an extradition treaty, living off his stolen millions."

I gulp at air. Gavin isn't here because he believes I've killed Tucker. He's here because he thinks I know where Tucker is.

If he's right... *Tucker is alive.*

I didn't kill him.

My head is pounding with this new information. These broken bits of knowledge I have to assemble into a coherent whole.

Tucker is alive... I didn't kill him... He somehow staged his disappearance to evade criminal charges... And left me behind, holding the bag.

What. The. Fuck.

It sounds crazy. And ridiculous. Like the plot of a bad movie. And yet... it doesn't feel wrong.

"So, I'm here," I gesture wildly at my IV and bandages and machines, "trussed up like a mummy while Tucker's living it up in the tropics, sipping mai tais? Is that what you're saying?"

"Calm down," he urges, which only inflames my temper more.

"Really? That's the best advice you've got? How about we switch places, and every time you ask a question someone either tells you to stop asking or drugs you so that you can't— Why are you looking at me like that?"

"Because you're going to be okay." Gavin's grin brightens as he reaches for my face, cupping it reverently between his palms. "I was so fucking scared, Poppy. But now... Now I know you're

305

going to be just fine. Everything else, *everything* else, we can handle, okay? But I really needed to see that spark to know for sure."

My small burst of energy and irritation burns away quickly and I collapse against his chest, exhaustion settling over me as the steady thrum of Gavin's heart beats beneath my cheek. "I've missed you," I murmur, the words so soft they're barely more than a shuddering exhale.

He presses a kiss to the top of my head. "Yeah. Me, too."

We fall silent for a while, each of us lost in our own heads. I'm almost asleep when he asks, "Does he make you happy?" There's an underlying note of reluctance in Gavin's voice, like every syllable was a painful effort.

I answer honestly. "He did. I thought he did, anyway. But not —" Pain clutches at my heart when I think about my babies. "Not for a while."

"But this trip, it was to celebrate your anniversary?"

"Celebrate... no." There's no reason to hide the truth from Gavin. "Things were over between us. It was really just a matter of filing for divorce to make it official."

"The decision was mutual?"

"I don't—" I rub at my throbbing temples. I may have wanted to kill Tucker, but eventually I would have come to my senses and done what rational adults do—hire a lawyer and move on with my life. Right? "I don't know."

"Okay." Gavin seems to sense my inner turmoil, shifting our position so that we're facing each other. "Let's back up. You remember flying down to Miami?"

"Yes."

"Do you remember where you stayed?"

"The Delano." There had been reporters broadcasting in front of the iconic oceanfront hotel.

"But do you *remember* it."

I close my eyes and concentrate. After a moment, I feel a blast of heat on my face, the taste of coconut rum thick on my tongue. "Yes. I remember having drinks there, by the pool."

"With Tucker?"

"Yes."

"What else?"

"We just stayed the one night. And then we drove…" My words fade as I recall getting into a car beside Tucker, a white Mercedes convertible, feeling like Grace Kelly with a scarf over my head and oversized sunglasses covering half my face.

Images rush at me, so many of them it feels like my head is going to burst. Mirrored aviators obscuring Tucker's eyes. A cloudless blue sky above an azure sea. Boats, hundreds of them. Then one in particular—an enormous, gleaming yacht, its flag silhouetted against the bright sky, hull riding high in the water. An immaculately dressed crew of eight lined up to welcome us.

I feel the gentle sway of the sea, relaxing and exhilarating all at once. The waxy surface of the gleaming teak deck beneath my bare feet.

"I remember the marina. I remember boarding the yacht and casting off. We sailed toward the Keys."

"He was an experienced sailor?"

I open my eyes. "Tucker learned to sail as a kid, I believe. His parents kept a boat at the Greenwich Yacht Club, in Connecticut. But the yacht came with a crew. Tucker didn't captain it."

"Can you remember if Tucker left the yacht at all? Did you go scuba diving together? Or explore the islands on your own, away from the crew?"

I take a quick breath and look away from Gavin, burrowing inside my jumble of memories to recapture a distinct memory of Tucker and me, together.

But it's like trying to punch through a veil as it dances in the wind. I'm only getting tangled up inside my own mind. Everything is blurry and confusing.

Not exactly everything. The emotion flickering to life inside me is the same one that has characterized much of the past nine months. *Betrayal.*

The thing about betrayal is that it has the strength to pervert logic, to turn rational people into zealots. Is that what happened between Tucker and I, in the warm waters just off the Florida Keys? Did I act to end our marriage, not by divorce, but by death?

"I'm really tired," I say, lifting my head and pushing myself back a few inches, needing some time to process my thoughts. And Sadie could come back at any minute—how could I possibly explain being cuddled up beside the FBI agent investigating Tucker's criminal activities? It's not like I ever told her about Gavin… *that* would be interesting to explain all these years later.

Gavin slides out from under me and stands by my bedside. "Okay. Get some rest. But you should probably know that the state police are bound to show up soon. You don't have to talk to them. You can push them off until you hire a lawyer."

"A lawyer? Won't that make me look like I have something to hide?"

"That's what they'll tell you, but they're going to investigate either way."

"Is it wrong if I talk to them, try to find out what they know?"

"No, it's not wrong, but—"

"I need to know the truth, whatever it is." I wasn't quite certain for a while there, but I am now.

Gavin sweeps his knuckles over my cheekbone. "Be careful what you wish for."

I savor the simple joy that rushes through me at his touch, but only briefly. There's no escaping the reality of my life. "I don't believe in wishes anymore."

Gavin glances away, his jaw clenching. When he looks at me again, his corneas are pebbles of obsidian glass, smoldering with a dark fury. "You married a thief, Poppy. But what he's stolen from you…" He shakes his head. "You're as much a victim as—"

"Don't call me that," I snap. "I'm not a victim."

My sharp retort makes him frown, a stubborn expression pulling at his features as if he's about to argue. But then he decides better of it. "I'll be back in the morning."

I toy with a loose thread in my sheet. "Do your bosses know about us?"

"Only what I've told them, that we grew up in the same town. I said we were acquaintances but nothing more. They'd be hard pressed finding someone who could prove otherwise."

I nod, remembering how I hadn't even wanted to share Gavin with my sister. On one of his messages from a few years ago, Gavin told me that his foster parents had passed. And if Doug is still around, and anything like he used to be, he'd hardly go out of his way to put himself on the FBI's radar.

"I pushed hard to come down here. I told my team I could get you to talk to me."

"Is that what you're doing now?" A fresh surge of fear coats my mouth with a metallic tang.

Gavin rears back, his face a map of every hurt I've inflicted. "No, Poppy. I'll come back later, in an official capacity. You can answer my questions or not. But right now, this is for me. When I heard you were taken to the hospital, I..." He looks away, swallowing heavily. "I had to come down here. I had to see you for myself. Help, if I could."

I didn't believe it was possible for my heart to break any more than it has already, but Gavin proves me wrong. "You always did want to be a hero."

His lips twist downward into a sad smile, possibly the saddest I've ever seen. "I tried to rescue you once before. This time, I hope you'll let me." He wraps me in his arms and presses a kiss to my forehead, adding, "I've never stopped loving you, Poppy. Never."

When he pulls away, the hollow laugh that trickles from me is as sad as Gavin's smile, leaving words I cannot say lodged in my throat.

I want to beg Gavin's forgiveness for pushing him away in New York when he came to me the week before my wedding, hurling lies at him like rocks. For avoiding him after he showed up at Worthington, explaining why he'd left Sackett, and what kept him away for so long. For never answering his messages or showing him how much I still cared.

But I can't.

Because I fell for Tucker's promises. I believed his lies. I'm wearing his ring. For better or worse, we built a life together.

That life is shattered now.

An hour ago, I was sure I was a murderer. A black widow.

But if Gavin is right, I'm the abandoned wife of a criminal.

Either way, I'm a fucking mess.

CHAPTER 44

FLORIDA

"Good morning, Mrs. Stockton. Thank you for seeing us. I am Detective Reardon and," he indicates the woman beside him, "this is Detective Diaz."

Gavin was right, the state police arrived first thing this morning. I study them now, debating whether to invoke my right to an attorney before answering their questions. Reardon is short and wide, with a bump in his nose, and the tip of it leaning slightly to the left. When he speaks, only the right side of his mouth moves, and the effect is almost cartoonish.

His partner is the same height, but only half as wide. Holding a small notebook and a pen, she wears a carefully impartial expression on her face, her eyes wide-set and intelligent. The brains to Reardon's brawn.

"We have some questions concerning your husband's disappearance," he continues.

I pick at the thin, nubby sheet folded below my waist, deciding not to lawyer up quite yet. "So do I, detectives."

Reardon frowns at my answer. "As I was saying, tell us about your trip to Florida."

I repeat the details I shared with Gavin just a few hours ago, ending with boarding the yacht in Miami and setting sail for the Keys.

"But you weren't on the yacht when you were found," Diaz protests, her hand poised over her notepad.

Another piece of memory slides into place. "There was a smaller boat on board. It can go places where the water is too shallow for a yacht."

Reardon give a low whistle. "If you say so."

"I do," I add stiffly. "Tucker and I used the smaller boat to explore the Keys on our own, just the two of us." It sounds romantic, and although this is where my memory is most blurry, I know it was anything but.

"How would you describe your husband's state of mind during your trip?"

I wrench my focus back to the detectives. "His state of mind?"

"Yes. Did he behave any differently than usual?'

I think back to the afternoon at the Delano Hotel. "He was distracted, on his phone a lot. But that's not unusual for him."

There is a hard set to Reardon's jaw. "Tell us everything you remember about your last excursion."

"I can try, although I don't remember much of it."

"Even the smallest details are helpful," Diaz reassures me.

I forge ahead. "The captain dropped anchor on the Gulf side of Key West, near the Marquesas Keys, and the crew packed champagne, and a light dinner for us."

"Dry Tortugas was your destination?"

I nod. Seventy miles west of Key West, the Dry Tortugas are actually a group of several islands, the largest of which, Garden Key, is home to Fort Jefferson, an abandoned military post and former prison.

"Is there anything else you can remember about the trip, or your last moments with your husband?" Diaz interjects. "Even the smallest detail."

What I remember is not wanting to go to Florida at all, but Sadie had convinced me that getting away from my empty nursery and the cold, dreary winter days in New York would be good for me. That it didn't have to be a trip to celebrate our anniversary, but a brief reprieve from the bleakness of mourning, an opportunity to begin moving forward with my life in order to honor my babies who didn't get that chance. Of course, I don't say any of this.

I think back, trying to remember something, anything about our time on the yacht, or the smaller boat we took out alone. My taste buds react faster than my brain. The briny, wrinkled bite of an olive. Creamy Camembert cheese and savory fig jam, spread on seeded, hand-cut crackers. "I think we opened a bottle of champagne, ate from the charcuterie pla—"

"The what?" Detective Reardon's eyebrows were raised as he leaned toward me.

"The charcuterie platter. It's an hors d'oeuvres plate. Cheese, cured meat, olives, crackers."

Satisfied by my explanation, he rocks back on his heels. "Okay, go on."

"There's not much to tell. I can taste the food, I can picture the way it was arranged on the plate. But that's all. The next thing I remember is waking up in the hospital." I gesture at the IV and my bandage-covered skin. "With a cracked skull and a dozen lacerations on my back and legs."

"Any drugs?"

"Sure, yeah. But you'll have to ask the doctor for specifics. I don't know—"

"Not here. On the boat with your husband." He lifts his hands. "No judgment, and we're not with narcotics, so you can be honest."

I blanch. "I don't do drugs, never have."

"Maybe you had too much to drink and blacked out. You sure you didn't open another bottle? Nice night. Anniversary trip with your husband. Shark-u-tree platter. It would make sense if you didn't notice, drank an extra couple of glasses."

"No," I say, pushing the word through gritted teeth.

"Why not? Wouldn't be the first time a girl had a romantic night with her guy, drank too much and couldn't remember what happened." He hoists one shoulder up, lets it fall. "Or maybe you do remember, but you're faking a black out rather than admitting an inconvenient truth."

Bile rises up my throat, hot and harsh. "Absolutely not. I would never drink to excess. Not after—" I close my mouth, pressing my lips together. Remembering a different hospital room, almost ten years ago.

"Not after… what?"

I shake my head, gathering my wits about me and schooling my expression into an aloof mask. "Nothing, just that I don't drink very much. It doesn't agree with me."

Their eyes linger on my face, sharp and accusing. "We've towed the boat to our forensics lab. You sure you don't remember anything else? Like maybe an argument, or any reason there would be blood all over the boat?"

"There's blood in the boat?" I wonder if Gavin knew this.

"Yeah, quite a bit of it."

Panic races through my veins, and I lift my hand to my head, fingertips brushing against gauze instead of hair. Of course, there is blood on the boat, I realize. *Mine*. "There's a four-inch gash on my head, cuts on my skin. The doctor said I must have bled a lot."

"Your husband's blood was in the boat too. Quite a bit of it."

Reardon's expression turns sly, almost victorious, as if he's caught me in a lie. My stomach goes queasy and I brace myself for what's coming.

"Mrs. Stockton, can you tell us why there was a knife on the boat with your fingerprints on the handle and your husband's blood on the blade?"

CHAPTER 45

FLORIDA

*C*hills race along the back of my neck, my heart pounding inside my ribcage like a trapped bird. My right hand twitches, and for a brief second, I picture the crimson splatter of blood, feel the smooth, warm weight of the knife's handle within my palm.

Could Gavin be wrong? His opinion came from his investigation of Tucker, not the boat where I was found.

Shit. Maybe I really did plunge a knife into his—

There is a knock on the open door and I look up, blinking my vision back into focus. Gavin strides into the room wearing a dark suit and carrying a gold badge.

"Hello, Mrs. Stockton, my name is Gavin Cross, I'm a Special Agent with the FBI." His eyes drill into me. *Play along.*

Of course, this is no game. And keeping secrets isn't as much fun as it used to be.

Reardon has no qualms about speaking up. "I don't care who you are, this is our witness."

Gavin pulls his gaze from mine, and the sudden loss stings. "Would you like to discuss this in the hall?"

The police officer adopts an aggressive stance. "No. You need to step off."

Gavin doesn't back down. "Look, you're a local cop, looking for a missing tourist. You have no idea who Tucker Stockton is. I'm willing to cooperate if—"

"You're willing to cooperate? Who do you—"

Detective Diaz puts a steadying hand on her partner's shoulder. "Sean, why don't we hear him out?"

Gavin ignores them both. "Mrs. Stockton, your husband was days away from being indicted in one of the largest money laundering schemes in US history."

Though he'd told me of Tucker's criminal activity, the sheer scale of it is an unwelcome surprise and I know it shows on my face.

Reardon folds his arms across his chest. "You can prove Stockton's illegal activities led to his disappearance?"

Condescension is woven into Gavin's words. "Our investigation is ongoing."

Reardon puffs up in response. "Well, until you—"

"Stop," I say, as loudly as I can manage. "Detectives, I'd like to speak with Agent Cross alone please."

"We're not through with our questions."

"For now, I'm through answering them."

Detective Reardon's face is like a bloated thundercloud as he stomps out of my room, his partner following.

"G—"

Gavin gives a quick shake of his head, then closes the door. He doesn't say anything until he is back beside me. "Are you all right? I got stuck on a call with headquarters, otherwise I would have been here earlier. I'm sorry you had to face them alone."

I reach out my hand and he takes it, our fingers intertwining effortlessly. "I'm fine, really." I fill him in on my conversation with the two detectives, then ask, "Last night, did you know that Tucker's blood was on the knife? His and mine?"

"No. That's why I was late. The report came in this morning."

"Do you still think this is all just a ruse to cover up his escape? Or..." I look away, feeling like the air's been knocked from my lungs.

Gavin grabs hold of my chin and forces my gaze back to his. "I do. And until we know for sure otherwise, so should you."

I manage a shaky nod, although the tension gripping my shoulder blades doesn't dissipate. "Will the Florida detectives come back?"

"Probably. But the case will be transferred to FBI jurisdiction."

"And you'll stay on it?"

"For now. I'll probably have to recuse myself soon."

"But not yet?" I feel better knowing Gavin's watching out for me. Although, if I am guilty, not even he will be able to save me.

"Not yet." He brushes a stray piece of hair from my face, gently tucking it behind my ear. "Those calls they asked about... Do you recall who Tucker was talking to during your trip?"

My brows push together over the bridge of my nose, and I rub at the line indenting my forehead. "I didn't pay much attention, and Tucker always walked away from me when he spoke on the phone."

"Could it have been Wren Knowles?"

Clearly Gavin has done his homework on Tucker, so I'm not surprised he knows about Wren. "No. It definitely wasn't her on the phone."

"How can you be so sure?"

"Tucker and Wren have their own shorthand, I always knew when he was talking to her." I pull at the sleeve of my hospital gown, feeling embarrassed to admit my husband's close relationship with another woman. "Is she involved?" Although it seems unlikely—Wren would take a bullet for Tucker.

"Her name has come up, but I can't say anything for sure."

"Can't or won't?"

"Can't." He cocks his head to the side, lips twitching. "I understand Knowles was your bridesmaid. Are you two close?"

"No. And frankly, that was at Tucker's insistence. Wren made no secret of the fact that she thought she should be the one wearing a white dress, not me." I splay my hands flat on the sheet, noticing my jagged nails for the first time. Tucker would hate that. "Wren has spent most of the past decade waiting for Tucker to wake up and realize that he chose the wrong woman."

He arches an eyebrow. "I can sympathize."

We fall silent for a minute. "I'm sorry, Gavin. I—"

He waves me off and stands up, walking across the room and leaning his back to the wall. "Last night, you said you were planning to divorce him."

"Yes."

"Why?"

I feel my eyes fill with tears and I know what I have to do. I have to tell Gavin the truth. The whole truth. Not just the scraps of memory I have from our time in Florida.

Everything.

I pat the bed beside me. "Please, come here. It's a long story." Dread squeezes my throat like a savage, replacing the oxygen in my chest with icy beads of terror. Once Gavin knows about *that night*, about my twin angels, about the hate I carried for my husband... will he still think I'm so innocent?

The world slows down as Gavin takes one step toward me, then two. Meanwhile, my heart is beating double-time, erratically flinging itself against my ribs. Gavin is an FBI agent. He knows what it takes to build a case.

Means: the bloody knife.

Opportunity: I was with Tucker on the boat.

Now, I'm about to prove I have motivation, too.

Once I tell him everything...

Everything will change.

But I never get the chance. Gavin's not halfway across the room when Sadie barges through the door.

"You can't be in here." Sadie's glare shoots sparks at Gavin, instantly pegging him as law enforcement. "Has my sister's doctor cleared you to speak with her? She's had a major head injury, for God's sake."

"Sadie, this is—"

"Gavin Cross." He extends his hand though Sadie makes no move to take it.

"You're that FBI agent." She turns to me. "You shouldn't be talking to him without a lawyer."

I could tell my sister about Gavin right now. And I should. If there was ever a time to come completely clean, this is it.

But I don't. Like a coward, I accept the reprieve.

I'm not ready for the two people I love most in the world to hate me.

CHAPTER 46

FLORIDA

Wealthy New York Financier and Philanthropist Tucker Stockton was reported missing earlier this week. He and his wife, Poppy Stockton, were exploring the Florida Keys on a leased yacht. The captain grew concerned when the couple, who were celebrating their fifth wedding anniversary, didn't return from an intimate jaunt using a smaller vessel.

Mrs. Stockton was found unconscious, with a head wound and other unspecified injuries, and was immediately transported to the Lower Keys Medical Center. Mr. Stockton, twenty-nine, has not been found.

The couple met at Worthington University as freshmen, marrying less than two years after their graduation. By all accounts, their marriage is a happy one, and Mr. Stockton is extremely successful and well respected among his Wall Street peers.

The U.S. Coast Guard, the Monroe County Sheriff's Office, and the Marine Enforcement Unit are searching for Stockton, and a forensics team is scouring both vessels for any evidence of foul play. Police have labeled his disappearance as "suspicious" but are not ruling anything out at this early stage in their investigation.

*T*he police seized my phone as part of their forensic examination. I gave my password to Detective Diaz without hesitation, although if they expect to learn much, they will be disappointed. A few pictures. To do lists. Emails, most of them mass mailings from retail stores or online shopping sites. Contact information for Tucker, Wren, my mother, and sister. Doctors. My dentist. My therapist. A few other people I haven't reached out to in months, if not longer.

They won't find any of Gavin's messages. He stopped leaving them after that afternoon in my apartment, the week before my wedding. And at Tucker's insistence, because I refused to drag my iPad with me wherever I went, I switched to an iPhone when I became pregnant so we could FaceTime while he was traveling. I lost everything from Gavin in the process.

Since Sadie walked in on me talking to Gavin, she's been at my bedside practically around the clock, which unfortunately means he hasn't. I used Sadie's phone to speak briefly with our mother, who lives in northern Maine now, courtesy of Tucker. She'd relapsed, again, a couple of years ago and after another long stint in rehab, Tucker discovered a place, a commune really, that believed in living off the land and avoiding all chemicals and additives, including caffeine, alcohol, and drugs. It works for her, and allowed Sadie to leave Sackett and move into Manhattan with me. The community also takes particular pride in remaining "unplugged." In my mother's case, ignorance is bliss.

According to Sadie, news of Tucker's disappearance has "grown legs." A few reporters had even trekked out to Worthington University to report from campus, standing right outside the dorm we shared during our freshman year. My thumb had hovered over the remote, unable to change the channel as the hair on the back of my neck stood on end, goose bumps sweeping down my arms and prickling my skin.

My years at WU belong firmly in the past. No good will come of unearthing that particular skeleton.

And from what Gavin told me, there are plenty of other skeletons in our closet, ones I had no idea about. The talking heads on the twenty-four-hour news programs are having a field day, and they don't even know about the criminal accusations being levied at Tucker. *Yet.*

On-screen, our marriage looks so glamorous, filled with luxurious vacations and black-tie galas. In reality, those vacations were usually business trips, with Wren joining us as often as not. And at most social events, I'd felt like a mannequin in a designer dress, so afraid of saying the wrong thing I barely said anything at all.

Tucker expected me to be perfect, or at least a perfect reflection of him. Anything less was unacceptable. Not just to him, but to me, too. It was almost as if, by marrying him, I'd been given a cloak of invincibility. As long as I looked like a Stockton and acted like a Stockton, I could think like a Stockton, feel like a Stockton. All the bad things that happened to Poppy Whitman—they never happened.

Walking down the aisle, I'd believed that each step toward Tucker took me closer to a fairy-tale life. Back when I felt like Cinderella about to marry her Prince Charming and live happily ever after.

How wrong I'd been.

I'd sworn to love, honor, and cherish Tucker Stockton. I'd married him with the best of intentions, planning to be a good wife. A perfect wife. The kind of wife Tucker deserved. Because of him, I could afford to work at TeenCharter. Because of him, I didn't have to worry about my mother. Because of him, our children would have opportunities I'd never dreamed of. They would never go to bed hungry, or become wards of the state, or rely on the charity of others.

The life I see on screen is not the one we lived. There are no photos of me sitting alone in our apartment, waiting on eggshells for Tucker to get home from the office, hoping he's in a decent mood. None of a pink-tinted puddle on a white sheepskin rug, or of our empty nursery. No reporter cutting to a video of Tucker and I in the hospital, saying a final goodbye to our babies.

A year ago, I thought Tucker and I had it all. He'd just taken over his family's business and I was pregnant with not just one— but *two* Stockton heirs.

Until I wasn't anymore.

The stability I'd been thirsting for my whole life was ripped away from me, ripped out of me. I learned that being a Stockton didn't guarantee happiness or security or anything at all.

No marriage certificate could patch the fractures and blemishes that marked our relationship, glazing it with a glossy sheen. Once we lost our babies, our elegant Manhattan penthouse became the loneliest place in the world.

For the thousandth time, I try to imagine my last moments with Tucker. Alone, on the open water, had we finally given up what little pretense remained of our marriage? Did I bring up divorce, as I'd planned? Had we hurled insults and accusations at each other?

What if Tucker refused to let me go? The man I married cannot tolerate defeat in any arena—maybe our marriage was no different.

At what point did it become violent?

If I believe Gavin, Tucker staged the scene to escape criminal charges. But Gavin doesn't have all the facts. He doesn't know that I've spent the better part of the past nine months wishing Tucker dead, fantasizing about a life without him.

But the detectives don't have all the facts either. They only just learned of Tucker's crimes. And they cannot possibly understand his uncanny ability to bend any situation to his benefit.

If Tucker knew he was about to go to jail, facing years behind bars… I have no doubt he would do anything he could to evade the law. Including faking his own death.

Will any of us ever know the truth?

CHAPTER 47

"Mrs. Stockton, it's always a pleasure to see you, although I regret the circumstances." There is something about Douglas Keene, in-house counsel for Stockton Capital, that is almost too slick, too cunning. But for now, the tall lawyer, with his graying hair carefully swept off his aristocratic features, is my best chance of understanding what was going through Tucker's mind on our last night together.

"Please, call me Poppy." I extend my hand and indicate the chair Sadie has pushed near my bed. "And thank you for coming down. You really didn't have to. We could have made our way back to New York."

"Nonsense. So, I've spoken with the Florida Police department, the FBI, the SEC, and Treasury. First of all, you are allowed to leave the state and go back home. I've taken the liberty of chartering a private plane. The pilot is waiting to bring you," he glances at Sadie, "and, of course, your lovely sister, back home. Have you been released yet?"

"Not quite yet. The doctor wanted to review the results of the MRI they gave me earlier, but he said if he's satisfied with the results, I'll be released this morning."

It doesn't feel quite right to leave Florida. Tucker hasn't been found—dead or alive. I haven't remembered what happened on the boat. And Gavin hasn't been back since Sadie kicked him out two days ago. But I can't just sit in a room, flipping back and forth between channels and doing nothing. I want to be back in New York, digging through our apartment for clues about the man I married. The man I thought I knew.

Either my husband has staged his disappearance and is somewhere now, watching his scheme play out.

Or… I killed him.

"Were you able to find out—"

"The questions you raised concerning your husband's business dealings, criminal or otherwise," Keene's smile drops, "I'm afraid I can't answer them."

I inhale a shallow breath, frustration tightening its grip on my lungs. "What do you mean? Why not?" That's the reason I called Keene in the first place.

"I'm legally barred from doing so. Everyone who works for Stockton Capital, from the secretaries to the managing directors, must sign non-disclosure and non-disparagement agreements. Even me. I can't talk about anything related to my work with you."

"But I'm Tucker's wife. I need to know what's going on."

Douglas lifts his hands, palms out. "I completely understand your concerns, but from a legal standpoint, my hands are tied."

"So why did you come all the way down here if you can't actually help me?"

"Wherever Tucker is, he would hardly want me to leave his wife to the mercy of government hacks looking to pin blame on the easiest target, which, the way I see it, is you." He adjusts the Windsor knot of his tie. "I'm here to ensure you arrive back in New York safe and sound. But beyond that, I've compiled a list of excellent criminal attorneys you should consider."

"Okay," I mumble, the enormity of the mess Tucker left me with finally beginning to sink in.

Keene isn't finished though. "However, in my opinion, there's only one person you should hire. If she'll take your case, that is."

I hadn't realized hiring an attorney would be such a difficult task. "Who?"

When he says her name, my stomach sinks. I must really be in trouble.

CHAPTER 48

My stomach dips as I eye the dozen or so reporters and cameramen gathered on the sidewalk outside the door to our building. "Can you please use the underground entrance?" I ask the driver.

Once Sadie and I are crammed into the elevator with all of our luggage, waving off help from a porter, I lean my head against the mirrored wall. "I keep expecting to wake up and discover all of this is just a bad dream."

"Well, if anyone can make lemonade out of lemons, it's you, Pops." The blasé tone of her voice scratches at my frayed nerves and I wonder if I've finally reached the limit to Sadie's empathy. She put her life on hold when mine fell apart and taking care of me has to be getting old by now.

But her words reverberate inside our small enclosure, taunting me. Sadie has no idea what loss—true loss—really is.

I do. It is like a vacuum, ripping out your hair, shearing off your fingernails, stealing your screams. No end in sight. Just unrelenting, unimaginable pain.

Until the very moment I held my dead babies in my arms, I

believed marrying Tucker would shield me from the worst life could throw at me.

I'd been such a fool.

Lemonade, my ass.

"I've buried two children. My husband, soon to be an accused criminal, is either missing or dead. And I might just be blamed for it. Those are not lemons, they're *tragedies*."

The elevator comes to a smooth stop and we maneuver our luggage into the quiet apartment. Isla left on a vacation of her own while we were in Florida and won't be returning for a few days.

I drop my bags at the door to Tucker's office. It's the one room in our apartment that had always been off limits to me. Tucker never explicitly said I couldn't come in, but just the way he always closed the door, even when it was just the two of us, told me I wasn't welcome.

In his office at Stockton Capital, Tucker has an enormous executive desk and an entire wall fronted by bookshelves. Here, Tucker has another desk, but it is smaller, with narrow drawers. No bookcases, just one file cabinet disguised as a decorative chest beneath the window.

Gathering up my nerves, I sit in Tucker's chair and reach for the handle of the top drawer.

It doesn't budge. Neither do the other four.

Locked, all five of them. I want to scream in frustration as I look for the key. It isn't taped inside the kneehole or to the back panel of the desk. It isn't hidden beneath the rug or in the damp soil of the potted orchid. The chest is empty, too.

Finally, I seize the letter opener from the top of the desk and jab it into the front of the top drawer. The wood around the lock splinters with each frenzied thrust, until the mechanism finally gives way, but my triumphant smile lasts only an instant before discovering it is as empty as the chest.

The weight of the blade in my hand feels welcome and

familiar as I attack the remaining locks, the jabbing motion activating a deep-rooted muscle memory that makes me envision my husband. Is this what I did to Tucker?

But furniture is not soft like skin, spongy like muscle. Each time the steel tip makes contact with the metal lock, or the mahogany wood, it reverberates through my arm, making my bones and joints cramp with pain.

Empty.

Empty.

Empty.

Empty.

Five locked drawers, not a single thing inside any of them.

My sister chooses that moment to poke her head through the door. "Have you discovered all of your husband's secrets yet?"

I grind my teeth to prevent saying something I'll regret and stalk off to the master suite. I need some space from her.

I still can't get my stitches wet, so I cover my head with a plastic shower cap and face the hot spray without turning my back toward the water. I feel battered and bruised—even more emotionally than physically.

I've spent years trying to fuse the disparate parts of me into one cohesive identity and, for a while, I thought I'd been doing a good job. But today I am like a demented child's toy. Barbie's body with a GI Joe's head, missing a limb and naked save for permanent marker all over me.

I am too overwhelmed to be outraged. Too exhausted to be embarrassed. I want to lather myself with every product in my shower, but I feel too fragile, too certain that scrubbing my skin might erase it entirely, inch by inch.

By the time I get out of the shower and dress in an oversized sweater and faded yoga pants, I just want to make a cup of tea and get into bed.

Deciding to do exactly that after I retrieve my bags from where

I dropped them outside of Tucker's office, I pull up short at the sight of Wren standing in the middle of the room, surveying the mess I made with undisguised horror. "What are you doing here?"

Wren spins around at the sound of my voice. "*Me?*" Her hands flap wildly at the empty drawers hanging from Tuckers desk like loose teeth. "What have *you* done?"

If there is a silver lining to Tucker's disappearance, it is that I no longer have to put up with Wren in my life. "Get out," I say coldly, pointing toward the front door.

"You'd like that, wouldn't you? Leave you in the apartment that Tucker's money bought, with everything he's given you."

Before I can respond, she yanks at an already open drawer and turns it over, feeling along the bottom and sides. Finding nothing, she tosses it aside and moves on to the next drawer.

"What the hell are you doing?" I could try to stop her, but I'm just as interested in anything Tucker left behind as she is.

Wren still hasn't answered when Sadie appears at my side. "What is she looking for?" she whispers, the two of us now staring at Wren as if she's an exotic animal at the zoo.

"I have no idea."

"Should I call security?" Wren moves on to the chest in front of the window, but when the last drawer bangs down on top of the rest, she is still empty-handed.

"No," I say, then direct my next words to Wren. "Whatever you're looking for, it's obviously not here."

"It has to be," she mutters, as much to herself as to me.

"This is ridic—" My tongue goes still as Wren grabs the painting hanging behind Tucker's desk and takes it off the wall, revealing a safe.

Sadie drags in a quick breath. "Holy shit."

We both take a few steps closer, peering over Wren's shoulder as she taps a code into the keypad. "Come on, come on," she grumbles, her first try failing. But on her second, there is an audible *click*, and she yanks at the rectangular metal door inset into the wall.

The safe isn't empty. Wren reaches for the stack of folders inside, flipping through pages and letting them fall to the floor in a stream of paper. "Fuck!" she screams once, then again. When she turns around, her face is red and blotchy, her eyes glassy and unfocused, the pupils blown. She looks like a drug addict who's just discovered the pharmacy she's broken into doesn't stock narcotics.

"Wren..." I say tentatively, not sure how to approach her right now.

She is shaking as she walks toward me, grabbing my shoulders with both hands, her long fingers like talons digging into my skin. "What have you done, Poppy? Where is Tucker's laptop, where are his papers?" There is a delirious look in her eyes I've never seen before, like she's come unhinged.

I shake her off, though I can still feel the bite of her nails when I reclaim my personal space. "I don't know. I haven't taken anything."

She blinks several times, then smooths down her hair. "Fine. Just tell me where he is, where he *really* is, and I'll go."

Another chip of my composure falls away. "You don't know?" If Tucker planned his disappearance, surely he would have told Wren. If there's anyone he trusts, it's her.

"Poppy, this isn't a game. The people Tucker—" She cuts off abruptly. "If you know what's good for you, you'll tell me where he is."

I cross my arms over my chest. "I don't know where Tucker is. What I do know is that the FBI is investigating Tucker's money laundering. And they asked about you, too. I might not know exactly how you were involved, but they're going to figure out your part in his scheme."

"You're lying," she says, but I can see that I've struck a nerve.

"Fine. Don't believe me. You'll find out the truth soon enough."

"The truth?" A humorless cackle spills from her bloodless lips. "You inserted yourself between Tucker and me freshman year, launching yourself at him with pathetic desperation, and now look what's happened. He's gone, and it's all your fault."

Half of what she's saying is true. From practically the first minute we met, Wren flat out told me that Tucker was off-limits. He was hers. But what did I do the second she looked away? I discounted her completely. I grew to want Tucker, too.

And I got him.

Be careful what you wish for.

"I have nothing to do with Tucker's business and you know it. Can you say the same?" A long beat passes as Wren weighs her options, a muscle in her jaw twitching as she looks between me and my sister. I add, "If you're here, trying to make me think that you weren't in on it with him every step of the way, you're wasting your time."

Wren's expression changes, as if she pulled a shade to hide her emotions. Without another word, she straightens her spine and walks out of Tucker's office, paper crinkling under her feet.

When the front door closes, Sadie turns to me with wide eyes. "Has she always been this crazy?"

"Probably." I shrug, glancing around Tucker's office and resigning myself to cleaning up the mess before going to bed. Another time, I would have stewed over Wren's performance, trying to analyze her motivation and intent. But right now, I can't be bothered. I have enough problems of my own without borrowing hers.

I kneel down and start gathering file folders.

"Why don't I do that?" Sadie offers. "It's my fault for letting her in."

"Don't be silly." I wave her off, forcing my mouth into what I hope is a reassuring smile. "It won't take long. I'll see you in the morning."

Whatever Wren left behind can't be very important, but I still want to look through it. I pick up the scattered pieces of paper one by one, sorting everything into its appropriate file. There are the purchase documents and deed for this apartment, his parents wills, our wedding certificate, medical records from my mother's various rehab stays, legal documents related to her arrest, and a few other innocuous looking contracts.

I'm about to put them all back in the safe when I realize I don't have the code to unlock it once I close the door.

Just before I turn away to drop everything onto the desk, my eye snags on something at the very back of the safe. Something almost indistinguishable from the steel enclosure. My nerves are already clanging in warning as I reach for it.

But the second my fingertips brush against the delicate silver chain, I know.

I know with a searing certainty that rips into me like a bolt of lightning.

The stack of papers I just organized into neat files once again flutter to the ground as I slide down the wall… clutching Gavin's moonstone pendant in my palm.

CHAPTER 49

NEW YORK CITY

*O*utside the windows of my bedroom, the setting sun plays peekaboo with New York City's most iconic landmarks. In the building across the street, there is a little boy stretched out on a rug, playing with LEGOs. One floor above, an older couple is seated at a small table, eating dinner. And one floor below, a woman about my age is laughing. Really laughing. Head thrown back, hair bouncing on her shoulders, her mouth open and smiling. I don't know if she's watching a comedy or having a conversation with someone beyond my line of vision. But I wish I did. I wish I could crawl inside her window, inside her body even.

When was the last time I'd let loose with even an exuberant giggle? When hadn't I been focused on pleasing someone—my mother, Tucker, a professor, Wren, Tucker's parents. On not making a mistake that would prove I was just an imposter hiding among them.

Even Sadie. As kids, we played together, but I was always taking care of her, reminding her of the rules, or keeping score.

Only with Gavin had I just let myself *be*.

I ignore Sadie's knocks, checking on me. And, even though I am desperate to hear Gavin's voice, I ignore his calls, too.

I spend half the night tossing and turning, trying to understand why Tucker had taken the necklace Gavin gave to me, lied about it, and kept it all these years.

Did Tucker purposely target me *that night*? Was my necklace a souvenir? A trophy?

Or had he merely viewed Gavin as competition and hoped that I'd forget about him without a constant reminder on my skin.

I spend the other half of the night mourning. Not my marriage, which has been over for a long time and had clearly been a mistake from the very beginning.

I grieve the days and weeks and months and years that I'll never get back.

Heartache that cuts so deep, the scars throb in tune with my pulse.

And the memories that shred a little more of my soul with every look back into the past.

I've wasted so much time, made so many wrong choices.

My entire life is up in the air right now, but there is one thing I know for certain. If I get through this, if I didn't commit the ultimate sin and wind up behind bars, I want to spend the rest of my life with Gavin. If he'll have me.

But first... First, I need to become my own hero.

I don't want to be rescued. I will never again hand over the reins of my life to anyone else.

Which is why, even though I'm operating on next to no sleep, I don't even consider postponing my meeting with Reese Reynolds. Every hero needs a sidekick, and in my case, the kind I need is a kick-ass lawyer.

I evade the reporters camped out in front of my apartment by leaving through the underground parting exit. Beneath my shirt, I am wearing Gavin's necklace. The clasp is broken, probably from where Tucker ripped it off my neck, but I used a safety pin to link the chain. I'll have to take it to a jeweler eventually, but right now I can't bear the thought of being without it again.

I've only been waiting in Reese Reynold's conference room a few minutes when she bursts through the door. Short and curvy, her lipstick is the exact same shade as her red suit, her blond hair cut and styled into a camera-ready bob. She is a familiar face on the evening news, a defender of high-profile, scorned, shamed women. Preferably attractive, high-profile, scorned, shamed women in the Forbes 400.

I am her perfect client.

She sits down and gets right to the point. "I've been following press coverage of your husband's disappearance very closely. I'm surprised it's taken you so long to contact me."

On TV, Reese looks like she could be a news anchor, with a wide, square jaw and unblinking hazel eyes. In person, it is obvious the blond comes from a bottle, her careful application of makeup hiding more years than she is willing to admit.

"You haven't just been following the case, you've had quite a bit to say." I haven't hired Reese based solely on Douglas Keene's recommendation. During the hours and hours of news coverage I devoured, she'd been the only lawyer who hadn't insinuated that I either knew where Tucker was or had something to do with his disappearance. The. Only. One.

"I can't say the same for you. You're allowing the press to tell your story, Mrs. Stockton."

"Please, call me Poppy. And that's because I have nothing to say."

"But you've spoken with the police and the FBI, correct?" At my nod of agreement, she says, "Tell me what you told them."

I do. Reese doesn't take notes or record me, and interrupts only occasionally to ask a question. When I'm finally through my throat is hoarse, and she stands up to pour me a glass of water from the carafe on the sideboard. I take it gratefully.

"It certainly sounds like you have a lot to say."

"Nothing that has helped to find him."

Reese's fingers curve over the back of the chair she'd been sitting in. "Let's talk this through a bit. Your husband went missing on trip to celebrate your five-year anniversary, yes?"

I sigh, about to explain that celebrate isn't exactly the right word to use, but she jumps in with more questions. "Your marriage, was it as happy as it appears? Champagne kisses and caviar dreams?"

"No," I admit, wiping a drop of condensation from the edge of my glass. "Not at all."

She remains unfazed. "Okay. Let me try to recap this situation from the perspective of law enforcement. We have two unhappily married people in a small boat, supposedly exploring an uninhabited island. Later that night, the wife is discovered in the boat, unconscious and with non-fatal injuries. The husband, a very wealthy man soon to be arrested for shady business dealings, is nowhere to be found. There is broken glass and a bloody knife. The wife's fingerprints are on the handle, and blood on the blade from the husband. Do I have my facts straight?"

I can't speak around the knot in my throat so I merely nod.

"Good. Now, let's try to solve the mystery. Scenario one, the husband fell or jumped overboard, either an accident or suicide. The blood on the knife came from the wife trying to reach for him, to save him. Unsuccessful, she falls and injures herself. Scenario two, husband attacks wife, she kills him in self-defense and is injured in the struggle. Scenario three, wife kills husband because she's furious that he's about to be arrested—"

"But I had no idea—"

"Fine. Then you kill him for some other reason," she concedes easily. "Scenario four, husband planned the whole thing and wife was in on it. The injuries, the knife, the blood—they're just to make it look like he's dead so he can escape arrest. Scenario five, husband planned the whole thing, likely with an accomplice, and wife was none the wiser. She's hurt when she tries to stop him. And scenario six, the mystery man."

"Who is the mystery man?"

"Exactly. Could be anyone. Actually, I'm being sexist. Mystery *person*. Someone, or group of people, murdered or kidnapped your husband. You were collateral damage." Reese finally pulls her chair out and sits back down, her unblinking eyes boring into me. "Six potential outcomes, and you are criminally liable in three of them. Are you willing to trust your fate to the toss of a coin?"

I definitely picked the right sidekick.

"No, I'm not."

"Good." She slaps the table with the flat of her palm. "First things first, I require a one-hundred-thousand-dollar retainer. I assume that won't be a problem."

"My husband handles the—" As soon as I realize where the rest of my sentence was going, I stop, my mouth still open. I haven't written a check or paid a bill in years. I have no idea how to access our accounts. But I'll figure it out. "It won't be a problem."

Reese reaches out a hand, covering one of mine. "This has been a shock, I know. You will have to face things—questions, doubts, accusations, realities—you never could have anticipated just a few days ago. I'll get you through it, but you're going to have to trust me. Can you do that?"

I agree, and she flashes a set of teeth so straight and white they look like Chiclets. "Good. Now, it's time to take control of the narrative. Of the three options where you aren't at fault, number one isn't interesting enough for the press to run with, and number six has too many unknowns to be interesting. Number five is your narrative. Your husband planned the whole thing, likely with an accomplice, and you were none the wiser. You were injured trying to stop him."

I'm still reeling from how quickly Reese broke down my case and came up with a solution. "How do we do that?"

"Sex."

I blink at her, wondering if I misheard. "Sex?"

"Clichés are clichés because they're true. Sex sells, Poppy. For our purposes, that means sex brings in the highest ratings. If we give the press a juicy story, they'll run with it."

"But, Tucker and I haven't had s—"

"Oh no," Reese interrupts. "This isn't about *you*. We need a woman to pitch as Tucker's accomplice *and* his mistress. Give me a name."

CHAPTER 50

NEW YORK CITY

J hadn't intended to call Gavin, or to walk to Central Park, but I couldn't bear to spend the rest of the day trapped inside. Taking advantage of the unseasonably mild winter day, I headed instead for one of my favorite spots, calling him on the way.

I extend the small bag of red, ripe raspberries I bought after leaving Reese's office. "It's not quite the same as picking it ourselves, but it's the best I could do."

He accepts it with an almost rueful grin, tossing a few berries into his mouth. "I guess you do still owe me."

The Ramble has always reminded me of the Sackett Preserve. At thirty-six acres, it's about the same size. And unlike most of the Park, its narrow, winding paths aren't meticulously tended and landscaped. The natural forest is allowed to grow wild here. All my favorite trees are present, plus several non-native and exotic species. It's a haven for birds, too. I've spent many afternoons wandering these woods, getting lost in my memories.

Especially on the days my old nemesis, bulimia, would beckon me. Tempting me with false promises of indulgence and then emptiness. Cramming myself so full that, for a few, fleeting

341

moments, even the most hollow, aching, barren places inside me were stuffed and sated.

"Consider it a debt repaid," I reply, smiling back. My chest feels lighter already, the stress and worry that has built up inside me dissipating with each passing minute I spend beside Gavin. I've forgotten how freeing it is just to take a deep breath.

"Now all we have to do is find a cave to hide out in and we'll feel right at home."

"We're almost a century too late for that, I'm afraid." At Gavin's interested look, I explain. "The original developers of Central Park found a cave as they excavated the site. It wasn't part of their plans, but they decided to line the entrance with boulders, and build a stone staircase leading into it. For years, it was a popular attraction. A play area for kids and a romantic spot for couples."

With his free hand, Gavin reaches for one of mine, our fingers naturally intertwining. "Yeah, caves are good for that."

Whispers of memory rush at me as we meander along the wooded pathways, afternoon sun slanting unevenly through the sparse leafy canopy overhead. "It didn't last though. By the turn of the century, the Cave had become a seedy, scary place. There was a suicide, several robberies, and an increasing number of homeless were using it as a shelter. The final straw came when over three hundred men were arrested for," I use air quotes, "annoying women."

"Annoying women… that's against the law?"

I nudge him with my elbow. "I think they meant harassing. But yes, I think annoying women should definitely be a crime. What do you think, G-man?"

He laughs and I want to wrap myself up in the warm, husky sound, make a cloak of it and keep it around my shoulders forever. "I think we'd need to build a few more prisons."

"Well, back in the nineteen thirties, New York decided to solve the problem by sealing off the Cave."

"Leaving men free to annoy women all over the city instead, I guess."

"Maybe the cops should do another sweep of construction zones."

"There's got to be a suggestion box somewhere. I'm sure they'll get right on it."

We fall silent for a few minutes, and when we come to a waterfall, Gavin points to a spot sheltered by an enormous weeping willow. "How about here?"

I nod, and we sit down like we used to, side by side, our feet outstretched in front of us. I take a raspberry from the bag and put it into my mouth, the tart juice flooding my tongue.

"So, how are you holding up?" Gavin asks.

"No." I shake my head. "I realize I'm a complete disaster right now, but can we please talk about you? Not because I need a distraction, but—" I break off, feeling out of breath for no reason other than I'm choking on a sudden rush of my own emotions. "I've really missed you, Gavin. But I don't know anything about who you are now, and what you've been doing for the past five years."

"Only the past five? It's been longer than that since we've spent any length of time together."

"True. But at least your messages allowed me small peeks into your life."

He frowns. "You never responded. I wasn't sure you ever got them."

"I did. Every single one." I sigh, tilting my head to rest it on his shoulder and squeezing my eyes closed as pain twists through me. I can see the hurt I inflicted on Gavin that day so clearly, his reluctance to believe the awful words I spewed. He stood there, giving me every chance to take them back, to take *him* back. But I hadn't. I'd been too convinced I was right. That the time for second chances had passed. That we were over. "I understand why you stopped though. I was really awful to you that day at my apartment. Really, really awful."

"Well, I did just show up out of the blue, the week before your wedding. I should have known better."

"No." My heart aches with regret. "*I* should have known better. I should have done better. And, I want you to know, I didn't... I didn't mean it. The things I said about you, about us, I didn't mean any of it."

Gavin swears beneath his breath and curves his arm around my waist, his hand slipping beneath my coat, his thumb sweeping across the sliver of skin between my sweater and slacks. "You don't know how good it feels to hear you say that."

His touch sends a scatter of goose bumps over my arms, the tiny hairs standing on end. "I'm so sorry."

"Don't be. You did what you thought was right at the time."

"Things would be so different if I had just—"

"Let's not go down that road. We're here now, together. That's what matters."

I release a shuddering breath. "Okay. You're right. So, catch me up. I don't even know if you're seeing anyone."

Gavin blinks at me, his eyes still interlocking layers of blue, from the palest robin's egg to the richest indigo sky. Lashes so long and thick they cast a shadow over the high crest of his cheekbones. His tawny hair is longer than it was the last time I saw him, and my fingers twitch with the desire to run my hands through it. "Starting with the most important information, I see."

A flush crawls up my throat, burning the tips of my ears, and I duck my head, embarrassed. *Technically, you're still married, Poppy. Don't make a fool of yourself.* "Sorry. You're right, of course. It's none of my business."

"Stop. I was kidding." Gavin reaches for my chin and brings my gaze back to his. His eyes rove hungrily over my face, twin flames of desire and vulnerability burning inside them. "I won't lie and say I've been a monk these past years. I tried to get over you, Poppy. I tried and failed. Because you're the only one who's ever claimed a piece of my heart. And you still have it, even now."

His candid admission knocks the breath right out of my chest, each gorgeous word wringing oxygen from my lungs until I'm dizzy with love and longing. "You know I don't deserve you, right? I'm a disaster."

"Luckily for me, it's not your decision to make."

My eyes drop to the silver scar marking the skin between his lower lip and chin, a final token of his father's misplaced rage. I lift my hand up, dragging my thumb over Gavin's mouth as an explosion of heat detonates somewhere deep in my belly. "Please tell me your mother came to her senses and forgave you."

"She did." His kisses the palm of my hand and I bite back a groan. Despite our outwardly casual conversation, my body is reacting to Gavin's proximity and touch in an entirely different kind of communication. "After she started seeing a guy who didn't get his kicks by beating her up every other week. They got married last year."

"That's really great, Gav. I'm happy for her."

"How about your mom, is she doing well?"

"Yeah. She lives up in Maine now. I called her last week to tell her what was going on and she rushed me off the phone because she didn't want to be late for drum circle." I roll my eyes. "Apparently, the last person to show up gets stuck with the bad banjo."

"I hate when that happens."

We share an easy silence for a few moments, and I can feel the years falling away like we're being pushed through an opening in the universe that was made just for us. The gravity between my heart and Gavin's is an undeniable force that has me leaning into him. My lips part, compelled by an instinctive urge to breathe his scent deep into my lungs, to swallow the energy sparking and dancing between us.

The spell is broken when a couple of tourists enter our clearing, using their selfie stick to pose in front of the waterfall. A chill breaks out over my skin and I jerk back, blinking my vision into focus. For several moments I am untethered, fighting to regain my sense of time and place while two strangers laugh and make ridiculous faces, completely unaware of us as they cycle through several poses before venturing off in search of the next Instagram-worthy spot.

Once they leave I exhale a ragged sigh. Gavin presses a kiss against my temple and curves his hand around the back of my neck, lightly caressing the tendons on either side of my spine. "I looked for you, you know," I say, my voice cracking. "When you stopped sending messages."

Gavin appears puzzled. "Looked for me... where?"

"Social media. Instagram, Facebook, SnapChat. Even Twitter."

His confusion works its way into a disappointed frown. "You could have tried calling me."

"I was married, Gavin. It wouldn't have been right."

"I don't do social media. But if I did, it wouldn't be all that interesting. After I left your place that day, I called up a contact of mine who worked in the New York Field Office and picked his brain for an hour. I figured if you were doing your thing, I'd better get my ass in gear and do mine."

I clear my throat, relieved to be talking about banal things for a little longer. My pulse is still racing and my breaths are shallow. "Did you always want to work in Financial Crimes?"

"Not really. It was only because—" He closes his eyes for a minute, almost wincing. "Fuck, I'm going to sound like a stalker for telling you this."

My curiosity immediately multiplies. "Tell me."

"I was trying to figure out what you saw in a guy like Stockton, so I read up on him and his family, their investment company. I never expected to find banking interesting, but I kind of developed a knack for it. Numbers don't lie." He turns back my way, his eyes open and trained on me once again. "One thing led to another and when a spot opened up in FC, I applied."

I have to stifle the urge to tie a bandana around Gavin's face. His stare triggers an alarm rigged deep within my body, somehow waking up every single cell and making them shake inside my veins. I feel jittery and tingly, like he's set off a chemical reaction I have no control over. Tearing my gaze from his, I look over at the waterfall. "How did you find out what Tucker was up to?"

"I can't take all the credit. One of my buddies from Quantico works in Art Theft. I stopped by his desk on our way to lunch and noticed a picture tacked to his bulletin board—"

I suck in a breath. "Wren."

"Yes. Apparently, she advises several collectors who are known to purchase black market art. I followed a hunch and learned that every single one of those collectors became a client of Stockton Capital after your husband took over."

"So you think…"

"He got into business with some really shady characters. Lines were crossed. I don't know how he found out about the pending indictment, but leaks happen. This isn't the first time someone's carried out an elaborate scheme to evade arrest."

I consider Gavin's assessment for a few minutes. He doesn't add anything else, giving me time to draw a conclusion of my own. But my mind quickly strays from thoughts of Tucker. I've wasted too much time thinking about him, worrying about him, trying to please and appease him. I don't want to waste any more.

And besides, I have more important things to discuss with Gavin. The truth… *my* truth.

Gathering all of my courage, I tug at the zipper of my coat and pull out the moonstone pendant tucked beneath my shirt

Gavin's eyes drop. "You still have it."

"Tucker had it, actually. I found it in his safe yesterday."

His brows knit together, an unspoken question in the crease of his forehead.

I fight against a sudden wave of vertigo and dig my hands into the cold dirt beneath me, bombarded by the sheer force of all the secrets I've kept from him through the years. Once I've found my center, clinging to a deep reserve of determination buried within my core, I dive back into the sea of confusion and concern swirling inside Gavin's gaze. "There's so much I need to tell you. Starting with the night I lost your necklace."

CHAPTER 51

NEW YORK CITY

Poppy Stockton, wife of missing Manhattan mogul, Tucker Stockton, has been discharged from her hospital in Florida and is now back in the luxury Manhattan apartment she shares with her husband, Tucker Stockton, who is still missing. In the meantime, Wall Street is buzzing over rumors that his company, Stockton Capital, may have been engaged in fraudulent, some are even saying criminal, activities.

"Turn that off, please." My voice is low, haggard.

Sadie vaults from the couch. "Poppy, you're finally back! How did it go?"

I drop my purse and fall back onto the pillows, sighing as I point at the TV. First things first. "Off."

Gavin and I spent hours inside Central Park, walking and talking and, in my case, crying. I told him everything. And it was hard. Really hard.

That night, of course. And the next morning, coming back from the hospital and having to face both Tucker and Wren when I could barely face my own reflection in the mirror. The choices

I'd made, including the middle-of-the-night truce with Wren. Working with Tucker on TeenCharter, forgiving him and eventually falling for him. I needed Gavin to know that our romance felt real to me. I believed I was in love with Tucker, shielding myself from everything wrong about our relationship... which was basically everything.

If Tucker had been within reach, he wouldn't have needed to fake his own death because Gavin looked ready to kill him. But for me, the worst was telling him about my babies. Through his eyes, I'd relived every excruciating moment.

I explained how angry I'd been, how vengeful. How everything I'd ignored and justified and excused came roaring back, drowning me within an endless ocean of rage.

Now Gavin knows the truth. My truth.

I asked him if he still believed I was innocent. Still believed that Tucker had faked his own death.

And he said *yes*.

Gavin is more certain of my innocence than I am.

Sadie grabs for the remote and a moment later, the screen turns mercifully black. "So, how did it go? You were gone so long I was starting to worry."

I have to tell her about Gavin. And I will, as soon as I fill her in on my meeting with Reese. I'm through keeping secrets. "It went well... I think."

"What does that mean?"

"Well, she basically broke down my options into six scenarios."

After I explain each of them, Sadie says, "You're going with number one, right? Tucker either fell or jumped overboard. He's gone, but it wasn't your fault."

I shake my head. "Nope. Number five. Tucker escaped, probably with an accomplice who definitely wasn't me."

"Why? You wanted to divorce him anyway. If Tucker is *gone*," it's clear Sadie means dead, "everything stops. The reporters will go away, the search will end. You can put this all behind you."

I run my fingertips inside the neck of my shirt, feeling for the warmth of the moonstone. Sadie is wrong. No matter what I choose, there is no light at the end of the tunnel. "Look, I understand you're trying to help—"

"Don't patronize me," she snaps. "I think you like the attention all this is getting you."

I suck in a deep breath, nearly choking on it. "Sadie, how can you say that?"

"Gee, I don't know. Maybe because you're hiring the most attention hungry lawyer in Manhattan. God, don't you want this all to end?"

"It's barely been a week! I don't think it's going away anytime soon." My flash of anger is replaced with guilt when I see the glimmer of tears in my sister's eyes. "Sadie, maybe you need a break. My mess doesn't have to be your mess. It's not fair to you."

"You want me to go?"

I choose my words carefully. "I want you to be happy, sis. That's all. You got me through the worst moments of my life. And this is awful too, but I'm strong enough now to deal with it on my own."

There is a flicker in her eyes, an emotion I can't read. "Just think about it," I add, reaching out to squeeze her knee before standing up and walking out onto our terrace for some fresh air.

Telling her about Gavin will have to wait. Again. I can't spring a decade's worth of lies on her right now.

When Sadie moved in with us it was supposed to be temporary. Just a few months until she found a job and an apartment and the babies were born. She never could have imagined what she was getting herself into. For months, my grief had known no bounds, poisoning every breath I struggled to take. Every pore of my body was clogged with guilt and shame and fury.

It was Sadie who found a therapist willing to make house calls when I couldn't get out of bed. And when I finally did but refused to leave the apartment, she'd dragged me out onto the terrace, insisting that there was still a whole world out there.

I will never forget that first afternoon, those initial moments outside. The buildings rising above me had appeared grim and imposing, like enormous tombstones with hundreds of seeing eyes. Every single one of them turning on me. Judging me.

I'd run for the edge, wanting nothing more than to put an end to the pain of living. Sadie tackled me to the ground, held me as I sobbed and screamed and raged.

I owe her my life.

I peer over the edge now. There is a lot of wind when you are nearly thirty stories above Manhattan, air gusting through corridors made of skyscrapers. Up this high, I can't smell the hotdogs and pretzels hawked by pushcart street vendors, or the exhaust fumes from buses and trucks and taxis. The air is different up here. Cold and sharp.

So different from the woodsy, earthy scent of The Ramble, where Gavin and I spent most of the afternoon. Now he knows everything there is to know about my relationship with Tucker. The good and the bad and the truly vile.

It's a lot to take in.

And while I did ask Gavin what he thought happened in Florida… I didn't ask what is happening now, with us. I know what I want to happen though. What I hope will happen, *if* I'm exonerated. *If* we have a chance at a future.

I want to fall asleep every night with Gavin's arms wrapped around me, the heat of his breath fanning my cheek, the rhythmic thud of his heartbeat pulsing through my chest. I want to wake up to the sweetness of his kisses and bathe in the warmth of his love. I want to build a life with the man I've never stopped loving —even when I believed I loved someone else. And maybe, one day, I hope our life includes children.

When I finally turn to go back inside, I pause at the sight of my reflection in the mirrored glass. I look frail, rather than merely thin. Wisps of blond hair have come loose from the pony-tail I'd secured at the back of my head, fluttering around my face like the silken strands peeking out from an ear of corn. My eyes are tired, with purple smudges beneath them.

Do I look like a murderer?

When Gavin came to my hospital room, he called me a victim.

I still hate that word now, every bit as much as I'd hated it ten years ago. Back then, I avoided it by pretending what Tucker had done was a meaningless slip up. An inconsequential mistake.

What happened in the Florida Keys was no mistake. And the consequences are mine to bear.

But I don't want Tucker's death on my conscience.

What I want is the chance at a future with Gavin.

Which is why I need Reese's scenario number five to be more than just a theory. I need it to be fact. He couldn't have done it alone though. Wren had to have helped him.

The more I think about it, the more it makes sense. We all flew down to Miami together: Tucker and I, plus Wren and Sadie. Wren loves the nightlife in South Beach and decided to tag along with us at the last minute. Sadie because she'd become a part of our family and it would have been rude to leave her out. She was going to get her scuba certification while Tucker and I explored the Keys on our own, then we were going to meet up with Wren and Sadie in the Bahamas before heading back to New York.

Did Tucker plan our trip knowing Wren was going to whisk him off on a private plane bound for Cuba? Gritting my teeth, I hold my head in my hands.

Remember. Remember, damn it.

Had Wren finally convinced him that she was the better choice? Did Tucker try to convince me to come with him? To live a life on the run together?

Was that when I picked up the knife? Had Wren tackled me to the ground as I stabbed Tucker, my head smashing into the floor, the glass fragments—from the champagne glasses, I assume— shredding my back and legs.

And then what happened? Did Tucker and Wren leave me there, hoping I would bleed out and die while they ran off together, eager to begin their new adventure?

The images in my mind are so real. The look of exhilaration on Tucker's face when he sees Wren speeding toward us. The steely glint of the knife in my hand. The sky a lavender dome above, the moon just a creamy crescent floating on the clouds as the sun melts into the horizon.

Goose bumps race up my arms as I gulp at air.

But I can't get past Wren's face yesterday, when she tore apart Tucker's office. She looked like she didn't know anything.

Had she pulled that stunt just to throw off my suspicions?

I yank open the door, the rush of filtered, purified, dehumidi- fied, temperature-controlled air like a slap across my face. It *has* to be Wren. I have the life she wanted, and if I don't pull myself together and start fighting back, she will bury me in it.

And then I'll never have the chance to see what the future holds with Gavin.

CHAPTER 52

NEW YORK CITY

*T*he smell of leather invades my consciousness a half second before I realize it belongs to the hand—the very heavy hand—covering my mouth.

Stifling my scream.

Everything inside me is operating at double-speed. Heart pounding, blood racing, nerves jangling—and yet my body is stiff as a board. Scared stiff.

"Shh." A hard whisper smacks my ear, breath hot and damp on my cheek. Adrenaline surges, sending every one of my senses into overdrive. The ambient lights of my darkened bedroom reveal a man with broad shoulders, smooth tanned skin, and a shaved head. His hooded eyes are firmly fixed on mine, and he doesn't look rough, or out of control. Which somehow makes the situation even more frightening.

The hand not covering my mouth presses into the pillow beneath my head causing me to roll toward him, the knee he'd set on the mattress digging into my hip.

There is way too much contact between us.

Living in Manhattan, it is impossible not to hear horrible stories of women being attacked in their own apartments. But usually, it happens in a ground floor bedroom without bars on the window, or a non-doorman building where anyone can press enough buttons and be buzzed right in. I am thirty stories up, in an apartment with an expensive, elaborate security system incorporating cameras, sensors, and high-tech locks. My own sister is just down the hall.

Oh my God, Sadie. I gasp, though no air makes it around his glove. But somehow, he must sense my concern because he says, "She is fine. It's you I'm here for."

This man—whoever he is—is not a common criminal, spontaneously deciding to rob or rape me. Tonight's visit has been carefully planned, expertly executed. He is a pro.

"I'm going to pull my hand away now. It would be a terrible shame to break that pretty little neck of yours." His voice is smooth, cultured, his accent Spanish, but with a hint of British, too. He reminds me of someone I met at Worthington, who had been raised in South America but attended school in England.

Those dark eyes narrow, and I notice he has extraordinarily long eyelashes. I am a sucker for long eyelashes on guys, they can soften even the hardest features. But tonight, on this man, it only makes him look more menacing. I swallow heavily and his stare follows the bob of my throat. "A real shame," he adds, the curve of his mouth sending another wave of unease rippling through my veins.

His hand lifts, just slightly at first, and my quick breath is the only sound in the room. His lips part, flashing teeth that have seen more than their fair share of coffee and nicotine but are perfectly even and straight. "I figured you for a smart girl. Glad you proved me right."

"What do you want?"

"Right to the point, I like that too. Your husband is a lucky man." He gestures at the empty space beside me before returning his focus back to my face. "Although not very smart. He obviously doesn't appreciate what is waiting for him in his own bed."

I shrink away from his appraising gaze, bile rising up my throat. He releases a soft chuckle, dragging a gloved finger along my thigh that had escaped from beneath my covers while I was sleeping. I am uncomfortably aware that I'm not wearing any underwear beneath my short nightie.

"Don't worry, *chica*, this is a business call. Normally, I would deal with your husband, but he is not here. He is not anywhere that I can find him, and I don't like not being able to find him. It makes me look bad, you see."

I see. "You work with Tucker?"

"That surprises you?" A cluster of hair hovers above his lip, too small to be called a mustache. It sits, like a fat beetle, just below his nose, moving with each word. I can't look away from it, wondering if it will be the last thing I ever see. "I don't look like a business associate of your husband?"

I rush to backtrack. This is not a man I want to insult. "No, of course not. I'm sorry. I just—"

His throaty chuckle cuts me off. "I'm just teasing. Your husband and I have never met. He always did his job, so there was no need. But now he's gone, and my bosses are concerned. And when they are concerned, they call me, and then I have to get involved. Do you understand?"

"Y-Yes. But I don't know where he is either."

His hand continues its ascent, moving slowly up my ribs, along the curve of my breast, his finger sweeping over my exposed collarbone. "Now that isn't the answer I was hoping for, *chica*. Are you sure you don't want to think a little harder?"

A tear escapes from the corner of my eye, dripping down my temple. "I don't know. Really. I've spent the past few days trying to remember what happened that night on the boat. But I don't, it's still a blank, and the doctor said my memories might never come back. Believe me, I want to find him as much as you."

He cocks his head to the side. "I'm not sure that's true."

"It is. If I don't wind up in jail, I'll live under a cloud of suspicion for the rest of my life, either as his co-conspirator, his murderer, or the stupidest woman on earth for not knowing what my own husband was up to."

I can't believe I am whining to a threatening stranger who has broken into my bedroom in the middle of the night... and yet the words keep coming. "His desk was cleared out by the time I came back from Florida. I'm looking for clues on Facebook and Instagram, for God's sake." Definitely not my proudest moment, but I had scoured Wren's social media, hoping to find something to bolster the theory that she and Tucker planned his escape together.

"And? What have you found?"

His eyes drill into me, finally halting the torrent of words pouring from my mouth. Even if I had proof Wren helped Tucker and is trying to frame me, I can't sic this man on her. I wouldn't wish this nighttime call on my worst enemy. "N-not much. Tucker traveled overseas all the time, to many different countries." I pause, anxiety clanging against my ribcage. "But I suppose you knew that already."

"Yes. I know this. The question is, in which of these places will I find your husband."

Tentacles of fear race up my spine, clawing at the back of my neck. I remember reading somewhere that the key to making it out of a dangerous situation is establishing a rapport with your attacker. "What is your name?" I ask now.

He arches an eyebrow. "You planning to friend me on Facebook?"

"No. Of course not. I—" I draw a shaky breath. "It's just... we want the same thing, I think. Maybe we can work together."

His lips twitch. "I've been told I don't work well with others." He looks down, and I curse my choice of nighttime clothing. My sweetheart neckline is showing way too much cleavage. "Then again, I've never worked with a woman before. Maybe I should reconsider."

"No, no, that's okay. It's fine, really. No problem." I am babbling. "This has to be some kind of misunderstanding, though. I mean, I'm sure Tucker didn't intend to get your bosses upset."

"Don't talk about my bosses."

I clamp my mouth shut at the implied threat, wondering if I've already said too much.

"Listen to me. I'm going to let you in on a little secret, *chica*. Your husband is a smart man, maybe too smart, although he has no common sense. Sometimes smart people are like that, they learn too much from books and not enough from life." He scowls, shaking his gleaming head. "He was very good at taking money, especially money that came from places America is not supposed to take money from, looks like it came from somewhere else. A lot of money. But now, your husband is missing. And so is the money. Just because he cleaned it, doesn't make it his."

I can't catch my breath. "He took your money?" *Who steals from people with assassins on their payroll?*

Tucker has always been smart, brilliant even. A good-looking savant with a powerful pedigree. He thought it made him invincible.

But who am I to judge? *I* thought it made him, and by extension *me*, invincible too.

We were both wrong.

And now it seems as if Tucker has left me holding the bag. An empty one.

Another soft, chilling laugh. "Not my money, no. Money belonging to the people who sent me. If I don't get it back for them, they will just send someone else. And someone else after that. So, you understand then, why we must find your husband." It isn't a question, but I nod anyway. "I will take your word that you don't know where he is, but you had better figure it out quickly. I am not a patient man."

He starts to stand, but then hesitates. "Co-conspirator," he whispers, soft as a sigh. "Is there a reason to believe you are as guilty as your husband? If you know where the money is… maybe I don't need to look so hard for your husband?"

My breath catches in the back of my throat as he stares down at me, his eyes becoming even colder, even darker. *No, please just go.*

But he doesn't. "You are beautiful, and beautiful women are often the most cunning." His gloved thumb sweeps over my trembling lips, his palm against my jaw.

"I don't know anything, I swear."

His full lips quirk as he sits back, dragging the Frette sheet and duvet off the bed. Inch by inch, I am exposed. "You know what else beautiful women are good at? Lying. I'll bet you are a good liar. How can I be sure you are being honest with me?"

I shake my head back and forth, a strand of hair catching at the corner of my mouth. "I'm telling the truth." A tear slides down my cheek, then another and another. "I don't know anything about money. Not even what's in our checking accounts." My voice breaks. "I don't even know how to pay my lawyer."

He exhales heavily and drops the linens. "Stop crying or I will give you something to cry about."

I sniff, wiping at my tears with shaking hands. "Sorry."

"This bastard I now have to hunt down, like an animal…" He reaches for my left hand, holding my enormous wedding ring up for a closer look and exposing a long, thin scar that goes from his jaw to his chin. "He kept you here, like a bird in a cage."

When he releases my fingers, his smile is more menacing than his scar. "Just don't fly free until I have the money, or I'll have to hunt you too."

CHAPTER 53

"*H*ey, sleeping beauty. You planning on waking up anytime soon?"

I wince at Sadie's strident tone, my head pounding as if I'd slept on a pillow of rusty nails. My memory of last night is a further assault.

The man in my bedroom.

His questions.

His threats.

The damp rag he'd put over my mouth, just before warning me not to tell anyone about his visit. The *or else* was unspoken, but it was there. Whatever the rag had been soaked in put me out immediately, and must be the reason for my killer headache this morning.

A bird in a cage, he'd called me. A pretty, perceptive phrase completely incongruous with the sheer menace of him.

He didn't know me, and yet he knew the most important thing about me. Despite my high thread count sheets, silk drapes, and Harry Winston rings, I am a prisoner. Captive inside a cage I willingly walked into.

Sadie regards me quizzically. "What's going on with you? Did you hit the bars last night or something?"

"Yeah, I snuck out when you weren't looking," I deadpan. "Can you just get me an Excedrin?"

Moments later she is back at my side, loudly shaking two pills from the bottle. I groan at the noise, but accept them gratefully. "The knock on your head hurting again?"

"Mm-hmm," I say, gulping water from the bottle on my nightstand. I cannot tell her about the man from last night. Sadie will always be my younger sister, and quite frankly, I am freaking out enough for the both of us.

"Okay, hopefully, these will work because your lawyer called. Said she was going to stop by to go over a few things with you."

My brain feels like a cruise ship trying to make a U-turn, heavy and ponderous. "Reese?"

"Unless you hired a new one overnight."

"Here?"

"Yep. Might want to get out of your pj's."

A strong sense of foreboding swirls in the pit of my stomach. Reese Reynolds making a house call? This can't be good.

And... shit. I need to pay her.

Your husband is missing. And so is the money. Just because he cleaned it, doesn't make it his.

Could Tucker have drained our personal accounts too? Alarm spirals its way through my intestines as I grab my laptop, logging onto my Internet browser before realizing I have absolutely no idea how to check our accounts. Tucker has always handled all of our finances. Even when I'd earned my own paycheck, it was deposited directly into one of our accounts and I simply used the credit cards Tucker gave me for my purchases. And if I needed cash, all I had to do was ask.

Who do I ask now?

∾

"I HAVE A PROBLEM."

Reese's expression remains impassive. "Problems are how I earn my fees."

"Yes, well, I guess you have your work cut out for you." I clear my throat, feeling a wave of embarrassment for ceding control over even the most basic necessity—access to a checking account —to Tucker. "I don't know how to access my bank accounts."

Reese leans back, arms folded as she appraises me critically. "Well, now, that is a problem. Although one that should be relatively easy to solve. Assuming, of course, that your husband didn't leave you penniless."

I chew at the inside of my cheek, afraid if I admit how plausible that scenario really is, my lawyer will walk out the door and never come back. I highly doubt my high-powered lawyer defends women who live in ten-million-dollar Manhattan penthouses pro bono?

Thankfully, she makes no move to leave. "What's your social security number?" she asks, pulling out her phone and making a call.

I answer, and she repeats it to the person on the other end of the line. "I need a full financial work-up on Mrs. Stockton immediately, and as soon as you're finished, I want one on her husband, too. And when you think you're done, you're not. I want shell companies, deposits, wire transfers, fund disbursements, fees. I want to see so far up Tucker Stockton's fiscal asshole I'm going to need a cigarette afterward, you understand?" She ends the call, regarding me with a satisfied smile on her face. "Okay then, now that that's settled, let's talk about your case."

She slides a photo toward me. "The knife. Take a look and tell me whatever comes to mind."

Shock ripples through me as I stare at the bloody blade jutting out from an ivory handle. "It's— It's from the charcuterie platter. I used it to cut the chorizo." When Detective Reardon asked me about a knife, I imagined something bigger, sharper, more lethal. "*This* is what I stabbed Tucker with?"

Reese frowns. "Do not admit to stabbing Tucker with anything, do you hear me?"

I nod, but inside I'm shaking. *I didn't do it. I didn't kill Tucker. I don't know how or why his blood got on the knife—but it wasn't because I'd intended to hurt him.*

"As far as the criminal case against you is concerned, at least your prints make sense now." Her phone buzzes and Reese squints at it. "Looks like my guy put together a preliminary financial snapshot on you already."

I try to slow my breathing as Reese downloads the report onto her iPad. She pats the chair beside her. "Come, let's go over this together."

I change seats, my brows drawing together as I study the information on screen. Beneath my name, is a bank account number and a dollar amount. $112,968.47. Below that are several credit cards. Various amounts, all under ten thousand dollars, have been noted beside each one. All three are marked "current."

Reese glances at my face. "What's wrong?"

"Two things. First, I haven't used that bank in years. And second, I only recognize two of the credit cards."

Her phone buzzes again and she picks it up, sighing. "Your husband's financial profile is proving more difficult. I can't say I'm surprised, given his wealth, occupation, and the charges he's facing. Tell you what, I'm going to email you this information, and you can try to figure out what's what. In the meantime, I'll head back to my office and see what I can discover myself."

I offer a tight nod. I can still feel the intruder's hand on my hip, hear the echo of his softly accented voice delivering icy threats. The next time he shows up, and I am certain there will be a next time, I'd better have something to tell him.

CHAPTER 54

NEW YORK CITY

I crawl back into bed with my laptop, then pull up the website of the bank I used in college. I enter the account number from the email Reese sent me, and fill a dozen boxes with my name, address, social security number, and a few other identifying bits of data. After confirming my email address, I am redirected to a secure portal and just like that, I have access to money I didn't even know existed a few hours ago.

But where did it come from?

Scrolling through previous statements, I go back months and then years to find the most recent deposit—a paycheck. In fact, those are the only deposits that were ever made into the account. Bi-monthly paychecks. The money in the account is the sum of my earnings from working at TeenCharter, all of which were paid out through direct deposits into my bank account.

Isla sorts our mail, leaving everything but catalogues, junk mail, everything concerning my mother, and the occasional birthday card or wedding invitation on the kitchen counter. Bills and bank statements either go directly to Stockton Capital or are left for Tucker in his home office. *No need for you to concern your-*

self with paperwork, he'd assured me. *I give it all to an accountant anyway.*

Out of sight, out of mind.

My lack of involvement in our financial affairs had never bothered me. Why would it? Money was never an issue.

Until now.

Taking another glance at my bank balance, I realize it's barely enough to pay Reese's retainer and Isla's salary, let alone basic expenses like food and the maintenance fees of our apartment.

There must be more money somewhere. I just have to figure out how to access it.

Turning my attention to the credit cards, I follow the same procedure as I did with my bank, logging onto the website and entering the account numbers and my personal data. But this doesn't give me the access I want.

Stifling a groan, I call the number on the back of my Black American Express card. The customer service representative is polite and friendly, patiently explaining that I am only an authorized user, not the actual account holder. Access denied.

My conversation with Visa is nearly identical.

But that still leaves one more card. The one that isn't in my wallet.

I call the customer service number listed on MasterCard's website. But the result is the same as the other two. Denied.

The stitches in my scalp feel tight around my wound, almost as if my head expanded with each wasted effort. Spotting the bottle of Excedrin Sadie left on my nightstand, I shake another into my hand.

Who else can I call?

The accountant.

Closing my laptop, I try to remember if Tucker had ever mentioned him by name. I am sure he would have used someone at Stockton, but there have to be dozens of accountants on staff, at the very least. Surely a confidentiality clause won't prevent Keene from forwarding my call to Tucker's accountant.

Cursing my complacency for the thousandth time in the past few days, I dial the main number for Stockton Capital and am redirected to Keene's line. If only I had taken even the slightest interest in our financial affairs at some point during our marriage, I wouldn't be in this position.

He picks up on the second ring. "Mrs. Stockton, you're ah—" he stops, the strain in his voice obvious. "It's kind of a busy time."

"I understand. It is for me, too. Um, I was just wondering if you could put me through to whomever dealt with our personal finances. I need to pay a few bills and I'm having a hard time getting information from my credit cards because I'm not an account—"

Keene interrupts. "I take it you haven't seen the news today."

"No. Not today. Why? What's going on?" I grab for the remote control on my nightstand.

"We're being investigated by the FBI. Trading has been suspended, computers and files are being seized." My jaw sags as the screen comes to life, showing a street view of Tucker's office building, a swarm of blue windbreakers carrying boxes with electronic equipment or reams of paper into a white van parked at the curb. "It's not a good time right now. I'm sorry. I really have to go."

He clicks off, and it takes a minute to realize the strange sound in my ear is a dial tone. I let the phone drop to the mattress.

The scene playing out on TV reminds me of watching the Coast Guard search for Tucker. All those people—on boats, on the beach, in the water, hovering overhead in helicopters. So many people looking for just one man.

All that effort, and they still haven't found him.

Clearly the investigation is expanding, the circle of suspicion widening. His wife. Our private life. Now his business. Everything is being torn apart in the search for Tucker.

I am living in a real life game of dominos.

Tucker, gone.

Stockton Capital, as good as gone.

Am I next? Will I spend the rest of my life in prison for a crime I'm now certain I didn't commit?

Crimes, really. All the buzzwords I've been hearing on TV swarm inside my head like angry wasps. Murder. Manslaughter. Money-laundering. Theft. Aiding and abetting a criminal enterprise.

Is Tucker watching this? How could he have let his happen?

I raise the volume.

Agents seized documents today at the Park Avenue offices of Stockton Capital, the Manhattan-based money management firm, executing court-authorized search warrants as part of their investigation into one of the largest cases of alleged money laundering in United States history. Sources have confirmed that this is a joint effort of the FBI, the Manhattan District Attorney's office, and the Treasury Department, although the SEC is expected to become involved shortly.

The screen changes to a montage of me and Tucker at our wedding, then at various black-tie events before showing footage of the search and rescue operation.

Since Tucker Stockton's disappearance nearly a week ago, authorities close to the investigation say they've been concerned about the potential for Stockton Capital associates to destroy evidence critical to the investigation. The firm hasn't returned messages seeking comment. We are tracking this story closely and will have more details for you as they become available.

The camera then returns to the network studio reporters.

You may remember, Tucker Stockton's wife, Poppy Stockton, was released from the Florida hospital where she was treated for injuries sustained during the fateful boat ride from which her husband didn't return. Sources tell us she's been questioned by the authorities though she has yet to be officially named as a suspect. However, Mrs. Stockton has retained the services of Reese Reynolds and we've reached out to the famed celebrity attorney for comment. So far, our calls have gone unreturned.

The back of my neck feels hot, as if warmed by the breath of someone chasing me. Like I am being hunted. The other reporter nods her assent and reads a lead-in for the next story.

Reaching beneath my sweater, I scratch at the cuts on my back, my hand coming away streaked with fresh blood.

"Hey, Poppy. Are you watching—" She stops talking when she pokes her head through my doorway and catches sight of the television screen.

"Yeah. I saw."

Her eyes probe mine. "Are you okay?"

I answer honestly. "I have no idea."

CHAPTER 55

"Thanks for coming," I say to Gavin, letting him pull me into his arms and exhaling a ragged sigh of relief and gratitude. I'd finally capitulated and told him about the man who'd broken into my apartment the other night.

"Poppy, you should have called me right away." Horror is written in the tiny creases extending outward from the corners of his narrowed eyes. "If your apartment isn't secure, you can't stay here."

I push my nose into the curve of his shoulder, breathing deep. Gavin still smells the same, even after all this time. Fresh laundry and pinecones. "I don't have anywhere else to go."

He rests his hands on the curve of my hips, pulling me flush against him. His voice turns gruff and protective, just about the most swoony combination there is. "Then you'll stay with me."

The idea of cozying up with Gavin at his place is far from unappealing, but I reluctantly shake my head. "You can't watch over me night and day. And besides, I have Sadie."

Gavin lifts his chin from the top of my head and looks around. "Is she home?"

"No. She's out. A spin class, I think."

I linger in Gavin's arms for a long while, drawing comfort from his solid bulk and gentle hold. God, it feels good to be held. After my miscarriage, I spurned every attempt at affection. I haven't wanted to touch or be touched, love or be loved.

But Gavin is making me want all of that again. He's igniting a passion inside me, the kind that sweeps you away on a frothy, white capped wave. But he will never let me get swept out to sea, alone and frightened. Gavin is my safe harbor, his commitment an anchor I can count on. I was wrong to ever doubt him, and I won't make that mistake again.

It will take time to fully immerse myself in another relationship, even with Gavin, because there is still much tying me to Tucker. Invisible wounds that have not yet healed. Potential criminal charges. The high-tech thug who let himself into my bedroom as if I'd rolled out the red carpet. Legally sworn vows. Complex financial arrangements.

I shift in his arms, hoping for a kiss. It's wrong, I know. We're standing in the apartment I shared with Tucker. But I feel like I might burst if I don't feel the press of Gavin's lips on mine, taste the warm mintiness of his breath, hear his ragged groan as our tongues slide together.

When he looks down at me, Gavin's eyes are glowing like blue flames. He's feeling what I'm feeling, I know it. But instead of a kiss on my mouth, his lips travel no farther than my forehead. I want to stomp my foot in frustration.

After everything I shared with him, Gavin is treating me like I'm made of fine porcelain, in danger of shattering at the slightest wrong move. "I won't break, you know. Not from you."

"I—"

"You think I'm fragile."

To my surprise, Gavin actually laughs. "Fragile? Poppy, you're the strongest person I've ever known."

Of all the things Gavin has ever said to me, this is by far my favorite. I pull away from him and swipe at the tears leaking from my eyes before they can fall. "Well, now that that's settled, I'll show you around."

Bringing him into my bedroom feels slightly uncomfortable, the mattress glaring proof that I've shared a bed with another man. Ridiculous, since it's hardly a secret. But Gavin makes no comment as he diligently examines every fixture and piece of furniture for planted cameras or recording devices, then checks out the windows for any sign that they've been tampered with or opened recently.

After looking inside both our closets, he casually asks, "What's next?"

My eyes automatically go to the closed door just beyond our bedroom. The nursery.

Gavin must sense the turmoil rising inside me. "You know what, I'll go have a talk with the security staff first—see what their cameras captured that night. When I get back, maybe I'll have a better idea of what I'm looking for."

I nod, blinking back the sting of hot tears. My babies' room is a sacred space for me. I could probably handle showing it to Gavin... but if he found evidence that that cruel, malevolent man from the other night had been inside, that he'd tampered with their things...

"Thank you," I murmur, walking with him to the front door on weak legs.

"Listen, before I go, I want to show you this." He pulls a folded piece of paper out of his pocket. A credit card statement for the one card not in my wallet. "This charge here, it's from a boat rental company in Key West. As you can see, it was quickly reversed. I called, and the boat was rented using cash, but they require a credit card number to reserve it and someone accidentally ran it before realizing their mistake."

"That's not my credit card," I say, quickly explaining the situation.

"Give this to your lawyer then. Not only is the card registered in your name, to your address, but the boat was rented by someone matching your description. The woman specifically asked for a fast, lightweight boat she could use to scuba dive off some of the more shallow keys, farther away. Sounds a lot like the Dry Tortugas."

"I've never rented a boat in my life, but even if I had, it makes no sense. Why would I rent a speedboat when we already had one, plus the yacht?"

"A prosecutor might argue that you needed a getaway vehicle. Another boat, anchored off the coast of the island."

"But I didn't get away. I'm still here."

"At the last minute, either you decided not to go or Stockton decided not to take you. There was a struggle, and he left you behind. Now you're lying to hide your involvement."

I feel my mouth go dry. "That's not what happened. Gavin, you have to believe me—"

"I do. And that's why I'm giving this to you. If you can prove someone else used this card, it will go a long way toward proving your innocence." His blue gaze is steady on mine as he tucks a lock of hair behind my ear, the pad of his thumb sweeping over my cheek. "The proof isn't for me. I don't need it. I know you didn't kill the bastard, even though he deserved it."

I'm reeling with gratitude at Gavin's faith in me, but I remember to put a restraining hand on his arm just as he turns to go. "Sadie might be here when you get back. I haven't told her about us yet."

He sighs. "There's a lot you haven't told her."

Gavin never understood why I kept him a secret from Sadie, maybe because he'd been an only child. He never had to share anything, or be responsible for a younger sibling.

"I will though. I promise." And I mean it.

After he leaves, I head into the kitchen to make making myself a cup of tea.

I've just taken my first sip when the front door slams shut and I hear Sadie drop her purse and keys on the side table. "Poppy, you home?"

"In the kitchen," I call out.

She sets down a square brown bag in front of me, along with a Snapple bottle. "I couldn't eat a burger and onion rings in front of you if you weren't going to have any, and quite frankly, I'm not in the mood to share so I just ordered for two."

I offer a wan smile as Sadie tears open her bag. She bites into an onion ring and groans. "Oh my God, these don't disappoint."

Surprisingly, my stomach gives an audible grumble and I reach into my bag too. Maybe taking a lunch break isn't a bad idea. I send an appreciative glance Sadie's way as I nibble at an onion ring. She wasn't kidding. They are piping hot, and deliciously salty.

"See, told ya." She grabs her burger with both hands. "Anything new to report?"

I finish chewing and twist the cap off my drink. "From who?"

"Anyone. Your lawyer, the FBI…" She glances at the TV on the wall, it's screen mercifully dark. "I haven't checked the news yet today."

I think about Gavin downstairs, combing through security footage for a glimpse of the man who'd broken into the apartment less than forty-eight hours ago. The credit card statement he gave me is in my pocket. "The FBI might be building a case against me as a co-conspirator."

Sadie barks out a laugh. "You?"

"It's not all that farfetched. Not if they think I rented the boat Tucker may have used to escape."

"Is there any proof of that? Or that Tucker's living somewhere as a fugitive?"

But I'm not listening. "Oh my God. What if that's what Wren

was looking for when she ripped Tucker's office apart the other day—proof that she'd helped him escape?"

"She could have been looking for anything. She's nuts."

Wren might be a lot of things. But she's not nuts. She's smart, and devoted to Tucker.

I pull out the credit card statement and push it across the table. "Someone used my name to rent a boat. Well, actually, they didn't intend to rent it with this card, they just gave the number to the person dealing with the paperwork. The card was run by accident and reversed almost immediately."

Sadie drops her burger, snatching up the piece of paper. After a long moment she tosses it back to me. "So what? They can't prove it was used to get Tucker out of the country. They can't even prove he's still alive."

"What about the credit card? The one in my name?"

"Poppy, you were at the Delano in Miami. Any place where there are rich tourists, there are identity thieves. I'm sure you just got ripped off."

"You're probably right." I take a bite of my burger, deciding it isn't nearly as good as the onion rings. "But it still doesn't explain how Tucker escaped."

Sadie stands up, dumping her barely touched meal into the garbage.

"I thought you were starving?"

She shrugs. "My eyes are bigger than my stomach, I guess." She turns on the faucet and washes the grease off her hands, lips pursed as if holding back a mouthful of words. I wait, knowing my sister won't be able to keep them inside for long. "Listen, I hate to say this again. But who's to say he escaped?"

"You think—"

"I don't know," she cuts in. "No one knows, right? But if you fell and cut your head, maybe he fell too. If your blood was on him…"

"Just say it, Sadie."

"Sharks. There, I've said it, okay? Those are shark-infested waters. And can't they detect blood in the water from like a mile away?"

My attention slides to the shelf just over Sadie's shoulder, to a photograph of Tucker from our honeymoon. He hadn't realized I'd taken it until I printed it and had it matted and framed. He'd been standing on the balcony of our villa in Bora Bora, the sea a stunning backdrop. He hadn't shaved yet, and his hair was still mussed from our early morning romp.

Tucker looked open, vulnerable. A good man with an old soul. A man I loved.

And I loved him then. Back when I believed the lies he told me. When I thought he was more good than bad. That we were meant to be.

Those days are long over.

But I still can't imagine that he's dead.

"What if Wren rented a boat in Key West and anchored it near Dry Tortuga? They took it back to Key West, and he boarded a private plane bound for Cuba. From there, he could be anywhere by now."

I glance at Sadie, noticing the bright spots of color on her cheeks. She is gripping the counter so hard her knuckles are white. "Are you okay?"

"Nothing a nap won't fix." She grabs for the strap of her purse sitting on the counter next to her half-full Snapple, knocking over the bottle. "Oh shit," she yells as it spills directly into her bag.

I jump up to help her, grabbing for the paper towels and sopping up the puddle.

"Damn it, it's all in my cosmetic case too."

"I've got this. You should go wash your makeup brushes with shampoo before they're ruined."

She shoots me an appreciative look and heads for her bathroom. "Thanks, sis."

"No problem. I'll just lay out everything to dry out here," I say, emptying the contents of Sadie's purse onto a clean dish towel. Noticing the wide open zipper of her wallet, I begin pulling out cash and cards and receipts and laying them on the towel to dry. It isn't until I am wiping out the inside of her bag that I notice the gold Mastercard with the now familiar account number.

With my name across the front.

CHAPTER 56

NEW YORK CITY

"*I* can't believe I did that." Striding back into the kitchen, Sadie pulls up short when she sees what I'm holding. "Poppy, I..." Her voice trails off as I lift my gaze to hers, my eyes glistening with tears.

"What? Are you going to say you can explain? How can you explain having a credit card with my name on it? How can you explain having this when, not two minutes ago, I told you it was the reason they think I'm behind Tucker's—"

All of a sudden everything comes together and I drop the card. "Oh my God, I've been so stupid. *It was you.*" The words leave my throat in a toxic whisper, burning the lining of my esophagus on their way out.

I sag against the kitchen counter, my head spinning. "All along. It was you, Sadie. Not Wren. You."

I wait for her to deny the accusation. There has to be something I'm missing, some explanation to put my world back into perspective. *Come on, Sadie. Tell me I'm crazy.*

As the seconds tick by, emotions flash across her face like the screen of a drive-through movie theater. Hatred. Jealousy. And

378

then I see something else, too. More than just a twitch of her lips, a glimmer in her eye. Pride.

A wave of nausea slams into me. Tucker and Sadie. Tucker and Sadie. Tuckerandsadie.

Tuckerandsadie.

But then she blinks, and for a moment I see past all of it. I see my sister. The one person I've always felt closest to, like we are two halves of the same whole. The only stability Sadie and I have ever had has been each other. Growing up, I shielded Sadie. Cared for her, protected her. And for the past year, during my pregnancy and after, when I was broken and empty, I thought she was doing the same for me. Returning the favor... in spades. Out of love.

When did her motivation change?

Because this, whatever *this* is, goes beyond mere sibling rivalry. Sadie isn't looking at me like a sister now. I am an obstacle in her path. A barrier to be breached.

An adversary.

"Yes," she finally confirms. "Someone had to step in. You lost your mind, remember? Could barely get out of bed, certainly couldn't be the wife Tucker deserved. I needed to do everything for you. Buy your prescriptions, force you into the shower, practically spoon feed you, for God's sake.

"Some of the drugs you were prescribed couldn't be picked up by anyone but you. Kinda hard when you refused to leave the apartment. So Tucker got me a credit card in your name and borrowed your license. All so I could take care of you.

"You thought you were so smart for getting into Worthington, so special for landing a guy like Tucker. But you didn't deserve him then, and you still don't. You got drunk and threw yourself at him, then you acted all holier than thou and treated him like a thug. How dare you!"

I feel like the wind's been knocked out of me. I never told her about *that night.* "How do you—"

"Tucker told me. He doesn't keep secrets from me, unlike you. It used to hurt when you kept things from me. But you know what, I stopped caring. I've had a secret of my own for months now, and you haven't even noticed. Serves you right, sis."

Spreading my palms flat on the cool marble countertop, I am so stunned by her cruelty that it jars loose a memory. Bright and vivid, it overpowers everything else.

Sadie, in a small speedboat, appearing out of nowhere. Tucker and I had been talking. Or rather, I had been talking to him. He was distracted, and I was trying to get his attention. I wanted him to agree to a divorce.

I lift both hands to my face, massaging my temples as though I can rub away the pain slicing through my skull. "It was you," I repeat, as if by saying it again, the awful truth will sink in. "This whole time. It was you."

"Of course, it was me. I swear, I can't believe you never figured it out. Actually, no," Sadie says with an almost manic chortle, "what I can't believe is that Tucker was ever into you in the first place."

Her condescending tone is a spray of salt on my wounds. "So you decided to take my place?"

"Ha! That's where you're wrong. I'm not a replacement. I'm the newer, better model. You couldn't hold his attention, or his babies. It was only a matter of time before he got rid of you, anyway."

Sadie's words are well-aimed arrows, the sharpened tips dipped in poison. Penetrating to the bone. Worse, so much worse, than the shards of glass doctors had spent hours picking from my skin. Those wounds will heal, most not even leaving a scar. But the cuts Sadie is inflicting now, these will stay with me forever.

The room blurs and I begin backing up, wanting to keep the kitchen island between us. "You really know how to kick me where it counts, Sadie."

She shrugs. "It's your fault we're in this mess. If you had just gone with us like we wanted, none of this would be happening."

"What do you mean? Why would I go anywhere with either of you?"

"Tucker tried to tell you about the business, about what would happen. But you refused to listen. He made plans, for all of us. New identities. Plenty of money. We would have had a nice life."

"A nice life, on the run from the US government and the criminals Tucker stole from—with my cheating husband and sister? Really?"

"You're so fucking selfish. Everything has to revolve around you."

Another memory, an extension of the other one, appears like a ghost, whispering at the edges of my mind.

Raised voices. Breaking glass. Falling. Pain. Then darkness.

"So you hit me in the head and pushed me into a pile of glass?"

"No one hit you. You tried to take control of the boat and you fell. There was blood everywhere. Tucker tried to pick you up and bring you into the other boat, and his hands got cut up from the glass too. The only way he would leave was if I agreed to drop him off and come back for you."

I scoff at her attempt to rewrite history. "Don't even. I was found alone, remember?"

"Only because the yacht captain was worried about a weather pattern coming up the coast. He sent his crew out looking for you and Tucker. By the time I came back for you, you had been airlifted to the hospital."

I chew on the inside of my cheek, trying to organize Sadie's self-centered commentary and my scattered memories into a cohesive timeline. "Why didn't you leave then? Why bother coming to check on me?"

"I thought about it. But I decided to find out if you had said anything first. And when the nurse told me you'd been uncon-

TARA LEIGH

scious since you were found, I decided to stick around and convince you to stay quiet."

"But… I didn't remember anything."

"An unexpected stroke of good luck. But then you had to go and hire Reese Reynolds. Making noise about Tucker faking his own death and having an accomplice. *Fuck*, Poppy. If it wasn't for you, I would be lying on a beach somewhere with Tucker right now."

She puts a hand to her belly, the corners of her mouth lifting into an eerie smile. "I'm giving him the family you couldn't."

The breath leaves my lungs in a rush and I lean against the nearest wall, quickly, before my trembling legs give out. My sister is going to give birth to Tucker's baby.

And yet somehow, her betrayal isn't as sharp a surprise as it should be. "You told me this. On the boat."

"Yes." She releases a humorless laugh. "I think that's when you knocked the champagne glasses out of the basket."

An uncomfortable silence descends. Where do we go from here? Except the *we* in this situation isn't me and Sadie. Her allegiance is to Tucker now. And if she wants him, she can have him. Which is exactly what I say. "You can have him, Sadie. Just go."

But Sadie only shakes her head. "I don't trust you, sis."

"What other choice do you have? I'm not going with you."

Her stare narrows as it drifts to a spot just over my head, a look of resignation settling over her features. "No, you're not."

The sun outside the window shifts, as if sliding out from behind a cloud, momentarily bathing my sister in soft white light and reminding me of my final moments with my babies. Our last goodbye.

And with it, reality finally hits home. I can't let Sadie go. No matter how badly she betrayed me, she is still my sister. Tucker will be caught, and if he's caught by the man from the other night… A shiver of fear shakes my spine. Sadie might not make it

382

out alive. "If you go to Tucker now, you'll be running for the rest of your life. You'll never be safe."

Sadie's eyes blaze with fire as she slams her hand against the kitchen counter. "See. I knew it. You don't want him, but you won't let me have him either."

My phone is in my bedroom. *Damn it.* I push off the wall, turning my back on Sadie. "Believe what you want, but I'm calling the police. It's for your own good."

I don't get two steps before I hear it, the sound of Sadie pulling a knife from the wood block beside the stove.

When I spin around, the sight of my sister bearing down on me, stainless steel blade glinting in her hand, seems like a dream. A terrible, terrible nightmare.

"Sadie, what the hell?" I squeak, backing away from her.

"I won't let you ruin all of my plans." Her face is a vengeful mask, almost unrecognizable from the sister I know.

Correction: the sister I thought I knew.

"So what, you're going to kill me?" I'm stalling, trying to buy time. Sadie is a Soul Cycle addict, small but fast. And she hasn't been dealing with a head injury and multiple lacerations all over her back. If she lunges, I am a goner. Somehow, I need to talk my way out of this.

"That's the idea, although, of course, I'll make it look like a suicide. I mean, it would be understandable, right? Your life is a complete train wreck. Husband a criminal who's gone missing. Assets frozen. Police questioning your involvement. Plus, there's your unhappy marriage to Tucker, and your miscarriage. Twins, so a double whammy." She speaks in a singsong voice, moving closer.

"You know what, you're right. Tucker is waiting for you. Why don't you just leave now? I won't say anything, I promise."

"Liar," she spits. "You're such a goody-two shoes, Poppy. Always have been. I wouldn't make it halfway down the corridor before you called the police on me. No. This is the way it has to be. You have to die."

My instincts kick in. I lash out with my forearm, knocking into Sadie's wrist and sending the knife skittering across the polished wood floors. Bone collides with bone and we both yelp, looking at each other in surprise. Sadie recovers first, spinning around to grab for the knife. I should probably race back to my room and barricade myself behind a locked door, but instead I pounce on my sister, jumping onto her back and sending us both sprawling.

"Ooof," she gasps, sucking wind.

The knife in sight, I army-crawl over her prone body to get it. Barely an inch away, my fingers outstretched for the handle, Sadie rears up, flopping me onto my back. Explosions of pain light up along my still healing skin, my skull smacking the hard floor. The edges of my vision blur, but not enough that I don't see Sadie wrap her hand around the knife and straddle me, her face flushed with exertion and rage.

"Get. Off. Me." I grunt, the pain in my head and back negated by a rush of adrenaline.

"Not a chance," she says, reaching for one of my flailing arms. "Just two quick cuts, you'll barely feel it. I'll throw you in a tub, stage it like a suicide. By the time your body is found, I'll be sipping daiquiris on a beach with Tucker." Sadie cackles. "Virgin for me, of course."

This isn't happening. I can't be fighting off my depraved lunatic of a sister who is intent on killing me to run off and join my husband.

But I am.

Swatting away Sadie's attempts to capture my hands, one of my nails draws a diagonal slash across her cheek. "Fuck!" she screams, holding a hand to her injured face as she stares at me accusingly.

"Let's just stop, okay? Right now." I freeze, my palms

outstretched to block the knife still pointed my way. "This is crazy, Sadie. We're sisters—no guy should ever come between us."

And at that moment—just before the thunderous sound of the front door crashing open, wood splintering around a booted foot, hinges being ripped from the frame—I see Sadie give the slightest shake of her head before drawing back the knife intending, I know without a shadow of a doubt, to kill me.

She never gets the chance.

Gavin points his gun, shouting for Sadie to drop the knife. My arms are shaking, fighting a losing battle to keep her from plunging it into my chest. Even so, I risk a glance Gavin's way. Just in time, I catch the almost imperceptible narrowing of his eyes, the clenching of his jaw. I don't have to see his finger twitch to know he is going to shoot my sister.

"No!" I scream, flinging myself up in an adrenaline-fueled burst of strength and wrapping my arms around her.

There is an explosion of pain in my right shoulder as Sadie and I jerk from the strength of the bullet that tears through both of us.

The knife clatters to the floor as Sadie's grip loosens, the two of us coming to rest in a tangled heap, our blood a fast-moving river heading toward the discarded blade.

EPILOGUE

SACKETT, CONNECTICUT

THREE YEARS LATER, POPPY

*W*e are the only ones at the cemetery this morning, and Valentina's tiny hand is soft and damp inside my own. "Belly Mama is here?" she asks, looking around the forest of gray headstones, most of them taller than she is. We've been coming to visit Sadie's grave once a month since her burial, but Valentina's only just begun stringing words together into sentences, and these are hard words to hear.

My throat tightens as I struggle to swallow the enormous lump of remorse blocking my vocal chords. "No, sweetheart," I finally manage. "Belly Mama is in Heaven. But she's always smiling down on you, and I know she'll love the bouquet you picked for her." A riotous assortment of wildflowers is clutched within her other hand, already wilting from the unusual heat and humidity of the morning.

Valentina's face brightens, and my heart immediately swells in response. It is a feeling I should be used to by now, after two and a half years with her. But somehow, every time I think I cannot possibly love this beautiful, mischievous, curious little imp more than I already do… I feel a surge of the purest love, so strong it nearly blows me over.

I cannot bring myself to hate my sister. She is Valentina's Belly Mama, after all. Even on that unthinkably awful day, I would have given my life to protect hers, and very nearly had. Luckily, the bullet that went straight through my shoulder had only grazed Sadie's abdomen. Another couple of inches to the left and we would both be dead. I still shudder to think of how close I'd come to never being given the gift of Valentina. Despite everything, I consider myself truly blessed.

Gavin and I live a quiet life with Valentina now, in Sackett. It's changed a lot since we were in school here. It still has a cozy New England vibe, but a burst of new construction in the past ten years has added new life to the old town. They even incorporated the school system into one district.

Last year, on one of our trips to the cemetery where I chose to bury Sadie, the same cemetery Gavin and I had explored as teenagers, we saw a sign for an Open House. A charming colonial that backed up to the nature preserve where Gavin and I first met and fell in love. We made it our home the very next month.

The life I shared with Tucker seems light years removed from the one I live now. My days are simple, trimmed of all the negativity and self-doubt that once cluttered my mind. Every choice I make is governed by love, and it is a flawless moral compass.

We find Sadie's headstone, which is right beside the headstone for my twins. They are buried together, just as they shared my womb together.

Tucker had wanted to bury them beside his parents, but I refused. We both dug our heels in, the last spark of our doomed marriage. Sadie had stuck up for me, I remember. Telling Tucker that it might help me process my grief if I chose their final resting place. So now, they all sleep beneath the stars together.

One day, when Valentina can understand, I will tell her about her angel siblings. But for now, I press a kiss to their stone as Valentina lays her flowers on the grass in front of Sadie's. There is no epitaph, just the facts. My sister's name and the years of her birth and death. Valentina runs her still pudgy fingers along the inscribed letters and numbers. Announcing each one in a proud baby voice. Eth. Ay. Dee...

Sadie didn't die from her bullet wound, or Valentina wouldn't be here with me. My sister received stitches and was sent to prison to await trail. Her lawyer asked for remand, offering Sadie's help locating Tucker if they allowed her to remain free until trial. But at the last minute, Sadie decided not to cooperate, holding out hope that she would be acquitted of all charges and then be free to join Tucker... wherever he was.

Wren was arrested for trafficking in stolen art. In exchange for a suspended sentence, she flipped on Tucker and shared everything she knew about his money laundering. And she knew a lot. The clients he got involved with, in an effort to hide losses on Stockton Capital's balance sheet and stave off critics who said the company had been better off under his father's leadership, were Wren's first. She made the introductions, a way of proving that herself to Tucker. Such hubris, all of them.

During the final days of Sadie's pregnancy, Tucker was located. As it turns out, even in countries with no extradition treaties, locals are suspicious of Americans who throw their money around. His crimes were reported all over the world, alongside his picture. But it wasn't the United States government that found him, much to Gavin's chagrin. No, he was found—and killed—by the men he stole from, maybe even by the man who came into my bedroom in the middle of the night.

I haven't been able to bring myself to look at the images that are too gruesome to be shown on network television, but are all too accessible online. Gavin assures me we are safe. Apparently, they reclaimed most, if not all, of the money Tucker had managed to hide overseas, and then they killed the man who had sinned against them. They might be murderers, but above all, they are businessmen. Hurting any of us would gain them nothing.

Just before Sadie gave birth, she begged me to raise her child. Her dream of a life with Tucker was gone, her conviction was inevitable, and she couldn't bear the thought of her son or daughter entering the foster care system. Neither could I. I took custody of Valentina mere hours later, choosing her name for its meaning—brave. And because she had the most perfect, heart-shaped face I'd ever seen.

We hadn't even arrived home before my phone rang with the news that Sadie had killed herself. She'd been on suicide watch for most of her pregnancy, crushed by the loss of the idyllic life she had envisioned with Tucker. But Sadie had loved the child they made together, and I'm eternally grateful she managed to hold on long enough to see her safely delivered. Even so, the news was a shock, and for the first few months of Valentina's life, I felt like I had murdered my sister and kidnapped her daughter. But as time went on, and we racked up milestones together—first smile, first laugh, first tooth, first steps, first word—Valentina and I became mother and daughter, in every way except for her birth.

Gavin and I learned how to become parents together. He usually handled the sleepless nights and diaper blowouts and colicky cries better than I did, soothing both me and Valentina at the same time. We became a family.

Financially, we are okay, too. As the Stockton's only grand-child, Valentina has an enormous trust fund, and between Gavin's FBI salary and mine as a program coordinator for Teen-Charter, we are comfortable. Everything else: the Manhattan apartment, international vacation homes, cars, art, furniture, Tucker's watch collection and all the jewelry he had given me over the years, including my engagement ring and wedding band —was all seized by Uncle Sam.

I don't miss any of it. We have a roof over our heads, food in the fridge, and love in our hearts. I found a therapist who has helped me process the trauma I'd experienced as a child and then a teenager, which sent me down a strange, distorted path. And now I'm living a life I didn't know enough to wish for. Not glamorous, not exciting, not excessive. Not even perfect, but that's okay too. Days of joy are made even sweeter by moments of sadness. The bright sheen of happiness is occasionally dulled by frustration. And my contentment is a steady, rising tide.

Looking at Valentina now, at her strawberry blond curls and upturned nose, listening to her breathy, lilting voice—I have everything I could ever want, and the only things that matter.

"Mommy, I'm ready to go home now," my daughter says, launching herself into my arms after finishing with the last number.

"Me too, sweetheart. Let's go."

"Bye, Belly Mama," she calls out as we begin walking back to our car.

"Bye, sis." I say more softly. *And, thank you.*

Gavin is waiting for us, holding our son. At three months old, he is still nursing and cannot be away from me for very long, so we tend to operate as a foursome whenever Gavin isn't working. I have another month left of my maternity leave, and I am soaking up every minute with my family. Jenny has been filling in for me and has done such a great job, I'm considering reducing my hours instead of returning full time.

My life so far has been completely unpredictable. I've known intense joy, and piercing heartbreak. I have no idea what to expect next year or the year after that or any of the years to follow. I can only hope that I spend every day loving the man who holds my heart in his hands and the children we're raising together.

"Hey, V," Gavin says, looking at Valentina through the rearview mirror, "how about we go for a walk in the woods while your little brother takes a nap? I think it's raspberries season."

She takes her thumb out of her mouth just long enough to chortle, "I don't like raspberries."

I laugh, casting a sideways glance at the beautiful man beside me. Even after all this time, just drinking in the sight of his tawny hair, strong jaw, and wide, warm mouth makes my stomach flutter. "That's exactly what your daddy said, too."

～

FIVE YEARS LATER, GAVIN

"Don't forget this, Daddy," Valentina says, tucking the poppy flower she picked from outside into the popsicle stick vase her brother, Declan, made at school.

"Never," I assure her, placing it on the breakfast tray the three of us have spent the past hour assembling. Sparing a final glance at the flour-strewn counters and sink full of dishes, I pick up the tray and grin. "Last one to wish Mom a happy birthday is a rotten egg!"

There is a split second where they both look at me, then each other. And then they're off, Valentina's blond ringlets streaming behind her and Declan's strawberry curls glinting gold in the morning sun as they race out of the kitchen, down the hall, and then scramble up the stairs.

I'm close enough behind them to see Valentina reach our bedroom door first. She hurls it open, allowing Declan to squeeze in front of her, then they both chorus loudly, "Happy Birthday, Mommy!"

Poppy obviously heard the stampede. She is propped against the middle of the headboard, the covers tucked around her swollen belly and a wide, beaming smile stretched across her beautiful face. "Has it really been another year already? I asked time to slow down when I blew out last year's birthday candles." She holds out her arms and Valentina and Declan climb in beside her.

Declan tilts his head to the side. "Your birthday wish didn't come true?"

Her eyes flick to mine before returning to our son and then our daughter. "I'm just being silly, sweetheart. All of my wishes have come true." Her voice cracks a little and my own throat tightens in response.

We have come so far, Poppy and I, only to arrive back where we started. I hated every minute of the time we were apart, all those lost years. And yet, this moment wouldn't be possible without them. In spite of everything, we are so damn lucky.

I am so damn lucky.

Setting the breakfast tray over Poppy's lap, Valentina points proudly at the flower. "Look, I picked a poppy just for you."

"And I stirred the pancakes," Declan says, then adds, "Daddy let me try flipping them, too. But I missed."

"You were really close this time," his sister kindly points out. "Right, Daddy?"

"Right. I bet next time you'll get it in the pan."

Declan stretches a hand over Poppy's belly. "Do you think the babies will like pancakes, Mommy?"

"I'm sure they will," Poppy says. "As soon as they get a few teeth."

"Drink this, Mommy." Valentina picks up the glass of orange juice and lifts it toward Poppy. "Make them wake up."

Poppy meets my eyes as she sips the juice. *Waking up the babies* has become a morning ritual. After what happened with her first pregnancy, she is vigilant about tracking their movements. But she is further along now than she was before. At just over thirty weeks, the chance of her delivering healthy twins is high, and getting higher every day.

Twins.

I still can't believe it. We started trying to expand our family when Declan was three. After a year, when Declan's kindergarten registration forms arrived in the mail, Poppy made an appointment with a specialist who suggested taking fertility drugs to increase our chances. They came with an increased chance of twins, too.

I wasn't sure we should. Raising two healthy children with the love of my life, every day is a gift. I worried we were tempting fate. Asking too much.

But Poppy has so damn much love to give. "Let's do it," she'd said. "The worst that can happen is nothing."

Months later, I've realized she was bluffing. So many things can go wrong. We can lose the babies. I can lose the three of them.

I love numbers. Complicated algorithms. Quadratic equations. Statistics and probabilities. But even I cannot compute the array of risk factors and potential outcomes. It's mind-boggling. And terrifying.

Thankfully, Poppy's pregnancy, though considered high-risk given her history, has gone smoothly.

Valentina and Declan each have a hand pressed to Poppy's belly, their faces pinched in concentration as they anxiously wait for their siblings to appease them. Seconds tick by and Poppy's expression shifts from amused to worried. I reach beneath the covers to squeeze one of her feet. "Give them a few m—"

"I got kicked!" Declan announces proudly.

"Me, too," Valentina says.

But I continue to watch Poppy carefully, knowing she won't breathe easy until she's sure she feels movement from both twins. It's only when she puts down the juice and whispers to me, "we're good" that I exhale the breath I didn't realize I'd been holding.

Poppy tucks into her breakfast, feeding bites from the mountain of pancakes on her plate, doused with butter and syrup and whipped cream, to Declan and Valentina and me for every one she takes herself.

Fuck, I'm happy.

Just sitting here on this bed, in this room, drinking in the sight of my family, drowning in the sound of their laughter.

Sometimes it hits me like this, hard. A punch in the gut that leaves me feeling completely hollowed out and yet bursting with all kinds of... *things* that don't have shape or weight to them, but are still so damn heavy.

It shouldn't surprise me though. Poppy has always done this to me. Made me feel. Made me want. Made me need.

The day I met her in the woods divided my life into two parts. *Before Poppy* and *After Poppy*.

Before Poppy, life sucked. *After Poppy*, aside from a few altercations with my foster parent's douchebag son, life was good. Really good. And every second spent with Poppy was fucking awesome.

Until the day my mom showed up. She was a mess, like she always was after one of my father's rages. But she'd left him, and I was all she had. If I didn't go with her, I knew she'd lose her resolve and slink back to him.

So I left.

I fucking left and a fucking storm blew in and ripped my fucking world to shreds.

I don't regret leaving; I had to. But I wish I'd done things differently.

I should have done everything differently.

I guess... I guess I thought Poppy's life would stay more or less the same. I thought she'd get my note and the phone and photos of us I had developed at the shop in town, and we'd keep in touch while I got my mom settled in a new life.

I didn't know we would spend nearly a year bouncing from state to state, usually because she decided to call my dad when she felt sad or lonely or just tired of moving. Then she'd come to her senses, or I'd see the look on her face and know what she'd done. And then we'd have to move again.

I couldn't have imagined that I'd end up killing my own father, or how much it would screw with my head.

And I definitely didn't know what Tucker Stockton—that entitled, arrogant, ass, fuck—would do to my girl. That he'd screw with her head so badly she lost faith in *us*.

I am hers and she is mine and we are us.

I had those words tattooed right over my heart after I left, at the first town that had a tattoo artist good enough to do them justice. They are the first thing I see in the mirror every morning, and the last thing Poppy sees every night, just before she rests her head over them. She says they give her the sweetest dreams.

I remember wanting to claw my marked skin off my body the day she pushed me away, just before her wedding.

I didn't shave without a T-shirt on for years, just so I wouldn't have to see the proof of what I'd lost.

I hated Tucker before I knew anything about him, except that he was the reason Poppy and I weren't together. As reasons go, it was a damn good one. And definitely all I needed.

Poppy still doesn't know this, but I stood outside the Metropolitan Club on the day of her wedding. I saw Stockton walk in. There was something about him. A shadow inside his eyes. Something rotten beneath his swanky, polished exterior.

What Poppy endured with him was awful. Her assault. The mind games and gas-lighting. Losing her first pregnancy, his affair with her sister, escaping the country. I'd give anything to have sheltered Poppy from every ounce of pain, every kind of tragedy.

I didn't. And I can't.

But I can love and honor and cherish her, just like I promised in an intimate backyard ceremony at the edge of the Sackett preserve, soon after Stockton's death certificate was issued. It wasn't worth jumping through the legal hoops involved in seeking a divorce when we didn't even know where her husband was. And, to be honest, we were too busy, too happy to think much about anything besides finding our way back to each other and becoming a family.

Though Valentina isn't my child by blood, she is every bit my daughter as Declan is my son.

And Poppy, the most magnificent woman I've ever known, is my wife.

Right now, my entire world is contained in the space of one mattress.

Yeah. Definitely one lucky son of a bitch.

Once the pile of pancakes is mostly depleted, I pick up the tray. "Who's up for a game of Uno?"

"Me!"

"Me!"

"It's my turn to shuffle," Declan yells, chasing after Valentina down the stairs. Our kids only have two speeds—completely still, when they're eating or sleeping, or running.

When I glance back at Poppy, all alone in bed, she looks a little forlorn. "What about me?"

"Don't you want to rest?"

She sighs. "I just woke up."

"You're sleeping for three."

"Are you just trying to keep me up here so you might actually win a game?"

I lift a brow. "Mrs. Cross, are you really trying to trash talk me into letting you play? The doctor said you should be taking it easy and those victory dances of yours have to be bad for your blood pressure."

Truthfully, I love that she gets competitive during our card games. She does let the kids win occasionally, and Valentina is getting so good she can sometimes win on her own. But when

Poppy wins, she is completely incapable of holding back her excitement.

Even now there is triumph in her smile. "Victory dance? So you're admitting that I am the superior Uno player?"

"I admit nothing," I say, biting down on my own grin as I turn to go. At the door, I pause. "So, when is Jenny getting here?" Jenny and Poppy have stayed close over the years, and now that Poppy is working mostly from home, Jenny often comes to visit. Today, she said she would watch the kids while I get Poppy out of the house for a bit of pampering and some time just for *us*.

She glances at the clock. "I didn't realize it was so late. She should be here any minute." The words are barely out of her mouth when I hear the doorbell, followed immediately by shouts of "Jenny's here!"

Poppy swings her feet out of the bed. "I'll get ready and meet you downst— *Oh no.*"

Her head is hanging low on her shoulders, her horrified expression aimed at the sudden wetness pooling between her thighs.

Even though it feels like my heart has relocated to my throat, I reach for reserves drilled into me from my time in the military. When in doubt, follow protocol. In this case, protocol means getting Poppy to a hospital as soon as possible.

Jenny takes one look at my face as I help Poppy down the stairs and instantly ushers the kids back into the kitchen with a clap of her hands. "How about we clean up the mess from breakfast and make your mom a birthday cake?"

I try talking to Poppy as I drive, blatantly ignoring street lights, stop signs, and speed limits, but Poppy is muttering to herself, or maybe to the babies.

I take her hand. "This time is different."

"No. No, it's just like before. I'm losing them, Gav. We're losing them."

My mouth presses into a hard line. I'm not sure how to argue with her. I'm not a doctor and I cannot feel what she is feeling. The best thing I can do right now is get her to the hospital quickly. My foot presses harder on the gas pedal, willing the miles to go by faster. Finally, I pull off the exit ramp, zigzag through a few side streets, and screech to a halt in front of the emergency room doors.

Poppy is taken by wheelchair up to the labor and delivery floor while I am segued by the administration check-in process. Insurance forms and sign in documents. It's only a few minutes but every second I'm not by my wife's side is an agonizing lifetime.

Finally, I'm released and I race down the corridor toward the bank of elevators, avoiding the crowd of people already waiting by throwing open the door to the stairwell and taking them three at a time. Four floors, eight flights. Poppy is already in a room just across from the nurse's station, and I can see the whites of her eyes as a team of doctors and nurses hook her up to machines, start an IV, and poke and prod at her.

I rush to her side, pressing a kiss to her clammy forehead. Whatever happens now, we'll get through it.

One of the doctors looks at me over his face mask. "You the dad?"

I nod. "Yes."

I think he smiles because his eyes crinkle at the corners. "Looks like your kids are about two months early. You couldn't convince them to sit tight a little longer?"

It hits me that he's joking. *Joking.* That means—"Are they okay?"

He jerks his chin toward one of the machines and glances at a nurse. "Turn up the volume on that, will you?"

A second later, the room is filled with that strange and beautiful sound, the *whoosh-whoosh-whoosh* of my babies heartbeats, still safe inside Poppy's womb. She blinks slowly, tears leaking from the rims of her eyes as some of the color returns to her face. "Is that... two heartbeats?"

"Sure is," the doctor announces. "We're going to have to start prepping you for a cesarean though since your babies are getting a little impatient. You two ready to become a family?"

Family.

I hold Poppy's face in my hands, the love I feel for her an endless well surging through my veins, pounding within my heart. "You've been my family since the very first day we met in the woods. You held up a deck of cards and told me you usually play Solitaire, remember?"

Poppy nods her head shakily. "I remember. I haven't had to play alone for a long, long time."

"I'll always be your partner. You and me."

"We are us," she whispers.

"Before kids and after. Before our vows and after. You are my everything."

WE ARE US is... a lot. A lot of emotion, a lot of story, and a lot of my heart and soul. If you'd like to know just how this story came to be, and maybe see a little further into Poppy's state of mind after *that night*, please keep reading.

A LETTER FROM ME TO YOU

The question I am most often asked about being an author is: Where do you find your inspiration? My answer is usually: *everywhere*. Movies and TV. Overheard conversations. The news. A story shared by a friend.

WE ARE US started with a source much closer to home. As a college freshman, I had a very similar experience to Poppy. And by similar, I mean exact in every way except that, of course, I was not assaulted by my fictional Tucker Stockton.

I was just a girl, a very drunk girl, who went into the room of a guy I thought was cute and nice. I remember flirting with him and kissing him. And I remember wanting to stop because the room started spinning and he was heavy and I felt sick and...

...And then I woke up in a hospital bed.

I was told what Poppy was told: that I was lucky to be alive, that there was evidence of sexual assault, and was then asked to consent to a rape kit.

Poppy's feelings, actions, and choices are all echoes of what I did, how I felt, and my own decisions. I refused the rape kit. I denied what had happened. And, shortly after returning from the hospital, I even found myself in a room with the guy who assaulted me (let's call him not-Tucker)

Not-Tucker apologized, sincerely, for what he did to me. He cried about his *mistake*, talked about his feelings, his regret, even his sister who he hoped would never experience what he'd done to me.

Not-Tucker didn't ask about my feelings, and I didn't volunteer them.

Like Poppy, I stood between two doors. *Rape*, with all that that four-letter-word entailed, or *mistake*. I chose mistake. Do I regret it? No, because at the time, to my barely eighteen-year-old self, the other option seemed so much worse. I wasn't thinking about right or wrong, black or white, silent or loud. I didn't want to make waves or be the subject of ugly, judgmental gossip. I felt horribly, achingly, alone. All I wanted was for the hurt go away and my life to go back to the way it was.

Of course, that didn't happen. I spent the rest of the year walking through campus, feeling like an open wound, terrified of running into not-Tucker. I considered transferring to a different school.

And I also fantasized about befriending not-Tucker. Why? Because I thought it would make what happened easier to deal with. Friends forgive each other. Friends don't skip class to avoid running into each other. Friends aren't terrified just thinking about running into each other in the hall.

I know now that my behavior isn't unusual. Survivors of sexual assault often pursue relationships with their attackers to regain a sense of control after it is ripped from them.

It doesn't make us weak. It makes us human.

Reading WE ARE US, you may have had a hard time understanding Poppy's choices. If you've never faced a similar situation yourself, it is nearly impossible to imagine. I hope that one day, victims of assault won't face so many negative repercussions to coming forward.

As for Tucker, although he was certainly a villain in my story, I purposely chose to show glimpses of his good qualities. Few of us are either all bad or all good. We are usually a messy mix of both, veering (hopefully) toward mostly good.

I don't believe that not-Tucker is or was a bad person. He did a horrible thing that, even now, I have a hard time defining as rape. Even now, I don't want to think of myself as a victim. From what I observed, *that night* was a wake up call to him. Not nearly as much as it could have been, had I chosen to press charges. But, in my gut, I truly believe that not-Tucker went on to live a kind and compassionate life, as have I.

Ultimately, I did not transfer schools. And unlike my fictional Poppy and Tucker, I had no further contact with not-Tucker after his apology (other than seeing him on campus occasionally). I put that night behind me, one day at a time—although it was hardly a healthy process.

I coped, if you can call it that, by retreating into myself and then later, by engaging in meaningless sex with countless men. I treated my body like it didn't matter. I thought, if I can give it away to relative strangers in clumsy, drunken one-night stands, then having my sexuality taken from me, just that once, while I was unconscious, shouldn't be a big deal.

But it was a big deal. Somehow those few minutes I couldn't remember became an event—a trauma—I'd never forget.

I also coped by binging and purging. Bulimia became like a friend, or at least a frenemy. I chased that feeling of fullness until fullness became pain, and then with my fingers down my throat, I made myself empty again. Light and clean. Powerful and in control.

There is so much of me in Poppy, but I feel that I should tell you, her miscarriage is not taken from direct personal experience. Although my first and second pregnancies were touch and go at some points, I never had to face that kind of loss. I can only hope that I've done justice to all of you who have.

There is no "right" way to deal with sexual assault or eating disorders or miscarriage, and I am not qualified to give advice in any of these areas. Below I've included contact information for places that offer help.

Thank you for reading WE ARE US and taking this journey with me. It hasn't been an easy road, but I'm so glad we made it through together.

May you find your own happily ever after,
Tara Leigh

NATIONAL SEXUAL ASSAULT Hotline
1-800-656-4673

RAINN: The nation's largest anti-sexual violence organization
https://www.rainn.org

NATIONAL EATING DISORDERS Association
https://www.nationaleatingdisorders.org

(800) 931-2237

MISCARRIAGE MATTERS
www.mymiscarriagematters.org

SHARE PREGNANCY and Infant Loss Support
www.nationalshare.org

ACKNOWLEDGMENTS

My readers—you are EVERYTHING!!! I love reading your reviews and value your honest feedback! And all those messages/posts/tweets/e-mails you send as you're reading—they make my day! **hugs** In so many cases you have become friends. Thank you for letting me into your lives!!

A huge thank-you to, Jessica Alvarez of BookEnds Literary Agency. Your career guidance is invaluable!

Lexi Smail, I am so thrilled we got to work together again— I could never have told Poppy's story without you!

Regina Wamba, thank you for this GORGEOUS cover! (and for putting up with me!)

Marla Esposito, thank you for your attention to detail!

Devyn Jensen, thank you for ALL THE THINGS!!!

Jenn Watson and the Social Butterfly PR team, thank you so

much for all the effort you've put into launching WE ARE US into the world!

My Beta Beauties:

Cindy, Thank you for your eagle eye and loving this story as much as I did.

Danielle, working with you is such a pleasure! Thank you for your feedback, encouragement, and friendship. You make my life a lot less stressful!

Lana, your voicemails about this story were #authorgoals! And your suggestions, as always, were invaluable!

Nadine, I love that you always speak your mind. Your honesty and thoughtfulness are a gift—thank you for sharing them with me. The love between Poppy and Gavin is much deeper because of you.

Nicole, thank you for your friendship, helping me with the VIPs, and all your screenshots!

Paramita, you are so enthusiastic and supportive. Thank you for convincing me I wasn't crazy and always making me smile!

Stephanie, thank you for making sure I got the medical details right and loving this story!

Yamina—thank you for your insight and encouragement. Your advice definitely make this story stronger !

Abby O'Shea & Christina Westrich, thank you so much for taking a chance on me. It is such an honor to be a part of The Romance Reveal Book Box, and I am truly grateful for the opportunity!

Lauren Layne and Anthony LeDonne of Last Word Designs, thank you for my gorgeous logo and website, www. taraleighbooks.com!

Moments by Andrea, thank you for the fabulous head shot.

Thank you to all the amazing bloggers and author assistants who have become a virtual cheering section for me, and I hope that I do the same for you. You are the unsung heroes in this wonderful place called Romancelandia and I am so grateful for your support.

I can fill the pages of this book with everyone that has made me laugh and smile and cry with your incredible reviews and personal messages. I hope you enjoy WE ARE US—believe me when I tell you, you are the reason I spend endless hours at my laptop.

My ARC Team, you remind me why I write. Thank you for your encouragement and honest feedback. Writing is a solitary endeavor, but because of you, it isn't a lonely one.

My Bookstagram Team, I am in awe of the creativity, energy, and effort to put into your pictures!

Grandma, you left me nearly twenty years ago, and not a day goes by that I don't miss you. For any smokers reading this—put the cigarette down. Think of the people in your life who will one day watch you struggle to breathe and, when you lose that battle, will miss you desperately.

To my family & friends—I adore you all . . . and I'm sorry for ignoring your calls when I'm writing!

Thanks to my mom for never ripping all those "bodice-rippers" out of my hands as a teen/tween, and to my dad for showing me what it means to work hard. (Who needs weekends or vacations, anyway?)

Stephen, thank you for being a wonderful husband and

supporting my dreams. I love you. Logan, Chloe, and Pierce, thank you for being such great kids & genuinely considerate of my writing time. I am blessed to be your mother.Our lives are enriched by our sweet rescue puppy, Pixie. The wonderful organization that brought Pixie into our lives is Goofy Foot Dog Rescue, and if you would like to welcome a dog into your family or donate to their organization, please visit their website: www.goofyfootrescue.org

And if you would like to see more pictures of Pixie and get updates on new releases, sales, and behind the scenes snippets, please sign up for my newsletter at http://bit.ly/TaraLeighNwsltr.

ALSO BY TARA LEIGH

ABOUT THE AUTHOR

Tara Leigh is a multi-published author of steamy contemporary romance. A former banker on Wall Street, she graduated from Washington University and holds an MBA from Columbia Business School, but she much prefers spending her days with fictional boyfriends than analyzing financial spreadsheets. Tara currently lives in Fairfield County, Connecticut with her husband, children, and fur-baby, Pixie. She is represented by Jessica Alvarez, of Bookends Literary Agency.

facebook.com/TaraLeighAuthor
twitter.com/TaraLeighBooks
instagram.com/taraleighbooks